Gone to Graveyards

by

Jack Watson

Gone to Graveyards is a work of fiction. Any similarities between the characters in this book and real people, living or dead, is coincidental.

Printed by Createspace
ISBN – 10: 154230427X
ISBN – 13: 978-1542304276

To Corporal David A. Semmler
Killed in Action, February 5, 1971

Other Books by Jack Watson

Over the Hump: the Coming of Age of 2Lt. Henry Watson

Two Voices Falling

Rear Echelon

Where have all the soldiers gone, long time passing?
Where have all the soldiers gone, long time ago?
Where have all the soldiers gone?
Gone to graveyards everyone,
Oh, when will they ever learn?
Oh, when will they ever learn?

Pete Seager
Where Have All the Flowers Gone

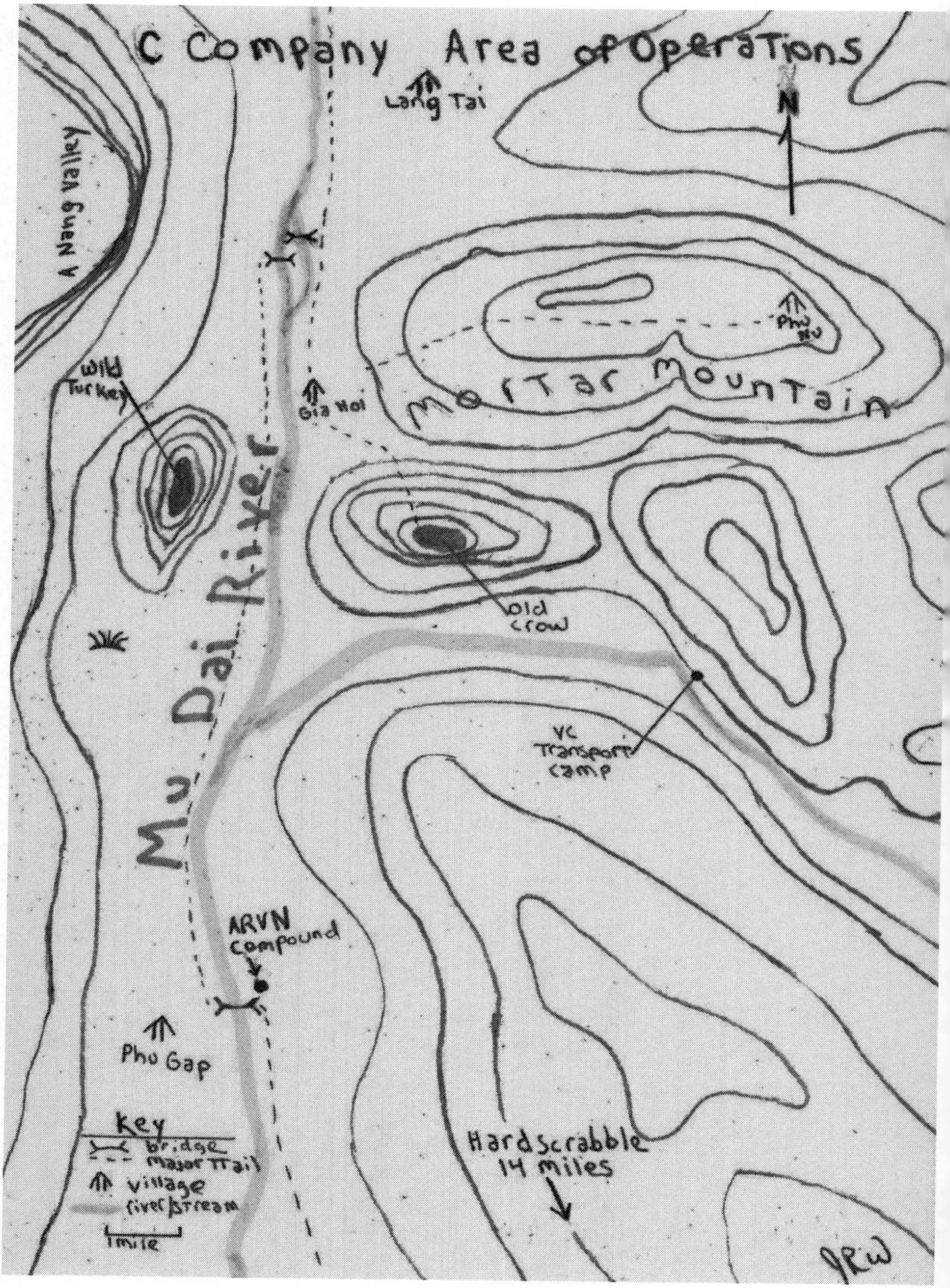

C Company Area of Operations
N
Lang Tai
A Nang Valley
Phu Nu
Mortar Mountain
Gia Hoi
Wild Turkey
Mu Dai River
Old Crow
VC Transport camp
ARVN Compound
Phu Gap
Key
bridge
Major Trail
village
river/stream
1 mile
Hardscrabble 14 miles
JRW

Gone to Graveyards

Prologue

Vietnam, the war, was not at all like you think it was unless, of course, you were actually there. Even then it was probably different than you remember. Looking at the pictures I took during my tour reminds me of how beautiful a place it was, with bright shining beaches and exotic rain forests--a patchwork landscape of rice paddies and quaint, thatch-hut villages. It's the things that happened there that made it ugly.

Time does that to you, or rather for you. Lets you remember ugly things as beautiful, scary things as exciting. It allows you to push the shortcomings of your past to the deep recesses of your mind where you can pretend they didn't happen. It's that ability that allows me to affect an appearance of sanity today; to walk among those who never heard a shot fired in anger as if I'm one of them. Either that or I was never crazy to begin with and the things I thought were real back then were just my imagination gone wild, which is even crazier still.

Forty years is a long time to remember something. It's an even longer time to try to forget.

Chapter 1

From the time I was young--eight, nine, maybe ten--I knew that someday I would be a soldier and that, if I was lucky, it would be in a time of war. I come, so I was told, from a long line of soldiers although, aside from my father, few of them actually fought in anything even vaguely resembling a battle. He--my father-- was killed, or rather died, in New Guinea not even knowing if I was going to be a boy or a girl. Both of my grandfathers served in World War I but neither saw any action. In a time before two-way radios, my mother's father trained carrier pigeons and never left the states. My father's father made it to France but was still at a training center when the armistice was signed.

My grandfather, the pigeon trainer, was apologetic about his role in the war and spoke proudly of *his* grandfather who was in the Union Army and once served a cup of coffee to Abraham Lincoln during one of the president's visits to the troops. My grandfather never mentioned Gettysburg, or Shiloh, or Appomattox, and since he said his grandfather *served* Lincoln a cup of coffee I assumed he was a cook and it was just part of his job.

Another relative, a great-great uncle or something, died in Andersonville Prison but there were no details. I liked to think he fought bravely, was maybe even wounded before he was captured, but knowing what I do now about the myths that surround war it's just as likely he surrendered early on thinking a confederate prison would be easier than the hardships of being a soldier and didn't find out until it was too late just how wrong a guy can be.

In any case, my passage to war was nothing like my forefathers'. No cramped troop ships, no long marches behind dusty caissons, no docks or streets full of flag waving patriots to see me off. I was flown to my war on a commercial jet complete with cushioned seats and pretty stewardesses who went out of their way to make our flight as pleasant as possible, knowing that some of us would not be making the flight back.

Like most of the young men--boys really--I was convinced of my immortality, my only fear being that I wouldn't measure up; that I might get someone else killed due to my own ignorance. And the closer we got, the more I started to believe what every enlisted man already knew--that the most dangerous person in the United States Army was a green 2nd Lieutenant at the head of a rifle platoon.

A bell dinged and the *fasten your seatbelt* sign flashed on the bulkhead over my seat. The pilot announced that we were now in Vietnam airspace and would be landing in about five minutes. I woke up the pimply-faced PFC in the seat next to me and told him to buckle up. Again, the pilot:

"The temperature at Cam Ranh Bay is a cool 96 degrees with not so much as a whisper of a breeze," he said, his voice professional, reassuring. "Local time is 1:23 in the afternoon, 1323 for you lifers." There were a few nervous laughs from the young enlisted men, but not many. Above the wing I could see the coast far ahead--a thin line of sand separating the blue-green of the South China Sea from the green-black of the land.

"We're going to be making a few turns and a rapid descent before we touch down, but nothing to worry about," the captain assured us. "It's all S.O.P. This is my eighth landing at this field and my stress level here is a lot lower than O'Hare or LaGuardia, so put your seats in the upright position, sit back, relax, and enjoy the show." The plane banked left and I could see the sprawling American compound in the distance. Fishermen worked their sampans around the rocky cliffs of several small islands that jutted out of the ocean to the north. The PFC leaned against my shoulder, trying to get a better look, then pulled back when I glared at him.

"Sorry, Sir," he said. I felt bad, but instead of saying anything conciliatory I turned back to my unobstructed view of where I would be spending the next year of my life.

We flew south along the coast, past the great warships, tankers, and cargo vessels nestled against the docks or lying at anchor in the harbor; past several small villages where mothers tended their children in the shade of palm trees and old men strung nets along the beach for repair. Beyond the sandy lowlands lay the lush foothills of the mountains. Fluffy clouds cast dark shadows across the jungle turning the vibrant greens black--a perfect metaphor, I was soon to learn, for the war that raged beneath the canopy.

Our descent gave the illusion of speed as the perimeter wire and guard towers flashed beneath us. A small city of wooden buildings protected by sandbagged walls as high as a man's waist streamed past my window. Jeeps and duce-and-a-halfs scurried along rutted roads carrying people and supplies from one part of the base to another. Soldiers lounged around artillery batteries and mortar pits waiting for a fire mission. In a matter of seconds we were over the runway where commercial jets shared tarmac space with military transports, fighters, and half a dozen species of helicopters, some parked in the open, others housed in their own sandbagged revetments. The runway was puddled from a recent rain, the concrete steaming in the humid air. The plane touched down and taxied to a stop, the engines still running as a quarter ton truck with a sign in the bed that said *follow me* pulled in front and led us off the runway where we parked, seemingly in the middle of nowhere.

Two Air Force enlisted men pushed a set of steps-on-wheels to the door and an army staff sergeant materialized at the front of the plane. "All right, listen up," he said in a voice that carried to the back of the plane. "We're going to do this quickly. From front to back you're going to deplane in a brisk and orderly fashion. Your duffle is already being loaded onto a deuce-and-a-half. Do *not* try to find your gear now. Go immediately to one of the busses parked outside and get on. First on go to the back and fill it up from back to front." I looked out the window and saw three busses--fifteen yards between them as if they were grunts on patrol--like they had been there all along. "Move," he said and disappeared out the door.

I could feel the heat as I moved toward the front of the plane. The stewardesses were by the cockpit door smiling and wishing us well. One of them, a pretty brunette with short hair pulled back in a braid, would occasionally reach out and touch one of the younger soldiers and for not the first time since we left the states I found myself wishing I was a 19 year old private instead of a 24 year old 2nd lieutenant.

The glare, the heat, and the humidity hit me the moment I reached the door and I had to squint to see the steps. By the time I reached the bottom my eyes had adjusted enough that I could see the first bus but a hand steered me away from it.

"Next bus," the airman said as the first bus pulled away. By the time I was up the steps, sweat was running down the valley of my spine. I started to take a seat near the front but the driver, a black, Air Force two-striper, yelled at me to move to the back. Perhaps he hadn't seen the bar on my shoulder. More likely he didn't care.

The bus filled quickly and the driver started pulling away as soon as the door closed. A Spec. 4 stuck his fingers through the wire mesh that covered his window and rattled it as if he were in a cage. “Where do they think we’re going to escape to?” he said, loud enough for the whole bus to hear and got the laughs he was hoping for. A platoon sergeant, probably back for his second tour, waited for the laughter to die down.

“It ain’t to keep you in, shit-for-brains. It’s to keep hand grenades out. Welcome to Vietnam,” he said. After a short ride the driver came to a stop behind the first bus, opened the doors and ordered us out. Several Vietnamese were milling around--picking up papers, carrying garbage bags, and pulling our duffle from the back of a deuce-and-a-half and throwing it in a pile. To a man, or woman, they were wearing straw hats, flip-flops, and black pajamas baggy enough to hide enough C-4 to blow up a whole fleet of busses.

We unloaded as the third bus pulled up behind us. Two more Vietnamese materialized and began pulling duffle bags from the pile and arranging them in neat rows. “Officers to my right, enlisted men to my left,” a sergeant with two rockers under his chevrons ordered. His voice was soft, his tone bored.

Once in our groups he walked to the officers’ section and planted himself in front of a young Spec. 4. “Specialist Witt,” he said with a glance at the boy’s name tag. “Do you want to spend the rest of the day saluting, or would you like to join the rest of the enlisted men?” The specialist looked at the lieutenant standing next to him on one side and the major on the other.

“You said--”

“I said *my* left. And I pointed.” The lieutenant next to Witt patted him on the shoulder and said *nice try* as the specialist left to join the rest of the enlisted men. “Senior officers, you may pick up your duffle and report to the orderly room for your room assignments. Specialist Williams will show you the way.”

Two majors and a lieutenant colonel went to the rows of duffle bags where a black specialist waited to help them find their bags. “Junior officers, you will get your duffle and report to barracks six,” he said pointing to a wooden building with *BARRACKS 6* painted above the door in letters a foot high. “Pick out a bunk and enjoy the air conditioning until someone tells you what to do next. The rest of you,” he said, turning his attention to the enlisted men, “follow me.”

He started walking away from officer country and, without looking over his shoulder because he had been at it long enough to know what was happening behind him, yelled "Leave your duffle. You'll pick it up later."

* * *

The *air conditioning* was a two foot square fan rattling on the floor at the end of a long aisle flanked by bunk beds on both sides. Two lieutenants and a captain lounged on their bunks either reading or staring at the new arrivals, looking for a familiar face. Other bunks had been made up but were empty, their temporary owners somewhere else. I dropped my duffle bag at the foot of an empty bunk. A thin mattress had been folded into thirds at one end and a pillow and bedding was stacked in a neat pile on the metal webbing that remained exposed. I picked up the bedding, laid out the mattress and flopped down. The mattress stunk.

"John Richards." A hand reached through the space between the upper and lower bunk.

"Sean Sullivan," I said, shaking his hand. I swung my feet over the side and sat up. "Nice, huh?" I said, looking over the bleak interior of the barracks.

"Depends, I suppose," John said. "If you're an eleven B you'll remember it fondly in a real short time." 11B was the army's designation for an infantryman. I stole a look at the single bar on his shoulder to see how familiar I could be.

"Then I guess it's nice," I said. "You?"

"Artillery," he said. "So what're we supposed to do now?"

Not much, as it turned out. We were taken to a warehouse where we exchanged our leather boots and stateside fatigues for jungle gear. The boots were made of leather and canvas, better suited to the tropical climate than the all leather combat boots we were used to. The jungle fatigues were made of a light weight synthetic that would dry quickly during the on again off again rains of the monsoon season. The pants were baggy with cargo pockets from hip to knee; the shirt looked like it was modeled after Captain Kangaroo's jacket, with extra big pockets and a long torso so it could be worn outside the pants.

Other than our wardrobe change and a trip to Finance to exchange our money for military script, we were free to wander the base and do what we wanted as long as we were in our barracks at 8

AM, 1 PM, and 6 PM for orders or duty assignments.

Surprisingly there was a lot to do. The war was expanding and so were the bases that supplied logistical support to the combat troops. Cam Rahn Bay was one of the biggest with units from the Army, Navy, Marines, and Air Force calling it home. There were PXs, BXs, rec buildings, outdoor movies, beaches, and four varieties of officers' clubs with cold beer selling for twenty cents a can. John and I were quick to discover that the Air Force and Navy clubs were nicer than the Army club and the beer came in glasses. We didn't even try the Marine club.

"So where ya from?" John asked as we waited for our first beer. We'd already covered the army part our histories.

"Hornell. New York," I said. "Not Hornell, actually. A small town near there that nobody ever heard of."

"I never heard of Hornell," John said.

"You?"

"Nebraska," John said, not even bothering to mention the town.

"What's that near?" I said.

"Fuck you," he said. The beers came, brought by a pretty Vietnamese girl. I gave her a dollar and let her keep the change. "Something about that Asian look," I said, watching her walk away.

"Yeah, well, that'll probably wear off soon enough," John said, but I noticed he hadn't taken his eyes off her either. The beer was cold and had never tasted better. "Jesus," John said after draining half his glass in one breath. "Maybe we should run a tab."

* * *

Six O'clock came quickly. Too quickly because we had trouble finding our way back to our barracks. We arrived just as the announcements were starting. The sergeant glared as I stumbled past him and crashed on my bunk. I was asleep in no time and slept right through evening chow.

When I woke up I had only a vague recollection of the previous night's announcements that included no mention of my name as far as I could remember. I wasn't as lucky at morning announcements. Maybe it was just the roll of the dice. More likely I was being punished for sleeping through last night's 'formation.' John landed on the duty roster too.

Chapter 2

Aside from six officers who were told to report to the orderly room for their orders, John and I were the only ones to draw duty. John was given the job of supervising three enlisted men assigned to pull cut-off oil drums from beneath the latrines and burn the contents using a few quarts of diesel fuel. We soon learned that 'burning shit' was a job usually done by the Vietnamese unless a soldier had screwed up bad enough to warrant such a punishment.

My job was supervising eight enlisted men assigned to filling sandbags and throwing them in the back of a three-quarter ton truck. It was hardly a job for an officer, not even a second lieutenant, but the message was clear. Sergeants couldn't give orders to an officer, of course, and I made the mistake of questioning it.

"Your name came up on the duty roster," the sergeant said, practically daring me to ask to see it. He wanted me to know who was boss and, knowing how things worked, I decided to cut my losses and stay awake for the rest of the formations.

My crew looked no better off than me, holding their heads and closing their eyes as we bounced along the road to the sand drop. I rode in the cab.

"So wha'd *you* do, Sir," the driver asked.

"A little too much celebrating, I guess," I said.

"Sergeant Kowalski's an asshole. Just play the game. You won't be here but a day or two. You an eleven B?" I nodded. "Bummer," he said and didn't say anything more for the rest of the ride.

I was sweating just watching the men work. The thought occurred to me to pitch in and help; it didn't seem right to just stand around doing nothing. But I had the feeling that Sgt. Kowalski might check on us and I didn't want to stoke his ire by appearing to fraternize. So I did the next best thing which was to supervise by doing as little as possible, including telling the men what to do. They worked at their own pace, drank warm water from a jug when they were thirsty, and waited for me to give them their breaks which were long and often.

By eleven o'clock the truck was only half full of sandbags and the detail was supposed to end at noon for lunch. "How many sandbags do you usually do in a morning?" I asked the driver. He was sitting on the shady side of the truck, his back against the side.

"Depends on how big an asshole you want to be," he said, standing up and looking into the bed of the truck. "Looks like you don't want to be an asshole at all," he said. "I wouldn't sweat it. The Army's just fuckin' with you. And them," he added, pointing his chin at the enlisted men. "You're not here because anything needs to be done the gooks can't do. Ya just pissed somebody off is all." I looked at my watch. The detail was still working but just barely. They were no more used the heat than I was. I pulled out my wallet.

"Why don't you to go get some cokes from one of the enlisted clubs," I said, handing him three dollars. Get a case. Is that enough?" I asked, meaning the money.

"More than enough," he said and hopped into the cab.

"Make sure they're cold," I said as he sped off. The detail stopped, wondering if his departure was a sign for them to quit; I decided to make an attempt at leadership.

"Keep working," I said. "If the pile's big enough when he gets back we'll call it quits for lunch."

The driver was only gone ten minutes but there was a respectable pile of sandbags waiting when he got back. "Good enough, Sir?" a PFC asked as the driver backed up to the sandbags.

"Yeah," I said. "Finish up the bags you're on and grab a cold one." I pulled the case of Cokes from the passenger seat and put it on the tailgate. The cans were icy cold and the condensation was beading up and running down the sides in wavy rivulets.

"Hey, thanks, Sir," came a chorus. They finished their bags, stabbed their shovels into the sand pile, and headed for the Cokes.

"What, no beer?" Already they were slipping into the more permissive relationship that existed between enlisted men and junior officers in a combat zone.

"Isn't that the reason you jerk-offs are here in the first place?" I said, enjoying the laxity as much as they were.

"Ain't that why you're here, Lieutenant?" another said, and they all laughed.

"Two apiece," I said, and like a good officer waited until everyone had taken their first can before I took one for myself.

*   *   *

The barracks was almost empty by the time I got back, most of the transients having already gone to lunch. I waited for John, assuming he would have waited for me if he got back from his detail first. I was laying on my bunk, eyes closed, when he came in. "Jesus, is that you?" I said, sitting up when I smelled his approach. He pulled the lapel of his fatigues to his nose and sniffed.

"Is it? I stopped smelling it two hours ago."

"Next time stand upwind," I suggested.

"There won't be a next time. Come on, I don't want to miss lunch."

"You're going like that? I ain't sitting next to you."

"You'll get used to it," he said. "Five minutes and you won't even notice."

We got back well before the one o'clock formation. Sgt. Kowalski was nowhere to be seen and the spec. 4 who took his place didn't seem to know anything about an afternoon duty roster. He welcomed three new lieutenants who arrived while I was on sandbag duty, gave them the usual spiel and held up a small sheaf of papers. "Sullivan? Sean?" he said, looking around. I held up my hand and he handed me my orders. My heart was pounding.

"Wha'd you get?" John said.

"Fifty-third Infantry. Where're they?" I asked. A second lieutenant standing next to me was mumbling something about the twenty-fifth.

"Fuckin' Delta!" he said, knowing that meant lots of VC, trench foot, and mosquitoes.

"Anybody know where the Fifty-third is?" I asked again.

"Central Highlands," the spec. 4 said. "Not too bad." I felt a wave of relief and finally noticed that John had gotten his orders too.

"How 'bout you?" I asked.

"156th Artillery. Let me hear you say 'Fire mission, over.'" I finally understood that we were in the same division and slapped him on the shoulder. We were scheduled to leave at eight o'clock the next morning.

Chapter 3

After gleaning what we could from our orders, John left with another artillery officer to get drunk. I was still feeling the effects of the night before so I stayed behind. I started to write a letter but didn't get past 'Dear Mom.' My head was just not into it. I stared at the paper until a few new arrivals lugged their duffel into the barracks. I recognized one as one of the cadets I went through OCS with but couldn't remember his name. He caught my eye and I saw the look of recognition on his face. He started over, then slowed, trying, I assumed, to remember my name. "Hey,…Sean," he said, pumping my hand.

"James," I said. That was his last name and as I read it off his name tag his first name popped into my head. "How ya doing, Fred?"

"Jesus," he said and looked around. "This empty?" he asked and threw his duffle bag onto the top bunk next to mine. "When'd you get here?"

"Yesterday. Leaving tomorrow for the Fifty-third."

"Jesus. So soon? I thought they'd give us some time to acclimate. We had a stopover in the Philippines and I thought I was going to die, but this!" Fred was from North Dakota and it was the end of January. "So what's the story here?"

"I was surprised too," I said, referring to the speed with which my orders came through. "You could be here for as long as a week from what I hear. Three formations a day. Other than that you're free to do what you want, as long as you don't fuck up." Fred laughed; I remembered that he was a bit of a fuck-up at OCS. I guess the army was desperate for infantry officers. "You hear from any of the guys?" I said, meaning the cadets in our class.

"Smitty's dead, man. Can you believe it?" I was stunned, my mind racing to process what he'd said. I hadn't been close to Smitty, no one was. But I had a hard time wrapping my mind around the fact that he was dead. We'd graduated from OCS a month ago, barely enough time for a short leave before shipping out. How could he have been killed already? Smitty, of all people.

Gerald Smith was one of those people you picked out of a

crowd right away; not because he was impressive, but because he was so unimpressive. He was short and skinny and further distinguished himself from the rest of our class by wearing the gray-framed glasses the army issued him. Physically, there was nothing about him that inspired confidence as a leader of men. Even the training sergeants overlooked him at first, appointing the taller, good-looking cadets to the leadership positions.

And Smitty did nothing to change anyone's initial impression of him. He fell behind in the runs, scored near the bottom in PT scores, and struggled with map and compass skills in our land navigation exercises. None of this was for lack of trying. It was painful watching him run the obstacle course. Not that he was awkward. He wasn't. In fact he probably would have been a good athlete if he'd been of average size and stamina. The pain of watching him came from the pain he put himself through just trying to keep up. He had an inordinate fear of washing out.

He put the same effort into the academic part of the program. He rarely went into town with the rest of us, staying behind to study instead. During field exercises he would pull out his map and compass during breaks and study the lay of the land even when we knew exactly where we were. Especially when he knew exactly where we were. I once asked him what he was doing as he leaned against his rucksack, his map plastered against his thighs while he sucked warm water from his canteen.

"Figurin' out what these contours look like in real life," he said. We had been taught the basics of reading topographical maps, but Smitty seemed to know that we would need a lot more than that if we were to be effective platoon leaders in Vietnam. He got so he could orientate a map with a mere glance at the compass and could then locate his position by matching the contours on the map with the surrounding terrain. "I'm getting pretty good at it," he said, smiling his crooked smile. "Just ask if you need help."

Six weeks into the program and the other cadets started looking to him during field exercises problems. The sergeants couldn't help but notice and, while his PT scores languished, his leadership scores started to climb.

For our final test each candidate had to lead a mission with a specific objective. It could have been as simple as getting from point A to point B in a given period of time. In this case the candidate would have to map out what he believed to be the fastest route given the terrain features on the map and use his leadership ability to get his team to their objective on time.

The sergeants gave Smitty the most difficult mission of all and he was given twelve hours to accomplish it. The mission was to move a platoon of thirty men to a VC base camp eight miles away and attack and destroy it with a minimum of causalities. The "VC", a platoon of infantry soldiers stationed at Fort Benning, would also have thirty men that they could deploy any way they wanted as long as at least twenty men were in the base camp at all times. All parties were restricted to an area bordered by roads, creeks, and other easily identified landmarks. Umpires would be on hand to rule on the outcome. Our training sergeants warned us that the 'enemy' would have Vietnam veterans among them who would like nothing better than to beat a bunch of officer candidates and to be on our toes. Clearly, they had saved Smitty for this final exercise for a reason. If we looked good, they looked good.

On the morning of the exercise we were given our mission briefing, the rules of the game, and a list of the equipment we would be allowed to take. Smitty studied the map as the rest of us looked on making our own observations and suggestions based on textbook tactics we had been learning for the past three months. After ten minutes Smitty asked the umpires who would be traveling with us--a lieutenant colonel and a captain--to leave the room while he briefed us on what we were going to do.

The colonel assured Smitty that they would have no communication with the enemy forces and that they needed to know our plans in advance in order to evaluate how well we carried them out. Smitty, who had never once stood up to our training cadre, explained that he didn't want them to prejudge or interfere with his plan before they saw how it played out. The colonel was not happy, but he left the room.

It was soon apparent why Smitty didn't want the umpires to know his plan beforehand because the colonel might not have let him go through with it. While it did not violate the letter of the rules, it did violated the spirit of the maneuvers and the rest of us were immediately on board. We knew Smitty was sticking his neck out and we were determined to show the veterans what we could do.

Smitty called the umpires back and then divided us into three squads. For equipment he decided to take one radio and one machinegun for each squad but left the 60 millimeter mortar behind. We would be taking no claymore mines, only a few smoke grenades, and three hand grenades apiece. Machine gunners and their assistants would each carry two, one-hundred round belts. Everyone else, except the radiomen, would carry an additional fifty rounds. Each squad would have an M-79 grenade launcher and everyone else not otherwise armed would carry an M-16 and 250 rounds of blank ammunition.

We were allowed three C-ration meals apiece and as much water as we wanted but Smitty told us to eat whatever we wanted as we packed up and to take only enough food for one meal. He advise the umpires to travel light as well as he planned on moving fast. Moving fast in Vietnam was rarely a good idea because of the threat of booby-traps and ambushes and I could see a look of impending disaster pass across the umpires' faces.

We packed quickly and a deuce-and-a-half took us to our jump-off point a mile away. The sun was just coming up as we formed our squads and when we were ready Smitty looked to the colonel.

"Whenever you're ready," the colonel said and instead of moving cautiously into the woods, we double-timed down the road we had just driven in on. We were in squad formations with the radiomen and machine gunners (the biggest and the strongest among us) appropriately positioned to keep the umpires happy even though everyone knew there was no chance of us being ambushed on the road. Smitty had a cadet we called Chubs set the pace because he was always last in our runs; we didn't want anyone falling behind.

After a half mile Chubs turned left on the road that was the western boundary of our area of operations. Smitty stopped and warned us as we ran past to stay on the shoulder. The rules did not specify if the actual road was in or out of bounds and he did not want the umpires to rule anyone dead for stepping on the blacktop. Another mile further on and we saw the wisdom of putting chubs in the lead. Sergeant Sims, a black staff sergeant, had been our P.T. instructor and he liked to lord his superiority over us by running us ragged while he ran up and down our ranks yelling so that even Chubs, who carried a few extra pounds of blubber, was in better shape than the average cadet in other platoons.

I was in the same squad as chubs and I could tell he was not even feeling it yet. In fact, Smitty had to tell him to take a break so the machine gunners and radiomen could catch their breath.

The captain, whose shirt boasted a CIB and a ranger tab, seemed to be enjoying the run. He ran on the road next to Chubs and had an expectant look on his face, eager to see where this unorthodox cadet was taking him. I had the feeling he had already figured it out.

Perhaps the colonel had too but he didn't seem as enthused as the captain. He did not appear to be struggling to keep up (he was traveling 30-40 pounds lighter than we were), but he did seem to be trying to look like he wasn't struggling. I suspected he was not in the same shape as the ranger captain, or even Chubs for that matter.

At every break the machine gunners switched weapons with their assistant gunners and one of the radiomen traded rucksacks with someone else because he got a stitch in his side.

Smitty seemed to be everywhere--reminding us keep our interval to keep the umpires happy, and checking to see if anything needed his attention. He did not give us phony encouragement or false praise, as if we were accomplishing something more spectacular than what Sergeant Sims had put us through. Instead, he made us feel that everything was under control and that we were all in the same boat, he no more than anyone else.

After ten miles the road took a sharp curve and Chubs called a halt. Smitty came forward and as the rest of us guzzled water and popped salt tablets he looked at the map and patted Chubs on the shoulder. It wasn't even nine o'clock and we were less than four miles from our objective. "Good job," he said and even though I couldn't see his face, I knew Chubs was beaming.

Smitty informed us that we would now leave the road and reminded us to stay alert and keep quiet. He moved a different squad to the front and put Hadley on point. It was then I realized that not only had Smitty been studying his books all those months, but also us. Smitty had no sense of direction. He was one of those people who could not walk in a straight line without looking at his compass every other step. Hadley, on the other hand, always seemed to know where he was in relation to where he had been and where he was going. He was a hunter and had demonstrated an uncanny ability to spot trip wires and unusual disturbances on the ground that might indicate land mines and booby-traps.

Now that we would be following more traditional tactics, Smitty briefed the umpires on his plan of attack. He showed Hadley where we were on the map and our objective. He shot an azimuth with his compass and pointed the way. "Four miles," he said, already speaking in a whisper. "Be careful."

We pushed through the dense vegetation that bordered the road and once under the canopy of the trees the forest opened up. There was little ground cover and the walking was easy, but after double-timing it seemed we were going at a snail's pace. For the first time, Smitty seemed anxious. He went forward to confer with Hadley. He pulled out his map, but without any major landmarks, and not being able to see more than fifty yards, Smitty was lost. "Where the hell are we?" he asked.

"'bout here, I'd say" Hadley said, pointing to a spot on the map about two miles from the enemy camp. Smitty looked at his watch. The colonel and the captain came up to see what was going on and Smitty tried to project an air of confidence.

"Pick it up a little," Smitty said, and then took his position near the center of the platoon. It wasn't long before the line stopped and Smitty moved up to see why.

"Listen," Hadley said. Smitty heard it too. We'd made better time than he'd thought and if we'd kept on the way we were going we would have missed the camp by three hundred yards. Three hundred yards *behind* it which would have put us four hundred yards from where we wanted to be for the attack. Hadley made no apology. He had found the base camp and figured being off by a few hundred yards was pretty good, and it was. Still, it left Smitty with a problem. We were within hearing distance of the camp and he had to get the platoon into position without so much as a broken branch or an unstifled cough.

"New plan," he said. The original plan called for us to set up an L-shaped attack using a small gully for cover on the south side of the enemy camp, and from whatever cover we could find on the west side. Now he decided to abandon the gully and hit them from the north and west. "Gully's probably full of booby-traps anyway," he said. The boobytraps would not be real explosives, but trip flares that would warn the enemy of our presence and cause the umpires to rule anyone near it dead.

Word was passed back and Hadley led us closer to the base

camp. Someone stepped on a branch and the snap sounded like a rifle shot in the still air. Everyone froze but the sound of voices from the enemy never stopped. They were further away, and talking louder, than we had thought. The line moved again, then stopped a few minutes later. Hadley crawled back. "They're just up ahead, milling around like they're on a picnic," he grinned. "One problem. There are a couple of guys outside the wire, probably putting up trip flares. Whaddya want to do?" Smitty thought a minute.

"Get the machine gunners and squad leaders up here," he said and then moved forward to see the situation for himself. By the time he got back the squad leaders and gunners were there and he moved them up as close as he dared. The men setting up booby-traps had returned to the camp and we could hear their voices clearly. They had acted just as Smitty thought they would, thinking we would make a textbook advance through the woods and not reach the base camp until after one o'clock. It was then just after ten. So far the element of surprise was on our side but there was still a lot that could go wrong.

Smitty pointed the gunners and the squad leaders to their positions. Machineguns would take up positions at the angle and both ends of the L while the rest of the men made up the lines in-between. The signal to open fire would be a shot from Smitty unless we were spotted by the enemy first. Then everyone would open up and get to their positions as fast as they could.

It turned out to be the latter case. Third squad was moving onto position when a "VC" they hadn't seen stringing flares on the north side spotted them. He yelled and third squad immediately opened up on him and then rushed forward, setting up positions just short of the flares. First and second squad did the same on the longer west side. In our haste the lines were ragged, but the cross-fire was judged effective, none-the-less. The "VC" stumbled all over themselves getting to their weapons, and return fire from the base camp was slow and weak. After five minutes the Umpires called a halt. They had seen enough.

* * *

Our training cadre was present for the debriefing and although we wouldn't know the results until it was announced by the umpires, we had filled them in on the mission and told them we were confident we had won. A large map showing the exercise area was at the front of the room, the Lieutenant Colonel standing off to the side, tapping his pointer on the floor to get our attention.

"Okay, let's get started," he said and we took our seats. "Well, this was one of the more unusual exercises I've been involved with and although it was primarily designed as a learning experience for our officer cadets, lessons can be learned on both sides. I'll start with what I observed from the aggressors' side. Cadet Smith was the assigned platoon leader and after the mission briefing he spent little time studying the map and finalizing his plan. Let's start with that. "Mr. Smith," he said, picking Smitty out of the crowd. "You were assigned a mission that would require you to lead your platoon through eight miles of enemy territory and you spent less than fifteen minutes developing a strategy for getting to your objective and launching the attack. Don't you think the lives of your men deserved more consideration than fifteen minutes, given the fact that you were allotted a full twelve hours to accomplish your mission?"

The colonel's tone was neutral but his demeanor was clearly negative and my elation over our victory quickly turned to one of foreboding. Smitty stood up and if he was experiencing the same feeling of dread I was, he didn't show it.

"I do, Sir," he agreed. "But when I saw the parameters of our area of operations, the plan I decided on just seemed so logical. I did consider a more traditional approach, briefly" he admitted, "But the key to my plan called for us to move quickly to catch the enemy off guard and I felt that every minute I spent considering alternatives could be better spent on the move."

"I was not permitted to be in the room at the time," the colonel said, fixing Smitty with his stare. "Did you ask the other cadets for their opinion on your plan, or once you came to your hasty conclusions was there no room for change?" For the first time since I'd known him I saw fear in Smitty's eyes. His whole body seemed to draw in upon itself as he realized that after all his hard work and preparation to become an officer, he might actually be washed out on the final day of our training. His Adam's apple rose and dropped on his skinny neck and his voice suggested that his mouth had suddenly gone dry.

"I don't remember exactly what I said," he said and his face flushed red. "Whether I made them feel their comments were welcome or not." A rivulet of sweat ran down his neck. "Perhaps I *was* too focused on the time element to allow for much discussion."

That may or may not have been true. I remember him saying "Comments? Objections? Anyone?" He only waited a few beats for someone to speak up and when no one did he immediately started breaking us up into squads. I could have spoken up on his behalf but I couldn't remember if I had misgivings about his plan at that moment or whether I felt my comments would be welcome or not. So I did what I did that morning. I kept my mouth shut, hoping Smitty's fate would not rub off on me. The Colonel seemed satisfied that he had taken this cocky cadet down a notch and was about to go on when Chubs spoke up.

"He asked, Sir," he said. "No one said anything. We were all on board." There were enough other cadets nodding their heads in agreement that I felt safe nodding too. Smitty sat down, clearly relieved, and touched by our support.

"If you don't know already how the cadets got to your position so fast--" the colonel said to the defenders, and here he took his pointer to the map. "After arriving at their jump off point, they double-timed back down the road, then turned onto the road that marks the edge of the exercise boundary and on up to this point here," he said, tapping the sharp bend in the road, "where they left the road and headed through the woods to your base camp. They traveled light and I'll have more to say on their equipment choices later."

"Sir." The lieutenant in charge of the defenders stood and without waiting to be recognized, questioned our right to use the road. "Isn't the road out of bounds? Why were they allowed to use that?" It seemed a direct challenge to the colonel's authority but he did not to take offence, another bad sign for us.

"I questioned that myself," he admitted. "It was never spelled out whether the road itself was in or out of bounds. That oversight will be corrected in the future. For our purposes, as soon as I saw what they were up to I decided that I would rule anyone who set foot on the road to be dead, but no one did. They stayed to the shoulder, but nice try Lieutenant," he said. A trace of a smile creased the corner of the colonel's mouth. I started to breathe a little easier but the colonel was not about to let us off that easy.

"That brings up another point," he said and he again looked at Smitty. "You moved your men for more than an hour and a half in single file without any flankers to protect you from an ambush. Aren't flankers standard procedure for platoon-sized operations? I appreciate your concern for speed, but don't you think not deploying flankers was taking too big a risk?"

"No, Sir," Smitty said, standing up. "There was no need to deploy flankers to the right because that was out of bounds. So if the defenders did ambush us it would have to be a linier ambush from the left. The vegetation was so thick along the side of the road I didn't think it would be practical to have flankers to the left. There would be no way to keep visual contact. I don't want to sound like a broken record, but it would have also slowed us down."

"And if you *had* been ambushed?"

"We were well spread out, Sir, and the rules left the defenders only ten men available for an ambush. If they ambushed the front of our platoon, the back would have deployed into the woods on their flank and we would then have had *them* in an L ambush." This time it was a Sergeant First Class with a 1st Air Cavalry patch on his right sleeve who took to questioning our ethics.

"Sir, The aggressors tried to get around the entire purpose of these exercises. We were supposed to simulate actual combat conditions they are likely to encounter in Vietnam. There are no out-of-bounds in Vietnam!"

"The Sergeant's right," the colonel agreed and before he could go on, Chubs spoke up again.

"Sir, for the past three months Sergeant Nichols has been drilling it into our heads that we have to deal with the situation as it is, not as we hope it is, or as we fear it might be. That's all we were trying to do." There was a murmur of agreement from the cadets and I stole a look at Sergeant Nichols who was leaning against the back wall, not even trying to hide his grin.

This angered the sergeant who had been caught off guard and unprepared when we opened fire on his position. His face turned red and spittle flew from his mouth as he yelled at Chubs: "And the situation is that if this really was Vietnam and you tried that crap your company commander would be writing a lot of letters home to your grieving mamas." This time Smitty didn't bother to stand up.

"Right from the start we knew your exact location," he said, his voice calm, his confidence back. "If this really was Vietnam we would have slept late and called in artillery after lunch." Even most of the defenders laughed at this and the colonel was grinning from ear to ear.

The tension broken, the discussion continued as an objective critique by the umpires about what each side did right and what they did wrong.

We were cautioned about our lack of security as we moved to our objective, but we were given high marks for Smitty's innovation and our quick response when our presence was detected before we were in position. We were judged to be a very cohesive unit, well trained, and well-conditioned. The umpires ruled we had won a decisive victory, killing ten of the enemy in the camp while another ten would have been able to escape. He ruled our casualties to be one dead and two wounded.

As we stood around congratulating ourselves, the ranger captain approached Smitty and asked if he had considered going to ranger school. Smitty answered that he had not. "Well, you should," the captain said and shook his hand. "Good job all around."

* * *

"Dead?" I said. "Smitty?"

"Can you believe it?" Fred said. "I got a letter from Rostankowski just before I left. He and Smitty only got five days leave after OCS. They landed at Tan Son Nhut and weren't there ten minutes when a 122 millimeter rocket hit the terminal. A piece of shrapnel hit Smitty in the back of his head. Rostankowski says he never made a sound. Killed him just like that. Wasn't even any blood hardly. Smitty! Can you believe it?"

I was in a daze. If anyone made it through Vietnam alive I always thought it would be Smitty. Smitty who would accomplish great things and get his men through safely. I couldn't wrap my head around it and when I finally did it left me more depressed than ever.

From the moment we arrived at OCS it had been drilled into us that to keep ourselves and our men alive we would have to master a wide range of military skills. Smitty did all that and more and it hadn't meant a thing. In the end he had gotten off an airplane, stepped into a building, and been killed and there was nothing he could have done to prevent it. He was just in the wrong place at the wrong time. Rostankowski, who graduated near the bottom of our class, was standing next to Smitty and hadn't received a scratch.

Chapter 4

Our convoy pulled out after breakfast the next day. A jeep with a .30 caliber machine gun mounted in back led the way while another took up the rear. Six deuce-and-a halfs and a ¾ ton truck filled with replacements were in between, the vehicles spread out like infantrymen on patrol.

We were sitting shoulder to shoulder on the side benches, our duffle piled in the aisle. Aside from two infantrymen who sat at the back, none of us had weapons. I had been placed in charge of the men in my truck. Nowhere in my training had I been taught how to react to an ambush when most of the men in my command were unarmed. The only order I could think of was *you two shoot back. Everyone else, hide.* Not inspiring leadership, to be sure.

The first mile was through a gauntlet of tin-roofed shacks populated by the hawkers, hucksters, pimps, and prostitutes who made their living off the desires of American servicemen. Dirty children squatted among the roadside litter while their parents and older siblings did business with the GIs who strolled among them.

Once free of what amounted to urban decay, the country-side opened up onto a tropical wonderland worthy of a postcard. Thatched-hut villages nestled in palm tree dotted islands surround by a sea of rice paddies, the green shoots waving in the breeze.

Small boys rode the backs of water buffalo, switching the beasts to greater effort as they harrowed fields yet to be planted. Young men manned primitive water pumps to keep the paddies full while old papa sans walked the dikes looking for leaks and watching the progress of their crop. Pretty girls in black pajamas and straw hats scurried along the road-side or across dikes carrying their baskets of produce on wood poles draped across their shoulders.

Young soldiers pulled out cameras and clicked away as if they were on vacation and such opportunities might not again present themselves before it was time to go home. Occasionally we caught glimpses of white sand beaches and the sparkle of sun off the ocean; I had to guard myself from thinking it wasn't going to be so bad after all.

We continued north along Highway 1 and without warning the

sky grew dark and we found ourselves in a soaking downpour. Cameras were stuffed away and shoulders hunched against the deluge. Water ran down our necks and chilled our backs and no sooner we were thoroughly drenched than the rain stopped as suddenly as it had started. The highway steamed and the air grew thick and oppressive. We passed through a small town with pink plaster houses, the walls surrounding them topped with swirls of barbed wire. Only a single iron gate, opening on the highway, interrupted the barrier.

We turned onto a dirt road and headed inland. Trees closed in around us and the soldiers in back tensed as the road wound around a small hill. One of them stood up, bracing a knee against the tailgate as he scanned the roadside ahead. He sat down once the hill was behind us but he seemed no less alert. Eventually the tension left him and a few minutes later we rumbled into a small compound under a banner that read *Welcome to the 53rd ID Jungle School–We make the best soldiers in the world better.*

If the purpose of the sign was to give me confidence in myself, it didn't. The news of Smitty's death had reminded me that I was not the best soldier in the world; not even close. But the sign gave me some relief in that it made me feel like I had a second chance.

Jungle school lasted five days and I devoted myself to learning everything I could about the guerrilla war I was about to face. Unlike Cam Rahn Bay, the camp was austere in the extreme. No officer's club, no movies, no PX. There weren't even any barracks. We lived in canvas tents and slept on the ground. There were no showers. Water for drinking and shaving came from canvas lister bags that hung like huge utters in the hot sun. There was no shade. If you were dirty you could strip and rub yourself down if the rain came when you weren't in training. All our meals were C-rations and no one was exempt from the program. Clerks, cooks, and mechanics took part in the same training as the infantrymen.

There was little new that I hadn't learned in OCS but what they taught took on a new urgency. Gone was the possibility that we might be stationed stateside or do our time in Europe, shining our shoes and getting ready for war with Russia. The games were over and the cadre made that clear right from the start with an afternoon sweep of the jungle outside the perimeter wire. We were issued weapons and ammo, but we were not allowed to chamber a round unless we made contact with the enemy. Only the cadre were locked and loaded.

The patrols were led by new sergeants and junior officers under the supervision of experienced cadre. We moved slowly with constant instruction--how to walk point, slack, and rear security. How to recognize booby-traps and the signs the VC left to warn their own people that one was near-by. We searched mock-up villages and listened to horror stories like the soldier who threw a grenade into a thatch hut and then flattened himself against the outside wall as if the grass would stop the shrapnel that killed him.

They showed us how to build bunkers and how to make fighting positions when the ground was too hard for entrenching tools. We learned how to locate tunnels and how to search them. We set up ambushes and re-learned what to do if we were ambushed ourselves. Doctors lectured about how to prevent heat stroke, trench foot, and venereal disease. We practiced bandaging wounds, applying tourniquets, and plugging sucking chest wounds. We were again shown the proper way to pack a rucksack: heaviest equipment toward the top, ammo, grenades and smoke grenades in the outer pouches where you could get at them quickly.

We practiced clearing jams in the M-16 and were warned against loading more than 18 rounds in a magazine to help prevent a jam in the first place. Radio procedure was stressed and everyone practiced changing frequencies because the radioman could not do it himself when the radio was on his back. Everyone pulled guard duty at night and ran patrols during the day to hone our skills and condition us for what lay ahead. The grunts complained but the clerks and other rear echelon types knew enough to keep their mouths shut and be grateful that jungle school would probably be the worst part of their tour.

Time passed quickly and then we were loaded onto trucks again and taken to LZ Hardscrabble, a two hundred acre compound of mud and dirt, wooden buildings, canvas tents, and sandbag bunkers surrounded by three concentric circles of wire--heavy mesh fencing, barbed apron wire, and a tangle of razor-sharp concertina wire. Guard towers alternated with sandbagged bunkers and open fighting positions every twenty or thirty yards.

Hardscrabble was the main base of the 53rd Infantry and was home to most of the support battalion and headquarters companies of the infantry, artillery, and engineer units. From the moment we arrived it was clear that the goal of the base commander was to get everyone to our assigned units as soon as possible.

I was assigned to C Company, 2nd Battalion, 605th Infantry Regiment. The orderly room was a shack about half the size of a one car garage with a sign over the door that read *C/2/605*. No company slogan, no inspirational motto, no claim to be the best of anything. Just *C/2/605*. The screen door banged shut behind me and a spec. 5 stood up from his desk and came to the counter.

"Yes, Sir," he said.

"Lieutenant Sullivan," I said and handed my orders across the counter. Without taking them the specialist turned and poked his head into the door behind him.

"Lieutenant Sullivan is here, Sir," he said and then turned back to me. "You can go right in. I'll watch your duffle."

I knocked on the door and stepped inside. There were two desks crammed into the small room. One had a brass plaque on the desktop engraved *Capt. Harold Messina*. The chair was empty. The plaque on the other desk had the division shoulder patch embossed in full color followed by *1Lt. William Avery X.O.* Lt. Avery did not stand or extend his hand so I saluted. "Lieutenant Sullivan reporting," I said. Lt. Avery tossed off a casual salute as if to say mine wasn't necessary even though his previous attitude said it was.

"Have a seat, Lieutenant," he said. I handed him my orders and he dropped them in his in-box without looking at them. I sat in a folding chair in front of his desk as he leaned back in his swivel chair. "So tell me something about yourself, Lieutenant," he said.

"Not much to say," I said, surprised by the command. "Came here right after OCS. This is my first assignment." He was obviously expecting more from me and gave me a few seconds to elaborate. When I didn't he went on.

"Thinking of making a career of the army?"

"I'm not thinking that far ahead. I guess I'll know if I'm cut out for this soon enough," I said. It was a lie and he knew it. He looked at me like I was a piece of dirt before deciding to big time me.

"Well I've been here for five months," he said. "Commanded a platoon at Benning before that and I can tell you Vietnam is nothing like you learned in OCS; commanding troops here is nothing like it is in the states, but you'll have to learn that for yourself." I noticed he wasn't wearing a combat infantryman's badge and I didn't for a second think it was because of any modesty on his part. He had never seen action. Probably hadn't even shouldered a rucksack since he left the states.

"I'm assigning you to first platoon. Sergeant First Class Nelson has the platoon now. You'd do well to listen to him." He showed me where the firebase was on a map thumb-tacked to the wall and traced the company's AO--area of operations--with his finger. He explained that C Company maintained two firebases, one held by one platoon, the other by the remaining two platoons. Weapons platoon, with two 81mm mortar crews, was divided between the two bases. "You'll be at Firebase Old Crow. A resupply chopper is going out there tomorrow morning. Report to Captain Messina. Be at the helipad by first light. Specialist Merry will get you squared away with the quartermaster."

With that I was dismissed without so much as a handshake or a 'good luck.' I left wondering why the CO was at a forward firebase while the XO manned the company headquarters in the rear.

* * *

I couldn't get to sleep, worrying that I would oversleep and miss my flight. The last time I looked at my watch it was after 4 a.m. and when I woke up it was to the sound of tracked vehicles rumbling past my tent.

I had traded in my duffel bag and state-side issue for a rucksack and combat gear the day before and had slept in my new jungle fatigues. I pulled on my jungle boots, slipped my arms through the shoulder straps of a very used rucksack, and headed for the tent flap before remembering the M-16 I had stowed under my cot.

The ground was wet from last night's rain and I ran to the helipad as fast as my untied boots allowed. Before I was halfway there a Huey thundered into view above the mess hall, heading west to who-knew-where. I could only hope it wasn't to Old Crow.

There were two Hueys on the ground when I got there, each with a ¾ ton truck backed up to the chopper's side doors. Two enlisted men were pulling cases of C-rations off the first truck and sliding them into the Huey while the crew chief distributed the load. The pilots were already in their seats, warming up the engines. "I'm supposed to hitch a ride to Old Crow," I yelled above the whine of the turbine. "C Company, second battalion?"

One of the men pointed to the other helicopter. I breathed a sigh of relief and went to the other truck. The pilots and crew chief were just arriving so I didn't have to yell to be heard.

"I'm going to Old Crow. Am I in the right place?" I said to the spec. 4 who was pulling gas containers from the bed of his truck and shoving them into the cargo bay.

"This is it. I'm by myself. Can you give me a hand?" he said, scrapping another container across the tailgate. I welcomed the chance to prove I wasn't the type of officer who wasn't above doing manual labor until he gave me the once over and I realized my new fatigues didn't have my rank sewn on. "New guy?" he said.

"Yeah." I dropped my gear and climbed into the back of the truck. "Gas?" I said, pulling one of the jerricans onto the tailgate. I couldn't imagine what a forward base would be doing with so much gas.

"Water," he said. "You *are* new." I didn't appreciate the sarcasm but accepted it as my due. The door gunners arrived just before we finished loading and without even making a pretense of helping out took their seats aft of the cargo bay. The one on my side pulled the beginning of an ammo belt from a metal box on the floor, laid it across the gun's feeding tray, and snapped it shut. The pilots started their warm-up procedure and I could feel the heat of the engine wash over me as I got the crew chief's attention.

"Catch a ride to Old Crow?" I yelled. He scowled.

"Shoulda told me that before. Gotta shift the load now."

"Sorry, I'm new," I said.

"No shit," he said. I might as well have had FNG--fuckin' new guy--tattooed on my forehead. The door gunner on my side gave the crew chief the finger when he turned to get the gunner on the other side to help him shift the load. After he had cleared a space I handed the crew chief my rucksack. He put it on top of a laundry bag bulging with clean clothes and then indicated a space next to the door gunner where I was to sit. He took my rifle and pulled the magazine from the well and set it aside. *What now?* I thought. He checked to make sure I didn't have a round chambered, replaced the magazine and gave the rifle back. Apparently I'd done something right. He said a few words into his intercom and the blades started a slow orbit above my head.

"Change of plans," he yelled into my ear as if unkind words had not been spoken only minutes before. "We got a pickup at Old Crow so that will be our last stop. You get the grand tour." I had no idea we were going anywhere *but* Old Crow anyway but I was grateful for any human contact that wasn't hostile. The side doors to the cargo/passenger bay had been removed so I scrunched back as far as I could and crossed my legs Indian-style. The door gunner tapped me on the shoulder and shook his head.

"That's rookie," he yelled. "Let your feet hang over. You won't fall out." I scooted forward until my lower legs hung over the edge. The sound of the engine grew higher in pitch and I could feel the aircraft grow lighter as we lifted off the ground. We hovered for a few seconds, then the nose dropped and we raced across the helipad, gaining altitude as we flew over the perimeter wire. We banked to the right and, gaining altitude, I could see the ocean off in the distance. Another bank to the left and the ocean dropped from view and I was looking at nothing but sky. At 3,000 feet we leveled off on a northwest heading.

From the air the ugly parts of Vietnam were washed clean leaving nothing but a beautiful, quilt-like landscape made up of a dozen shades of green rice paddies stitched together by lines of brown dikes. The lowlands soon gave way to the highlands. Villages grew farther apart and the jungle seemed to swallow everything but the rivers, still muddy from an early morning rain. The door gunner said something into his intercom and a moment later fired a short burst into the nothingness, testing.

Our first stop was an ARVN outpost that would have been invisible had it not been for the fallow rice paddies and millet fields surrounding it. The dirt road they were guarding ran along the edge of the clearing before crossing a small river by way of a one lane wooden bridge. On the other side were acres of working rice paddies and a small village; nothing of any military value. It was like the South Vietnamese soldiers were there just to make the government's presence known.

The outpost was so small we had to land outside the wire. Three soldiers ran forward and pulled off the supplies indicated by the crew chief–nine cases of C-rations and a box of batteries for their radio. No water cans, no laundry bags, and no ammo. The compound consisted of two bunkers big enough to hold three or four men each and a few fighting positions around the perimeter. We were on the ground for only a minute or two.

Five minutes into the air the crew chief tapped my shoulder and pointed to a compound the size of a football stadium atop a mountain. “Old Crow,” he yelled. I nodded and started studying the terrain from the perspective of one who would soon become very familiar with it at ground level. I no sooner formed the impression that it was rugged country than the chopper banked sharply to the left, the ground momentarily disappearing from view. Two minutes later we made our approach on another compound on a narrow ridgeline almost half a mile long. The compound was the size of a football field without the end zones, the slopes along the sidelines dropping off to the east and west.

“Wild Turkey,” the crew chief yelled and I remembered Lt. Avery telling me that was the base manned by C Company’s Second Platoon. At first glance the ridge seemed to have little to recommend it as a fire base. It was long and narrow, the ground an inhospitable platform of rock with no shade. There were no fences or apron wire to mark the perimeter, the ground too hard to take a stake, just a double row of concertina wire held in place by a few sandbags. There were more bunkers here than at the ARVN compound and they were higher and closer to the perimeter, so cramped were they for space. A mortar pit had been built at the south end of the camp where the approach of an attacking force would be the longest.

Despite its shortcomings I could see why they had chosen this site. It held the highest ground around and the slope to the east was steep and offered little room to maneuver once crested. A platoon of well-armed Americans could hold off a much larger force for a long time, even defeat them if they had adequate air and artillery support.

Soldiers materialized on both sides of the chopper as soon as we touched down and the crew chief started shoving boxes, bags, crates, and cans to the sides where they were pulled off by the infantrymen. Our chopper several hundred pounds lighter, the crew chief waved the soldiers off, the supplies littering the ground around our skids. When they were clear, one of the soldier gave a thumbs up; we lifted up and, nose down, raced across the compound, over the mortar pit, and were gone.

The chopper swung east across a narrow, river-bottomed valley and in less time than it had taken to unload at Wild Turkey we were over Old Crow.

Old Crow was bigger than Wild Turkey; more oval than linier, the more forgiving mountain top having been bulldozed flat to give the compound room to spread out. Tons of earth had been pushed aside, spilling over the slopes and creating embankments too steep in places for an enemy to scale. A tangle of concertina wire was sandwiched between two rows of apron wire for the perimeter. A zigzag entrance had been left open on the north side opposite an open dugout that I assumed was a machinegun pit.

An 81mm mortar pit ringed by sandbags was situated toward the east end of the compound and contained a bunker that served as the camp's ammo magazine. The Helipad was located far enough away so as not to interfere with the mortar, the space between taken up by a volleyball court and a canvas canopy that provided shade for the lister bag and extra containers of water.

It seemed like the entire camp turned out for our arrival but only a half dozen soldiers were positioned to unload the chopper, standing just off the helipad amid a jumble of empty water containers they were eager to exchange for full ones. Two men stood a short distance away, their feet spread wide to hold down the corners of a poncho spread out beneath them.

Puddles from last night's rain dotted the low spots of the helipad--a square of ground soaked in oil to hold down the dirt, but which also kept the water from soaking in. It would have to evaporate on its own.

A smoke grenade had been popped to indicate wind direction for the pilot and a soldier in a camouflaged helmet stood amid the green swirl, guiding us in. The bare-headed soldiers waiting to unload the chopper ducked their heads as an explosion of dust and dirt billowed outward from the edges of the helipad. The poncho ballooned and snapped around the ankles of the men holding it down providing glimpses of the boots and lower legs of the dead soldier underneath. Once the skids touched ground the crew chief waved the squad forward and motioned me off.

The men worked quickly to unload their supplies, parting just enough to let me through as I pulled off my rucksack and ran in a crouch off the chopper pad where two men waited to meet me.

"Lieutenant Sullivan?" One of the men shouted. He was tall and skinny with a balding pate that looked like it had been shaved clean like the rest of his head only a few days earlier. His jungle fatigues carried no mark of rank but because he carried the unmistakable air of military authority I addressed him as a superior.

"Yes, Sir." I yelled it like a recruit in training, not out of deference, but to make myself heard.

"Captain Messina." He held out his hand and I shook it. His fingers were long and delicate in the way a piano player's might be, but the skin was rough, the grip firm and quick. "Come with me," he said. The soldier next to him was younger than Captain Messina and because he took my rucksack for me I took him for an enlisted man.

The men were pulling off the last of the water containers when the two holding down the poncho stepped back, allowing the rotor wash to blow it away. Grabbing the dead soldier under the knees and armpits, they carried him to the chopper and slid him onto the deck of the cargo bay. One man lingered longer than the other, then patted the dead man's leg as if he were still capable of comfort before running clear of the chopper.

"Don't let that spook you," Captain Messina said as the helicopter cleared the perimeter. "First man we lost in three months." I nodded my head, not sure what to say to that. At the third bunker, the man carrying my rucksack hurried ahead.

"Your new home," he said, dropping into a trench. "I'll catch you later." He took another step down, ducked his head, and disappeared into the cave-like hole in the ground.

"That's Lieutenant Holder," Captain Messina said. "You'll get along." He said it in such a way that I assumed I'd be sharing the bunker with him.

"Yes, Sir," I said as if his statement was an order. I was very much aware that I was no longer a transient and needed to start making an impression. And not just on the CO. On everyone, including the enlisted men. Especially the enlisted men.

Chapter 5

Captain Messina's bunker also served as the communication center. Like the other bunkers, it was sandbagged three feet above ground level and dug down another three feet below that. Still, Captain Messina had to duck once inside to keep from hitting his head on the log roof. Two PRC25s sandwiched a bigger, stationary radio on a dirt shelf carved out of the front wall. Wire antennas snaked through the sandbags and up to the roof for better reception. An enlisted man sat in a lawn chair, the bank of electronics spread out in front of him.

"All set?" he said.

"Yeah, thanks," Captain Messina said. The enlisted man got up and Captain Messina motioned me to the chair.

"Hey," the PFC said as he passed me on the way to the door.

"Hey," I said. The captain opened a chair for himself as I sat on the frayed nylon webbing, wondering if it would hold.

"We monitor two frequencies at all times," Captain Messina said. "Battalion and company. Battalion's on the big set. The third set's for air, artillery, dust-offs. Sometimes the alternate company frequency if there's too much chatter going on. Hasn't happened yet. Not since I've been here anyway. You're taking over first platoon. They're in the field now. Watch out," he said, coming out of his chair toward me. I scooted my chair aside and he picked up the handset from one of the PRC 25s. "X-ray One, X-ray One, this is X-ray Actual, commo check, over." There was a static burst followed by:

"X-ray Actual this is X-ray One, I got you lima charlie. How me? Over."

"Same same," the captain answered. "Be advised your new platoon leader has arrived. You can spread the word, over."

"We're celebrating already, Sir. Over," the RTO—radio/telephone operator--said after a short deliberation.

"I'm sure you are, X-ray One. Out," Captain Messina said. "That was Specialist Cisco. He's your platoon RTO, if you want to keep him. I hope you have a sense of humor." I wasn't sure how to answer that.

"To a point, Sir," I said. His hawkish face gave away nothing.

"Sergeant Nelson has the platoon now. Lt. Barons DEROSed two months ago. He was very popular with the men. Maybe too popular, so you're up against that, but don't let that influence you. Is this your first command? I haven't been back or I'd have reviewed your 201 file."

"Yes, Sir. Right out of OCS," I said, not wanting to raise his expectations.

"Well, that might not be a bad thing," he said. "Things are different here." I noticed he'd said nothing about Sergeant Nelson--nothing good, nothing bad; not even that I would do well to listen to his advice as the XO had. It was standard practice to advise 2nd Lieutenants to listen to their senior sergeants and I was left wondering why he hadn't.

"Lieutenant?" Captain Messina said. My mind had been drifting.

"I'm sorry, Sir" I said, searching my mind to play back what he'd just said. "Leadership style?"

"Yes. Do you have a preferred style of leadership?" he repeated. If I'd learned anything at OCS it was that you shouldn't become too familiar with your men. Beyond that, all the greats--Grant, Lee, Washington, Bradley, Patton--had their own unique way of leading.

"Not really, Sir," I admitted. "Just to try and find the right distance to keep from the men, I guess." It sounded grossly inadequate even to me but Captain Messina seemed neither pleased or displeased with my response.

"Well, you're probably eager to get settled in," he said, getting up from his chair. I took his cue and stood up as well. "Did you have a chance to zero your weapon before you left Hardscrabble?"

"No, Sir," I said.

"We have a makeshift range out past the Helipad. You should get that done sometime today," he said, leading me to the door. "We'll talk again. Good to have you here, Lieutenant." He shook my hand and I went out into the bright sun, shielding my eyes and trying to remember which of the more than a dozen bunkers in the compound was mine.

* * *

My bunker was smaller than it looked from the outside, the double thickness of sandbags taking up a lot of space. A small window of sorts had been built into the back wall as much for light and air as to provide an exit for a blast from outside should we be attacked. Lt. Holder, Gary, introduced himself and gave me a tour.

"This is mine, that's yours," he said indicating the dirt beds dug into the side walls. "And this is ours," he added, sweeping his hand across the floor space. "I hope you didn't bring furniture."

"Nice," I said. A crate stenciled *shells, 8, mortar, 81mm, HE* was pushed up against the back wall along with a two cases of C-rations.

"The table is a pullout," he explained, indicating the wood crate. "And I grabbed you a case of Cs." I lifted the cardboard lid on my case and noticed it had already been opened.

"You stole my pound cake, didn't you?"

"I was going to. But I decided to wait and see if I was going to like you first."

"I appreciate the opportunity," I said.

"The air mattress works," he said, nodding to the deflated rectangle of rubberized canvas on my bunk. "You just have to re-inflate it every day or two. Yours I did steal after Lt. Barons left. You can steal it back when I leave."

"When will that be?"

"Seven months, three days."

"I look forward to that."

"Me too," he said. I sat on my bunk and leaned back against the wall, feeling a sprinkle of dirt fall as I did. "Was that one of your guys that went out this morning?" I asked, not sure if that was something that was talked about.

"Yeah," he said. "Stupid."

"You get attacked yesterday?"

"Last night. Mortars. It happens every now and then. Never more than a few rounds and unless you're on guard duty everyone just sits it out in their bunkers. Unless you hear small arms fire, then it's everybody out. Usually it's nothing."

"So what happened last night?"

"First round lands in the wire and this new guy on perimeter guard starts yelling an' screaming that we're getting hit, like we don't know that already. Miller, that's the kid that got killed--he was our medic--he thinks the new guy's screamin' that *he* was hit so he goes runnin' out there to help when the next round lands ten yards away; knocks him unconscious. He probably laid there five minutes before anyone even knew he was hit. And since he was the only medic in camp….. not that anybody could have done anything for him anyway." He stared at the floor for an awkward moment before saying what he was thinking. "At least it wasn't anything *I* did. New guy feels like shit though." I couldn't think of anything to say.

"Captain Messina says I should zero my weapon. We got anything in the way of targets."

Gary lifted the lid on the mortar crate and rummaged around inside and handed me a sheet of paper with five targets on it. "Half of this is yours, by the way," he said, indicating the crate.

"Which half?" I said, noticing that it was filled to the top with a variety of junk.

"The bottom half," he said.

* * *

The target range was a piece of plywood leaning against the perimeter wire and a few sandbags on the ground fifty yards away. There were no tacks but the plywood was so splintered with bullet holes that it I could impale the target on them. There was one guard on duty atop the commo bunker; everyone else was in their bunkers, out of the sun. Still, I knew I would be under close scrutiny for a while so I was careful not to violate any of the safety rules while handling my weapon. I lay on the ground, spread my feet, and nestled the barrel into a groove in one of the sandbags. I switched the selector switch from safe to semi-automatic, held my breath, took careful aim, and squeezed the trigger.

Men came swarming out of their bunkers in various stages of dress, rifles in hand, bandoleers bouncing off their chests, looking around to see what was going on.

"Hey! You're supposed to yell *fire in the hole* before you do that," the guard on the commo bunker yelled. Other's muttered and cursed before lumbering back to their bunkers.

"Sorry," I said in a voice that didn't carry far.

"Fuckin' new guys are gonna get us all killed," one man said loud enough for me to hear. I could only hope that wasn't true.

* * *

Captain Messina wasted no time putting me to work. He gave me the midnight to 2:00 AM radio watch and I was grateful for the opportunity to feel useful. The sergeant of the guard woke me fifteen minutes before my shift and, as there was nothing to do but put on my boots, I got to the commo bunker early. A PFC was sitting in the lawn chair when I got there.

"Oh, hey Sir," he said, not getting up. "PFC Masonis," he said.

"Lt. Sullivan," I said. I offered my hand and he shook it.

"Yeah, I know," he said. "Get your weapon zeroed okay?"

"Yes. Appreciate your concern," I said. He laughed. "So just what is it I do here?" I made no pretense of knowing anything because I didn't.

"It's real easy, Sir. We're X-ray Kilo. If any calls come in for us you just answer them. You probably won't get anything from battalion. That's this one," he said tapping the big radio. "Other than that it's just calling for sit reps every hour on the hour. That's what we call situation reports," he said when he saw my look of confusion. When my expression didn't change he said: "I'll show you. It's a little early but that don't matter. X-ray One, that's your platoon, is in the field. They're in ambush so they can't talk unless it's important so we do it for 'em." He picked up the handset from one of the PRC 25s and pressed the transmit button. "X-ray One, X-ray One, this is X-ray Kilo. If you have a negative sit rep, break squelch twice, over." He spoke just above a whisper and waited until two short static bursts came through the receiver. "Roger, X-ray One. X-ray Kilo, out…. They have their radio turned down low at night. That breaking squelch is just pressing the transmit button so they don't have to talk. If you have–" He stopped when another transmission came over the radio.

"X-ray Six, X-ray Six, this is X-ray Two, if you have a negative sit rep, break squelch twice, over." Another pause and then two more static bursts.

"That was second platoon, over at Wild turkey?" the PFC said. I nodded that I understood. "Besides the platoon in the field, we always have one squad outside the wire at night, either on ambush or a couple of LPs. Tonight second platoon has an ambush out but that's all you should be hearing from the company net. If you have any problems, just wake up Captain Messina. He don't mind." I assumed Captain Messina bunked behind the poncho liners hanging across the middle of the bunker. The PFC got up and I took his seat.

"What if they don't respond?"

"It's probably nothing. Usually someone forgot to change the battery, or they fell asleep. Keep trying for five minutes. Just don't never raise your voice. Then wake up Captain Messina." He started to leave, then turned back. "Officers don't usually do radio watch at night," he said. "That's just the Captain breakin' you in. He's big on training the new guys." With that he was gone and I was left with nothing but the radios to keep me company.

My shift dragged. Except for the sit reps there was no traffic on the radio. I was nervous that I would mess up my first sit-rep so I waited for second platoon to call there's in before calling for first platoon's. I got a strange sense of accomplishment, taking the sit-rep from my platoon, and wished the RTO on the other end knew it was his new platoon leader calling to make sure they were all right.

It was warmer outside the bunker, but a light breeze cooled my face and arms. I was too keyed up to go to bed after my shift so I climbed on top of the commo bunker and sat down on the sandbag fighting position.

"Tough first day?"

I almost jumped. A sliver of moon was just visible above the mountains to the west so that the man sitting next to me was nothing but a black silhouette against a less black background. How I sat down next to him without seeing him I didn't know. "Are you on guard?" I asked, regaining my composure.

"Sorta," he said. We sat in silence for an awkward moment.

"Yeah," I said, thinking of my target practice fiasco. "Tough first day." He struck a match and I could see a shock of red hair splayed across his forehead as he lit a cigarette, cupping his hand around the flame and shaking it out as soon as it was lit.

"Lot to learn," he said.

"Like light discipline?" I said. He laughed quietly.

"Can't see a shielded cigarette as far away as you think, but you're right," he said, taking a final drag and grinding it out on a sandbag. "Main thing to remember is one of us is always here to help. You just have to be open to it."

One of the first things we learned in OCS was to never appear unsure of yourself so I wondered how to ask for help without losing the men's respect. I opened my mouth to ask but when I turned my head the soldier was gone.

Chapter Six

I slept fitfully that night, my air mattress worse than Gary said. It was flat well before morning and I laid in bed, pretending to be asleep until someone stuck his head in the bunker.

"Captain wants to see you, Sir," he said. "Both of you."

"Thanks," Gary said and turned to wake me.

"I heard," I said, sitting up. "Shit! I've got to shave."

"You can do that when you get back," Gary said. "It's not a big deal as long as you do it every day. Unless you're in the field." I grabbed my fatigue shirt, still sweaty from the day before.

"How often do we get clean laundry?" I asked.

"Once a week," he said. "One set on, one set at the laundry. After a while you acquire a third set as people rotate out or whatever." I had seen an example of *whatever* when I'd arrived the day before. "Except for socks," he added. "Socks are community property. Take as many as you need until the next resupply."

"What about underwear?"

"Don't even bother. Nobody wears 'em except for sleeping if it's real hot. Unless you want crotch rot, which you'll probably get anyway. You can label yours if you want but nobody really bothers. Koreans run the laundry. They do a good job. " I took off my underwear and put on my pants.

"You can use the marker for your name too," he said, noticing my shirt had no name tag. "And your butter bar," he added, meaning my lieutenant's insignia. "If you're lucky the laundry will sew on real ones when they see the marker. Ready?"

"Let's go," I said, my boots tied.

"Your rifle's part of your uniform here," he said when I didn't grab mine as I headed for the door. "Goes with you everywhere."

On the way to the commo bunker we ran into Gary's platoon sergeant--a tall, stocky, black man who, despite the dusty boots and faded fatigues looked every bit the army sergeant. "Hey, Lieutenant. Captain Messina wants to see you," he said. Gary stopped.

"We're on our way," he said. "Sergeant Jackson, this is Lieutenant Sullivan. He's taking over first platoon." SFC Jackson's handshake was quick and firm, a man who made direct eye contact.

"Welcome to Charlie Company, Sir. Yeah, I saw you on the firing range yesterday. Don't let 'em get to you," he said, meaning the rest of the enlisted men. "My first day in the field I saluted my CO. That was in Korea. I'd probably be an E-8 now if it weren't for that." He smiled. Saluting an officer in the field in a hostile fire area can target the officer to enemy fire. It's not considered good form.

"He bunks with Sergeant Nelson," Gary said as we went on our way. "He's a dick."

"Sergeant Jackson?!" I said, turning back for another look.

"NO!" Gary said. "Sergeant Nelson. You heard about him?"

"No. What about him?"

"He's a dick," Gary said.

* * *

We ducked into the commo bunker--TOC (Tactical Operations Center) as everyone called it--and I followed Gary's lead by leaning my rifle against the wall once inside.

"You wanted to see us, Sir," Gary said.

"Take a seat," Captain Messina said, opening another lawn chair. He took a chair facing us as we sat down.

"I want you to do a sweep outside the wire before lunch," he said, looking at Gary. "You lead it personally. The usual mission, but more importantly I want you to familiarize Lt. Sullivan with the terrain. Has anyone explained our escape plan in case we get overrun?" This he directed at me.

"No, Sir."

"Show him that before you go," he told Gary. "Also you're going to put out some LPs tonight." Again he looked at me. "You'll be going with them. Pair him up with one of your squad leaders," he told Gary. "It's the only time you'll have to do this--sit a listening post--but it's the best way to learn what it's all about." I nodded that I understood; that nothing was beneath me. "Your platoon is due back in two days and you don't go out again for another ten or eleven days after that. During that time I'll be running you ragged between here and Wild Turkey just to familiarize you with things. Actually, you got here at the perfect time in the field rotation. Gary had to take his platoon out for six days the day after he got here, remember that?" he smiled, looking at Gary. "Course, he had Sergeant Jackson," he said as if that made up for any inexperience a new lieutenant might have. He said nothing about Sergeant Nelson.

"Any questions?" There were none. "Before lunch then."

"Grab a radio," Gary said as I picked up my rifle. "One with a frame."

Once outside I slipped my arms through the frame's shoulder straps. "Easier to carry," I said.

"Actually, I'm going to have you carry it on the sweep. Familiarize you with our call signs and shit. But first…" He led me to the back side of the perimeter where a bull dozer had pushed loose dirt off the back slope. There was no apron wire along this stretch, just a single row of concertina wire held in place by steel poles. At one point two poles had been placed close together. From a distance it looked as if there was only one but up close I could see that it was where two ends of the slinky-like wire met. The wire had not been fastened to the poles. Instead, D-rings had been attached to the razor wire that could be lifted off the poles to create a gap in the perimeter. "This is our escape route if we get overrun," Gary said. "If that happens the captain shoots off a red flare. When you see that, everybody pulls back to here. First person here pulls off the wire. Don't push it down the hill or you'll get caught on it when you slide down." The slope at this point was so steep that the tops of trees a short distance away were at eye level. "Pull it all the way back to the next stake and leave it there. Then slide down and di di mau." I looked at him. "Get the hell out of here. It's Vietnamese."

"What if the gooks are–"

"Hopefully they won't be back here. They've probably already scouted us out well enough that they know they can't get up this slope."

"That's what Montcalm thought," I said.

"Who?"

"Battle of Quebec?" I said.

"Not familiar with it," Gary said. "Anyway, we have a few fighting positions back here, just in case." I didn't see any.

"Where?"

"Back here," he said leading me away from the wire. "Against the back of our bunkers. That way we can watch the wire without having to worry about our backs." The fighting positions were not dug in but were sandbagged enclosures two feet high that a man could lay inside for protection while fighting back. "Oh, and get out quick. As soon as they see our red flare, Wild Turkey is going to call in artillery. On the compound. We'll have about two minutes. And don't forget the wounded." He led me to the front of the bunker and yelled inside. "Sergeant Fischer!"

"Yo, El Tee," Sergeant Fischer said, sticking his head out.

"We're going on a sweep. Get your men ready."

"We went last time."

"Breaking in the new lieutenant," Gary said. "I want you there."

"Oh, okay. Hey, lieutenant," Sgt. Fischer said, giving me a nod. Whether that was the real reason Gary wanted Sergeant Fischer's squad to go or not, I couldn't help but admire the way Gary had handled the sergeant's protest, making him feel as if he wanted his best men for the job.

"El Tee?" I asked as we walked back to our bunker.

"L.T.--Lieutenant," Gary said. "Things are different here."

"I noticed," I said.

* * *

Gary gave me a quick lesson on how to pack for a short mission such as a sweep around the compound. No rucksacks, only what we could carry on our pistol belts: a one quart canteen, battle dressing, ammo pouch with four magazines, and another canteen pouch, this one holding three or four hand grenades. He carried an extra bandoleer of ammo across his chest and a shoulder harness to distribute part of the weight of his pistol belt to his shoulders. Everything else went in our pockets.

As I was adjusting the shoulder straps of the radio pack the bunker went dark. "Here we go," Gary said as the sound of raindrops on the roof turned into a din of heavy downpour. "Check the radio and then we'll go," he said, turning it on for me. I had done communication checks dozens of time in training but now my mind went suddenly blank. "We're X-ray Three, TOC is X-ray Kilo," Gary said. "Just ask for a commo check." I took a second to run the words through my head before I pressed the transmit bar.

"X-ray Kilo, X-ray Kilo, this is X-ray Three. Commo check, over." I released the bar and waited.

"X-ray Three, this is X-ray Kilo. I got you Lima Charlie, how me?" I didn't understand the transmission even though it had come over loud and clear. Gary saw my panic and grabbed the handset.

"X-ray Kilo, X-ray Three, we got you same same, out." He handed me the handset and I hung it on my shoulder strap. "Lima

Charlie–loud and clear," Gary said. "Captain Messina sometimes uses 'five by five.' Been a while since I was an FNG. That's a–"

"That one I know," I said.

The rest of the squad was waiting at the gate, soaked to the skin, their bush hats dripping a steady stream of water down the backs of their necks and in front of their eyes. They gave me the eye, knowing I was the reason for their misery. Gary gave the order to lock and load. I already had a round chambered, thinking that was one of the things that was different over here, and had to fake chambering a round as a spec. 4 led us out the zigzag path through the wire.

"Call TOC and let them know we're outside the wire," Gary said.

"X-ray Kilo, X-ray Kilo, this is X-ray Three. We're outside the wire, over."

"X-ray Three, X-ray Kilo, roger, over."

"X-ray Three, out," I said and hung the handset on my harness feeling very much the soldier.

It took us an hour to circle the small compound and within the first five minutes I felt the shoulder straps from the radio pack burrowing a groove into my shoulders. Five more minutes and I felt my feet squishing in my boots, the extra weight of the water seeming heavier than it probably was. We stayed on a trail leading down the mountain for about fifty yards and then turned off the path and followed the contour of the hill.

Several times Gary pointed out where good listening posts or ambush sites might be set up and why. Occasionally I heard radio chatter from my platoon as they reported in and felt a sudden brotherhood with them. The slope got steeper as we worked our way around to the back side of the mountain. The men started slipping on the slick ground, grabbing fronds and placing their feet at the base of trees to keep from sliding. I could see what Gary meant when he deemed it an unlikely avenue of approach for the enemy.

Staying on track was exhausting. My legs burned and I opened my mouth to catch some rain, not wanting to be the first to pull out my canteen. Finally the point man stopped.

"Take a break, El Tee?"

"A little farther," Gary called back. No one made any pretense of being quiet. It might have been because of the noise of the rain, but I suspected it was more likely they felt safe so close to the compound. Still, it seemed careless and I wondered if Gary hadn't gotten too familiar with his men. The envy I had felt for that relationship only moments before I now saw as a liability. I wondered if the FNG in me was overreacting. Twenty yards farther on Gary called a halt. The point man sat on the ground while the rest of us kept moving forward, our interval collapsing until we were all gathered into a close group. *One grenade would get you all*, I could practically hear the sergeants at OCS yell. I sat down, digging my heels into the soft earth to keep from sliding.

"Wait here. I'm going to show Lieutenant Sullivan our exit plan from back here," Gary said. I groaned inwardly and struggled to my feet.

"You can leave the radio here," one of the men said, helping me out of the harness. "It's a hike and you're, you know, first platoon." The rest of the men laughed and Gary told them to knock it off and not good naturedly. They did as they were told and I started to admire his leadership style again.

The back slope of the compound was even worse than Gary had described it. Seventy degree at least, the rocks and dirt gullied from the rains and sliding downhill from its own weight even as we watched. Even Wolfe's men couldn't have scaled it.

"I see what you mean," I said.

"That's not going to make it through the monsoons," Gary said, meaning the slope. "Let's get back."

Chapter 7

Captain Messina was true to his word. He kept me moving to the irritation of third platoon who had to baby sit me. That night five men from Gary's platoon set up three LPs outside the wire and I went with them. Together we went downhill and then, in groups of two, spread far enough apart that we could fire in any direction without worrying about hitting the compound or the other LPs.

I was paired with a young buck sergeant with a Hispanic accent. He picked a small, depressed patch of ground that was still boggy from the day's rain. The mosquitoes were vicious; so vicious I had to swallow my pride and admit that I'd forgotten my repellent. "Man, don' never go nowhere without it, especially during the rains," he whispered, handing over his bottle. "Don' be stingy. I got plenty," he added, watching me squeeze a little dab into my palm.

"New Guy," I said.

"I know. Tha's why you wich me," he said. Unlike during the sweep, we talked in hushed voices, the night taking away any sense of security spawned by the light of day. "You take the firs' watch, Sir" he said, making no pretense of putting me in charge. "You know how to do sit-reps?"

I answered by miming two fast squeezes on a handset, the last of the daylight turning everything into dark silhouettes. Sergeant Cortez had carried the radio to our LP but now it lay on the ground between us, community property. Before we left he had rubbed camouflage stick over the frequency controls to black out the glow of the dials and now called in to report that we were in place. His voice was little more than a whisper and he turned the volume down so that the reply from TOC was barely audible.

"Jez don' mess with the volume, Sir," he said. "An' no more talking on the radio unless we been foun' out." A thought occurred to me, so basic I wondered why I hadn't thought of it before.

"What if I see something? Or hear something? How do I let TOC know?"

"Jez wake me up. You jez break squelch real fas'," he said, holding his hand close so I could see his fingers twitching. "That'll alert the other LPs an' TOC will ask you questions you can answer by breaking squelch. But wake me firs'."

I did not have to wake Sergeant Cortez once that night. I don't think he slept. After the sun went down the jungle came alive with all sorts of sounds that caused me to sit up and strain my ears. I did not want to overreact and cause a false alarm; worse, I did not want any VC to sneak by us. Twice I was scared enough that I was about to wake Sgt. Cortez and each time he was already awake.

"Animal," he would whisper, as if in his sleep. When the moon came up the jungle floor turned into a maze of shadows. Trees and boulders, if stared at, seemed to move and take on the shapes of men. Once I heard a voice say "Fuck you," as clear as could be and I sat up, leveling my rifle toward the sound. Sgt. Cortez sat up too and put pushed the barrel of my rifle down.

"*Fuck-you* lizard," he said and allowed himself a laugh. "Sorry, Sir. Forgot to warn you 'bout them." I suspected he hadn't forgotten anything.

It was a long night, three times interrupted by rain. Gary had warned me against taking my poncho. Too noisy. I took my nylon poncho liner instead. It didn't keep out the rain, but it kept me warm and acted as a security blanket throughout the night. When the black jungle turned green, we stood up for the first time. Sgt. Cortez picked up the wrappers from the food he had snacked on during the night, explaining that they often used the same LPs and didn't want the VC to find them and booby trap the site. Most of the things he told me I had learned at OCS; others were new and I was amazed at how much I still had to learn.

Sgt. Cortez put on the radio and handed me the handset. "Tell TOC we're on our way in so don' nobody shoot us." Moments later the two other LPs did the same.

* * *

No LPs went out the following night. Instead, Captain Messina had me go out on an ambush with a different squad from Gary's platoon. No one had specifically put me in charge. It was understood that the ranking soldier was responsible, but that was not the same thing. Again, a buck sergeant led us outside the wire just as it was getting dark. We went down the mountain paralleling the trail until the sergeant found a spot he liked. "This look good to you, Sir?"

"Looks good, Sergeant," I said, unable to see much of anything. The men set up their claymore mines to cover the trail and we then pulled back a safe distance and set up a linier ambush. In my mind I questioned why the sergeant hadn't set up a more effective L-shaped ambush but said nothing. Sgt. Henry set up the watches and I spent another uneventful night in the jungle. At least I didn't have to embarrass myself by borrowing someone's mosquito repellant.

Late the next afternoon the TOC radio watch stuck his head outside the commo bunker and yelled: "First Platoon, coming in!" I had been reading inside my bunker and put down my book, put on my boots, grabbed my rifle, and went outside to get my first look at my platoon. I need not have hurried. I had expected the rest of the compound to turn out too but everyone went about their business as usual. The work details had finished their work before the sun reached its zenith and most of the men were in their bunkers, staying out of the sun. Only one person was on guard, sitting in a lawn chair on top of the commo bunker as if he were lounging on a beach.

It was ten minutes before the point man broke the crest of the hill. The rest of the platoon followed, their interval compressed to a few feet. *One grenade would kill you all.* They were a bedraggled-looking bunch--tired, dirty, unshaven--and had a hang-dog look about them, as if they had lost friends when in fact they hadn't even made contact with the enemy. Their faces showed none of the relief I expected that they had all returned safely, no joy that their six day ordeal was over. Just a worn-out, dispirited, look. Captain Messina was at the gate to pull back the wire and welcome them back. A few went to the lister bag and, holding their mouths under the spigots, drank their fill. Most though, those who had been more disciplined with their water use, went straight to their bunkers to crash.

I picked Sergeant First Class Nelson out from the rest of the platoon by his face, years older than the rest of the men. Other than that, he looked no different than the rest of them. I expected him to look for me too, to come over and introduce himself, but he didn't. Alone, he walked to his bunker. At the entrance he stopped. I thought for an instant that he looked my way but before I could be sure he disappeared inside.

* * *

Two hours later it rained again, another downpour that lasted fifteen minutes. A few men from my platoon, Sergeant Nelson included, came out, naked, and tried to scrub a week's worth of filth from their bodies before it stopped. Most though, slept through it. I gave Sergeant Nelson a half hour to get himself together and then went to his bunker.

"Knock, Knock," I said, immediately regretting my tired attempt at levity. I stuck my head in and saw that Sergeant Nelson was asleep. Sergeant Jackson was sitting at a make-shift desk, writing a letter. "Sorry," I said. "I'll come back later."

"No. That's okay," Sergeant Jackson said. I stepped inside as he punched Sgt. Nelson's air mattress. "JIM! Lieutenant Sullivan here to see you." Sgt. Nelson rolled on his side and squinted my way.

"Afternoon, Lieutenant," he said.

"Sergeant." He swung his feet over the side of his bed, rubbed his eyes and then pointed his chin toward the door as if ordering me out. He followed me out into the sun which seemed to hurt his eyes.

"What can I do for you, Sir," he said as if this were not the first time we' met.

"Nothing," I said. "For now. Just wanted to introduce myself, maybe get your take on the platoon." He did not offer his hand and, as the time for a handshake seemed past, neither did I.

"Not much to tell," he said, dropping the *Sir*. "Just a platoon of grunts. No better or worse than any other, I guess." I suspected that wasn't true. Whatever the case, he had not answered my question and I took an immediate dislike to him. I should have called him on it but there was something intimidating in his manner and if that was his intent, it worked. I said nothing.

He looked older than I had expected, based on his rank. Women of a certain age, I suspected, might find him attractive in a rummy sort of way. His face showed early signs of wrinkling and the skin had a spongy-looking quality to it, his nose and cheeks a spider-web of red capillaries. He had the look of someone well into middle age but I suspected drink had added years to his appearance.

"Maybe another time," I said. "Sorry to have disturbed your sleep."

"Probably should be reporting in anyway. Let me know if I can do anything for you," he said and then headed over to TOC.

"Yeah, like clueing me in on the rest of the platoon," I said when he was out of earshot. "Fuck you."

* * *

I had planned on calling a meeting with all the sergeants from my platoon and later a platoon meeting with all the men the next day but Captain Messina had other plans for me. Second Platoon was going out that day and he detailed me and a squad from my platoon to catch a ride on the resupply chopper to help hold Wild Turkey while they were on their mission.

The company was undermanned and therefore so were the platoons. Gary had 31 men in his platoon and I had 30. Second Platoon, because they alone manned Wild Turkey, had 36 men plus a four man mortar crew and a full-time RTO in their TOC. Because of their extra manpower they ran four squads with eight men each. Three of those squads went on patrol when it was their turn while the fourth squad stayed behind to hold the fort. This caused bad feelings among the men in Gary's and my platoons because that meant one squad from second platoon got to sit out a mission every fourth rotation. Second Platoon claimed they deserved it because they pulled more LPs and ambushes. Both factions had a point.

I took third squad with Sergeant Little because it was their turn. Sgt. Little was a soft-spoken black man from Missouri who had gotten his third strip for reenlisting after his two-year commitment was up after being drafted. There were only three other black men in my platoon, all of them in Sgt. Little's squad, a situation I found too out of proportion to be a coincidence.

Second Platoon was ready to leave when we got to Wild Turkey. Lt. Petros introduced himself, pointed me to the squad leader he was leaving behind and left, his platoon stretching out along the ridgeline before disappearing down the gentler slope to the north.

Staff Sergeant Fote showed me around but there was little to see. I decided to lodge in the TOC bunker and perhaps pick up a few more tidbits from the radio chatter. The bunkers were taller here than Old Crow--and hotter--having been built on solid rock instead of being dug into the ground.

Captain Messina's decision to send me to Wild Turkey turned out to be a good one. It gave me the chance to familiarize myself with both Wild Turkey and the men in Sgt. Little's squad. The day after our arrival I ask Sgt. Fote to take me on a sweep around Wild Turkey and since my goal was to familiarize myself with my own men as much as it was to get the lay of the land, we took Sgt. Little's squad with us.

Sgt. Little was a steady, low key leader that the men responded to with little question, the only exception being Specialist Nolan. Nolan was a burly black soldier with three chains around his neck--one for his dog tags, the other two with a peace sign medallion and black fist carved out of wood.

The orders he didn't question, he bitched about. Sergeant Little seemed unperturbed by the rebel in his squad. When Nolan wanted to know why he had to do something, Sergeant Little had two responses--either it needed to be done or it was his turn. He did not allow himself to be drawn into an argument and the job always got done. For my part, unless I addressed him specifically, Nolan ignored me as if I wasn't even there.

Outside the wire the squad appeared as cohesive as could be expected. Inside the compound the black and white soldiers gravitated to their own kind, Sgt. Little excepted--a sign of the times. Racial tensions were high in the states and that was reflected in the Army as well.

* * *

Second Platoon was as dirty and bedraggled as my platoon was when they returned from their mission, but there was something different about them I couldn't quite put my finger on. Outwardly they seemed more vocal, happier to be back. But it was more than that. Something I felt more than saw or heard.

We caught the next resupply ship back to Old Crow and I was disappointed to find that Gary's platoon had already left on their mission. Gary and I had bonded quickly and I was surprised at how much I missed him when he was no longer around. As usual, though, Capt. Messina didn't give me time to brood. No sooner did we return to Old Crow than I was summoned to his bunker.

"Take a break," he said to the enlisted man on radio watch when I came in. I recognized him as one of the men from my platoon but beyond that I knew nothing about him.

"So how's it going? Getting a feel for things?" Captain Messina asked, motioning me to a chair.

"I think so, Sir. Slowly."

"How are you and Sergeant Nelson getting along? Any problems?"

"No, Sir." *Other than the fact that he's a fuckin' asshole.*

"Good. You'll be going out as soon as Third Platoon gets back. What do you think of your platoon so far?"

"Kinda early to tell," I said, avoiding any mention of Nolan or my concern that all the black soldiers were in one squad. "They seem to know what they're doing." Some chatter came across the radio but Captain Messina kept talking as if he hadn't even heard it.

"Lt. Barons ran a tight platoon. It was his for almost a year, and the last two months it was Sergeant Nelson's. You need to make it your platoon. Lt. Barons was a good officer. But without good leadership men can lose their edge quickly and it takes time to get it back. It doesn't happen overnight and pep talks won't work on these men. You have to lead by example, but I'm not telling you anything you don't already know. From what I've seen you have the right idea. Excuse me," he said, reaching for one of the handsets.

"This is X-ray Kilo Actual. Let me call you back in one five, over." Captain Messina apparently had the ability to block out only those radio transmission that didn't concern him. He laid the handset down and resumed our conversation.

"I'm appointing you morale officer. We've been without one since Lt. Barons left," he said.

"Morale officer?"

"War is hell. But it can also be boring as hell. Not much to do out here and make-work details don't cut it in a combat zone. Lt. Barons started a little library," he said, opening the lid on a wooden crate that once held mortar rounds so I could see the books inside. "He also got balls and baseball gloves for Wild Turkey and volleyball equipment for us, but the men need new things every once in a while. I've been keeping you busy but when you get into the routine of things you'll see there's a lot of down time and you know what that leads to." I didn't because I had yet to experience an excess of down time since joining the army.

"Is this for the whole company, Sir, or just–"

"The whole company. Lieutenant Petros is the laundry officer; Lieutenant Holder is sanitation officer. I have supply and everything else. Any questions?" I had none. "Good. I want you run an ambush tonight. One squad. Take a different squad than you took to Wild Turkey. It's your ambush. Don't take Sergeant Nelson. Have him set up the guard roster and make him sergeant of the guard. Time you started taking charge."

* * *

I took out Sgt. Allen's First Squad. It was raining when we left and I directed the point man to a spot near the place Sgt. Henry had picked when I went out with his squad, assuming it was a location I could not be faulted for choosing. As it turned out, the location didn't matter. It was so overcast there was no light from the stars or moon and it rained so heavily the NVA could have marched a battalion up the trail and we wouldn't have seen or heard a thing.

The rain continued on and off for the next 36 hours and when I was awoken the following morning it was to tell me that the south slope of our compound had collapsed during the night and I was to pick a work detail to replace the perimeter wire that had gone downhill with the dirt. I picked Second Squad because they were the only squad left that I hadn't yet worked with.

A thirty yard section of the back slope had caved in leaving a concave bulge in our perimeter, the concertina wire half buried twenty yards down the slope. There was no fixing the slope; the only thing to do was pull the wire back up the hill and reset it on ground that was still stable. A PFC, eager to prove his worth, volunteered and before anyone could stop him he started down the slope which quickly collapsed under his weight, sending him and a half-ton of mud sliding down the hill. The dirt kept going but PFC Murphy--thereafter nicknamed Audie, after the World War II hero Audi Murphy--was stopped by the wire.

The more he tried to extricate himself, the more tangled he became, the razor wire cutting him to shreds. I took the rest of the squad out the front gate and around the mountain and we cut him out with wire cutters. Embarrassed, Audie insisted his cuts were mere scratches but our medic, Doc Ertel, disagreed and spent the next half hour cleaning and bandaging the lacerations.

We had to throw grappling hooks into the wire from above and haul the tangled mess out of the mud slide and up the slope before we could reset the wire. Even then there was a gap in the wire because of the added distance the bulge created; we had to splice new wire onto the old to close the gap.

It took us all morning and part of the afternoon to complete the job. It was miserable work and we were all scratched and bloody before we were done, but the men worked well together despite all the cursing. More importantly from my point of view, I felt as if I had earned a small amount of respect from the men by pitching in and tolerating their bitching as if it were their due.

Chapter 8

Third Platoon came in late the next morning and my platoon left right after Gary's debriefing. Captain Messina had assigned us the same patrol area Third Platoon had just worked. The company hadn't made contact in almost a month; he thought the VC were lying low and would let their guard down after Gary's platoon left--not expecting another patrol in the same area for a while.

My platoon had already assembled at the gate when I left TOC. It was drizzling when I went into the debriefing and already the men's bush hats were soaked and dripping from the brims. I went to my bunker, sloshing through the puddle that had accumulated on the floor over the last few days. I was slipping my arms through the shoulder straps of my rucksack when Gary came in.

"Bandoleer first," he said.

"Oh yeah," I said.

"Relax, Lieutenant. They won't leave without you."

"A little nervous, I guess," I said. I slipped out of the rucksack, crossed my bandoleer across my chest and then got into my rucksack again. "How's my hair?"

"You look nice. They're gonna love ya," he said. I ducked out the door and joined my platoon at the gate.

"Okay, let's go," I said as if I'd led my platoon on six day missions hundreds of times before. No one moved. I stole a quick glance at Sgt. Nelson for a clue but he just stood there like the rest, enjoying my humiliation.

"Who takes the point, Sir?" Sgt. Little finally said. Did that mean I was supposed to pick someone to take up the most dangerous position in the platoon? I didn't know.

"First squad take the point. Third squad, rear security," I said and Sgt. Allen's squad took up position at the gate.

"Where to, Sir?" Spec. 4 Patterson said.

"Phu Nu first," I said. "Then the usual swing through Mortar Mountain." Mortar Mountain was the name the men had given to the mountain across the valley where they believed the VC set up for their mortar attacks on Old Crow. Dozens of sweeps through the area had failed to find the site and Captain Messina wanted it. Bad.

"You do a commo check yet?" I ask my radioman as we worked our way through the wire.

"Yes, Sir."

"Where's your antenna?"

"Right here, Sir," Cisco said. "No sense calling undue attention to myself." He had pulled the antenna over his shoulder and rubber-banded it to the shoulder strap of his rucksack. On my first radio watch Captain Messina had hinted that my radioman was a bit of a wiseass but so far he appeared to be nothing short of professional.

"Good idea," I said.

"Thank you, Sir. If there's anything I can do to make your stay here more pleasant, just let me know," he said. And there it was.

"I'll do that, Specialist," I said. The rest of the platoon was out of the compound, badly bunched up but already starting to spread out. I was eager to take charge but waited to see if they would maintain a correct interval on their own. We worked our way down the trail, violating everything I learned at OCS. But the path was bare of vegetation so that any tripwires would be readily visible, any mines exposed by the erosion, so I kept my mouth shut.

Specialist Patterson moved at a slow but steady pace. The weight of my rucksack, which at first felt reassuring, was now throwing me off balance, the straps already making themselves known on the boney parts of my shoulders. Twice I slipped, sliding a few feet down the slope on my rear but there was no laughter. Others were having the same problem. The drizzle continued and a small stream marked the middle of the trail until the ground leveled off. It had taken twenty minutes to get off the hill and already I was soaked through, my 65 pound rucksack having taken on another few extra pounds of water.

We crossed a small stream and continued north for half a mile before cutting across a cluster of rice paddies. The rain had stopped and several villagers were tending their crop. They watched us while going about their business. Specialist Cisco stopped, waiting for me to catch up.

"Gia Hoi," he said, pointing his chin toward the village. "They're friendly, as far as we know." An old mama san glared at us from under her conical hat and spit a stream of betel nut juice into the water. "Friendly being a relative term," Cisco said. We sloshed through the paddies, avoiding the dikes where booby traps might be set. The mud sucked at our boots making each step an effort and by the time we reached the jungle and started up Mortar Mountain my legs felt as if I'd just run a marathon in full gear. The faces of the men behind me showed nothing but the dull expression of every beast of burden I had ever seen--the blank look of the powerless to affect their own misery. Cisco dropped back again.

"The men won't think any less of you if you want to take a break, Sir," he said.

"Let's get away from the village a little more. Stay in line. I'll tell the point." I made an effort to move at a good pace to dispel any notion the men might have that I was calling a break because of any weakness on my part.

"You can give the men a break when you find a good spot," I told Patterson when I reached the front.

"Good a place as any," he said, swinging his rucksack to the ground. The slack man turned to the man behind him and I could hear "break" being passed down the line. I sat down myself, leaning against my rucksack to take the weight off my back and shoulders, and pulled out my map. I located Gia Hoi, and then took a guess.

"This where we are?" I said, tapping the map.

"About," Patterson said. The slack man, called Slick-slack, Slick for short, leaned over and gave his own assessment.

"More like here, Sir" he said, indicating a spot considerably farther behind my guess. "Takes a while to get used to the scale. An' not many landmarks once you get into the jungle. Plus these maps aren't worth a shit. There's a trail down here on the valley floor that swings up to Phu Nu but it's all overgrown," he said drawing an invisible line with his finger. "And another trail here, higher up. But this way's safer. Plus we've got a bet with Third Platoon. Whoever finds that VC mortar site first. You want in on that, Sir?"

"What's the bet?

"Two cases of beer. With ice."

"Sure," I said and then turned to Specialist Patterson. "About ten minutes," I said, meaning the break. "You don't have to wait for me to give you the word." I dragged myself to my feet and headed back to my place in line. Along the way I passed men smoking, drinking water, adjusting their packs, or napping. I should have gone all the way to the back of the line to make an appearance but I knew we had a long haul before the day was through and I decided to grab a drink and close my eyes for a few minutes myself instead. Besides, Sgt. Nelson was back there and I didn't want to deal with him just yet. Wasn't even sure how to deal with him.

Around one o'clock we stopped for lunch. The men gathered in groups of two or three but otherwise kept in line and stayed spread out as they drank warm water and ate cold C-rations out of cans. Doc Ertel handed out salt tablets and made sure everyone took them. I decided to stop putting off the unpleasant and grabbed a can of spaghetti and meatballs and joined Sgt. Nelson. Sgt. Nelson was at least ten years older than me and he hadn't impressed me as being fit to begin with, what with his drinker's complexion and a roll of fat around his belly. I was curious as to how he was holding up.

"How ya doin' Sergeant Nelson?" I said. He looked up from his can of beans and franks and eyed me without expression.

"*I'm* doin' just fine. How are *you* doin'?" he said. My face went hot. In fact, he looked better than I felt and if I had underestimated his stamina, I felt certain I hadn't underestimated his disposition toward me. I decided to be the better man and play to his ego.

"Good," I said, pulling out my map. "Where you figure we are? About here?" I pointed to a spot about an inch from the location Slick had shown me earlier.

"About. Hard to tell when ya can't see a hundred yards ahead. 'Sides, I ain't been keeping' track. This is your show." I stood stock still. My heart was pounding and I felt my ears go hot. *So that's how it is, you fuckin' bastard,* I thought, but kept my composure.

"Thank you, Sergeant," I said, standing up and walking back the way I had come. "And if I get killed it'll be your show so you better fuckin' keep track of where we are."

"Sir?" another man said as I walked by.

"Nothing," I said. "Just talking to myself."

"Don't go looney on us yet, Sir," he called after me. "You just got here."

* * *

"Not gonna eat?" Specialist Cisco said as I jammed my spaghetti and meatballs into my rucksack. I said nothing, afraid of what might come out of my mouth. "Gotta eat some something, Sir."

"You're not my mother, Cisco," I said, turning on him. "Get that through your head right now." For a moment I thought he was going to cry.

"Yes, Sir," was all he said. He sucked his spoon clean, stuck it in his shirt pocket and tossed his empty can off to the side.

"And bury that, or hide it under a bush. Ya wanna lead the gooks right to us?!" He buried the can under leaf litter making me feel like the biggest asshole second lieutenant in the history of the United States Army. "We leave in five minutes," I said.

"Uh…Sir?" he said, getting his gear ready. I looked at him as if to say *what now?* "We usually change points every hour or two, depending. Kinda stressful up there," he added as if I didn't know what stress was.

"Tell Sgt. Little he has the point," I said, then changed my mind. "Never mind, I'll do it myself." Give me a chance to look like I know what the hell I'm doing for a change.

* * *

Despite his tough talk and demeanor, Specialist Nolan was not part of the point/slack team. Instead it was two white kids, Brokovitch and Turner who alternated between the point and slack positions. I checked on them occasionally and found they did not have the sense of place that Patterson and Slick had.

We went through two more point rotations before I went to the front to find out where we were again. "Somewhere in here, Sir," Specialist Patterson said, running a finger across a mile of green. He looked at Slick who just nodded. "Everything looks the same in here," he said, meaning the jungle.

"Should be a big gully around here somewhere," Slick said, pointing to a place on the map where the contour lines took a loop toward the higher elevations. "Thought we would have reached it by now but it can't be too far away. Take that right up to the trail if you want an exact location," he said.

"That would be nice to know. Five more minutes," I said.

We hit the gully shortly after the break and followed it uphill until the radio buzzed.

"They want you up front, Sir," Cisco said. "He wants everyone to be quiet." I passed the word back and hurried forward, my thighs burning every step of the way. Patterson and Slick were sitting just below the trail. I leaned forward and looked both ways, like I was crossing a street. To the right the trail dropped out of sight and then reappear thirty yards farther on.

"Good job," I said.

"What now?" Patterson asked. I looked at the sun, now just a flicker of light through the jungle far to the west.

"Think we can get around to the back side of Phu Nu before dark? I'd like to set up an ambush close to the village."

"You're not going to sneak up on Phu Nu. Or any other village for that matter," Slick said. "Fuckin' dogs will give you away every time."

"I'd shoot every dog in Vietnam, it was up to me," Patterson said. "But El Tee Barons wouldn't let us. Hearts and minds and all that shit."

"What does Sgt. Nelson say?"

"Sgt. Nelson's chicken shit. He'd shoot every dog *and* person in Phu Nu if he thought he could get away with it."

"Too close to his pension now, though" Slick added. I should have told them to knock it off but I was enjoying the rare moment of camaraderie too much.

"Then I guess this trail's our next best option." I said and waited for comments.

"Sure," was all Patterson said.

"Okay, let's drop back down, parallel the trail, and just before dark come back up and set up a half mile or so from the village. Maybe get lucky." Slick waited a moment before he spoke.

"It's okay to use the trail for a little while," he said, going against everything I'd been taught. "This slope is killer on the hips. And there's still enough light to spot booby-traps."

"Time for a point change anyway," Patterson said. "Brokovitch loves that trail shit. He finds a booby trap? You'd have to shoot him in both legs to stop his struttin'."

"Okay," I said. "You fall in behind Little's squad when they come up. Let's be careful." I still wasn't convinced walking the trail was the right call but my hips were hurting as much as anyone's.

* * *

Once on the trail the pace actually slowed. Apparently Specialist Brokovitch dreaded the thought of missing a booby-trap even more than he enjoyed finding one. I started to worry we weren't going to get to our ambush site before dark when shooting erupted from the front of the line. The platoon stopped. Men were crouching, lying down, their weapons pointed into the jungle, their eyes searching for movement.

My heart was pounding, not knowing what to do. The small arms fire was soon joined by Sgt. Little's machine gunners. I had yet to make a move or issue an order when Sgt. Nelson ran past me. I followed like a trained dog until we reached the point. Brokovitch and Turner were firing short bursts at a bend in the trail thirty yards ahead while the two black machine gunners sprayed a wide swath across the entire front. Sgt. Little and Specialist Nolan were also in the fight, the M-79 man hanging back, too far away for his canister rounds, too close to use his grenade rounds. Sgt. Nelson made a quick assessment and called a halt to the shooting, Specialist Nolan emptying the rest of his magazine before obeying.

"What is it?" I gasped, a lame attempt to look like I was in charge.

"Gooks, Sir," Brokovitch said. "At least two that I saw." He looked at Turner.

"Could have been more behind them," Turner said. "I saw at least one weapon," he added, to my great relief.

"Okay. Good job. Stay down," I added because I couldn't think of anything else to say. Behind me I heard Specialist Cisco calling in the contact, people doing their jobs without being told. Ahead a weak voice called out and everyone opened up again, then stopped on their own.

"Chieu hoi!" Sgt. Little yelled. *Chieu hoi* was the name of the program encouraging the Viet Cong to defect to our side. In this case Sgt. Little was asking him if he wanted to surrender. The man answered again in what sounded to me like gibberish.

"What's he sayin'?"

"Who knows?" Sgt. Little said. "If he wants to give up all he has to say is *Chieu hoi*. Pretty sure he's hit, Sir. What do you want to do?" I waited for a suggestion from Sgt. Nelson but he didn't even look my way.

"You call it in?" I said to Cisco, stalling for time.

"Yes, Sir."

"Good. Tell the other squads what's going on."

"I'm sure they were listening in, Sir," Cisco said. Of course they were. Stupid. The light was fading fast. The dark green of the jungle was turning black and the sky was the color of old lead. Again the Vietnamese called out, a long spiel no one could understand. I tried to pick out the words *chieu hoi* but everything sounded the same.

"Hold your fire," I said. The man was obviously behind cover or he would have been dead by now. I wanted to send someone forward and take him prisoner but the thought that I might get one of my own men killed stopped me cold.

"Want us to check it out, Sir?" Sgt. Little asked. He seemed willing but I didn't want to risk it.

"No. Let's pull back a ways and set up an ambush. Maybe they'll come back for him." I left Sgt. Little with the two machine gunners to watch the trail while the rest of us pulled back about twenty yards. I heard one of the gunners say something about me being hard core. I assumed by his tone that he approved of a leader who would leave a wounded enemy to die a slow, agonizing death on the off chance that we might get a few more if his friends came back to get him. The truth was, I didn't know what to do and pulling back to set up an ambush was the first thing that popped into my head. I pulled Sgt. Nelson aside.

"I want you to set up an L-shaped ambush with second and third squad facing that way," I said, pointing up the trail. "I'll set up first squad to cover anyone coming up the trail the other way. Make sure everyone knows their field of fire."

"Not a good idea, Lieutenant," he said. It did not escape me that he avoided calling me *Sir*."

"Why's that, Sergeant?"

"I'm sure that would look very good in OCS, but not out here. Not with these guys."

"Because?"

"Because they're not used to it. You can set up your silly stakes and mark out your fields of fire, but when the shit starts flyin' and you can't see your hand in front of your face these guys are going to be shooting all over the place. You'll be lucky if they don't kill more of us than the gooks. Sir."

I wanted to tell him to just follow orders but the fact that this was the first time he had offered his advice convinced me he was right, especially since I felt he offered it more to keep himself from getting shot than to keep me from making an embarrassing mistake. There was a trace of gray through the trees to the west and I did not want us fumbling around setting up claymores in the dark.

"Okay. We'll set up an NDP right here. Machine guns facing up and down the trail. Claymores all around. Better hurry," I said. "Getting dark." I pulled Sgt. Little and his machine gunners back and made a final check of the perimeter.

The usual procedure was to have the platoon leader and his RTO set up a command position in the middle of a night defensive perimeter but our small platoon made our perimeter so small that that seemed impractical. Instead, Cisco and I took up a position across the trail from Sgt. Little's machine gunners. The wounded man occasionally called out and it wore on my nerves. I tried to think of other things but it didn't help. I was too keyed up to sleep so I took the first watch.

The man's cries for help grew farther apart. My mind was racing, questioning the things I might have done wrong. Was setting up the NDP right on the trail the right thing to do? Would the circular perimeter allow enough fire power to be brought to bear if the VC did come down the trail? Would the gooks guess we were ambushing their wounded comrade and ambush the ambushers? Did the men set their claymores out far enough, or with the backs to a tree so the back blast wouldn't hit us? Should I have asked the squad leaders to check?

You don't even have to ask. If you need help, just be open to it. I turned at the sound but there was no one there. I caught a glint of star light reflecting off someone's glasses just before they disappeared into the dark. *Smitty?* I thought. Isn't that what he once told me, if I needed help… No, that's crazy. Nellis? He's small, wears glasses.

The wounded Vietnamese moaned, too weak now to speak. One of the machine gunners coughed; another man gasped when his partner elbowed him to stop his snoring. A crackle came over the radio, then my call sign, asking for a situation report. I squeezed the transmit button twice, grateful for something to do, then listened to the sit reps for the other ambush and the three LPs the company had out that night. The moon was now up, a quarter crescent blurred by the clouds. The wounded man groaned again and I wished him dead, for his sake as well as mine. I looked at my watch. 6:15. Eleven hours to go.

I looked up the trail, watching the trees take shape in the moonlight. I looked across the trail at the machine gunner on guard, his black face nothing but an outline. His hand came up, squashing a mosquito on his neck, then applying more repellent. I heard Captain Messina's voice calling to me again, a soft whisper in the night. Another hour had passed, another sit rep. I heard a noise and turned toward the sound, saw the machine gunner do the same. *Easy, don't panic. Probably just an animal. Another predator on the hunt.* Was my silent advice meant for the machine gunner or myself? I was glad he heard the noise too. Not all on me. The leaves continued to rustle, slowly fading to nothing.

The moon disappeared and the sky opened up, the rain coming hard and heavy. The man groaned again, this one sounding more like a moan of happiness. I pictured him turning his face to the sky and opening his mouth to catch some rain, trying to get one last bit pleasure before he died. Men were waking up around me, pulling poncho liners from their rucksacks, wrapping themselves up to fight off the chill. Cisco slept through it.

The rain stopped. Another sit-rep and Cisco woke up to the sound of our call sign. He looked around, trying to figure out where he was. "Oh," was all he said. Then "My watch, Sir?"

"Yeah," I said. I could hear movement as other watches changed around me. Cisco shivered and pull out his poncho liner, wrapping it around him to keep in his body heat.

"Okay, I got it, Sir," he whispered and sat up taller as I settled in. "He dead, Sir?"

"Yeah, I think so," I said realizing the moan I heard when the rain started was the last sound I'd heard from him.

"Good," he said and put his rifle where he could get at it quickly.

Chapter 9

I couldn't sleep. I was awake not only for my watches, but for most of Cisco's as well. It wasn't until his last watch that exhaustion finally caught up to me and I fell asleep.

"Lieutenant." Someone was shaking my shoulder. "Lieutenant Sullivan." Again the Goddamn shaking. "It's morning."

The sun wasn't up yet but the eastern sky was lighter than the rest of the world so it wouldn't be long. "Right," I said and looked around the perimeter, saw the restlessness of the men. I grabbed my rifle and made my rounds. "Okay, let's go. Get your claymores in. Let's get the hell outta here." There were no arguments. Our NDP was at our last contact with the VC and they knew the jeopardy that put us in as well as I did. Better.

Cisco was already packed up when I got back. I stuffed my poncho liner into my rucksack and before I stood up automatic fire broke out upslope from our perimeter. I dove to the ground. More shooting. Someone screaming for a medic. My men were being slaughtered. Brass shell casings rained down around me. Sgt. Little's machine gunners running past me, setting up their gun. Cisco put in a new magazine and then laid low, his ear to his handset.

"X-ray Kilo, X-ray Kilo, this is X-ray One. We are in contact at this time, do you copy, over." I buried my head as a machine gun opened up near-by. Ours? The noise was deafening. I looked around. Men were lying down, looking for cover, firing into the jungle.

"Not at this time," Cisco said. "More later. Out." He picked up his rifle but I yanked it from his hands.

"We need help! Air support. Call air!" I yelled. My voice sounded far away and I wondered if Cisco even heard me. His eyes were big; all he could do was stare at me, a look of bewilderment on his face. I reached for the handset but he snatched it away. "We need help!" I yelled, trying to get through to him. A bullet threw a spray of dirt into my face and when I looked up the jungle was gone, replaced by a field bright with sun. I looked around. Panic-stricken men were running past me, a gray-clad horde splashing across a creek in hot pursuit. A sergeant with an Irish brogue was grabbing every blue jacket he could get his hands on; trying to stop the rout, get his men in line.

In the distance I saw a church steeple poking above a line of trees, Manassas Junction invisible behind a ridge to the south.

The sergeant was livid, screaming at an officer whose horse was practically trampling his own men in his panic to get away. He saw a lieutenant running his way and grabbed him by both shoulders, shaking him as if that might clear his head.

"Rally yer men, Sir. For God's sake draw your sword and use it." The Lieutenant's eyes were wide, seeing nothing but the Confederate infantry closing in behind him. He tried to struggle free of the sergeant's grasp; the sergeant threw him to the ground in disgust. He turned, seeing me for the first time. His expression said he hadn't expected to see me, but was not really surprised either. "Ya shavetails never change, do ya?" he said. "Never let 'em see yer fear," he said looking at the panicked mob in blue running for the nearest tree line. "No matter how skeered ya are, don't let yer men see it." Then, seeing no Union men between him and Bull Run that weren't either dead or dying, he turned and joined the rout.

"Lieutenant! Lieutenant?" Specialist Cisco's eyes were as wide as agates.

"Yuh." I looked around. The noise was as loud as ever, the men firing on full automatic, the machine guns chattering in six or seven round bursts, the boom of a shotgun blast as the M-79s let loose with canister rounds. One of my men was face down twenty yards out from our perimeter, caught in the crossfire and yelling not to detonate his claymore. What I couldn't hear was any shooting beyond our own lines.

"Hold you fire! Hold your fire!" I yelled, hurrying along the line until the shooting stopped.

"Jesus Fuckin' Christ, you guys almost killed me!" PFC Nellis rolled onto his back, drawing his foot up to where he could get a good look at it. Doc was already there, pulling Nellis's hands away so he could see for himself.

"Sgt. Burkholtz! Take your squad and check it out," I said, pointing to where the enemy fire came from. "Sgt. Little. Check out the guy from last night. Any weapons, documents, bring them back. Nolan, go with him." Nolan was standing only a few feet from me. He looked me in the eye and brought his right hand to his forehead. I closed on him in a second, got in his face.

"What the hell do you think you're doin'?" I hissed. Nolan didn't flinch.

"Acknowledging your order. Lieutenant," he said. He brought his hand down, a smirk on his face. Nolan was taller than me, solidly built, his eyes looking for a fight.

"Nolan!" Sgt. Little yelled. Nolan waited just long enough to let me know he wasn't afraid of me or my rank, then turned and walked away.

"He's bad news, Sir," Sgt. Nelson said, appearing beside me. "The whole bunch of 'em," he added, looking in the direction of Nolan and Sgt. Little. My anger shifted to Sgt. Nelson but I said nothing. "Outta nip that in the bud," he advised. *And just what the hell were you doing the whole two months before I got here?* I thought as he walked away.

"Sgt. Little's not like that." Cisco said. "Stevens either."

"What about Caulkins?" Cisco shrugged.

"He's just Nolan's home boy," he said. I needed to exercise some control over…anything. Sgt. Allen's squad was gathered around Nellis, trying to see how bad he was hit. Trying to be a part of it.

"Doc, you need all those nurses?!"

"No Sir," Doc said.

"Sgt. Allen!" I yelled and the squad started to disperse. My mind flashed back to the first moments of the firefight. What the hell had happened!? What the hell *was* that? How long was I out of it? Hundreds of M-16 casings littered on the ground, at least three magazine's worth at each fighting position. But on full auto a man could fire twenty rounds in five seconds so that didn't tell me much. I joined Doc to see how Nellis was.

"How ya doin', Nellis?" I said.

"Ask Doc. Jesus Doc, take it easy!" he said, his foot jerking back from the pain. His glasses were smudged with so much dirt I couldn't see his eyes.

"He'll be out for a while. Two more like this and you get to go home," Doc said referring to the rule stipulating that if a man earns three purple hearts he gets to go home no matter how much time he has left on his tour. Doc was blotting blood from the gaping wound on the Nellis's ankle so he could pick out the bone fragments.

"Shit. This should be enough to get me home, don't ya think, Doc?" Nellis asked. He flinched again when Doc hit a nerve." Doc didn't answer, continued to work on the foot. There were no shell casings on the ground. Nellis hadn't fired a shot, keeping his head down while bullets from both sides whizzed over his head.

"Them or us?" I asked.

"I got hit right off," Nellis said. "It wasn't us."

"Lots of open field around Phu Nu," Cisco said. I hadn't seen him join us. "We can get a chopper in there."

"Call 'em now."

"I already let them know we have a WIA. They have a crew standing by. We can call again when we get there."

I couldn't look him in the eye. I was just starting to realize how badly I had panicked, trying to call for air support because a few VC had taken potshots at a platoon of heavily armed Americans. It wasn't even a few. Sgt. Burkholtz returned and reported that, based on the shell casings, there were only two of them.

"Any blood trails?" I asked

"Naw. Too much cover between us and them. They didn't stick around long," he said, making me feel even more foolish.

Sgt. Little returned with a Chinese SKS and reported that the man wounded the night before was dead. There were no documents to say who he was and no blood trail to indicate that the other man seen with him had been wounded. I was just glad he had a weapon.

Getting Nellis to the LZ was harder than I expected. He couldn't bear weight on his foot so Doc fashioned a crutch from a tree branch; Nellis's gear was distributed among the rest of the platoon. An axe would have made making the crutch easier but no one was carrying one. I also noted that not one person in the platoon was carrying an entrenching tool. That would have to change.

Everyone had to check out the dead Vietnamese as we passed. He appeared to be in his mid-thirties but it was hard to tell. He had been hit once in the lower abdomen; another bullet had broken his femur which was sticking out of the wound like a piece of bloody porcelain. He died laying on his back, his eyes and mouth open. It must have been a lonely and painful death; it didn't take long to satisfy my curiosity.

The people at Phu Nu knew we'd be coming and had all night to booby-trap the trail. Three times the line stopped and Brokovitch called me forward to see the boobytraps, either for my education or to show off his skill. I wasn't sure which.

"Whaddya ya do with it now?" I asked.

"Take 'em back and dispose of 'em. Can't use them because the gooks sometimes cut the fuses so they explode as soon as the spoon comes off." He reached into the brush on the side of the trail and closed his hand around the grenade. "Fuck!" he said, making me flinch.

"Jesus Christ!" Turner snapped. "How many times have I told you not to do that!"

"Fuckin' safety pin!" Brokovitch said. "They sometimes replace the grenade pin with a safety pin 'cause it slides out easier. Here, hold this for me, Sir," he said, and handed me the grenade. "Fingers tight around the spoon." I did as I was told as he wrapped electrician's tape around the grenade and spoon to hold it in place. "If it's a grenade pin I keep it. I'm makin' a necklace for my girl back home," he said.

"Lovely," I said.

Phu Nu was a small village nestled into a jungle alcove on a gently sloping interruption of the mountainside. Separating us was a 200 yard wide field planted in yams and other vegetables suitable for the soil. There were no dikes for cover should we be attacked during the medevac. There were also no people to be seen--no one cultivating the fields, no one tending the water buffalo, no one gathering firewood for the noon meal. Text book OCS problem.

Cisco called for the dust-off and we moved out into the field. We hadn't gone ten yards before the dogs started barking. Shortly after reaching the yam field Brokovitch stopped. He reached into the leafy recesses of one of the plants and pulled out a bamboo stake, its tip cut to a razor sharp point and angled in such a way that it would slice into a man's shin just above the boot.

"Punji sticks!" he said, holding it up for all to see. "Keep away from the plants!" The men did no such thing. Every plant that concealed a punji stick, and many that didn't, were summarily executed by a few well-placed kicks and stomps. Hearts and minds, I thought to myself.

"Leave 'em," I yelled. "Set up a perimeter. Let's go." Cisco came up beside me. There was a buzz of activity over the radio.

"Five minutes out, Sir," he said. Sgt. Nelson, Doc, Brokovitch and I left Nellis on his own while we cleared the LZ of punji sticks. We heard the chopper before we saw it. Cisco pulled a smoke grenade from his rucksack, ran to the center of the perimeter and tossed it.

"What's their call sign?"

"Dust-off Seven." he yelled. I pressed the transmit bar.

"Dust-off Seven, this is X-ray One, over." A yellow plume of smoke was starting to billow up from the yam field. Dust-off Seven acknowledged my transmission.

"Dust-off Seven, this is X-ray One, we have smoke out. Please confirm, over." The Huey burst over the tree line to the north, the barrels of its machine guns bristling out its sides.

"X-ray one, this is dust-off seven. I have yellow smoke, over." He flared away from us, gaining altitude as he assessed the situation. Cisco's arms were raised over his head, the smoke from the grenade drifting lazily toward the village.

"Dust-off Seven, X-ray One. That's affirmative, over." The chopper circled back.

"X-ray One this is Dust-off Seven. I don't like that village there. I'm going to come in cross wind from the south, Over."

"Roger, Dust-off Seven. Out." I turned to tell Cisco but he could see for himself. The chopper made its approach over the trees, Cisco directing him with his arms. Yellow smoke exploded outward from the grenade canister, the men on security watching their sectors for signs of trouble while the chopper was at its most vulnerable.

Doc helped Nellis to the chopper, Brokovitch right behind carrying his gear. Once all was aboard they ran back the way they had come. Cisco gave the pilot the all clear and before I knew it the chopper was a distant hum, fading away to the west.

It suddenly occurred to me that I hadn't said a word to Nellis since we left our NDP. No words of comfort or encouragement, no joke to ease his anxiety, no word of thanks, no expression of sadness over losing a valuable member of the platoon. No words that he would be missed simply because he had been here, a part of us. Nothing. The evacuation had gone off without a hitch. So why did I fell like shit?

Chapter 10

There was no question as to what we would do next. I passed the word: "We're going to search the village. Sgt. Allen's squad will cordon it off. Everyone else will search the hooches. Pair up and watch each other's backs. We're looking for weapons and other contraband, not souvenirs. Be nice. Hearts and minds, people."

Such talk marked me as naive among the more jaded veterans, but I believed in the platitude. We had already killed one of their own--a husband, brother, father. There would be no point inflaming them further. We gave Sgt. Allen a few minutes to surround the village and then went in.

The Vietnamese made a poor show of ignoring us, pretending they were going about their usual routine as if we weren't there. Mama sans puttered around their cooking pits as if preparing to make breakfast but no fires had been lit, fearing it might tempt us to torch a hut or two. We too had lost a man.

Old men sat in the shade, eyes down, smoking while they contemplated the dirt. The dogs, having tired of their barking, slinked off as we moved among them. Children looked at us curiously; a few approached, only to be scolded by their mothers and pulled away. There were no males between the ages of fourteen and sixty to be seen.

Cisco and I took one of the hooches near the village well. I dropped my rucksack by the door and ducked inside, leaving Cisco on watch outside. There wasn't much to search. There were a few makeshift chairs but little else in the way of furniture. Sleeping mats served as beds; there were no desks, no tables, no floorboards to pull up. The floor was a clay platform raised to keep the rain outside. A rectangular stand sat against the far wall, draped with an embroidered cloth. Old pictures in brass frames sat on the cloth as did a glazed vase with joss sticks flowering out the top.

"Cisco, get in here," I said and he came inside. "What's this?"

"Some kind of alter to their ancestors," he said. "They burn incense to worship them or something. I'm not sure." We took the things off the top and tilted the altar back to look underneath. Cisco held the altar while I pulled out the things hidden underneath: a silver teapot, small engraved spoons, some jewelry, a cup of coins.

"Put the altar back the way it was but leave this stuff out," I said. "Let them know they're not getting away with anything. I'll check out the back rooms." The back rooms turned out to be a single room divided in two by a ratty sheet hung from a rope. Clothes hung from pegs pounded into the bamboo frame of the hooch; more sleeping mats had been rolled up and stacked in the corner. The place smelled of urine and feces. I pulled the curtain aside and the smell washed over me. An old woman lay on a mat under a blanket, her brown skin deeply wrinkled from decades of toil under the sun. Her eyes sparkled and her mouth opened in a big, toothless grin, as if she was happy to see me. She mumbled something I didn't understand and held out a withered hand. I took it as she babbled on about something. It seemed she would go on forever if I didn't let go of her hand.

"Sorry to have bothered you," I said, backing away. "Have a nice day." She nodded her head vigorously, still smiling and babbling. I pulled the curtain behind me and left the room. "Let's get out of here," I said.

The rest of the platoon was gathering around the well, filling their canteens and bullshitting while Sgt. Nelson interrogated a middle-aged woman in his pidgin Vietnamese. "VC a dau?" he kept asking to which she kept answering *No VC. No VC.*

"Yeah, then who the hell was that shootin' at us this morning!?"

"No biet," the woman said.

"Bullshit. You biet plenty."

I didn't have to ask if anybody found anything; the villagers had plenty of time to hide anything incriminating. Sgt. Allen's squad was coming in too--breaking the cordon before I told them to--but I didn't say anything. The VC were not going to attack us while we were in the village with their own people. "Okay, finish filling your canteens and let's get out of here," I ordered.

* * *

We left the way we had come. The punji stakes pointing the way we were going, the men walked carelessly, neither avoiding nor targeting the plants that might hide them. Their anger spent, they did what infantrymen had been doing for centuries--trudging somewhere other than where they already were. I stopped just before the jungle swallowed me up and looked back at Phu Nu. Already wisps of smoke were starting to appear above the hooches as mama sans started their fires for the morning meal. I turned away and fell into line behind Specialist Cisco.

* * *

We spent the next two days patrolling during the day and ambushing trails at night. After my mistake setting up an NDP on a trail near our last contact with the VC, I had Sgt. Nelson set up our ambushes while I pretended to be busy with other things. I had to admit he not only knew his job but how to handle the men. The ambushes were always well positioned, the men professional.

On our third night out Cisco woke me up during his watch. Old Crow was being mortared and Captain Messina wanted us to listen for the whump of mortar shells leaving their tubes. I strained my ears but the only sound I heard was the distant explosions of rounds hitting Old Crow. The attack lasted only a few minutes; five minutes later Captain Messina was back on the radio to let us know there were no casualties and asking if we had a fix on the mortar's position. I told the men to be alert in case the VC used the trail we were ambushing to return to their homes.

They didn't. We spent the next three days covering as much of the mountain as we could but found no sign of the mortar site. It was, as Cisco liked to say, like looking for a mortar in a jungle. At first the men were eager to find it but their enthusiasm lasted less than a day before lapsing into the malaise of putting one foot in front of another. Their bodies were wearing down and their minds were wearing out; no one felt it more than me.

There is no way to prepare yourself for the strain of carrying 70 pounds of gear through rugged terrain for six days other than to do it again and again and again. I was not prepared but felt the need to prove I was so on our last full day out I announce that we would be going to the top of the mountain and work the ridge line on our way back to base. This was met with the expected grumbling and eventual acceptance as we began the grueling trek uphill. Four hours later Patterson came upon a trail and called me forward.

"Whaddya want me to do, Sir?" I had long ago regretted my decision to go to the top. I was traveling as light as I could--no extra radio batteries, no claymore mine, no machine gun ammo. I had even cut back on C-rations so I would not embarrass myself by fagging out. But I was beat and not sure I could make it to the top.

"Where's it go?" I asked.

"Not sure. Probably the same trail we were on at Phu Nu. Just never been this far west before," he said. I pulled out my map but it showed no trails going to Phu Nu. On paper the village just sat there like an island in a vast ocean of green. "Wanna follow it?" he asked. Slick slack looked at the map.

"Probably goes to Gia Hoi. Right on our way home, Sir," he said hopefully.

"Forget it," I said. "We still got one more night out here." I studied the map again. "Where do you think we are?" Slick made a wide circle on the map with his finger.

"Okay," I said after some thought. "We follow the trail until you find a good place for an ambush. Then we lie low and set up just before dark. We'll see where the trail goes when we head home tomorrow."

"Good plan, Sir" Slick said and patted me on the back.

* * *

We had nine hours to kill until dark. I had one squad far enough back from the trail that they could remain hidden if anyone came down the trail and close enough that they could engage them if any weapons were seen. The rest of us stayed fifty yards further back. Ghosting, the men called it--being there but not doing anything other than relaxing. I put a few men on LP, still within eye sight, and rotated duties so that everyone would get some down time. Men slept, cleaned their rifles, talked quietly, rearranged the contents of their rucksacks, put on dry socks; then cursed when a downpour soaked them again. The ambush squad reported some activity on the trail--wood cutters coming or going, farmers carrying sacks of grain or rice--but no weapons were seen. Normally their bags of produce or bundle of sticks would be searched for contraband but we did not want to ruin our ambush by revealing ourselves prematurely.

At dusk we set up a linear ambush with a 50% watch. Cisco and I were in the middle with Sgt. Burkholtz's squad. Sergeant Little and Sergeant Allen and their partners would anchor opposite ends of the line. They, and only they, were to trigger the ambush. Depending on which way the gooks were going, the ambush was to be triggered just before the lead elements left the kill zone. The idea was not to have the first person to see them open fire on the lead element and have the rest of them get away.

It started to rain a little after seven o'clock. It soaked through my poncho liner and started working into my fatigues when I got a rush of adrenalin. I don't know if I heard them, saw them, or just felt them first but I was suddenly aware of two figures moving quickly past me on the trail. They were there and just as quickly gone, disappearing into the rain and the darkness in the direction of Sgt. Little's squad. I shook Cisco awake.

"Gooks. Two of them. Headed that way." He looked the way I pointed, then the other way. There was nothing to see. I braced for the explosion of gunfire I expected to hear coming from Sgt. Little's direction but there was nothing but silence. Had I imagined it? The shadowy forms had appeared and disappeared so quickly I started to doubt my own senses. I waited another minute, long enough for any following elements to appear, and then moved down the line.

"What the hell is going on?" one position after another asked.

"Did you see them?"

"Yeah, two of 'em," was always the answer until I got to Sgt. Little's position. Sgt. Little was asleep, not his watch. Nolan's head snapped up at my approach. He was sitting, his rifle across his lap, his poncho liner wrapped around his shoulders. He had a look of surprise on his face at seeing me and for the first time I saw fear in his eyes. He started to say something but I cut him off.

"What the hell are you doing?" I hissed. Sgt. Little came awake instantly.

"What's going on?" he whispered.

"Two gooks just strolled by your position. Going that way," I snapped.

"I was awake," Nolan said, ignoring the fact that I had never accused him of being asleep. "Nobody came by. I would have seen 'em." He was looking at Sgt. Little, as if he was the one he had to answer too. I grabbed his shirt and his eyes flashed.

"Everybody else saw them. Everybody!" He looked me straight in the eye.

"Nobody came by," he said again. I could feel my chest tighten as I tried to contain my anger.

"Stay awake," I said, pushing him back as I released my grip on his fatigues. Everyone had the same question as I worked my way back to my position and to everyone I gave the same answer.

"Somebody fucked up," I said. I didn't say who. They'd figure it out for themselves soon enough.

* * *

I kept the platoon in ambush an extra hour after daybreak hoping to catch the two that passed us the night before but the only people to go by were the two woodcutters we had seen the day before. We stopped them--the look of surprise on their faces strangely satisfying--checked their IDs and let them go.

"When Luke the Gook finds out he walked right by our ambush last night he's going to shit his pajamas," PFC Murphy said. Sgt. Little was stone-faced. Nolan acted as if he had done nothing wrong.

"What the hell were you thinking, putting Nolan in one of the most important positions in the ambush." I said when I got Sgt. Little alone. He must have known what was coming and had the rest of the night to come up with a bullshit reason which might even have been true. Instead, he looked me in the eye and said: "It was a mistake. It won't happen again." My anger drained away as if through a sieve. I had made enough mistakes myself in the last week to last my whole tour.

"Forget it," I said. "Let's get outta here. You take the point."

As Slick guessed, the trail led to Gia Hoi. We looked for the men we had seen on the trail the night before but all the men of military age had IDs. No booby-traps or punji sticks surrounded the village and if the villagers weren't friendly, neither were they hostile. Children came up to us, smiling and staring. Some of the mothers called them away. Others let their kids gawk at us and take the handouts offered by the less jaded among us while the veterans looked on in disgust. I too felt the need to be the benevolent GI, to see the smile on a kid's face, but kept my C-rations to myself rather than suffer the disapproval of the more seasoned among us.

We got back to Old Crow a little after noon.

"Well, look who got lucky his first time out," Gary said as I tossed my gear on my bunk.

"I hear you had a little excitement yourself," I said.

"Probably retaliation for the gook you got. I hear Nellis is going to be okay."

"Might get him a ticket home though. Chipped the ankle bone pretty bad."

"You can fill me in when you get back," he said. "Captain Messina wants to see you."

*   *   *

"Lt. Holder said you wanted to see me, Sir?" I said. Captain Messina offered me a seat without dismissing the enlisted man on radio watch so I knew I wasn't in for a reprimand for losing a man.

"Congratulations, Lieutenant," he said. "That was our first kill in over a month. Something I can give to battalion anyway."

"Thank you, Sir. I can't take much credit though," I said, ready to admit the man was hit before I knew what was happening.

"Of course you can, just as I will. Just as Major Dempsey will, and so on up to LBJ. That's the way this game is played, sad to say. Nellis is fine, by the way. They sent him to Cam Rhan Bay for further evaluation. I guess in addition to the other damage the fibula is fractured so he'll be out for some time."

"I'm glad to hear that, Sir. That he'll be okay I mean."

"Anyway, I'll let you clean up and crash for a while. You can fill me in in more detail tomorrow." I thanked him and started to leave. "Oh, and I already put you in for a CIB. Nellis and Murphy too. They were the only ones in your platoon not to have one."

I hadn't even thought about the Combat Infantryman Badge. I had a big grin on my face as I left.

My moment of glory was short lived. Captain Messina summoned me to his bunker early the next morning and this time he told the radio watch to take a break. I thought someone had complained about the way I set up the NDP the night before Nellis got hit but I was wrong.

"So tell me about the ambush your last night out. What happened?" I gave him a straight forward account of how I set up a textbook ambush on a trail that allowed for the maximum number of enemy soldiers to enter the kill zone before the ambush was triggered. Two men walked through the kill zone, I said, but the ambush was never triggered.

"Who fucked up?" He was steaming, thinking how easily the one kill he had reported to battalion could have been three.

"I put sergeants at both ends of the ambush," I said in an attempt to deflect personal responsibility. "Sgt. Little and Specialist Nolan were at the trigger end. Specialist Nolan was on watch."

"He was asleep?" Captain Messina said and I knew the next question was going to be what I did about that. The fact was I was all but certain Nolan was asleep. It was a court martial offence and I had done nothing more than chew him out. I had known from the beginning that Nolan was bad news and if I was honest with myself I would have to admit that the reason I hadn't taken official action against him was racial; I didn't want the other black men in the platoon to think I was prejudice.

"I can't be sure, Sir," I said. "It was dark. And raining. I could barely see them myself. The gooks."

"But you did. And so did everyone else on watch." I was amazed at how much he knew.

"I believe so, Sir."

"Nolan should've never been put at the trigger position," he said and he was right. It had been Sgt. Little's decision to put him there. Maybe he wanted to give Nolan more responsibility to make him a better soldier. Or maybe he just wanted to keep the platoon's biggest worry close where he could keep an eye on him. I don't know because Sgt. Little never said and I could think of no better response than the one Sgt. Little gave me.

"It was a mistake. It won't happen again," I said.

"I'm sure it won't," he said. "That's not why I called you in here. These things happen. I don't expect you to tell me every mistake you make. What I won't tolerate is a soldier under my command covering up a mistake by withholding valuable information." I had no idea what he was talking about. I could only look him in the eye and wait. "I'm not happy that you let two VC walk right by you without firing a shot. The bigger issue is that you didn't tell me about it." I was still confused. He had just told me he didn't expect me to tell him about every mistake I made. "Two gooks out after curfew is intelligence. Not a big deal by itself, but a small piece of a big puzzle. If the same thing is going on in the rest of the battalion's AO, or at regimental or division level, that could be a sign that something big is in the works. That's what our guys at G-2 do--make big deductions based on lots of small bits of information. You deny them that information and Americans die. Got it?" I did.

"Yes, Sir. It won't happen again," I repeated.

Chapter 11

We got resupplied later that afternoon. Life at Old Crow was so tedious that even the resupply chopper was anticipated like a USO show. That day's chopper had something almost as good. In addition to the usual C-rations, water, mail, and clean laundry, they dropped off six thermite containers of hot food, something different from the twelve entrees available in C-rations. It also had an additional delivery for me--PFC Thomas Boyd. Boyd had been assigned to third platoon but Captain Messina gave him to me when it became clear that PFC Nellis would not be returning anytime soon, if ever.

The Chopper landed in a downpour. PFC Boyd slid off like he had been traveling in helicopters all his life. He took a second to take in his new surroundings and then loped over when he saw me waving. He was tall and lanky and moved as if carrying a rucksack was his usual means of getting around. He reminded me of a cowboy with his saddle thrown over his shoulder.

"Boyd?"

"Yessir," he said and put his hand out as if that was how he normally greeted officers. His grip was quick and firm.

"I'm Lt. Sullivan. You'll be with me." I looked at the M-14 that hung from his hand as if it were an extension of his arm. "They run out of M-16s?" He was wearing his helmet and rain ran off the front, partially veiling his face.

"No, Sir. Just a better weapon," he said. "Actually, I'd like to go to sniper school. It's just three weeks and I think I could be of more use if I got fixed up with one of those scoped Remington 700s." I just looked at him. This kid didn't waste time.

"Why don't you grab some hot chow first. You'll be bunking with Murphy," I said, introducing him to the PFC whose eagerness to please had entangled him in a web of concertina wire. "I think you two will get along just fine."

* * *

I was spooning hot chicken tetrazzini out of my canteen cup and washing it down with pre-sweetened Kool-Aide. My mail had finally caught up to me and I had six letters waiting for me on my bunk, five from my mother and another from an old high school friend. The rain continued and a puddle was working its way through our door. The gloom of the bunker was partly alleviated by a string of small Christmas tree lights that Gary had hooked up to a radio pack battery.

"So what's your new guy like?" he asked.

"Very confident," I said.

"That doesn't sound good," Gary said. He wiped his mouth with his hand and then wiped his hand on his pants, a small pleasure he allowed himself on laundry day.

"Not cocky though," I said. "Wants to go to sniper school. You ever hear of a Remington 700?"

"Uh uh," Gary said, shoving another spoonful into his mouth."

"Me either." I glanced at my letters, still unopened, but resisted the temptation to read them while eating. My pleasures were few and far between and I wanted to make them last.

"Letter from a girl friend?" Gary said.

"No. No girlfriend. There was this girl in college I'd been keeping in touch with but I kinda broke that off before coming over here. Now I'm wishing--"

"Don't," Gary said. "You're better off. Just one more thing to worry about." He opened the ammo crate on the floor and rooted around in it. "Beth," he said, handing me a picture--a typical yearbook head shot. Everything about her looked soft--soft hair, soft eyes, soft skin.

"Why don't you put it up so I can enjoy her too?"

"Get your own girl," he said, taking it back.

"Serious?" Gary shrugged. I took it the uncertainty came from her.

I mixed some green beans with the last of my chicken tetrazzini. "I need ideas. Did I tell you I'm the new morale officer?"

"It's bullshit. Don't worry about it," Gary said. "He's just gotta fill a slot is all."

"Still…" I said.

"You wanna raise morale? Kill gooks and don't get your own men killed doing it. That's what raises morale. You didn't see it in your guys?" he said, referring to our last mission. "I did. Forget about the two that got away. Your guys were flyin'. The rest of the company too. My guys are jealous."

I had a flash of memories play backward in my mind--the burst of gunfire from the jungle; my moment of panic; my … vision, or whatever it was; the silhouette that reminded me of Smitty telling me… what? *If you need help you don't even have to ask.* That triggered another memory--the kid on top of the commo bunker my first night at Old Crow telling me the same thing: *one of us is always here to help. You just have to be open to it.* It was crazy.

"By the way, who's that kid from your platoon?" I said. "Red hair. Smokes."

"Nobody with red hair in my platoon," Gary said. "Why?"

"Nothing," I said, wishing I hadn't brought it up. "Just something he said." But I didn't want to let it go. "Maybe his hair just looked red. It was dark. I only saw it when he lit his cigarette."

"No redheads in my platoon," Gary said again. "Just Doc. And he got killed the night before you got here."

* * *

I read my mother's letters first. She had little to say other than how much she missed me. Strange because she had never expressed any such sentiments the four years I was away at college. She told me she loved me and hoped I was well but avoided any mention of where I was or what I was facing. I imagined that she was the good soldier's wife while my father was away too, getting himself killed in New Guinea.

The letter from my friend was more interesting--news about old friends, who was doing what, who was married, who was pregnant, everything that was going on in life without me. Then he got to the real reason for his letter. He had just finished his master's degree and had been notified by the draft board that he had been reclassified as 1A. He wasn't sure if he was going to be called but didn't want to take the chance. He wanted my advice.

"Question." I said. Gary was laying on his bunk, eyes closed.

"I'm ready."

"Friend of mine. 1A and nervous. He's been going with this girl for two years. Could be the one but he isn't sure. Should he: A--marry her and get reclassified. B--get on the waiting list for the navy or air force and hope for an opening before he gets drafted and ends up living like a rat in a hole in the ground…"

"So you've already written him?"

"I just added that last part," I said. "Or C--do nothing and hope his number doesn't come up."

"B. Or A," he added after some thought. "A or B. Not C. Definitely not C."

*   *   *

After being in the field I found the next few days relaxing. I pulled radio watches, assigned my squads to ambushes or listening posts when it was our turn (I didn't go on these myself anymore), and basically fucked off. My routine stayed the same after second platoon returned and Gary's platoon went on their mission, but my outlook changed. I felt a tightness in my chest whenever I remembered that after Gary got back I would be going out again. I didn't even have to think about it. It was always there, that feeling that all was not well, that something awful was waiting for me outside the wire. The feeling became even more intense one day when I was on radio watch and a bunch of chatter involving D Company came over the battalion net. Captain Messina heard it too and came out from behind his curtain. He turned on a spare radio and tuned it to D Company's frequency. At first there was nothing.

"Are you sure you have the right frequency, Sir?" I said. Captain Messina shot me a look that said *didn't you learn anything on your first mission.*

"They're in contact," was all he said. After reporting the initial contact the RTO became just another infantryman fighting for his life. His job was not to provide a play by play for our entertainment. He wouldn't get back on the radio until the radio became more helpful to his platoon than his rifle.

Finally the radio crackled. The RTO reported that they were taking heavy casualties and he requested gunships. Plural. To make his case he adjusted the casualty figures he had apparently reported earlier. He was now reporting 3 KIAs and another 5 wounded. My mind was a blur. KIAs? Our guys? Not enemy kills? Is that what he said?

The radioman's voice was outwardly calm, but I detected the tension behind the mask. One dust off could handle the WIAs but he asked that a second helicopter stand by in addition to the one he had requested earlier. I could hear the chatter of automatic weapons in the background, the thud of the M-79s, the explosion of hand grenades, the screaming of men in battle. It was just getting started.

And then it was over. The enemy withdrew before the gunships arrived. A different voice, this one high pitched and excited, was now reporting five men killed and eleven wounded, almost half the platoon. He asked for two dust offs equipped with winches and baskets to penetrate the jungle canopy. He also asked permission to extract what was left of the platoon when they could get to a place where choppers could land. Their lieutenant was dead, he said, and they were no longer an effective fighting force. He made no mention of enemy dead.

Chapter 12

"Have a seat." I leaned my rifle against the wall and took the lawn chair opposite Captain Messina. He had a map spread out on an ammo crate, oriented toward me. "I'm sending you on a combat assault," he said. "Four slicks will pick you up and insert you here," he said, pointing to a small circle he had penciled onto a sea of green. It doesn't show but there's an oblong clearing there maybe a hundred fifty meters long. I've seen it. Grassy with a few bushes surrounded by jungle. You're familiar with CA tactics?" I said I was, leaving out the part that I had only practiced it once at OCS. Basically, I knew how to get on and off a chopper without getting my head split open by the tail rotor.

"Tell me," he said. With my finger I traced a straight line on the map within the circle he'd drawn.

"Land the choppers in a straight line. Deploy off both sides. Run twenty yards away from the chopper. Get down and provide security. After the choppers leave, send a squad to secure the tree line. Then follow with the other squads." It almost sounded too simple, like I had forgotten something. Apparently that was good enough.

"I want you to patrol as much of this area as you can," he said, making a wide circle with his finger. "Look for any signs of recent activity. Battalion thinks something big is brewing out that way. Anything beyond this ridgeline is D Company's AO. Keep out of there. We don't need you guys bumping into each other unexpectedly." Friendly fire casualties were not unheard of in the jungles of Vietnam and no one wanted to write a letter to a next of kin telling them their son had been killed by another American. I looked at the ridgeline. The approach from our side showed an increasingly steep slope, almost too steep to climb. The contour lines on the other side were even steeper, merging at one point into a single dark line more than a mile long--a sheer cliff.

"I don't think that will be a problem," I said in an attempt to show off my map reading skills.

"Still," he said. "This is where D Company lost half a platoon." He tapped the spot once, his finger bouncing off like it was too hot to touch. "You're looking for NVA if you haven't already guessed," he said meaning North Vietnamese Army regulars, well-armed and well trained. "Draw rations for six days. You leave tomorrow as soon as third platoon gets back. Questions?"

"No, Sir," I said. I grabbed my rifle and headed for the door.

"You're just there to find them, Lieutenant" he said as I reached the band of sunlight streaming through the door. "Don't take on more than you can handle. We're not Marines," he added, tapping a finger to the side of his head.

* * *

The slicks came in two at a time, their wiper blades slapping the drizzle from their windshields. I jumped on the first chopper along with Cisco, Doc, and one man from each of the three squads. I squeezed in next to the crew chief and tapped his head set. He plugged an extra headset into the overhead, handed it to me and held up a finger for me to wait. Once airborne and circling until the other ships joined us he gave me the okay.

"You the flight leader?" I said into the mic.

"No, Sir. That would be Mr. Twitzel. Blue one." Behind their visors I couldn't tell which of the two pilots I was talking to. Worse, I had no idea if I could talk to Blue One on this thing.

"Could you tell him to land us in a straight line?" I said.

"No problem, Sir," he said. The intercom went quiet while he relayed my message.

"You gonna be able to find that clearing in all this?" I said, referring to the weather.

"If not, we'll just drop you off anywhere. That okay, Sir?" When I couldn't think of a comeback right away he took me to be humorless. "We'll find it, Sir." he said. I handed the crew chief the head set and took a seat on the cargo deck between Murphy and Turner, our legs dangling out over the skids. The third grunt was on the other side with Doc and Cisco. Cisco should have been on my side but it was too late to change now. If that was the worst thing that went wrong on the assault I would be happy.

I felt I had been gaining the respect of the men and wanted to cement it with a smooth insertion. I had called the platoon together earlier that day and gone over everything, diagramming in the dirt the way the choppers would land and how we were to deploy. I went over it twice and then ask Sgt. Allen to repeat what I had just said.

Then Sgt. Little. When I asked Sgt. Burkholtz he just said "We got it, Sir," his tone suggesting I was insulting them by preaching things they had learned through experience long before I boarded my flight to the Republic of Vietnam. I also ordered that one man in the platoon would carry an axe and one man in each squad would carry an entrenching tool.

"An axe?!" It was PFC Romansky, a short, assistant gunner in first squad who was already overburdened with three hundred extra rounds of machinegun ammo.

"D Company had to use a jungle penetrator to get their wounded out. It might come in handy."

"C-4 is lighter," Romansky said, meaning the plastic explosive the engineers used to blow up stumps, among other things.

"One axe," I said. I didn't have to see the looks of disapproval on their faces; I could feel them.

"Sir," It was Sgt. Burkholtz. "We're never in one place long enough to dig in," he said, referring to my order about the entrenching tools. "Plus the noise an' all." I considered giving in on that. The men were carrying sixty-five to seventy pound packs as it was."

"One per squad," I said, trying to make the four pound shovel seem as inconsequential as possible, which it was, to everyone but the guys carrying it.

* * *

When the other choppers were in the air we banked to the west, dropping low off our mountain and accelerating just above the tree tops. The Mu Dai River--the men called it the *Muddy*--rushed by below, a brown ribbon trapped inside a green chasm. Two minutes later the crew chief yelled for us to get ready. The door gunners readied their guns and suddenly the clearing was directly beneath us. One of the choppers appeared off to the right. Something was wrong. This was not what I'd asked for. Not what we'd rehearsed. The choppers flared--mine and the one to our right. I had no idea where the other two were. Even before the choppers leveled, even before the skids touch the ground--troopers were jumping off, their boots hitting the grass and then splashing into the water beneath. I found myself following, my feet on the skids, then, suddenly, dropping through space. My knees buckled as the weight of my pack drove me to the soft ground, my face underwater. I came up sputtering and ran forward, crouching when I came on line with Murphy and Turner. They were jumbled up with the grunts from the chopper that had landed to our right, looking as confused as me.

The choppers were already over the trees at the far end of the clearing, banking to the left and leaving me with the mess they'd created. I had asked for the choppers to land us *in* line, not *on* line. Hadn't I?

"Sir, What the fuck--"

I turned around and saw the same confusion with the men from the other two choppers. Cisco was standing ankle deep in water, turning around in circles, pretending to be talking on the radio, looking for me. "Hey, Moe! Moe! Where the fuck are ya, Moe?!" he yelled, falsetto. The men were watching, laughing.

Sgt. Nelson ran toward me with Sgt. Little's squad. He squatted next to me while Sgt. Little and his men kept running, securing the tree line. "Quite the clusterfuck, ey Lieutenant?" Sgt. Nelson said. He had an ill-concealed grin on his face, clearly enjoying my humiliation.

"Quite a clusterfuck, Sergeant," I admitted. He had started the business of bringing order to the confusion and all I could do was take over and try to regain some of my dignity. Sgt. Little was in the tree line, giving me the all clear signal.

"Second Squad," I yelled as if everything was going as planned. "You're next. Go. Go! Let's get out of this clearing." Sgt. Burkholtz's squad ran past. "On line! On line! Spread out!" I yelled, even though they were already on line and well spread out. "Third squad, line up on me. Get ready!" I grabbed Cisco by his shoulder strap and yanked him down to my level. "Cut the shit, Cisco," I hissed. His face dropped and he couldn't meet my eyes.

"Just having some fun, Sir," he apologized but I was having none of it. "Now is not the time. Did you call in a cold LZ?" I was forgetting my priorities and once again Sgt. Nelson took over.

"The rest of you, let's go!" he said leading them toward the tree line. Cisco stood up.

"Yes, Sir," he said and started running. It felt more like he was running away from me than following Sgt. Nelson and that gave me a small feeling of satisfaction. I was the last one off the clearing, leading from behind.

"What the fuck was that, Sir?" Sgt. Allen said once I got there.

By now everyone was drenched from the marsh and the rain. Water was dripping from trees, dripping from jungle hats, dripping from noses, dripping from gun barrels.

"I don't know," I said. "I told them to land *in* line, one behind the other. They landed *on* line." That wasn't completely true--I hadn't said *one behind the other*--but I wasn't going to take the rap. If the flight leader wasn't sure what I meant he should have asked for clarification.

"I thought you said it was a clearing," someone else complained. "That's a fuckin' marsh."

"Take it up with Captain Messina," I said, regretting my words as soon as they were out of my mouth. "Let's get the hell out of here. Check your weapons. Make sure they're not blocked." I pulled the charging handle on my M-16 and saw that I'd forgotten to chamber a round. I looked down the barrel and saw nothing but black. I hit the muzzle with the heel of my hand until enough mud came out that I could see daylight and then gave it a few more whacks for good measure. I looked around to see if there was anyone else in the platoon who was more fucked up than I was. Back to square one, I thought.

* * *

The weather at Hardscrabble had kept the choppers grounded until late afternoon so we had gotten a late start. Now we had barely an hour to find and set up an NDP and we used most of that putting as much distance between the clearing and us as we could. The NDP was not ideal but it would have to do. The mosquitoes from the marsh seemed to have followed us and the rain washed off our repellent as fast as we applied it. We ate a cold meal and settled in for a restless night.

The rain contined. At first the men kept shifting positions, trying to keep away from the water streaming off the mountain but eventually they realized the futility of it and got as comfortable as they could where they were. We had a 50% watch but few could sleep. After midnight the rain let up but that only brought more mosquitoes. When not on watch we tried to find relief under our poncho liners but they kept out the mosquitoes no better than they kept out the water.

The break in the rain lasted half an hour and then started again, alternating between a drizzle and a downpour. The temperature dropped and by morning everyone was cold and miserable. We left at first light and by seven o'clock the temperature was 80 degrees and the rain kept falling. We stopped for breakfast and I hunched over my can of scrambled eggs and ham, spooning the mixture of protein and congealed fat into my mouth while water pooled in the depressions I had excavated with my spoon.

"Is this what they call a continental breakfast, Sir?" Cisco asked. Sometimes I couldn't tell when he was joking. "'Cause we're like on another continent?"

"Yours is," I said. "'Cause we're in Asia and you're eating spaghetti. How can you eat that shit in the morning?" He looked at my eggs and ham.

"How can you eat that shit at all?"

"Good point," I said, grateful that we were back on speaking terms. Cisco deserved the chewing out I gave him at the marsh but it was hard to stay mad at him for long. He had taken a bad situation and made the best of it in the only way he knew how, by making a joke of it; the men had laughed, whether at me or the situation I wasn't sure. What I was sure of was that if men can still laugh in bad situations, their morale is good and I could always count on Cisco to give the men a laugh. He tilted his face to the sky and squinted through the drizzle.

"Looks like rain," he said.

"Shut up and eat," I said. He tipped his can until all the water ran out.

"Excellent idea, Sir," he said.

* * *

I drove the men hard for the next two days, walking the thin line between being a tough leader and being an asshole. The rain did not let up until late the second day when the sun came out and our fatigues started to dry. We hadn't seen any sign of the enemy--or anyone else for that matter--so I called a break for a full hour to give everyone time to cook a hot meal and clean their weapons.

We had been patrolling the mountain side in a switchback pattern that now put us halfway to the top. The rain started again before the hour was up so there was a minimum of grumbling when I had them get back on their feet again. We spent another miserable night in the rain but at 1500 feet the mosquitoes were not as bad. By noon the next day we had run out of gentle slope. We stopped for lunch and as we ate another cold meal Sgt. Nelson came up to me.

"What now, Lieutenant?" he said. "Not even a Montagnard could live on that slope." Montagnards were a tribal race that lived in the densely jungled mountains that the Vietnamese found too steep to farm. Until that moment I had not considered going any higher but Sgt. Nelson had a way of pushing my buttons. He had done what a senior sergeant was expected to do during our insertion. He had put order to the chaos but his gloating had made it seem like just part of our pissing contest. I wanted to show him who was boss.

"We're not done till we reach the top," I said.

"That's nuts!" he said, his pink face glowing red. "You'll never make it."

"I don't plan on going alone," I said.

* * *

We hadn't gone far when I started to think Sgt. Nelson had been right. The slope was almost 50 degrees and if the map was right it would be closer to 60 before we reached the top. The rain continued and the mud turned to slop. Every step had to be planned--a solid outcrop or a protruding root, anything that would give a foot purchase. We were no longer zigzagging, we were going straight up the slope, the men using their free hand to grab a root or sapling, their packs pulling them down while their arms tried to pull themselves up. Sometimes the saplings would come loose from the thin soil and the man would slid back, only to start over again.

The line disintegrated. Men spread out, looking for untrod dirt where they could get better footing. Rifles were handed back so two hands could be used to pull oneself up. Then two rifles were handed back up so the man behind could follow. Men were pushed from behind and extended a hand from above. I could hear the cursing from fifty yards away--damning the rain, damning the mountain, damning me. I did nothing to stop it. There was no one around to hear us but us. A rifle went off and everybody froze.

"Sorry," came a weak apology. I called a break to rest and check their safeties.

I was exhausted. And ashamed. Ashamed that I was putting my men through this just to prove something to an asshole sergeant. Now they were paying the price, and so was I. My quadriceps felt like they were going to snap and I hoped someone else would cramp up first so I could call off the whole thing and still save face. And if it was Sgt. Nelson who cramped up, so much the better.

I pulled myself over to a small tree where I could rest without sliding down hill while I tried to figure out what to do next. My head felt light and my eyes refused to focus. I took off my hat, wiped my eyes and blinked, the rain having stopped without me noticing. The jungle looked thicker now and the men were moving on without me. They were back in line, moving slowly, mechanically, one foot ahead of the other. They were worn and ragged, almost skeletal in appearance; their helmets--they were now wearing helmets--rolling on their heads as if the liners had rotted away. One of them turned my way, noticing me for the first time. He looked surprised to see me, then not so surprised at all. He fell out of line and worked his way over to me. He sat down, laying his M-1 on the ground next to himself. He wiped his eyes on his corporal's stripes and brushed the hair from his eyes. There was something familiar about him, but I didn‘t recognize him as someone in my platoon. He looked me in the eyes as if to see what I wanted, why he had been summoned.

"Steep," was all he said. His face was gaunt, his skin yellow, an open sore oozing from the side of his neck and I had the impression that the moisture running down his face was more sweat than rain. His eyes too, seemed to have a hard time focusing. He was far more exhausted than anyone in my platoon. Someone called from the line.

"Sean!" We both said *What* at the same time. He turned to the man who had called our name, then back to me, staring at my name tag.

"I'll be along in a minute," he said. The other man looked at me and just said *oh*. He had no rifle, just the baseplate for a 60mm mortar strapped to his back. He hitched his pack higher, slipped, and then continued clawing his way up the mountain.

It was then that I recognized the man in front of me--recognized him from the picture that sat on our mantle since before I was born. He looked different from the happy, fit-looking soldier that smiled from behind the glass but still, how could I have not recognized my own father?

"You look like your mother," he said. "I thought, if you were a boy she was going to name you after *her* father." I couldn't do anything but stare. He made no effort to reach out and touch me, to touch my face, to brush a lock of hair from my forehead. He was as much a stranger to me as he had always been. Another voice from the line called to him.

"Sullivan, you okay?"

"Be along in a minute," he said. He studied me again. "Is it still Vietnam?" he asked, curious. I nodded that it was.

"Hard to keep track sometimes," he said.

"What–"

"I've got to get goin'," he said when someone called his name again. "You want something. What is it?" I couldn't remember at first. I looked again at the men of the 41st Infantry Division as they struggled up the treacherous terrain of New Guinea.

"How…How do you do it? Keep going, I mean. When you're so…" I remembered finding my father's death certificate when I was young. I had always liked to think that he had died gloriously in battle and asked my mother what the FUO–fever of unknown origin–meant in the cause of death box. My strong, scrapping father, killed by a mosquito. I looked into his vacant eyes and almost cried. I knew he would not make it to the top. "Why?" was all I could manage.

"Because that's where the Japs are," he said. He looked at my shoulder, noticing the black bar the Koreans had sewn on at the laundry, and thought of an answer that might help a young second lieutenant. "You've got to give them a reason," he said. "A purpose. And I don't mean that God and country crap. Something that means something to them right *now*. That's what keeps them going. You shouldn't have to look far."

"Lieutenant Sullivan!" The voice was familiar but it took a second to register. It was raining again, but the vegetation had thinned and the helmeted men who and been fighting their way up the slope were gone. It was Doc. He worked his way over to me on hands and knees, his bush hat dripping water like a veil. "The men are pretty whipped, Sir," he said as if that alone would make his meaning clear.

"Yeah, me too," I said. Doc waited for me to say more and when I didn't he went on.

"I'm worried about heat stroke," he said. "It's over a hundred degrees. And the humidity…." He didn't have to say it. It was like a sauna. I should have asked him pertinent questions about the men's condition but instead I recited the mantra recited by drill sergeants in every training class they ever gave when the going got tough.

"Have them take two salt tablets and drive on," I said. He looked as if he were disappointed in me and I felt like a sack of shit.

"It's more than that, Sir. I'm worried about cramps. Or an accident. Or an ambush," he added, reaching. "You can't get a dust off in here, and we sure couldn't carry anyone out." I wasn't worried about that. A large enemy force couldn't occupy this terrain for long, and a helicopter could lift out anyone with a sprained ankle with a jungle penetrator. But I got his point. What had my father said? Men need a reason. A purpose. What was he trying to tell me? That without a good reason I shouldn't demand the most of them? Or that I should come up with a good reason whether I had one or not? I had put myself in this position for no other reason than my own ego and I was stuck with it. To abandon my goal of reaching the top was the right thing to do and I knew it. What, though, would be the consequences? Would that gain me respect in the eyes of my men, or lose it? I looked at Doc's face and could see the face of every other man in the platoon--worn, exhausted, demoralized.

"I'll talk to the men. Thanks, Doc," I said.

I left my pack and worked my way back down the slope, talking to the rest of the platoon, singly or in small groups--telling them the same lie so often that by the time I was done I believed it myself. I told them that the top ended in a sheer cliff that would give us an unobstructed view of the valley where D Company had lost 16 men. I told them we were going to the top to see if we could spot any signs of an enemy build up and if we did we would call in artillery and air strikes and get the bastards that got D Company, and by the time I was done that's exactly what I hoped would happen. By the looks on their faces I could tell that they wanted it too.

The slope got steeper, the soil and vegetation thinner, the rocky outcrops more numerous the closer we got to the top. The cursing got louder as the men slipped and fell and pulled themselves up the mountainside, but the grumbling was gone. They wanted to get to the top as much as I did. It was personal now. PFC Murphy was the first to reach the ridgeline and I was not far behind.

"Ya gotta see this, Sir! Unbelievable!" he said, extending his hand to pull me up the last few feet. The map did not do justice to the vista before me. The ridgeline curved for almost a mile in both directions, like a giant amphitheater. We were perched on a piece of rock and dirt only a few feet wide. Behind was the slope I had just climbed, in front a cliff that dropped straight down more than 300 feet before reaching a talus slope of loose stone that went another hundred feet before disappearing into the jungle below. The valley went on for miles before being cut off by another range of mountains far in the distance. I could see no villages, no roads, no fields of rice or millet or yams. Nothing but the tops of trees for as far as the eye could see. Even Jim Beam--D Company's base camp--was swallowed up by the jungle.

"Jesus," was all I could say.

"The NVA could hide a whole division down there," Murphy said. It was obvious even to a FNG PFC. There was no way we were going to spot an enemy build up through that canopy. If their presence was that obvious, air reconnaissance would have spotted them long ago. If they were to be found it would be because some unlucky grunts bumped into them by accident, like the platoon from D Company that was almost wiped out.

I returned my attention to the rest of the platoon, those who had already reached the top encouraging those still struggling up the slope; some of the stronger men even going back down to help the weaker ones with their packs and weapons. The once orderly line had disintegrated into a ragged mob scattered over several acres of some of the worst terrain imaginable as they tried to find the path of least resistance to the top. A festive air descended on the mob, small celebrations breaking out along the ridge as each person reached the summit. I looked for Sgt. Nelson but could not see him anywhere down below. Somehow he had reached the top without me noticing.

There was no order and I was glad none of my OCS instructors were on hand to see the mess I had created. On the other hand, I had never been prouder of myself--or my men--for what we had done. I let disorder reign while I caught my breath and the men enjoyed their victory over the mountain.

"Damn, Sir," Cisco said, all smiles as he picked his way along the ridgeline toward me. I suddenly realized that my near-constant shadow had become separated from me, finding his own best way to the top. "Sorry, Sir," he said. "But, damn!" He looked at the slope he had conquered and then over the cliff that marked the end of his ordeal.

"Everybody make it up okay?" I asked.

"Want me to do a head count?"

"No. I'll do it." I wanted my victory lap. I had earned it and no one was going to take it away from me. The rain was starting to let up and I had regained enough strength in my legs to make the rounds. I dropped my pack and started off in the direction Cisco had come.

"Hey, El Tee. We stayin' here tonight?" Cisco asked. I stopped and turned back, making sure I had heard him right. The title *El Tee* (Lt.) was not bestowed lightly. It was more than an obligatory sign of respect. It was an implicit admission into their ranks, a proclamation that I was not just their leader; I was one of them. It felt like I had just been awarded the Combat Infantryman Badge all over again. The difference was, this time I felt I'd earned it.

"Can't waste this view," I said.

I worked my way along the ridgeline, playing the leader concerned about the welfare of his men, when I realized it was no longer an act. I was proud of them and I did care. Other men also called me El Tee. It was as if they had called a secret meeting and voted on whether I deserved the honor. Only Doc seemed sullen about our accomplishment. I took him aside.

"I appreciate what you did back there," I said, looking down the slope. "You were right. I was pushing them too hard. It's your job to tell me when the men's health is endangered. Don't stop doing that." He smiled.

"Sir, I think our lives are in danger here. I think we should get out of Vietnam as soon as possible."

"I'll talk to the captain when we get back," I said.

The platoon was spread out for a hundred yards and I consolidated our line on the widest part of the ridge available which was never more than a few yards wide. I placed our machine gunners at the ends of the line and told the men to get into groups of four; that we would only keep a 25% watch for the night. The men were tired and no one would be sneaking up on us here. I told them to pay particular attention to the valley, to watch out for fires or other indicators of a human presence. I also gave them permission to have a hot meal as long as they kept the glow of their heat tabs below the ridge line. Cisco was on the radio when I got back. He put his hand over the mouth piece as he handed me the handset.

"Captain Messina. I called in our position. He wants to talk to you." I took the handset.

"This is X-ray One Actual," I said.

"This is X-ray Actual. I have your coordinates. Please confirm, over." Cisco was ready. He handed me a paper with the coordinates already coded into letters.

"Checked them twice, sir," he whispered.

"This is X-ray One Actual. Our coordinates are Hotel Whiskey Whisky Foxtrot, Lima Bravo November Bravo, over." There was a pause as Captain Messina checked the coordinates on his map; another pause as he considered how to confirm what he suspected without giving clues to our location to any VC or NVA who might be listening in.

"X-ray One, X-ray Actual. Did you go where Jack and Jill went? Over."

"Affirmative, X-ray Actual. Over." Another pause, whether from disapproval or awe, I couldn't tell.

"Anything to report? Over." The sun was starting to break through the clouds low in the western sky. In light of our accomplishment I felt I could get away with a little levity.

"Not yet. Looks like we might have a nice sunset though, over."

"Roger, X-ray One. Keep me posted. Out." Cisco and I exchanged grins.

* * *

Sgt. Nelson joined Cisco, Doc, and me in our headquarters watch group. He was his usual, reticent self. "Not much of an escape route," he said, looking out over the cliff. He was right, but I knew it was just a dig. He liked to criticize, but the only time he offered alternatives was when he thought my mistakes were serious enough that they presented a real danger; in this case, he didn't.

"I don't think that will be a problem," I said, putting my last spoonful of beans and franks into my mouth.

"I hope not. It's a long drop," he said, making sure Doc and Cisco were aware of the predicament I had supposedly put them in. I could feel Doc and Cisco looking at me, waiting for my response.

"A long drop," I sighed. I tossed my empty can over the edge and leaned against my rucksack, wishing for once that I smoked so I could light up in a display of how relaxed I felt.

Chapter 13

It wasn't a good sunset. The clouds closed in again and the rain returned so that we could see little of what might be going on in the valley. Sometime after midnight red and green tracers spit at each other far up the valley, but they were so far away I couldn't hear the gunfire above the rain. It lasted only a few minutes and a short time later I heard the boom of a single artillery round off in the distance. An illumination flare burst over the site of the firefight, its magnesium glow swinging beneath a small parachute. Three more rounds were fired, enough to turn night into day for a small section of the valley. Then all was quiet again except for the fuck you lizards who seemed to like the rocky heights. Like the firefight had never happened, at least for us. I could only guess what D Company's morning reports would say.

The sun was barely visible through the fog and trees when I woke up. Cisco was making coffee. Sgt. Nelson was giving me the evil eye.

"Been here a long time, Lieutenant," he said, rubbing his cigarette out across a rocky outcrop. The valley was totally obliterated by the fog. It was like looking at a cloud, from a cloud.

"Sit tight," I said. I picked up my rifle and made the rounds, pissed off that no one had woken me earlier. Men were eating hot breakfasts, drinking coffee, smoking, bullshitting.

"Hey, El Tee, we staying here all day?"

"Twenty minutes," I said. "Eat up." Groans all around.

"Forget it," I said, and then, just to make conversation: "You hear all those fuck you lizards last night?"

"Those weren't lizards." I recognized Nolan's voice. Everyone was laughing. Everyone but Nolan who had a nasty smirk on his face. I would have thought it funny too had it come from anyone but him. I force a smile, pretending I could take a joke.

"Twenty minutes," I said again. There was a lively discussion going on when I reached the next group.

"Hey, Lieutenant Sullivan. You'll know. What's our motto?" PFC Romansky said.

"Our motto?"

"Yeah. You know. Like the Marines have *semper fidelis*--always loyal--an' the Coast Guard is *semper paratas*--always prepared. What are we?"

"Semper tirades," I said. "Always tired."

"Really?" Everyone else laughed. Several called Romansky a dumb ass. "No. Really, Sir. What is it?"

"I don't know. We leave in twenty minutes."

"You didn't learn that in officer school?" Romansky persisted as I walked away.

"No. Twenty minutes."

"Hey, El Tee. We should plant a flag or somethin', ya know." It was Patterson, point man for Sgt. Allen's squad.

"A flag?"

"Yeah. Like at Iwo Jima. Somethin' that says we were here." Making it to this point was hardly the same as the Marines taking Mount Suribachi but I couldn't deny them the simple pleasure of proclaiming their accomplishment to whoever might follow.

"You find a flag, we'll plant it," I said.

Fifteen minutes later he came to our mini headquarters along with the rest of the platoon. Murphy had a small flag--the kind they hand out at parades--and Doc wrote C/2/605 and the date on one of the white stripes with a marking pen. Cameras came out of nowhere and the men took turns taking pictures of the platoon, me and Sgt. Nelson front and center against the back drop of the fog-covered valley. Finally, Doc pulled out a suture kit and 'sewed' the flag to a small branch at the top of the ridgeline.

"Let's get the hell out of here," I said when the last picture was taken.

"And never come back." Amens all around.

* * *

Getting down the slope was almost as hard as getting up. Men were slipping and sliding, colliding with boulders, trees, each other. Our clothes torn, our bodies bruised and scraped, we grabbed for anything that could slow our descent but it was never enough. It took only a half hour to reach the bottom of the steep slope it had taken us three hours to climb the day before. There were no major injuries but Doc spent an hour treating cuts and scrapes before we resumed our reconnaissance.

We spent the next three days patrolling. We again worked the mountainside in a switchback pattern but found nothing--no villages, no booby-traps, no signs of people other than one site with C-ration cans littering the ground. They were rusty and half covered with forest litter. Stained water, swimming with mosquito larvae, filled them to overflowing; there was no telling how long they'd been there. It could have been weeks. It could have been years.

We crossed several trails but none wide enough to suggest they were made by people, what fresh tracks there were suggesting they were made by deer or some other creature of habit. The routine was monotonous and the men got sloppy. With my newfound stature among them I felt comfortable reminding them to stay alert, keep their interval, and take their salt tablets.

On our fifth night out I called in our position about a klick from the clearing where we had been dropped off and asked for an early extraction the next morning. Captain Messina set a time of 10 o'clock but told us we had to make a complete reconnaissance of the area before the choppers would come in. Pilots did not like to make extractions from the same LZ where they were dropped off unless they were sure it was secure. The VC often left ground units alone while they were on patrol, hoping to get them, and a few helicopters, during the extraction when they were at their most vulnerable.

We set up our NDP for the night, having gone back to the SOP watch ratio of one man on, one man off, and waited for daylight. The mosquitoes were back in force and after a restless night the men were eager to get to the LZ, as if that would make the choppers arrive before the scheduled time. We moved slowly, patrolling as we went and still got there three hours early. We would need all of it.

The rain had raised the marsh a foot, flooding the adjacent jungle so that our search of the circumference would be a slow slog. For the first time I sent out flankers. The three flankers on the marsh side were to go into the water and probe the bottom with sticks to find shallow areas where the choppers might land. The flankers on the outside were to stay as far away from the water as they could and still maintain visual contact, keeping a constant lookout for signs of an enemy ambush. It took two hours to circle the marsh and another half hour to return to the place best suited for the extraction. Sgt. Nelson didn't like it.

"They ain't gonna wanna set down in this," he said, meaning the marsh. "Bottom's soft. They'll get stuck." He was telling me this now, having known the entire time that this was the only LZ around. He took my lack of response to be skepticism. "My first tour was in the Delta," he added to prove his point.

"What do you suggest, Sergeant?"

"It's your platoon, Lieutenant," he said. "They'll have to hover. Tricky with a full load."

I called over the flankers who had walked the marsh. "Where's Simpson?" I asked.

"Burnin' off the leeches," Murphy said. "His pants came unbloused."

"Never mind, you'll do," I said to Murphy and Boyd. "Get some extra poles. Use the axe," I said, eager to prove that carrying one was not a useless gesture. "Mark out an LZ big enough for four slicks, far enough out so the rotors won't hit the trees but no more than knee deep." They ignored my suggestion to use the axe, there being plenty of dead branches lying around. When they were done I called them in.

"I'm just gonna go out a little more. It feels like it's leveled off," Murphy said and took two steps before disappearing into the reeds. He came up splashing and coughing, gasping for breath and making swimming motions toward shore. But he was not moving, his feet stuck in the mud. Twice his head went under. I ran out to help but Boyd got to him first, extending a pole and pulling him out. What might have been a tragedy quickly turned comical as Murphy splashed to land, ripping off his shirt and screaming about leeches. Doc no sooner calmed him down, assuring him there were no leeches on his body than Murphy noticed he had lost a boot in the muck and started in again, pulling his pant leg up and swatting at every piece of swamp debris that had plastered itself to his skin.

"Audie fuckin' Murphy. 'Fraid of a little ol' leech," Caulkin's said.

"Yeah, well why don't you take a swim if you're so fuckin' brave," Murphy answered back.

"Semper wet," Caulkins said.

"Semper assholes!" Murphy spat, flicking a rotting piece of vegetation Caulkin's way. "Where's my hat? I lost my fuckin' hat." It was good to hear the men laugh.

* * *

The choppers came in low, a light drizzle and lingering fog

limiting visibility. I informed them of the situation and that there would be no smoke to guide them because of all the water. We would load onto the choppers from the shallow side only, while the pilots tried to hold the ship in a hover. Speed would be of the essence.

The flight circled the marsh, the door gunners firing occasional bursts into the jungle to provoke a response from any VC that might be hiding there. Satisfied, the slicks made their approach from the west to give them the longest 'runway' possible when they took off.

The water roiled as the rotor wash slammed the surface. They landed in unison, the back of their skids brushing the water as they flared, and then settled into a level hover--a water ballet of aluminum hippos. Four sticks of grunts splashed forward. Doc and Cisco were the first to our chopper. Doc pulled himself onto the skid, his hands clawing for purchase on the deck as the chopper tilted to the side. The crew chief grabbed Doc's rucksack to help him on but Cisco's pack, heavy from the radio, threw him back into the water.

"Rucksacks off! Throw them on first," I yelled. The door gunner was out of his seat, grabbing rifles and packs as fast as they were handed to him, the crew chief shoving men and equipment to the door gunner on the other side while the pilots tried to hold the ship level. As each man climbed aboard the chopper sunk lower into the water. I could hear the engines whine, fighting the weight of seven waterlogged men and their equipment. By the time it was my turn the skid was touching bottom, sinking into the muck. The chopper ahead of us was already loaded but blocking our take off. I could see our pilots struggling with their controls, waiting their turn. The lead chopper was moving slowly forward, its nose down, the front of the skids dragging in the mud. Suddenly it broke free and lunged forward like a race horse out of the gate. For a moment it looked like it was going to somersault but the pilot pulled the nose up in time to prevent a disaster.

We were now clear for takeoff but the extra time on the ground had buried us deeper into the muck. I smelled the odor of burning oil, imagined the tachometer needle deep into the red, but felt no lift. The pilot eased off the throttle and the chopper again settled into the mud. He moved his control stick slowly, first to one side, then the other, increasing the RPMs and rocking us out of the muck. The ship suddenly broke free. Men yelled as the ship titled so far to the left that the rotor slapped the surface of the water on that side. The pilot overcorrected and for a moment we were swinging like a pendulum before he throttled forward, the front skids plowing through the water until we were free of the drag. The jungle loomed ahead, the windshield a deadly green. We banked sharply to the left, everyone grabbing anything within reach to stop their slide. Suddenly the green turned to gray and everyone was cheering.

The third chopper in line was already racing across the marsh, its skids slapping our wake. He had a longer 'runway' than we had but it was clear it was not long enough and when they banked to the left the chopper's momentum took them so close to the jungle that the tips of the rotor hit the tops of several trees, the leaves and small branches exploding into space.

The last ship had been sitting too long. It tried to lift up only to be sucked back down by the mud. Wiggling back and forth or trying to plow forward were no more effective. It was too heavy. The other choppers circled, providing cover while the fourth ship struggled like a mammoth in a tar pit. As we swung around for the second time I could see Sgt. Little's squad jumping from both sides of the chopper. Bent over, they tried to lift the chopper free to little effect. They tried to get into a rhythm--rocking and lifting, rocking and lifting. Sgt. Little and Nolan had climbed over the skids and were underneath the chopper, their faces in the water as they lifted with their backs and legs.

On the third try the chopper sprang free sending several men sprawling into the mash. The pilot steadied the ship and inched it forward, the skids dripping water and mud. The men followed along--holding on to the skids like they were carrying a casket. The chopper stopped and the men scurried aboard while the chopper settled back into the water. The last man was still standing on the skids when the pilot started moving the ship forward, slowly accelerating and gaining altitude as the man was pulled aboard. The ship rose slowly but steadily and with the extra room for takeoff they cleared the jungle at the end of the marsh without banking or touching so much as a single leaf.

Chapter 14

Dead skin was still coming off. Two days of scraping my feet with my bayonet and it was still coming off in mushy gobs. And it wasn't just me. The entire platoon had trench foot from the constant wet of our mission. Simpson had it so bad that Doc sent him back to Hardscrabble where they were treating him with fresh air, antibiotics, and clean sheets. Everyone chalked it up to the weather, but I knew the climb to the top of the mountain had made things worse. I drew my bayonet through pinched fingers, watching the pasty glob gather before falling into a puddle of water. The ground was saturated and even though the rain had stopped, the walls glistened with the wet and dripped wherever there was a protruding root or outcropping of dirt.

"What the hell are you doing?" Gary said, ducking through the door. He leaned his M-16 against the ammo crate and elevated himself onto his bunk, away from the mud.

"Cleaning my feet," I said, stating the obvious.

"Well don't drop your dead skin on the floor. It stinks."

"I'll clean it up," I said. "I'm done anyway." I had pulled too hard on some live tissue and my feet were freckled with blood." I dabbed my feet with a clean towel and then left them to air out until Doc arrived to torture me with his daily dose of alcohol. Gary pillowed his field jacket and laid back.

"Captain wants to see you," he said.

"What about?"

"I don't know. He doesn't confide in me."

"Shit," I said. I grabbed a pair of dry socks and pulled them on, carefully.

"And if I have to hear about your great assault on Mount Everest one more time I'm going to shoot one of your men."

"Make it Nolan," I said.

"I'm serious. Jesus." My boots were still damp but there was nothing I could do about that. Even the air was wet. I unlaced my boots half way and eased my feet in. "My guys are sick of it too. Now they want to go, just to shut your guys up." I laughed.

"Yeah, well my guys weren't too happy about it at the time," I said. "I thought I was going to have a mutiny on my hands for a while there."

"Even your extraction. Braggin' like it was some great adventure. Sounds to me like it was fucked up."

"It was," I admitted.

"Well, seems like shit doesn't stick to you," he said. I just looked at him. "Forget it," he said. "Ya done good."

"Two men in the hospital and the rest of the platoon on profile. I'm not sure Captain Messina would agree with you on that." I laced my boots up tight so they wouldn't flop around.

"Yeah, remind him of that," Gary said. I grabbed my rifle and ducked out the door.

"And get that dead skin out of here!" Gary called after me.

* * *

"Have a seat," Captain Messina said. "How're the feet?"

"Good," I lied. "We should be able to do our share of ambushes and LPs…starting tomorrow."

"Williams, grab some chow," Captain Messina said. The radio watch thanked him and left. "I don't think your medic would agree with that," he said but there was little more he could say. I didn't control the weather and he was the one who picked a marsh for an LZ, thinking it was a field. "That's not why I called you in here. One of the chopper pilots wanted to know the name of the black buck sergeant on his ship. I assume that would be Sergeant Little?"

"Yessir," I said. I had no idea where this was going.

"He's putting him in for a Bronze star. They want another witness. Did you see what happened?" I wasn't sure what he was talking about.

"You mean during the extraction?" Captain Messina nodded. "Yeah, most of it," I said. "In bits and pieces. We were circling. But it was everyone, not just Sgt. Little."

"The pilot says it was Sgt. Little who ordered the men off the chopper and got the whole thing going. In these cases the award usually goes to the man in charge. And in this case, rightly so, wouldn't you say." I agreed.

"I just assumed the pilot or the crew chief ordered them off and they just did what they were told," I said.

"Uh uh. Type something up before you leave. Let's get this thing going. Anybody else you saw that should be singled out for recognition?" In my mind I saw an image of Sgt. Little and Specialist Nolan climbing over the port skid and going under water three times before they got the chopper out of the mud.

"No, Sir. Everybody else was just doing their part," I said, telling myself that was technically true.

"Don't hesitate to put those who deserve it in for an award," he said. "It's good for morale. As long as they deserve it. Otherwise it just pisses everyone else off."

"Yes, sir. Like I said, I wasn't aware the whole thing was Sgt. Little's idea."

"It's your job to find these things out," Captain Messina said. "And speaking of morale, you've done a pretty good job with your platoon. What about the rest of the company?"

"The rest of the company?"

"Perhaps I didn't make myself clear before. I made you morale officer for the entire company, not just your platoon. Have you given any thought to that?"

"Oh yessir," I said, thinking fast. And the first thing I thought was that I was going to kill Gary for telling me being morale officer was a bullshit assignment. My mind flashed to Romansky wanting to know what the Army's motto was. "Well, I was thinking how, you know how some units have a motto or slogan for their unit? I noticed that we didn't have anything like that. No insignia or motto hanging above the orderly room door. I thought we could have, like, a contest. See who could come up with the best motto or something. Maybe have some kind of prize for the winner."

I've always been able to come up with excuses for my failings on the spur of the moment. I prided myself on it; that my mother or teachers or whoever, usually bought what I told them, I was that convincing. I waited but Captain Messina's face showed nothing.

"What else ya got?" he said. I put my mind to work and remembered that Captain Messina was big on training.

"Well, I haven't worked it all out yet, but on the last mission I was thinking about what would happen if Doc got wounded. We've all had first aid training, but what if he was hurt bad and was losing a lot of blood before we could get a dustoff. None of us knows how to start an IV or give an injection of morphine or whatever. I was thinking he could give us--the whole company--some training sessions on that stuff. Same thing with radios. All our RTOs are just eleven Bs humping Prick 25s. Why don't we get a real RTO to come out, show us how to break down a radio, maybe some quick fixes if one breaks in the field, stuff like that. Knowin' all that would give everyone confidence. Raise their morale." Captain Messina didn't say anything for a long moment.

"Okay, get going on that?" I wanted to make sure there was no misunderstanding this time.

"Which one?" I said.

"Both," he said. "The training seminars *and* that motto thing. Good ideas. Now, I wanted to talk to you about Sgt. Nelson. He's been putting in for a job in the rear ever since Lt. Barons left. Before that even. The battalion quartermaster position is opening up in two weeks. I was thinking of putting him in for it. What do you think? Do you think you're ready to run the platoon by yourself?" I thought of Sgt. Nelson, his bad attitude, his antagonism toward me.

"I feel I've already been doing that," I said. Captain Messina's lips tightened, but he said nothing for a moment.

"It's an E-8 slot. It would be a promotion. Either that or he'd have to work above his grade. I take it you don't think he deserves another rocker?"

"No, Sir."

"Neither do I," Captain Messina said in a rare moment of sharing his opinion of a subordinate with me. "I'll see what I can do. It may take a while to replace him. Make no mistake--you still have a lot to learn. In the meantime, if Sergeant Nelson gets the job you'll need an acting platoon sergeant. What do you think of Sgt. Little?" I wasn't prepared for that. All three squad leaders impressed me as capable in their roles but I never thought of any one of them as being better than the others. Captain Messina misinterpreted my silence for disapproval. "The reason I asked is that Sgt. Little has more time in grade than the other two, so unless there's a good reason why you don't think he's up for the job, or unless to think Sgt. Allen or Sgt. Burkholtz can do better, Sgt. Little will get the job." My mind was racing; I could think of nothing that made Sgt. Allen or Sgt. Burkholtz more qualified for the job than Sgt. Little.

"No, Sir," I said. "Sgt. Little is fine."

"Good!" Captain Messina said. Clearly, Sgt. Little was his first choice. "Start giving him more responsibility, but don't tell him why. Nothing's for sure yet so don't say anything. About the bronze star either. It should go through based on what I've heard, but you never know. You sure have a way of turning your missions into adventures, Lieutenant," he said in such a way that I couldn't tell if it was a compliment or a criticism.

*   *   *

"Thanks, buddy," I said, ducking inside.

"What?"

"Telling me the morale officer assignment was bullshit." I leaned my rifle against my bunk and sat down. Gary had left his entrenching tool fully extended in plain sight so I would know he had taken care of my dead skin. A puddle had formed where he had scooped up the pasty skin and an inch of dirt along with it.

"It's not?"

"No," I said and gave him the gist of my conversation with Captain Messina. "Still haven't figured him out yet," I said.

"Captain Messina?"

"Yeah. I mean, why's he out here, anyway? He never goes on patrol."

"He's gone out a couple of times," Gary said. "He took your platoon out once before you got here. I think he was worried about Sgt. Nelson after Lt. Barons left. Nothin' ever came of it, though. I'm sure Nelson had his shit together when the captain was around. Plus, this is his second tour. He was an advisor with the ARVNs in '65 so he's seen his share of shit. Plus I don't think he thinks much of Lt. Avery."

"That was the other thing. What's he doin' back at Hardscrabble? And I keep seeing him on the resupply chopper."

"You want him out here?"

"No, but--"

"Neither does Captain Messina. He's a chickenshit. An' all that shit about ridin' around on the chopper? Merry? The company clerk? He told one of my guys that he saw this record Avery keeps of every time he goes up and for how long. Soon as he has enough hours he can put in for an air medal." A plate-size patch of dirt fell from the wall, landing on the floor with a splat. "I'm enlarging the place," Gary said. He scooped up the pile with his entrenching tool and deposited it in the depression he made when he threw out my dead skin.

"You in scouts?" he continued. "There's always that kid who

collects patches and merit badges just to have them on his uniform. Does as little as possible to earn them, has his parents sign off on everything. That's Avery. Merry said he once asked the captain to sign off on a CIB for himself because Hardscrabble got mortared one night. Closest round probably didn't even wake him up. Messina went through the roof. Told him if he wanted a CIB he'd give him a line platoon for the rest of his tour. That shut him up."

"So how'd he get to be XO? Stay in the rear?"

"I dunno. I guess Captain Messina hates paperwork."

* * *

Doc Ertel rolled up his tourniquet strap and put it back in his medical bag. "Any questions on arterial bleeding?" he asked. The sky was clear and the men were enjoying a rare moment of blue above their heads.

"What do you do with the rest of the leg, if it's like, not attached anymore?" This from one of the new guys in Gary's platoon.

"Doc sells it to the Gooks. Tells them it's dog?" Cisco said, and everyone laughed. Messing with the new guys was *the* main pastime for the veterans.

"No, I'm serious," the new guy said. "What happens to it?" For a moment, Doc didn't know what to say.

"If I think you're not going to make it I put it on the dustoff so it can be buried with you," Gary's medic said. "Otherwise I just toss it away." The new guy gave a nervous laugh and then looked around when no one else joined in. "Oh, you're serious," he said.

Setting up my first training session was easier than I expected. I just told Doc I wanted him and 3rd Platoon's medic to give a training session reviewing what the men had already been taught about first aid and to teach them how to handle emergency situations they hadn't been taught in case the medic was unable to provide care. They were already in their second hour and the men showed no sign of boredom.

"Now if he's lost a lot of blood and it will be a while before he can be evacuated," Doc said, pulling out a bottle of clear liquid, "you're going to need to replace the lost fluids. Look for pale skin, a weak pulse, loss of consciousness. I need a volunteer to be the patient," he said, unwinding a plastic tube attached to a needle. There was an outburst of laughing and jostling among the men.

"Somebody expendable. Murphy," someone suggested which was followed by unanimous agreement from my platoon.

"No, this job calls for someone of unquestioned courage," Doc said. "A man of proven leadership. A man who's willing to sacrifice his own men to accomplish his mission. A man with the guts to scale the highest summit to--" Doc was drowned out by the cheering and clapping as all eyes turned to me. Men were slapping me on the back and pushing me forward. "Lt. Sullivan, will you come up here please?" Doc said. The men were going wild. I looked to Captain Messina before things went too far but he just shrugged as if there was nothing he could do. I had no choice but to go along and hope the demonstration would just be a simulation, that no blood would be spilled. I worked my way to the front, only vaguely aware of the pats and slaps to my back. "Next I need a volunteer to--"

"Oh, me! Me!" Cisco yelled, tripping over the crowd as he scrambled up to join me. More laughing and cheering. Apparently my occasional abuse of Cisco had not gone unnoticed by the rest of the platoon.

"Easy," Doc said, pulling the needle away and mugging for his audience. "Well, at least one of our volunteers is eager." He waited for the uproar to die and then got serious which made me even more nervous. He rolled up my sleeve, then tore open an alcohol pad and rubbed the disinfectant in the crook of my elbow. The peanut gallery grew quiet, the laugher more nervous than raucous. Only Doc knew how far this was going to go. Even Cisco was starting to look nervous.

"Next you want to restrict the flow of blood at the bicep," he said, handing Cisco a long rubber tube. He showed him how to loop it around my arm and had him pull it tight. I felt a pinch as the rubber contracted on my skin. Next Doc took the cap off the needle and handed it to Cisco. "The point of the needle is beveled. Be sure the longest part--the pointy part--is down, closest to the vein. Here," he said, pointing. I flinched as the tip of the needle touched my skin.

"We haven't even done anything yet," Cisco said and everyone laughed. Doc put his hand on Cisco's and gently eased it down.

"Have the needle at a low angle, about fifteen degrees to the arm. You want the needle to go into the vein, not through it. Use the fingers of your other hand to keep the vein from rolling when you push it in." The men were shifting around; some stood up, trying to get a better view. Cisco took a breath.

"Okay, El Tee. You're going to feel a little prick, followed by a few minutes of excruciating pain as I dig around looking for the vein," he said. I felt a sharp pain; then nothing as a drop of blood appeared in the tube. There was complete silence for a moment and then a loud cheer as everyone realized that that was exactly what was supposed to happen.

"Perfect," Doc said. "Normally I'd then release this clamp but I don't want to waste a perfectly good bottle of plasma on a second lieutenant. Here *or* in the field." He showed how to stabilize the tube for transport; then removed the needle, taped a gauze pad over the puncture and Cisco and I returned to our places to great applause.

Apparently that was the grand finale. Several men came up to look over the medic's equipment and ask questions. I went up too, to congratulate the medics on a great presentation. Captain Messina was there too, adding his compliments and telling Doc Ertel (Gary's medic was going out on patrol the next day) that he was sending him on the next resupply chopper to Wild Turkey to give a training session to Second Platoon.

"Nice job, Sean" Captain Messina said, using my first name for the first time as we walked back to our bunkers. "The men seemed to enjoy that. I learned something myself. What's next?"

"Mortars," I said, "I've already talked to Sgt. LoPresti. They'll give a presentation after we get back from our next mission."

"Good. Contact Lt. Petros and have him arrange to have his mortar crew give a training session to Second Platoon. Wait until Doc does his thing over there. Give them an idea of how it should be done. They did good, huh?"

"Yessir," I said.

Chapter 15

The call to stop came from the rear. It traveled forward like a wave. Tense, urgent. My chest tightened even before I saw what caused the need to stop. They were a hundred yards above us on the trail heading to Phu Nu--two mama sans and three kids, one of them an infant hugged tight to its mother's breast. They were moving fast, scurrying. The little girl was old enough to keep up but the boy was being dragged along at a pace too fast for his little legs. The women kept their eyes to the ground but the boy looked right at us, pointing and jabbering. His mother kept yanking him forward and scolding but the boy persisted. The woman stopped, spun around and slapped him in the face. "Yap di," she hissed. Shut up. The boy cried but his mother had accomplished her mission. The boy was so intent on keeping up, he no longer noticed us. I moved forward to the point, picking up Sgt. Little on the way.

"Think they saw us?" Turner said.

"They saw us," I said.

"I didn't think we were that close to the trail," Brokovitch said, a hint of apology in his voice.

Third platoon had just come back from a patrol in the same area. Gary had lost a man to a VC ambush and come up with nothing in return except an American ammo pouch when they tossed Phu Nu the following day. An old man was hauled off in a chopper for questioning which everyone knew would reveal nothing. Phu Nu was near where Nellis had been shot in the foot on my first mission and it was now on Captain Messina's pink list. Pink, as in commie.

He rarely sent back to back patrols to the same area but he made an exception for this mission, thinking we might catch the VC off guard. Our plan was to pass well below the village, circle around and set up a series of night ambushes along the trails.

"What now?" Brokovitch said. I said nothing, thinking.

"Well, we can't keep going the way we have been," Sgt. Little said, stating the obvious. Sgt. Nelson had left the platoon for the quartermaster job. Sgt. Little was now acting platoon sergeant and I regretted my decision to give him the job soon after he took over. Shy by nature, he had been slow to assert his new authority. This was the first time he'd spoken up and I took it as a positive sign.

"I still want to get behind that village before nightfall," I said.

"Whatever we do, we better do it fast," Brokovitch said. As point man, he'd be the first to go down if we gave the VC enough time to set up an ambush.

"Okay, let's drop down the hill a couple hundred yards and keep going the way we have. If they set up an ambush, at least there will be a lot of jungle between us and them. Maybe we can get around them before they have time to set up."

Brokovitch set a quick pace but we were not moving as fast as the mama sans. After almost an hour on the move the patrol stopped. My first thought was that Brokovitch was taking a breather until I saw Sgt. Little running toward me at a crouch.

"Brokovitch is spooky, Sir," he said. "Somethin' ain't right." No sooner were the words out of his mouth than all hell broke loose. I ran forward and AK rounds were soon hitting the ground around me, whizzing past my head. I took cover behind a tree, fired a short burst toward the muzzle flashes up the hill and then ducked behind the tree again. Sgt. Little ran past me and I followed because I didn't know what else to do. Brokovitch was lying on the ground, not moving. Caulkins and Stevens had set up their machinegun behind a small boulder and were firing long bursts up the hill and ahead of them. I kept running, firing wildly until I saw a stream of smoke heading right at them. I stopped, frozen in my tracks. Caulkins flattened himself against the rock. Stevens, intent on putting down surpressing fire, never saw it coming. The rocket hit the ground right in front of them, the concussion knocking me flat.

My head spun and a chill run down my spine, only adding to my confusion. There was a simple response to the situation we were in but I couldn't think what it was. I couldn't breathe. I opened my mouth to yell for help but no sound came out. My body went cold. I opened my eyes to a world turned upside down. I could see enemy soldiers advancing toward me, but they were farther away now, a half mile at least, and down the hill instead of up. I tried to suck air into my lungs but my diaphragm was paralyzed. It came suddenly, in a cold rush of air that stung my lungs, but never had air tasted so sweet. I gasped several times and tried to focus.

The Americans occupied a narrow strip along a small river in a landscape of black and white, rock and snow; the Chinese, in their quilted jackets, were pushing hard against the American line.

"Goddamn him!" I was standing in a trench, the major next to me fuming as he watched the scene without the use of the binoculars that hung around his neck. "I told him! I told him a dozen times!"

"Who?" I said. It was then that he looked at me, registering no surprise at my presence wearing only my thin jungle fatigues to protect me from the frigid Korean winter.

"Major Peabody," he spat and turned his attention back to the front. He picked up his radio in a gloved hand and started calling in orders. "Look at that," he said, pointing to a sector off to the left where a concentration of Chinese troops were pushing back a quarter mile section of the American line. "Wilson! Where's that artillery?" he yelled.

"Coming, Sir," a voice answered from the bunker behind us.

"And where the fuck is air?" There was no answer to that. "Thinks he's some Goddamn second lieutenant or something," he said, referring to Major Peabody. "Trying to live down his name or some silly shit like that. Now I have to commit *my* reserves to *his* sector." The Chinese were now splashing across a ford in the river. Those American who didn't fall back were quickly overrun. I waited, expecting to see the units on either side of the hole shift to fill the gap but there was no movement on the American side. "Goddamn him to hell. He doesn't know what the Fuck's going on. That why *you're* here?" he growled, casting a steely glance my way.

"I…I guess so, Sir," I said. I assumed there must be *some* reason I was there and that was as good a one as any. I ducked as an artillery round exploded half way up our hill. The major barely flinched.

"What the--"

"That's not ours, Sir" the artillery observer said. He had brought his radio outside so he could see better. A smoke round exploded three hundred yards behind the Chinese troops that were breaking through the American line. "That's ours," he said.

"Well get 'em on target, Captain," the major said. "Sometimes you have to distance yourself from the action so you can see the big picture." This he directed at me. He turned, noticing the single bar on my shoulder. "Mmmm," he said. "Mentally, if you can't do it physically," he added just before another artillery round landed farther up the hill, covering us with a shower of frozen dirt.

"Sir. Sir, are you okay!" I shook my head, blinking my eyes to clear them.

"Yuh," I said, still trying to digest what the major had said. I looked around, trying to make sense of everything. The sounds of gunfire, the yelling of men, the muzzle flashes of the VC, seemed far away. Brokovitch was moving now, crawling toward our machinegun position. Doc was laying down next to Stevens, unable to give him the care he needed lest he be shot himself. Caulkins was laying on his side beside Stevens, yanking on the gun's bolt handle, trying to clear a jam. I could see the bent bipod and the buckled cover assembly blocking the feed tray. The gun was useless.

Nolan was behind a tree, sticking his gun out at every lull in enemy fire, shooting wildly in their direction without exposing himself. I did not see Turner anywhere. I was on my feet, running, Cisco following me to the protection of an uprooted tree. Behind me, the rest of the platoon was bunching up, unable to move or return fire without shooting over the men in front of them.

The muzzle flashes from the VC sparkled like a string of Christmas tree lights. I could see their position in relation to ours as clearly as if they were lines drawn on a map--a problem to be solved from our tactics workbook in OCS. The solution: a textbook flanking maneuver. The first thing we learned.

"Rivera, Romansky!" I yelled. "Get your gun up here." A second B-40 left a smoky trail over our position and exploded harmlessly behind us. Rivera yelled for cover fire and he and Romansky ran forward, almost slamming into Cisco and me behind our root and dirt wall.

"Shit, man," Romansky said as an enemy round found a weak spot in our cover, spraying us with dirt as it came through. We all crouched down.

"I think there are six or eight of them. Maybe ten," I said, not telling them anything they hadn't already figured out for themselves. The VC were behind a downed tree, the large trunk giving them complete cover except when they stuck their heads up to shoot. We had to get around them.

"See that rocky ledge over there?" I said, pointing to an outcrop just wide enough to give a machinegun crew cover. It was directly downhill from the ambush and would give us a clear shot at the VC behind the fallen tree. It couldn't have been in a more perfect place.

"Gotcha, Sir," Rivera said. Boyd thumped against the trunk of the tree next to me, his M-14 looking big and useless in a situation like this. Everyone was on automatic. He ducked under the trunk to the other side where he found the room he was looking for. With the butt of his rifle he bashed the dirt between two large roots until he broke a hole through to the other side. Rivera and Romansky joined him on the other side. From the length of the ammo belt I could tell they hadn't yet fired a shot.

"Cover fire," Rivera yelled. He waited a second for our gunfire to reach full pitch; then he and Romansky dashed to their new position. Boyd was squeezing off rounds as fast as he could pull the trigger. I could tell he didn't have a visible target. Rivera and Romansky reached their position unharmed. As far as I could tell the VC didn't know they were there. They set up quickly and opened fire. I could see the .30 calibre ammo chopping through tree branches--splinters and dead leaves flying everywhere. They were firing long bursts with barely a second break between, not worried about running out of ammo or burning out the barrel. It was over in less than thirty seconds. Those who hadn't been hit were on the run. I only saw one fall before the rest disappeared from sight and he managed to get away too.

I ordered a cease fire and as Rivera let his gun cool off the rest of the platoon rushed forward, running around the downed tree to the other side. Turner let loose with a full magazine. "None of that shit," I yelled. "Unless they're reaching for a gun."

"He was, Sir" Turner said. Someone laughed.

"I mean it," I said. Two other gooks were dead, those closest to Rivera's machinegun, riddled with holes. Sgt. Allen was pulling on the arm of another man who had wedged himself as far under the tree trunk as he could in an effort to hide.

""Dung Ban! Dung Ban," he begged as he was pulled out, his free arm up as high as he could get it. He was hit in both legs and had another hole high up in his abdomen. He was bleeding badly.

"Got a blood trail here," Murphy shouted. He was near where I saw the one VC go down. Boyd was running up to join him.

"Forget it. You two set up security til we can get outta here," I ordered and then went to assess our losses. Stevens' entire upper body was peppered with shrapnel. Goo was running from where his left eye used to be and he kept spitting up blood and pieces of teeth.

The blood was a mix of dark maroon and bright red. These Doc ignored, bandaging instead the wounds that dotted his chest like the measles. I was surprised to see how pink Steven's flesh was under his dark skin.

"How ya doing, Stevens," I said. I didn't know his first name.

"Fucked up," was all he could get out before he started into a fit of coughing. I felt at a loss. I patted his shoulder, nodded to Caulkins who was holding his hand.

"Ya did good," I said to both of them and I meant it. God knows how many men we would have lost if they hadn't kept the VC's heads down in those first critical seconds. "You'll be fine," I said and looked at Doc. Doc mouthed the word *fast.* I turned to my ever-present shadow.

"On the way," Cisco said. It was obvious we couldn't get Stevens out from our present location without a jungle penetrator. Hanson had been shot in the arm, a nasty wound that shattered his humerus and punctured an artery. Doc had applied a tourniquet and splint but only a hospital could stop Stevens' bleeding. I had no idea what to do next. My mind was a mess. Sgt. Little came running and sliding down the hill, holding his rifle out to the side for balance.

"We're right below the village, Sir," he gasped. "We can get them out same place we did Nellis." I could have kissed him.

* * *

It took us fifteen minutes to reach the yam field. The dustoff wasn't there yet so we stayed in the cover of the tree line. Doc started an IV on Stevens; then asked Hanson how he was doing.

"Good," was all Hanson said. His hand had turned blue and he stared at his shattered arm as if he couldn't understand what had happened to him while Doc fashioned a sling.

"You're next, Sir," Doc said, taking his bandage scissors from his shirt pocket. I pulled back. "Relax," Doc said. "I'm gonna cut off your sleeve, not your arm." It was then that I noticed a hole in my fatigue shirt just below the left shoulder. It was a small tear, the fabric around it dark with blood. I said nothing, as if I knew I had been wounded all along, had soldiered on despite my injury.

"Two minutes out," Cisco said. Sgt. Little watched as Doc pulled off my sleeve. I was surprised at how little blood there was. The hot shrapnel had cauterized the vessels as it sliced through the muscle.

"Sgt. Little," I said and for the first time since I'd known him I saw fear in his eyes. It took several seconds for what this meant for him to register.

"Yes, Sir," he said and started giving orders to set up a perimeter for the dustoff. Doc was poking around in my arm while I tried to act disinterested, as if it was nothing, which it was compared to Stevens' and Hanson's injuries.

"Think it's time to trade that in for an M-16?" I said. PFC Boyd was holding the plasma bottle above Stevens, his M-14 lying on the ground next to him. Stevens lay perfectly still, his eyes closed. If Doc hadn't just put in an IV I would have thought he was dead.

"No, Sir. Not yet," Boyd said. His tone was edgy. I was trying to make a joke but he took it as an *I told you so* comment.

"Jesus, Doc!" I said as his probe scraped across the metal in my arm, sending an electric charge clear down to my fingertips. I could hear the chopper but not yet see it. A plume of blue smoke was sprouting forty yards out into the yam field.

"It's deep," Doc said. "Nothing I can do here." I said nothing, embarrassed that I hadn't put up so much as token resistance to abandoning my men to a buck sergeant while I went back to the safety of Hardscrabble. Sgt. Little came trotting back.

"All ready," he said. He looked at me, his face blank, but I knew that underneath he was waiting for me to say 'Good job. I'll take it from here.'

"Don't take any unnecessary chances," I said instead. "You can ask for an extraction, your call, but I don't think you'll get it." Doc was on his knees, checking on the wounded VC. "How is he?" I asked, but I could already see. No one had made any attempt to stop his bleeding. More important things to do.

"Dead," Doc said. The chopper appeared over the tree line at the far end of the field, banking into its approach. Doc applied a bandage to my arm while the rest of the stay-behind crew gathered up the equipment that would be going back with us.

"Leave the M-60," Sgt. Little said. "We'll hump it out." It was heavy and useless; I looked at Sgt. Little. "Don't want the gooks to think we only got one gun," he said. He was right. Adams and Talltree had DEROSed. Sgt. Nelson was back in the rear. Simpson was still on profile and Slick Slack was on R and R. Now, with me, Stevens, and Hanson gone the platoon was down to 24 effectives.

There would be a lot of eyes on the dustoff; most of them could count and all of them would be mad that we had just killed four of their own. Maybe five. I nodded to Sgt. Little that keeping the gun was a good idea.

The chopper flared and we ran through the expanding circle of smoke and debris. I looked at my arm, disappointed that my blood had not yet soaked through the bandage. I could feel the eyes of the platoon on me as I let the crew chief to help me aboard, letting my left arm hang loose at my side as if it were useless. I watched, embarrassed, as Stevens and Hanson were slid onto the deck, their fatigues soaked with blood, the medic hanging Stevens' IV on a hook suspended from the overhead.

The dustoff lifted up, spun on its axis and then raced across the field. We gained altitude quickly and as we banked away I caught a glimpse of my platoon--a ragged circle of boys in an exposed yam field full of punji stakes and the worst thought imaginable popped into my head--I was glad I was not still with them.

Chapter 16

It took twenty minutes to get back to Hardscrabble but it was enough time for the natural sedatives that had flooded Hanson's body after he was hit to wear off. He was doing his best not to scream, gritting his teeth and cursing under his breath. I put my hand on his good shoulder and told him to hang on, we're almost there, but it was like he didn't even hear me.

"Can't you do anything for him?" The flight medic was leaning over Stevens, adjusting the IV drip. He looked at me, shook his head. My blood ran cold as I realized he thought I was talking about Stevens. "I meant him," I said, pointing to Hanson.

He pulled a vial of morphine and a syringe from his aid bag. "Hey, Stevens, how ya doin'?" I said, my mouth close to his ear so I wouldn't have to yell above the noise of the chopper. His chest was rising and falling in a slow, shallow rhythm; a clear liquid tinged with red oozed from under the bandage covering his left eye. He opened his good eye, squeezed it shut, then opened it again. He looked at me, trying to place me; trying to figure out why I was on the chopper with him. He opened his mouth to say something but it was too much for him; he closed his eye again and went back to the business of breathing.

The medic nudged me away and went back to Stevens, placing his fingertips on the side of his neck. He held it there for several seconds and then said something into his intercom. I looked at Hanson. The medic had written a giant M and the time on his forehead with a marking pen. Already his eyes were starting to glass over as the morphine worked its magic.

"Almost there," I said, but he no longer seemed to care.

Hardscrabble didn't have a forward aid station. Instead it boasted a small hospital complete with three operating rooms, its own X-ray, labs, a recovery room and a twenty-bed ward. As soon as we landed a team of nurses pulled Stevens onto a stretcher and rushed him into one of the buildings adjacent to the helipad. The flight medic jumped off and he and another medic helped Hanson off. The nurse took one look at him and called for a gurney. No one said a word to me; I simply followed behind like a lost puppy.

Stevens was nowhere to be seen when I got inside. Hanson lay on his back while a nurse removed his splint and bandage. The doctor checked the wound, the nurse handing him fresh gauze pads and dropping the used ones on the floor as he soaked up the blood. A medic appeared on the other side of the gurney. "Get three units of whole blood ready," the doctor said. "Make it four. Let's not fuck around." The medic checked Hanson's dog tag and left. The doctor took a hemostat from his shirt pocket, poked it into the gaping wound and clamped off a vessel before loosening the tourniquet. Blood gushed from a hundred small veins and capillaries and then subsided to a slow seep. The nurse soaked up the blood and checked the clamped artery.

"It's good," she said.

"Can you make a fist?" the doctor said. Hanson made a fist. "Now open. Good. Wiggle your thumb." Hansen wiggled his thumb. "You're gonna be fine," he said and turned to the nurse. "Get him to X-ray and call Doctor O'Shaughnessy. When you get the pictures, take them to three and scrub up." He turned to leave and noticed me for the first time. He glanced at the bandage on my arm which I was glad to see had a quarter-sized circle of red where the blood had finally soaked through, my red badge of courage.

"What's with you?"

"Piece of shrapnel," I said. He didn't even bother to take off the bandage.

"Audrey, you busy?" he said, stopping a nurse who was walking by.

"Just going off shift," she said. She was short, with a nice face and thick hair that was matted to her forehead and curling, sweaty, around her ears.

"Can you take care of this guy first?" he said.

"Sure." The doctor started to leave; then noticed my bars.

"By the way. Your medic did a nice job on the arm," he said, meaning Hanson's.

Audrey--Lt. Kostanciak, I saw by the name on her fatigues--pulled a pair of bandage scissors from her shirt pocket. "That it?" she said.

"That's it. Shrapnel," I added so she didn't think it was just a scratch. She bent her head over the bandage and started cutting. Her hair was dark at the roots and where the sweat stained it against her skin but it was lighter at the back and on top where it was bleached by the sun. "My medic said I had to come in. Too deep for him." I'm not bad looking and I wanted her to look up, see my face, but her attention was on my arm. She peeled the bandage off and looked at the small hole, no longer bleeding.

"Ouch," she said in a tone that was neither sarcastic nor sympathetic. "Two more and you get to go home," she said. The standard response to minor wounds had gotten around.

"Keep looking," I said.

"It has to be in separate incidents."

"That was a joke," I said.

"Oh. Yeah," she said and forced a smile. A sense of humor would have been nice but it wasn't a deal breaker for me.

"Doc said it was in deep," I said. She pulled a probe from her breast pocket and cleaned it with an alcohol wipe.

"Want me to numb it up?" she said.

"I'll try being a man first. See how it goes." She finally looked up, forced another smile, and went back to my wound, my face causing no more interest in her other than as just another patient. The probe went more than an inch into my arm and when it hit the shrapnel I pulled back like a knee jerk reaction.

"Uh huh," Audrey said. "Enough of being a man for one day?" I suspected men were not on her list of favorite things.

"Yes, ma'am." I said.

"Sit down," she said. "I'll be right back." Apparently my wound wasn't worth contaminating an entire operating room.

She returned with a cart full of medical supplies and gave me an injection deep into the skin next to the wound. "Give that a minute," she said and then busied herself unwrapping her instruments and laying them out on the cart.

"Where'd you do your residency?" I said, trying to loosen her up.

"Here," she said, not even turning around. "Everybody works above their pay grade here." Her tone couldn't have been more disinterested if she tried. While she was busy getting everything ready I took the opportunity to check her out. She was trim, and pretty in a girl-next-door sort of way. Not a raving beauty, but I was sure that at Hardscrabble she would not be starved for male attention. She turned back to me, her hands gloved in latex, and began pressing the skin around my wound.

"Anything?" she said.

"No." She put the probe in and I could feel her tapping on the shrapnel but there was no pain.

"Good?" she said, all business.

"Good," I said. She poured disinfectant into the wound, cleaned the area around it, and picked up the scalpel.

"I'm just going to open it up a bit so the shrapnel comes out easier." She put the blade into the wound and pulled it out in one smooth motion. For a moment there was nothing; then the hole filled with blood which began running down my arm. "Hold that," she said, putting a gauze pad over the wound. I enjoyed a moment of pleasure before she pulled her hand from beneath mine, then laughed as she put on new glove.

"What?" she said.

"Nothing," I said. She picked up a hemostat which I assumed she was going to use like a pair of pliers. "I just realized how filthy I must look to you."

"Relax. I'm used to it, Lieutenant," she said.

"Sean," I said. For the first time she looked at me as a person instead of as a wound and gave me a genuine smile.

"Sean," she said, as if remembering how lonely I must be. How lonely we all were. Her eyes were a soft brown, the color of polished cedar. "Okay, let's see what we have," she said. "Press hard for five seconds and then take the pad away." I pushed on the pad and when I lifted it up the hole looked deep and dark and empty of blood. She put the instrument in the hole and as it refilled with blood she slowly worked the shrapnel to the surface. When it was out I put the pad over the wound as she held the jagged piece of metal up for me to see. It was about the size of a marble, but rough and ugly-looking. She put it on her cart and picked up the bottle of disinfectant.

"Pressure," she said. I pushed and when I pulled the pad away she poured the liquid into the wound, flushing out as much contaminate as she could as my blood and disinfectant spattered on the floor. She handed me a fresh pad, letting the blood flow freely before she took my hand and pressed it back to the wound. It was only an instant, that tender moment, and then she was on to the business of preparing her suture kit as if nothing had happened between us. It tried not to consider that, for her, nothing had.

Five stitches and the job was done. I barely noticed when she finished, so intent was I on the fall of her hair, the pink of her skin, the curve of the *U.S. ARMY* on her fatigues above her breast. "You've done this before," I said as she put a clean gauze pad over the stitching and taped it down.

"A few times," she said and handed me a bottle of pills. "One a day until they're gone," she said. I wanted the piece of shrapnel but didn't want to look like a jerk, asking for it. She saved me the embarrassment. "Souvenir," she said. I held out my hand and she dropped it in my palm; then started cleaning up the mess we had made. I didn't want it to end. I wanted to find an excuse to spend more time there and walk out with her when she was done.

"I'd like to see how my men are doing," I said, which was true even if it wasn't my main reason for asking.

"They'll be needing more than five stitches," she said. She wasn't trying to be mean but that didn't stop me from feeling any less pathetic. "Come back after supper. It'll be a while before they're ready to see anyone."

"Right," I said and started to walk out through the doors I came in through.

"That way," she said, pointing me down a corridor to the right of the helipad entrance. "We have to keep that way clear."

"Right," I said again. I read the doctor's names on the office doors on my way out. The door at the end of the corridor was propped open so I could hear the downpour outside long before I got there. I decided to wait it out under the awning until it let up, or until Lt. Kostanciak showed up, whichever came first.

"You still here?" she said, joining me under the awning.

"Waiting for the rain to let up," I said. She eyed me suspiciously.

"I'd think you infantry types would be used to a little rain." Rather than meet her expression I gazed into the downpour.

"When I have a choice, I usually pick dry," I said.

"Well, when I have a choice I usually choose to eat lunch. Mess hall closes in ten minutes," she said. She put her fatigue hat on, preparing to run.

"Uh, Where is it?" I asked even though I could clearly see it. I was hoping she'd say *follow me* but instead she pointed the way.

"That building over there. The one with the *mess hall* sign over the door. It was nice meeting you, Sean," she said, hunching her shoulders and dashing into the rain. I was right behind her, splashing through the low spots as the monsoon drenched my hat and shoulders. I pulled ahead at the last second and held the door for her.

"Thank you," she said, slapping her hat against her leg before stuffing the brim into her waistband. I was embarrassed at how aroused I was. Disappointed too, that she hadn't extended the conversation beyond politeness. She went through the chow line, pointing to the things she wanted and thanking the Vietnamese help who waited on her. She had the spaghetti. I took two cheeseburgers and fries. I followed her to the beverage dispensers and filled a large glass with milk while she drew a glass of red Kool-Aid.

"Mind if I join you?" I said.

"I'm not–" she said, then changed her mind. "Sure." I followed her toward the back of the mess hall, past a low partition that separated the officers from the enlisted men. She ignored two empty tables and took a bench seat at a table already occupied by two other nurses and a young captain I took to be a doctor.

"You're late," One of the nurses said. She was a stunner, with natural blond hair and pouty lips; the kind that, with a little lipstick, you'd see on the cover of a magazine.

"Last minute customer," she said. "This is Sean. Sean--Barry, Karen, and Marlene." I shook hands with Barry and nodded to the girls. Marlene, the pretty one, gave me a smile that faded as quickly as it had appeared.

"Purple heart or bar fight?" Karen asked, noticing my bandage and cut-off sleeve. She was a tall, willowy girl with a sharp, hawk-like nose. Her eyes were small and beady, furthering the predator-like impression of her face.

"Shrapnel," I said and searched for something more to say. Should I make light of it? Say how lucky I was compared to Stevens and Hanson? Two more and I get to go home? The moment passed. I left it at *shrapnel*. Karen started asking me questions--where was I from? How long had I been here? What I wanted to do when I got out--the kind of conversation I wanted to be having with Audrey. Or Marlene. But they were engaged in their own small talk. Both gave the impression they were glad Karen was taking care of the pleasantries for them. Karen seemed happy too. Barry, I noticed, was wearing a wedding ring and wasn't interested in either of the conversations going on around him.

I was barely into my second cheeseburger when Audrey and Marlene got up and said their good-byes. They didn't even ask Karen if she was coming. They just smiled and left. I wanted to say something to Audrey—*thanks; nice meeting you; hope to see you again*--but she didn't meet my eyes and I was left with nothing to say but *see ya* to their backs as they left. Karen was still jabbering away like a school girl with a crush. She kept fussing with her hair and the more she talked, the more I couldn't help but notice that, aside from being a little on the skinny side, her figure wasn't all that bad.

Chapter 17

I had several hours to kill before Stevens and Hanson would be out of surgery and ready for visitors so I went to our company orderly room and reported in. Spec. 5 Merry jumped up as soon as I came in. "Hey, Sir, how ya doin'?" he said and before I could answer he leaned into the XO's office. "Lt. Avery, Lt. Sullivan is here," he announced. "I went over to the hospital to see how you were doin' but you were already gone," he said, turning his attention back to me. "Stevens and Hanson were still in surgery. How ya doin'?" he said again, looking at my bandaged arm.

"Lt. Sullivan, glad to see you're okay," Lt. Avery said. It seemed odd being called Lt. Sullivan by another lieutenant but I supposed that was Lt. Avery's way of reminding me that he was a first lieutenant and I was still a second. We were not equals. "Come in," he said. I stepped past him into his office. He rounded his desk and sat in his chair. "Take a seat. Glad to see it's not serious, the arm. You had us worried. By the way, good job, from what I hear."

"Good job?" I said.

"Four enemy KIAs and a blood trail. I'd say that was a good day's work."

"I have two seriously wounded men who might not agree," I said. I expected him to get defensive but he didn't.

"This is war, Lieutenant. These things are to be expected." I felt my face burn. I didn't need some rear echelon chicken-shit lecturing me about war.

"I guess I expected better of myself," I said. Lt. Chicken-shit leaned back in his chair, lacing his fingers behind his head.

"You'll feel different after you've been here a while," he said, playing the time in-country card. I wanted to ask him how many bones he'd seen sticking out of flesh; how many pints of eye fluid he'd watched dripping down a man's face during the two months he was in Vietnam before I arrived. I held my tongue, but he couldn't have helped but read my expression. "Well, I'm sure you want to grab a shower and get a hot meal, so I won't hold you up. Draw a new fatigue shirt at supply. Tell Sergeant Dozier I said to write it off as a combat loss," he added, like he was pulling strings for me. "Old

Crow is getting resupplied tomorrow. Check with Aviation. I assume you'll want to be getting back to your platoon as soon as possible." The platoon would be in the field for three more days so I saw no hurry to get back.

"Unless Captain Messina has an urgent need for me, I thought I'd stick around a while and check in on Stevens and Hanson," I said, not asking permission. "I'll check in before I leave," I said and walked out without any further military courtesies.

I signed for a new shirt and kept the old one. The pants I was wearing were fine and I didn't want to be walking around with all new fatigues like I was some fuckin' new guy. My rifle and the rest of my gear had been turned in by Aviation and I left it with supply, showing Sgt. Dozier what was mine and telling him I'd pick it up when I went back to Old Crow.

The enlisted shower room was closer so I draped my new shirt over my shoulder and went in. There was one other soldier there, a hard faced teenager that I took to be a fellow boonie rat, his shower head trickling slowly. Not a good sign. I could still go to the officer's shower but I wasn't in the mood. I left my clothes on the bench and turned on a shower. A good flow started, sputtered twice, then settled down to a dribble.

"Where's the fuckin' rain when ya need it, huh?" the other guy said. Definitely a boonie rat.

"No shit," I said. There was a nasty sliver of soap on the floor, but no nastier than my skin so I picked it up.

"I heard C Company got into some shit today, you hear about that?" He was unusually chatty for a naked man and I wasn't in a talkative mood to begin with. I just wanted to take a shower and crap out for an hour or two.

"Uh huh," I said. The other guy made a slow twirl under the shower, his final rinse, then went to the bench to towel off.

"I heard one of the guys might not make it," he said. "Fucking B-40 or sumpthin'."

"He'll be okay. Lost an eye though," I said. He stopped toweling off, looked at me for the first time, noticed my bandage.

"You the lieutenant?" he finally said.

"I'm the lieutenant," I confessed. He put his towel on the floor, scuffed his feet on it and started dressing.

"Heard the officer's shower had lots of water," he said.

"Maybe for the field grades," I said and the boy laughed. I scrubbed up as best I could, then started my own body twirl. The young soldier finished dressing, then gathered up his things.

"Sorry about your guys, Sir. There are times I'd give an eye to get outta this fuckin' place," he said and I almost believed him.

"Good luck to you, soldier," I said.

"You too, Sir," he said and walked out.

* * *

Hanson was awake, staring at the ceiling. The patient ward was small--twenty beds and a desk where a nurse was busy filling out charts. Another was changing the dressings on the stump of a man's leg.

Hanson didn't recognize me at first. "Hey, Hanson," I said. He looked at me blurry-eyed, then placed the voice.

"Hey, El Tee." His voice was weak, his eyes unfocused. "Hey, could you…" He reached for a Styrofoam cup on his bedside table, his face grimacing with the movement. I put the cup under his mouth, felt the last of the ice sloshing against the sides. His mouth gaped like a fish as he found the straw and sucked. He was plastered from chest to forearm, a metal bar between the two keeping his upper arm at a fixed angle. A large rectangle had been cut out of the cast at the site of the break so they could treat the wound.

"Just ask a nurse if you need something," I said.

"They always look pretty busy," he croaked. I aimed the straw toward his mouth again and he sucked until there was nothing left. "Thanks."

"It's their job. It's what they're here for," I said. He blinked, losing his train of thought, then lowered his lids as if about to sleep. "So wha'd the doctor say? About your arm?" He swallowed hard, licked his lips. An IV was dripping clear liquid into a vein somewhere under the sheets.

"Said it would be good as new." A small smile creased his face. "I'm done, Sir. Going home." I smiled back.

"Lucky you," I said. I could tell he was trying to stay awake for my benefit. "Tired?"

"Doped up," he said. "Feeling no pain, Sir." I put my hand on his shoulder.

"Well, listen, you get some sleep," I said. "I'm just going to check on Stevens and I'll see in the morning."

"Stevens didn't make it, Sir," he said.

I remember little after that. I said something that I hoped would be comforting, spoke to the desk nurse. I only remember fragments of what she said--*four hours, multiple injuries, internal bleeding, nothing we could do.*

I remember walking toward the mess hall but ended up at the O Club instead. I was wearing my filthy boots, my grungy pants, and my new fatigue shirt with no insignia on it but no one questioned my right to be there.

I went straight to the bar and ordered a scotch and soda, then changed my mind. "You got Old Crow?" I asked.

"Jim Beam," he said; I nodded that that was okay. He poured a generous shot.

"So what's with all the fire bases named after bourbons?" I said as he took my money.

"Beats me," he said.

"Lieutenant fucking Colonel Billy Bob Redneck," the man sitting next to me said. He was already glassy-eyed and I was eager to catch up. I drank half my drink and put the glass down.

"Huh?" I said.

"Lieutenant Colonel Billy Ray Pigfucker," The lieutenant said. His fatigues were clean, but well worn. "He was the engineer who built those bases so he got to name them. At least that's what I hear. He was from Kentucky sooo…You with Second Battalion?"

"C Company," I said. It took a moment for that to register.

"Oh," he said, then motioned the bartender for two more, one for me and one for himself.

"Jack Miller, A Company. Formerly of Old Granddad," he said. We shook hands. The bartender put our drinks in front of us and Jack pushed his dollar through the damp. "Sorry to hear about--"

"Thanks," I said, not sure myself if it was for the drink or the sentiment. I drained my first glass.

"Let me guess. You thought you were going to go an entire year without getting any of your men killed?" There it was. Right out in the open. It should have hurt, but I found the words strangely comforting.

"Something like that," I said.

"How fuckin' dumb are we?" he said. He raised his hand in a toast and I clinked his glass.

"Pretty fuckin' dumb," I admitted. "You said *formerly*."

"Formerly what?"

"Formerly of Old Granddad."

"Small confession," Jack said. "I'm outta the shit now. I'm XO until my year's up. Actually, acting CO. Best fucking job an eleven B can have. XO I mean. At least it will be when a real captain shows up. No pain, no real responsibility. The hardest decision I'll have to make is whether to shave in the morning or at night."

"And which do you prefer?"

"Night. Right before I come here. When I'm neither fucked-up or hung-over. It's a small window of opportunity."

"Smart man," I said. "I would have been proud to serve under you." He raised his glass again.

"Toooo….?"

"Stevens," I said, realizing I still didn't know his first name. "Specialist Four Stevens."

"To Specialist Four Stevens, who gave his life for…something." We clinked glasses again. "I've given too many of these toasts," Jack said. "I hate this fuckin' place."

* * *

I don't know how long I'd been there or how many bourbons I'd had but after Jack left I no longer felt the need for company. I ordered a fresh drink and started for an empty table, almost tripping over a chair on the way. *Asshole*, I said about the person who left it right where someone could walk into it. I pushed it aside and made my way to a table against the far wall and staked my claim.

I sat down, noticing Marlene and Karen sitting at a table with a third nurse I didn't recognize and two other officers. Karen was chatting up some captain and when she saw me she raised her hand in recognition, smiled, and refocused her attention on the captain. Probably a finance officer or some shit. Marlene and the other nurse were talking to the other guy but nothing as intense as what was going on between Karen and Captain Courageous. She really did have a nice body.

I went to the bar, got another drink and left it at my table while I went outside to urinate. No just walking out to the wire here. They had piss tubes complete with privacy shields on three sides, probably in deference to the nurses. The piss tube I found myself in front of had a big funnel sticking out of it, probably put there by some joker. Or maybe not. I was having a hard time hitting even that. *I must be fucked up* I thought as I spattered my boots and laughed, which didn't help my aim any. I laughed even harder, thinking how proud I was that I could even hit the ground, considering how much I'd had to drink.

My drinks were undisturbed when I got back and I finished the one I'd already started. Maybe I did recognize that other nurse after all. Was she the one who had wheeled Stevens to the OR? *How the hell would I know, shit-for-brains? You weren't even there yet.* Jesus, I couldn't even pick a pronoun and stick to it. *I'll bet it was her, though. 'Smatter?* I thought, glaring at her. *Your shift end before he was out of the woods? Break time?*

Audrey came in. She took a chair from another table and sat down next to Marlene. Marlene leaned close and said something to her. Audrey looked over. *I'll be right back* I could almost hear her say. Marlene grabbed her arm but Audrey ignored the warning, came over.

"I'm sorry about James," she said.

"James?" I said.

"Your friend," she said. So that was his first name.

"He wasn't my friend," I said. "He was one of my men."

"One of your men then," she said. I made a grand gesture of offering her a chair but she didn't take it.

"I heard if you were still alive when you got off the dustoff you had a 99 percent chance of making it," I said. An image of me flirting with her while Stevens was dying on the operating table flashed before my eyes and I suddenly hated her.

"Where'd you hear that?" she said. All I could do was shrug.

"I'm sorry," she said again. "I know how you feel."

"You don't know shit," I said. She looked at me, her eyes going all puffy. "I'm sorry," she said again and then turned away and hurried toward the door. Marlene got up, started after her, then changed her mind and headed straight for me.

"She doesn't need another asshole in her life right now," she said, then turned and followed Audrey out the door. *So I'm not the only asshole?* I remember thinking, and then answered my own question: *No, just the biggest one.*

Chapter 18

It wasn't the worst hangover I'd ever had, but probably in the top three. I remembered little from the night before. Shards of memory flashed into my consciousness from time to time but I couldn't put my mind to anything beyond the needles of pain bouncing around in my brain. I wanted nothing more than to be back at Old Crow, lying on my deflated air mattress, my eyes closed to the world.

I went to Aviation HQ and asked about a lift to Old Crow and they told me a resupply chopper would be leaving around 3:00, give or take an hour. The clock on the wall looked like it was 11:25, give or take an hour. Too late for breakfast, too early for lunch. The O Club would open soon but I was not one of those hair-of-the-dog types. Alcohol was the last thing I needed. I remembered my promise to Hanson and went to the hospital, conflicted over whether or not I wanted to run into Audrey. Marlene's warning echoed in my ears.

Hanson's bed was empty. There was only one nurse on duty and she was busy passing meds. She looked vaguely familiar.

"Excuse me, I'm looking for Specialist Hanson. He was here yesterday? The arm?"

"He was evaced this morning. We get them to Japan as soon as they're stable enough to make the trip," she said.

"Oh," was all I could manage. I stood there, thinking there must be something more I should say, ask, but for the life of me I couldn't think what it was.

"You're the guy from last night," she said. The other nurse at the table, I guessed.

"I'm the guy from last night," I admitted. She waited for more. "Listen, I'm sorry. I….Just tell Audrey…I–"

"You should be the one to tell her, but she's in surgery," she said. "I wouldn't advise looking for her anyway. You don't want to run into Marlene." She wasn't smiling, but there was no meanness in her voice either.

"Thanks," I said.

"You're welcome," she said. It was more sympathy than I

deserved so I was all the more grateful for it.

I left through the receiving room where I first met Audrey, hoping she'd be there. She wasn't so I kept walking down the corridor toward the exit, but found myself standing in front of Dr. Fletcher's office instead. His door was open. Major Fletcher, Division psychologist, according to the name plaque next to the door, was sitting at his desk doing paper work. He must have felt my presence because he looked up. I didn't move.

"Can I help you?" he said.

"No. No. I was just…" Just what, passing by and thought I'd stop and have a mild seizure?

"Come in," he said. "Shut the door." I stepped in but didn't shut the door.

"No, that's okay. I can see you're busy," I said but made no move to leave.

"Crossword puzzle," he said, turning the newspaper so I could see the truth of it. He stood up and came toward me. "Have a seat and tell me about the world outside these four walls." He stepped past me, closed the door.

"Doesn't that bother the paranoids?" I said, an attempt at humor.

"Are you paranoid?" he said.

"I think people are trying to kill me." Another attempt at humor. Not original.

"They probably are. Well, that was easy," he said, taking his seat. I laughed for the first time since…forever." He smiled and I took the chair in front of his desk. "The door thing eliminates claustrophobia too so there are just a few hundred more disorders to go through and we can send you back to…"

"Old Crow," I said. Then the silence psychiatrists are known for. Be quiet long enough and the patient will say something revealing.

"I'm not crazy," I finally said.

"Ever read *Catch 22*?" I nodded. "So if you aren't crazy that would be a statement of fact, and if you are crazy you wouldn't know it, so…" I wasn't falling for it this time. I made him finish his thought. "This is my second tour and I haven't met a crazy person yet. Just a lot of people reacting to the stress of war the best way they know how. And I'm a psychologist, not a psychiatrist. I'm not qualified to decide whether you're crazy or not."

"What are you qualified to do?"

"Determine whether or not to refer you to a psychiatrist who can determine if you're crazy." I was starting to like this guy.

"If you're trying to snow me with a lot of big words, it won't work."

"Officer?"

"Lieutenant. Sullivan. Sean."

"Hiram," Major Fletcher said. "Everyone calls me Hi." He was tall and beefy with a crew cut so close it left nothing but bare skin at the peak of his skull. He looked more like a lineman, or a marine, than a psychologist, but his voice was easy on the ears and he gave off an air of trust. He did not take notes.

"What do you know about hallucinations?"

"Hallucinations?"

"Seeing things that aren't there?"

"Things like?" I hadn't thought this through at all. Now the silence worked in my favor. Gave me a chance to think what I was going to say, make it sound not so crazy after all. Maybe that's all I really wanted--assurance that I hadn't lost it completely only two months into my tour.

"I panicked my first time under fire. Froze," I said. "Just a coupla gooks shooting wildly in our direction, but you'd think I just landed on Omaha Beach the way I reacted--yellin' at my RTO to call in air support; pissin' my pants for all I know." I paused to see his reaction but he showed nothing. "Anyway, suddenly, it's like I wasn't there anymore. I was like in a different place entirely… in the middle of this Civil War battle. Like I was actually there, in person, ya know. I saw it just as plain as day. Everybody was runnin'. Everybody but this union sergeant. You know, with those big, oversized chevrons?" Major Fletcher nodded that he knew.

"Anyway, he grabs this young lieutenant. Grabs his shirt and gets right in his face, screamin'. Tells him he has to stand tall, set an example, but it's like the lieutenant doesn't even see him. All *he* sees is this screamin' hoard of rebels splashing across this creek after him. The thing is, then the sergeant turns and sees me for the first time. But it's not like he didn't know I was there. It's like he knew I was there all along. Like he was just waiting for the right moment. So he's just lookin' at me--real sad like--and says, just as calm as can be--*never let 'em see your fear*. Next thing I know I'm back to reality, like I was never even gone in the first place." I was suddenly aware that my heart was racing, reliving that moment. I looked at Major Fletcher. His turn.

"How long were you …gone, for lack of a better word?"

"Not long, I don't think. My RTO was lookin' at me funny, askin' if I was okay, but it was like it was only a few seconds. I don't know, really. Not as long as it seemed to be, I'm sure of that. When I was at Bull Run, I mean. That's where I thought the battle was. Doesn't matter."

"What happened then?"

"Well, my men were shootin' like crazy an' it didn't seem like anyone was shootin' back so I called a cease fire. Turned out there were just two of them. Gooks, I mean. One of my men was shot in the foot. That's it. Like I said, not the epic battle I first thought," I said, raising my eyebrows in a self-deprecating gesture.

"First time under fire--most men don't have the poise they think they should. I don't think what you experienced is all that unusual."

"Getting into a time machine and going back a hundred years isn't unusual?"

"Well, not that part. But that trance-like state your radioman saw? The mind is an amazing thing--all those neurons and chemicals connecting up and firing just the right circuits at just the right time. It's a wonder we don't get short-circuited more often. Even experienced soldiers have experienced it. Washington at Brandywine? The same day the Japanese bombed Pearl Harbor they also bombed our air bases in the Philippines. MacArthur was said to have been paralyzed. Couldn't give an order. Just stood there with his B-17s parked in nice, neat rows while the Japanese took them out in one straight pass after another. Who knows where their minds were when they were needed most. At least you got some good advice to act upon." I thought about what he had said, trying to relate it to other similar incidents. He seemed to read my mind.

"Was that the only time something like that happened?"

"No," I said. I told him about the most recent incident. How I had made a mistake that cost me one man dead and another wounded; that my mistake would have been even more costly had it not been for my intervention with the major during the Korean War. I didn't mention my conversations with the dead medic from Gary's platoon, the Smitty thing, or the incident with my father. I wasn't in the mood for reasonable explanations for what I thought was real, or a psychoanalysis of my fatherless childhood. Major Fletcher gave me a sympathetic look and my connection with him suddenly vanished. I hated myself for having revealed myself like that. Wished I had never stopped in front of his door in the first place.

"You've been under a lot of stress," he said, in his most rational tone. Here it comes, I thought. "Seeing one of your men die? It's natural that you might question your culpability, even healthy…" Yeah, yeah, yeah. On and on, the same old crap. Men die in war, Nobody's fault…I didn't need this shit. I looked at my watch and even though I still had plenty of time to catch my flight back to Old Crow I stood up and made my excuses. He caught up to me at the door, placed his hand on the knob as I reached for it.

"You're not crazy," he said. "Everyone has their own coping mechanisms. I had a kid in here two weeks ago who imagines what everyone in his platoon would look like dead so it won't be such a big shock if they do get killed."

"Very comforting," I said, sarcastic. He took the knob and opened the door.

"I have maybe two or three appointments a day," he said. "If the door's open and you feel like talking, about anything, don't hesitate to stop in." I nodded, my natural tendency to be polite, but couldn't bring myself to thank him.

* * *

Staff Sergeant Dozier came out from the back when he heard the screen door bang shut.

"Headin' back?" he said.

"Yeah. They said you had my gear."

"Uh huh," he said, my rucksack suddenly appearing on the counter. "What's up with you and Sergeant Nelson?"

"Nothing. Why?"

"He was over here, asking for your shit. Said you could pick it up at Battalion. I told him I already sent it back to Old Crow. Thought he might just want to fuck with you."

"Thanks," I said. He turned and started for the back room. "You been havin' trouble with your M-16 jamming'?" he called over his shoulder.

"No, why?" I said and it occurred to me that yesterday was the first time I had fired it other than on the rifle range. He came out from the back room and handed me the rifle.

"The extractor looked worn so I had it replaced." He'd done more than that. I could tell just by looking at it that he'd given it a thorough cleaning.

"Thanks," I said.

"I just turned it in at Ordinance. They did all the work." I put my rucksack on and, even though I wasn't in the mood to see Lt. Avery, I checked in at the orderly room. Specialist Merry stood when I walked in.

"Just letting' you know I'm headin' back to Old–" I didn't have time to finish my sentence. Captain Messina came out from the room he shared with Lt. Avery.

"You okay?" he said. I said I was fine and that was the end of that. Stevens was dead and there was nothing more to be said on that account. "I came back to see Hanson but he was already gone. I've got a shit-load of paperwork to get caught up on so I'll be staying here a day or two."

"Anything new with my platoon?"

"They set up an ambush outside Phu Nu last night but nothing'. You hurt them bad. You did a good job." He looked at his watch. "You in a hurry or you have time for a drink at the O-Club?" It was like I'd just been accepted to into an exclusive fraternity–Sgt. Dozier intervening on my behalf with Sgt. Nelson, Captain Messina offering to buy me a drink. I wasn't sure if it was because I'd just lost a man or because we kicked some ass or because I'd been wounded. In any case, I hardly felt like I deserved special treatment.

"Gotta catch the resupply chopper," I said as if I was disappointed.

"Gary's in charge," he said needlessly. "I should be back tomorrow or the next day."

I picked up the rest of my stuff in the transient tent and headed over to Aviation. Lt. Avery never came out to see me. I assumed he was off pretending to be doing something essential for the company while Captain Messina was there.

Chapter 19

I got back to Old Crow shortly after 4:00 and spent the rest of the day in the commo bunker listening to the radio chatter and following First Platoon's movements on the map. Apparently Sgt. Little was not the get-out-of-Dodge type, but he wasn't reckless either. They were still in the neighborhood of Phu Nu, rarely moving until just before nightfall when they set up their ambush.

"Did the same thing last night," Gary said. "Different place though." Being in charge while Captain Messina was away, Gary had taken up residence in the commo bunker. Neither ambush site was on a trail but he would have a good view of the village should any gooks try to sneak in or out during the night.

"I told him not to go looking for trouble," I said.

"He seems to know what he's doin'. He does most of the radio communication himself." I usually let Cisco do it and Gary's comment sounded like a criticism of me.

Gary went to bed when the first radio watch of the night came in; I stuck around to do the first sit-rep so they could hear my voice and know I was back. Then I laid down, my head propped against the wall and didn't hear another thing until morning.

Captain Messina returned just after noon bearing gifts--a cooler full of ice and three cases of Falstaff. Gary and I sat in the shade of our bunker guarding the cooler while his platoon's share of the beer got cold. The rest of the beer was stashed in the commo bunker.

"Oh, forgot to tell you," Gary said. "We got the votes from Wild Turkey." We had given the men two weeks to come up with a company motto and we turned in our votes just before we left on our mission.

"And the winner is…" I said.

"PFC Fisher. A very talented young man," Gary said.

"Which one was that?"

"Semper Humping." I laughed. There were eight entries, most of them following the 'semper' theme which had quickly made the rounds--Semper Filthy, Semper High, Messina's Marauders, Out to Get You. Fisher had cemented his win by including his own artwork of a Sad Sack, bent over and sweating under the weight of an oversized rucksack.

"Captain Messina was okay with that?"

"He's giving him a three day pass to Hardscrabble to cut it out of plywood, paint it and hang it above the orderly room door."

"Avery's gonna shit."

"Yeah." A Spec. 4 shuffled over to get his beer. "You have absolutely no self-control, you know that, Harper?" Gary said opening the lid of the cooler. Harper took a beer, held it in front of Gary and shook it, cold water spattering all over his face.

"Eat your heart out, El Tee," he said and then realized what he'd done. "Now see what you made me do?" he said, making a move to trade the agitated can for a new one.

"Uh uh," Gary said, closing the lid and taking Harper's beer. "No self-control and no respect." He rolled the can across his face and the back of his neck before handing it to me.

"Don't mind if I do," I said, giving myself a cold facial before tossing to can back to Specialist Harper.

"Mean, Sirs," Harper said.

"Fuck up?" I said once Harper had left.

"Just a wise ass. I'm putting him in for sergeant when Cortez leaves."

"Gotta love the army," I said.

"Uh huh," Gary said.

*   *   *

My platoon got back just after one o'clock the next day. It was raining and they looked beat. There was none of the grab-ass swagger you might expect from a platoon that had just recorded the highest body count in the battalion in more than a month. Stevens' death had taken that out of them. They came through the wire like whipped dogs--heads down, rifles hanging from their hands or resting on their shoulder like hoes on a sharecropper. I was at the gate when they came in. They greeted me wearily, asking about Hanson, occasionally about me. They had heard the radio chatter, knew one of the evacuees was KIA, figured out the rest.

The ice in the cooler had melted to a few small slivers floating among the Falstaffs. They took their cans and went to their bunkers where they could get out of the rain and wish there had been enough beer to get fucked-up on. Doc hung around the cooler until everyone else had left.

"So what happened to Stevens?" he asked.

"I don't know," I said. "He made it to surgery. He was there a long time but…he just didn't make it." Doc said nothing. "The doctor told me you did a good job. He told me that," I said because it was the right thing to do. A partial truth. The compliment was for the work Doc had done on Hanson's arm. "Hanson too. He could have bled to death."

"How's he doin'?"

"Good. They shipped him off to Japan. He'll be okay." I didn't tell him I only saw him once; that I was asleep--hung-over--when he was evacuated.

"How 'bout you?" he finally said. "Let's see it." I unbuttoned the cuff and struggled to get the sleeve above the wound. "Just a couple of stitches. Five," I said, glad that Audrey had to widen the wound before removing the shrapnel.

"They give you anything?" he said, pulling the sleeve back over the wound.

"Pills. They said you could take the stitches out."

"Five days," he predicted. "See me a couple of times before that. Don't want it to get infected. Glad you're okay, El Tee," he said, no resentment that I'd left the platoon with what, in Vietnam, amounted to a scratch.

"Thanks," I said. "How'd everything go?"

"Good," Doc said. "We hung around the village for a couple of days but didn't see nothing. I think they pretty much had enough."

"No problems?" I was fishing for his feelings about Sgt. Little.

"Nolan got a case of the ass is all," he said. "Nothin' new."

"What this time?"

"Having to hump the busted up M-60. You know." I did. I didn't know a single white guy who liked Nolan. I never knew what the black guys were thinking.

"How'd he get stuck with it?" I asked.

"Sgt. Little, I guess. He's the biggest guy in the squad so…"

"How'd it go with Sgt. Little?"

"Good. He's…he did good. Everything went well."

"Good," I said, ashamed to find myself disappointed that Doc thought a buck sergeant could run the platoon as well as me.

* * *

Sgt. Little was already there when Gary and I got to TOC.

Captain Messina had started asking both of us to attend each other's debriefings so we could learn from each other's experiences. Sgt. Little was sitting on an ammo crate. Gary and I took lawn chairs.

"Lt. Sullivan, why don't you start?" Captain Messina said. I gave him a brief rundown of the mission up to the point where we spotted the two women and their kids on the trail above us and then went into more detail.

"We were closer to the trail than we'd thought and it was obvious we'd been seen. We discussed the options--me and Sgt. Little--and I decided to keep going the way we were but to drop down the slope a couple hundred yards in case they set up an ambush." I went to the map on the wall. "When we got here, just below the village, our point man saw something suspicious and stopped. That's when they opened up. At least two AKs, some M-16s, a B-40..." I looked to Sgt. Little.

"We recovered an SKS too," he reminded me.

"Right. Thanks," I said. "I think Hanson got hit right off. The B-40 that got Stevens was the same one that hit me, took out our machinegun." My mind flashed to the scene in Korea. The icy chill of the air. The major watching his lines break before him. The race between both sides to get their artillery on target. I blinked twice, looked around. Everyone was staring at me. "We were putting down suppressing fire but they were pretty well dug in. Behind a downed tree actually. We were exposed. There was a rocky outcrop just ahead of us on their flank that afforded good cover. I ordered our other gun crew to take up a position there and they made short work of them." I returned to my chair.

"How many you think there were there all told?" Captain Messina asked. I'd replayed the whole thing over in my mind too many times to count but I could only guess.

"It all happened pretty fast," I hedged. "Eight, maybe ten."

"Eight," Sgt. Little said. He looked like he was as surprised to hear his voice as the rest of us. "I saw four running away, including the one that got hit. Could have been more," he admitted.

"Eight then," I said. The ones I saw running I saw only as a blur. The fog of war. "That's about it. We called for the dustoff and went up to the clearing to wait for it. I turned the platoon over to Sgt. Little and went out on the dustoff.

"Anything else?" Captain Messina said. This is the one thing I admired most about the army--the opportunity they gave you to admit to your mistakes in an atmosphere free from the threat of incriminations, to confess your sins without inviting censure. In the written report it would fall under the title 'Lessons Learned' and no after action report would be considered complete without it. There was always something that could have done better and you were expected to recognize that fact and learn from it. It allowed you to state your fuck-ups in the positive light of a learning experience--a teachable moment for others who could benefit from your insight. If the shit were to hit the fan, it would not be at the debriefing.

"I didn't think the mama sans would get back to the village in time for the gooks to set up an ambush. As it turned out, changing our route completely would have been the better option. Even dropping farther down the hill would have made a big difference.

"Sgt. Little, your turn," Captain Messina said.

As far as I could tell Sgt. Little had never been to a debriefing before but he took his cue from my presentation and went from there. He reported on the two days he had lingered around the village. He kept most of the platoon well back into the jungle but he also kept a two man O.P. at the tree line, keeping an eye on things. He had given the men on O.P. a green light to engage any bad guys they saw on the condition that they were certain they were armed and that they would get at least one KIA. He did not want to give away his position for nothing. After two days of nothing they started back, avoiding the trails and looking for the mortar position that had been harassing us. He pointed out the location of their last NDP before they returned to Old Crow the next day. It was close enough that they probably could have gotten back that night if they had pushed, but their mission called for them to be out one more day. I kept my smile to myself. Tired and emotionally drained, he had taken his time so as to get back at a respectable time. They had been ghosting. Not a problem for me. I had done it myself. Good for morale if not overdone.

"We could have been more aggressive in our patrolling," Sgt. Little admitted, "but we were down five men and a machine gun. If we made contact I wanted to be sure it was on our terms." I didn't know if Sgt. Little knew he was supposed to go into things he should--or could--have done differently, or if it was his own honesty that made him admit to his caution. It didn't matter. I was unexpectedly proud of him. I had left the platoon in better hands than I thought. I could see why Captain Messina had nudged me in that direction and I wished I had seen it myself.

"Very good," Captain Messina said. "Lt. Sullivan?" I shook my head. I had no questions. "Lt. Holder?" Gary shook his head too.

"Recommendations for medals? Above and beyond?" He looked at me, then Sgt. Little. I waited to see if Sgt. Little had anything to say while images of that day flashed through my mind-- Sgt. Little running past me to the front after the first shots were fired. Stevens and Caulkins exposing themselves to put down suppressing fire before the B-40 knocked them out. Doc laying down next to Stevens, unable to give him the care he needed without getting his head blown off, Rivera and Romansky running across open ground to set up their machine gun, Rivera falling, scrambling the last few feet to the rocky outcrop on hands and knees."

"Everyone just doing their jobs," I said.

"Then unless there are any objections I'll put Stevens and Hanson in for the bronze star in addition to their purple hearts. You'll get that too, of course," he said to me, meaning the purple heart. The bronze star was for an act or bravery, but it was also given to combat soldiers who simply did their jobs well over an extended period of time. Stevens and Hanson had certainly met that criteria.

"Okay, then," Captain Messina said. "Sgt. Little, I want you to write up the after action report. You were there for the whole mission." Was that a slam on me? Sergeants rarely wrote after action reports if an officer had been on the mission, and I was there for the actual combat. Sgt. Little looked stunned.

"I don't--"

"It's not a big deal. Lt. Sullivan can help you with it. Can you type?"

"No, Sir."

"Long hand will do. Merry can type it up later. Any questions?" There were none. "Thank you, gentlemen." Gary and Sgt. Little headed for the door. Captain Messina touched my arm, held me back.

"Don't help him too much," he said. "Just steer him in the right direction. I want to see how he does." I got the message.

I caught up to Sgt. Little before he got to his bunker. "Good job.

Captain Messina was impressed," I said. He smiled, said nothing. "Stop over after lunch and we'll get that after action report taken care of. It's not that big a deal," I assured him.

* * *

I was still eating--beans and franks, with some help from Gary's Tabasco sauce—when Sgt. Little showed up. "Oh, Sorry, Sir. I can come back later," he said.

"No. No," I said, waving him in.

"I can see you two want some alone time," Gary said, heading for the door. "Take the sock off the door when you're done." Sgt. Little didn't get the reference. College joke. I stacked three ammo crates to make a desk and positioned them in front of Gary's bunk. Sgt. Little sat down; I gave him a pad on which I had written *After Action Report* at the top along with the date. Under that I had written *Mission:* and three lines below that *Mission Brief:*

"Where it says 'Mission', write what our mission was: go to Phu Nu and look for gooks, but don't say gooks. Engage them as appropriate…Keep it simple. One or two sentences. Use your own words." Was that patronizing, k*eep it simple*? That's what I would have said to anyone, isn't it? I kept my mouth shut, watched him struggle for the right words, cross something out and try again. I finished my beans before he was done.

"Is this okay?" he said. "Our mission was to go to the village of Phu Nu and look for VC or NVA. If we found them we were supposed to engage in combat, but if there were too many of them we were supposed to just call it in. On the way we were supposed to look for them too and find where their mortar site was."

"Perfect," I said. It wasn't, but good enough. I told him how to write a summary of the mission and when he was done with that I explained what was meant by *lessons learned.* He seemed stumped.

"What's the biggest mistake we made?" I hinted. He thought a long time.

"Walking into the ambush," he finally said.

"And how could we have avoided that?"

"Like you said at the debriefing, drop down farther?"

"Uh huh. Or?"

"Change direction completely? Get to the back of the village another way?" He knew what to do. He told me himself right after we'd been spotted by the mama sans. It was the thought of putting the words on paper that troubled him.

"And when should we have done that?"

"After we was spotted."

"Then that's what you write." Again he took pen to paper. It took a long time, with long pauses to think and an even longer time to get it down on the paper. When he was done he handed the two page document to me. I was immediately stunned by his penmanship. It looked as if it had been written by a girl. He wrote with a large, fluid hand. His loops were graceful, the 'I's dotted with small circles. Each letter was perfectly formed, the words uncrowded and easy to read. The context itself was less fluid. He often struggled for the right word and his syntax was not very smooth. Despite all that the report was complete, concise, and unambiguous. Spelling and grammatical errors would be corrected by Specialist Merry when he typed it up.

"Good," I said and handed it back to him. "Just sign and date it and you're done." His signature was even more elaborate than the rest of his writing. A John Hancock by the name of Clarence O. Little. Until that moment I had never even thought of him as having a first name other than Sergeant. I wondered what the O stood for but didn't ask. I couldn't think of any 'O' names any better than 'Clarence' and didn't want to embarrass him. He handed me the report.

"You wrote it. You turn it in," I said and he started to leave. "You'll be acting platoon sergeant until we get a replacement for Sgt. Nelson," I said, stopping him at the door. "I'd like to relieve you of your duties as squad leader during that time. Who's got the most time in grade as a Spec. 4 in your squad?" He looked at me for a long moment before replying.

"Nolan," he finally said.

Chapter 20

Before Gary's platoon left on their next mission our mortar crew give a training session on the use of the 81mm mortar, something not covered in light weapons infantry training. Sgt. LoPresti proved to be a natural teacher. He tailored his talk to the needs of the grunts, spending little time on the use of aiming stakes and how to operate the elevation and traversing knobs. Instead, he concentrated on things they might be asked to assist with should someone on the mortar crew be killed or wounded. He broke the men into groups and had his crew demonstrate how to set the propellant charges on the rounds and then had the men with the most time left in country set charges for different ranges.

He then demonstrated how to drop the round into the tube without getting their hands blown off and let them drop the rounds they had prepared into the tube. Every explosion on Mortar Mountain was accompanied by a raucous cheer, as if hitting the mountain was a sign of their proficiency.

When the session was over, Cisco asked everyone for a moment of their time. The men moaned, eager to get out of the sun, but Cisco was always good for a laugh and everyone stayed.

"Thank you," he said, taking his place at the front of the gathering. "Last night I was going through some of the orientation materials we were all given when we first got here and I thought now might be a good time to review--" Boos and catcalls and thrown pebbles only caused Cisco to speak louder. "To review some of the excellent advice MAC-V gave us but which many seem to have forgotten. I'm talking about the *nine rules*," he said, holding up the small card they had been issued at jungle school. "Can anyone tell me even *one* of the nine rules of good behavior that should be followed so as not to upset the people whose country we have invaded? Yes, PFC Murphy," Cisco said when he saw a hand.

"When you kill someone, don't cut off their ears." Cisco waited for the laughter to die down and looked at his card.

"Very good," he said. "While earectomies are not mentioned specifically, I think that would fall under rule number two: understanding the life of the Vietnamese and honoring their customs. The Vietnamese believe that they can't go to heaven if their body isn't whole and, as Americans, I'm sure we wouldn't want anyone to spend an eternity in hell just because they believe in such nonsense. After all, what are we fighting for if not for the right of people to worship as they please?" This pronouncement was met with great applause. "Anyone else?" When no one spoke up he read from his card. "Rule number one: remember we are guests here. We make no demands and seek no special treatment. What does this mean in practical terms?" he asked rhetorically. "Simple common courtesy," he said. "Wipe your feet before entering a hootch to toss it for weapons and contraband. Don't track outside dirt onto their inside dirt. How would *you* like it if someone tracked dirt into *your* bunker? Do onto others.

"Number three: treat women with politeness and respect."

"Even the whores?"

"Especially the whores," Cisco said. "Whores are our friends. It is the most intimate contact we have with our Vietnamese hosts and we should not squander the opportunity to make the most of it. Please and thank you go a long way to winning their hearts and minds. Who knows how to say *please* in Vietnamese?"

"Prease?" More laughter.

"That's Japanese," Cisco said. "*Xin*. Let's all try it--Xin may I fuck you?" Everyone repeated the phrase. "And thank you--*Cam on*. Cam on for letting me fuck you. Again." Again everyone repeated the phrase. "And don't forget to pay them. Very important.

"Don't attract attention by loud, rude or unusual behavior," he continued, skipping down to rule seven. He gave the mortar crew that had just dropped a dozen high explosive rounds on the quiet countryside a nasty glare. "I'm not saying that blowing communists to smithereens doesn't have its place, but is all that noise really necessary?

"Number eight: Avoid separating yourself from the people by a display of wealth or privilege. I mean, how does it look, us flying around in helicopters while the gooks have to walk everywhere? Can you think of anything more pompous? Yes, we're the richest nation on earth, but it's just bad manners to throw our wealth in the faces of the people we're trying to conquer. Captain Messina?"

"I agree. No more CAs," he promised. "We walk to our objectives. Choppers for dustoffs only."

"And beer runs," someone added.

"And beer runs," Captain Messina agreed.

"And finally," Cisco concluded, paraphrasing from the card. "Remember, you are members of the United States *Fuckin'* Army. At all times conduct yourself in a manner that reflects honor upon yourself, your unit, and the United States of America!" Thunderous applause and cheering.

"You have anything to do with that?" Captain Messina asked as the group started to break up.

"No Sir. That was all Cisco."

"Well, there's precious little entertainment around here," he said. "Sgt. LoPresti did a good job too. We should have started something like this long ago. What's next?"

"M-60," I said. "Most of these guys haven't fired one or broken one down since AIT. Thought it might be a good idea for when one of the gunners DEROSes. Or gets hit." Captain Messina nodded. "And I was thinking about getting a real RTO to talk about radios. Any idea where I might get one?"

"Sims," he said. "But better get him quick. He's getting short."

"Where would I find him?"

"Wild Turkey. He's in Second Platoon." I remembered him. Skinny black kid always sitting in front of the radio bank. I'd always thought of him as just another grunt putting in his time on radio watch. I walked Captain Messina back to the TOC bunker, thinking it was as good a time as any to approach him with another problem.

"Got a minute?" I said before he ducked inside.

"Yuh," he said and I ducked in after him. "Miller, take a break. You missed a good training session." Miller got up from his chair.

"I heard all the laughing. Never thought of mortars as all that funny," he said.

"That was Cisco."

"Oh," was all he said, then called over his shoulder: "Lt. Avery wants to talk to you."

"I'll call him," Captain Messina said, and then to me, "What's up?'

"Kinda on the same subject as morale, Sir," I said to make it seem as if it was within my sphere of responsibility. "But it also goes to the smooth change of command."

"What?" he said.

"Well, I've been giving Sgt. Little more responsibility, like you said, and I'd like to relieve him of some of his duties as squad leader."

"Uh huh."

"Well, there's no clear chain of command below the rank of Sergeant. I mean there are four spec. 4s in Sgt. Little's squad alone and—"

"The spec. 4 with the most time in grade is next in line. Everyone knows where they stand."

"Yes, Sir. But the person with the most time in grade may not be the best person to take over, and until someone gets promoted to sergeant…" I was afraid Captain Messina was going to ask which spec. 4 in Sgt. Little's squad had the most time in grade but I suspected he already knew.

"There are ways of working around that--transferring spec. 4s around between squads. That works to our advantage anyway, so the new squad leader doesn't find himself ordering around friends."

"Yes, Sir. But that takes time. I was thinking more of a situation where a squad leader is killed or wounded and someone has to take over right away." As I said before, I was always fast on my feet when it came to talking my way out of, or in this case, into something.

"So what's your idea?"

"Promote one Spec. 4 in each squad to corporal. It's the same pay grade so it won't cost the army anything and it would allow us to have the right person as second in command at the squad level." I was talking too fast, a dead giveaway that I was not confident of my position. I forced myself to slow down. "Plus it would be good for morale. The hard stripes, I mean."

"For the people who get them maybe," Captain Messina said. I had no response for that. "When's the last time you saw a corporal?"

"Basic training," I admitted.

"The army is trying to get rid of them for some reason, but I agree with you. I never liked those specialist ranks anyway." He seemed to be on my side so I kept my mouth shut, let him think it over. He was in no hurry. "Okay, write up a justification for battalion. Put it under my name. Ask for ten, one for each squad. Use all the arguments you used with me and any more you can think of, but no grasping at straws. One weak argument makes your whole case weaker. Three days," he said.

"Thank you, Sir," I said and started to get up.

"While you're here," he said. "How much do you know about Sgt. Little?" I wasn't sure what he was getting at.

"He's a good soldier," I said. "A good leader. The men respond to him. Quiet. Not the usual sergeant." I remembered a time when we were setting up an NDP for the night. I didn't like our position and decided to put out an LP in Sgt. Little's sector. He was eating supper in the gloom of dusk when I gave him the order. He responded with his usual *Yes, Sir.* Nolan echoed Sgt. Little's reply, only it came out *Y'Suh*, like he was an Uncle Tom carrying out the white man's orders. Sgt. Little showed no reaction but as I walked away I heard him say "Hanson and Nolan, you got LP tonight." Hanson bitched and the rest of the squad laughed quietly, but I heard nothing from Nolan. I turned my head just in time to see Nolan give Sgt. Little a nasty glare while Sgt. Little calmly drizzled the juice from his canned peaches over the top of his pound cake.

"He's DEROSing in a couple of months," Captain Messina continued, meaning Sgt. Little. "And his enlistment will be up shortly after that. Did you know he was drafted?"

"I guess I never really thought about it," I admitted.

"He'd done well and re-enlisted when his time was up with the promise of making sergeant." I waited for the rest. "It's part of our job to keep good soldiers in," he said. "Has he mentioned anything to you along those lines?"

"No, Sir," I said. I didn't mention that Sgt. Little and I rarely talked about personal matters.

"Well, he's been an E-5 for two and a half years. I'm thinking of putting him in for staff sergeant. Make his re-enlistment bonus a little more enticing should he be thinking about staying in. How much help did you give him on that after action report?"

"Hardly any. A little guidance. The writing is all his."

"Good."

"He's doing a staff sergeant's job anyway. All the squad leaders are," I said.

"I know," Captain Messina said. "The army spends a fortune on weapons and supplies but they like to get their grunts on the cheap. So you see no reason not to give him a rocker?"

"No sir. He deserves it," I said.

"Okay. Thanks. Nothing about this, okay? The corporal thing either. I hear any rumors, I'll know where they came from."

* * *

The resupply chopper came in fighting off a light drizzle and gusty winds. I was there with the usual crew to help unload and then jumped on, along with Specialist Ferris. Ferris was going back to Hardscrabble for a week of ghosting before his time was up and he went home--a small perk Captain Messina granted his grunts when they got short. Getting killed was one thing. Getting killed with only a few days left on your tour was another.

My reason for going back was less cheery. Apparently Captain Messina was happy with the training sessions I had set up but thought I needed a little training myself. At our last meeting he was not impressed with my knowledge of the men in my command and ordered me to spend a day at PRB going over the platoon's personnel files. Knowing the background of the men I commanded, he said, would make me a better leader.

We dropped off more supplies at Wild Turkey, Jim Beam, and Rebel Yell and then landed in blue skies back at Hardscrabble. I shook hands with Ferris and thanked him for his service. The truth was I barely knew him. He was one of those soldiers without whom the army could not do without--the vast majority that fly under the radar, quietly doing their jobs without drawing attention to themselves or their deeds. Captain Messina was right. I didn't know enough about these men. I didn't even know Ferris's first name or where he was from. I hadn't even known he was short. I located PRB, introduced myself to the clerk who handled our company's records and told him what I was there for.

"No problem, Sir. Just that the 201 files are arranged by company in alphabetical order. They're not broken down by platoon. Give me a list, or you can pull them yourself?" He pulled out a file drawer labeled *C & D/2/605*. "All the way back to here, Sir," he said pulling up a cardboard divider half way back. He went back to his typing while I leafed through the files, pulling those with familiar names and making a stack on the floor. I also was curious about Gary, Lt. Avery, and Captain Messina but their files weren't there.

"I'm missing the files on Lieutenants Holder and Avery and Captain Messina," I said. The Spec. 5 stopped typing.

"Officer's files are kept separate. You'll need permission from your CO."

"Not important. Any place I can look at these?"

"Ponzini's on R&R. You can use his desk," he said, indicating the desk next to his. I thanked him and dropped the files on the empty desk. "It would help if you kept them in alphabetical order for when I put them back. Sir," he added.

"Any problem if I go to lunch first?" I asked. I was hoping to see Audrey. I had no idea what I was going to say, other than sorry, but since getting back to Old Crow I had not been able to get her out of my mind--the way her hair was plastered to her forehead while she cleaned my wound; the confidence of her voice; the curve of her fatigue blouse. Most of all though, I couldn't shake the look in her eyes when I told her she didn't know shit when she tried to empathize with me at the officer's club. She popped into my mind at the most unexpected times, and the most expected times, like just after crawling into my bunk before falling asleep.

"Uh uh," he said. "Just put them on my desk if I'm not here when you finish."

"I can put them back," I said, trying to be the helpful officer.

"No. I've got them in order. I don't want them fucked up, Sir. No offense."

I timed it so I got to the mess hall about twenty minutes after it opened--not enough time for Audrey to eat and leave before I got there, and late enough that I could stick around until the mess hall closed without drawing too much attention to myself.

It seemed that cheeseburgers and fries were always on the lunch menu, plus something else, different every day. Today's something else was some kind of chicken-in-gravy served over toast so I had that. The milk was real so I took two glasses and a Styrofoam bowl of wilting salad. I took a seat in the officers section facing the door and tried to act like I was there for no other reason than the food.

An hour went by and Audrey still hadn't showed. I finished eating, then went back for a cheeseburger, fries, and a glass of brown Kool-Aid--probably a mix of flavors--but it was cold and tasted good.

Karen had been in earlier with the captain I had seen her with at the O club, and another captain that also looked familiar--one of the doctors, I think. But she was not looking around and I didn't want her to see me anyway. The mess hall was almost empty except for a few late comers and three Vietnamese women who were working their way through the tables, cleaning up for the next meal.

"You fina?" The mama san was wiping down my table, clearly wanting me to leave so she could finish cleaning up. Her hair was still black and silky but already her teeth were rotten, stained purple from chewing betel nut. She could have been 35; she could have been 55.

"Yeah, I'm finished," I said. I picked up my tray and took it to the drop-off window. The glare of the sun was blinding after being indoors and I almost ran into Audrey as I put on my hat. She stopped, Marlene taking two steps past me in a failed attempt to keep Audrey moving.

"What are you doing here?" Audrey's voice was flat, her face still in surprise mode. Not a happy surprise either. It took me a moment to gather myself.

"Catching up on some admin stuff. I'm glad I ran into you," I said. Marlene came back, a step past me, as if she was trying to block me out.

"You comin', Aud?"

"Yeah," she said. She took a step forward; I put my arm out to stop her and immediately pulled it back. Marlene turned on me, the protective mother. Audrey stopped.

"I'll be right there," she said. Marlene held her stare just long enough to make me uncomfortable, then turned and went to the door.

"Look, I'm sorry about…the other day," I said. "I was--"

"Forget it," she said. She looked me straight in the eye and then looked to Marlene, holding the door for her. My hand went out again, touching her sleeve ever so briefly.

"No, really. I was…" What? Drunk? Hurting? An asshole? All of the above? "Having a bad day," I said.

"Don't worry about it," she said. "There's a lot of that going around." She held my look for a fraction of a second and before I knew it she was gone. I watched her disappear into the mess hall, her hair, too short for a ponytail, exploding from the rubber band pulled tight to the back of her head. My heart was pounding so hard I could hear it beating in my ears.

Chapter 21

"Whaddaya think?" Sgt. Little looked past the rice paddies, more yellow than green as the monsoon's came to an end and the harvest began.

"A lot more men than las' time I was here," he said. The rest of the platoon was bunched up behind us. Sloppy. I got a queasy feeling in my gut. I turned to Cisco.

"Tell the men to spread out and stay alert. We're not on break." Cisco squirmed out of his rucksack and disappeared into the brush. The men in the paddies and the village were dressed in black pajamas, straw hats, and sandals--the usual wear for farmers. Take away the straw hats and the sickles and they looked no different than the Viet Cong. A few women and older children were there as well, carrying the sheaves back to the village where they would be dried for threshing. "VC?" I said. Sgt. Little shrugged.

"Maybe," he said. "They can be pretty cozy." Sgt. Little had been to Phu Gap only once and the only time I had seen it was when the chopper that took me to Old Crow for the first time dropped off supplies at the ARVN compound across the river.

The compound was barely visible through the trees lining the Mu Dai River. Manned by a single squad of ARVNs, their main job was to protect the village and guard the bridge over the river. They were also supposed to patrol the area and engage or report any VC activity but that rarely happened.

Captain Messina had long suspected that the ARVNs and VC had an unwritten understanding not to mess in each other's affairs. Both sides needed the bridge and neither side wanted a fight. Captain Messina rarely sent his men into the area lest the ARNVs take it as a slight and when he did it was without the ARVNs knowledge. It was also with the understanding that we keep a low profile. Basically, we were on a recon mission.

I could see movement in the compound but most activity was in the paddies on our side of the river where the men, women, and children of Phu Gap toiled in the hot sun. Only the village's two water buffalo, their jobs done, had nothing to do. They lazed in their wallows, swishing flies with their tails.

"Whaddya make of that?" I said, pointing toward two mama sans scurrying across the paddy dikes toward the bridge. They were carrying two baskets each on carrying poles that rested across their necks and shoulders. We watched as they crossed the bridge and disappeared into the ARVN compound.

"Probably just selling bread. Or rice," Sgt. Little said. Cisco came back through the brush, excited and out of breath.

"They just took two prisoners," he gasped.

"What? Who?" I had given specific orders not to engage unless we'd been spotted.

"Murphy and Boyd, I think. I just know they got two gooks and came right back."

"Shit," I said. "Who else is on the net?" I asked.

"Everybody," Cisco said.

"Stay here," I said. "And don't call it in. Goddamn it." I snatched up my rifle and hurried toward the rear. Our line was a mess. Everyone wanted to see the prisoners and I had to get them back in place before I could find out what had happened. It was PFCs Boyd and Murphy who had taken two young males prisoner. They were dressed in black pajamas--no straw hats--and were wearing the traditional Ho Chi Minh sandals made from old tires.

"Hey, Sir--" Boyd started but I cut him off.

"What the hell did I say? We're on a recon mission. That means--"

"We saw them coming down this trail, over there," a scared Murphy said. "And we were pretty sure they'd seen us--"

"Pretty sure?!"

"They saw us, Sir. For sure," Boyd said and I started to cool off. Both were gung ho, but Boyd in particular had impressed me as being pretty level headed. He rarely fired his M-14, still waiting for a real target that had yet to present itself. He showed no remorse for his actions and his confidence in himself persuaded me that he had done the right thing. "We took these off them," he said, handing me a small handful of papers.

"And check this out, Sir," Murphy said, pointing to a puckered patch of purple skin on the older man's calf. "That look like shrapnel to you? Or a gunshot wound?" I didn't know what old wounds looked like but if I had to guess I'd guess they looked like the purple patch of wrinkles on the older man's calf.

"Could be anything?" I said. I looked at the papers but they meant nothing to me. Two appeared to be ID cards. "Which goes to who?" I asked. Boyd flushed and admitted that he forgot to keep them separate. I compared the pictures on the cards to the faces of the men. The younger one looked like his picture and there was a date in one of the boxes that I assumed was his date of birth, indicating he was seventeen years old.

"Sgt. Allen says they're civilian IDs," Boyd said. "If they're registered with the government they're supposed to have one." I looked at the boy, pointed to the photograph and then to him.

"You? Nguyen Dinh Ba? You?" The boy nodded his head.

"No VC. No VC," he said. He jabbered something else while making hoeing motions with his hands.

"Check out the other one," Murphy said. I handed the boy his ID card and gave the other papers, except for the ID card, to Boyd.

"Get Sgt. Allen over here," I said and Murphy, still eager to appease me, hurried off. The age of the other prisoner was hard to determine but he was definitely much older than the sixteen that showed on his card. If I had to guess I'd say he was somewhere between twenty and thirty. "You?" I said, going through the same pantomime I did with the boy. He nodded his head happily.

"No VC," he said and imitated the boy's hoeing motion. "Bullshit," I said. The man just smiled nodding his head as if agreeing. Murphy returned with Sgt. Allen.

"What do you think, Sergeant?" I asked after filling him in. Sgt. Allen looked at their hands. Both had hands that were rough from labor but the older man's lacked the pronounced calluses that bulged just below the fingers of the boy's palms.

"This one might be okay," he said, pointing to the younger prisoner. "But this guy's got Victor Charles written all over him." I took the papers I had given Boyd and handed them to Sgt. Allen.

"You make anything out of any of this?" Sgt. Allen shook his head.

"No maps, but that don't mean nothing," he said. He took the one picture from the lot, an amateurish photo of a pretty girl dressed in a flowing white gown. She appeared to be in her early to mid-twenties. He showed the picture to the two prisoners. "Who?" he asked, swinging his finger so it pointed first at one, then the other. The older man looked nervous but made no move to answer. The boy pointed to him and then quickly looked down. Sgt. Allen squared off with the older man. "You mama san?" The man looked confused. Or scared. It was hard to tell.

"No biet," he said.

"Bullshit. He's lying, Sir. It's either his wife or his girlfriend. He ain't no sixteen, I'll tell you that."

"Blindfold him," I said. Boyd took off his sweat band and tied it around the man's eyes. "Come 'ere," I said. I grabbed the younger boy by the shirt and pushed him ahead of me until we were out of ear shot of his companion. Sgt. Allen followed.

"VC? Him?" I said, pointing to the other prisoner. The older man was squatting on his haunches, PFC Boyd looming large behind him, his M-14 pointed at his back. The boy looked frightened, not sure what to say.

"No," he finally said, shaking his head unconvincingly.

"No VC?" I said. I made my voice as threatening as I could, realizing as I heard it that I was not pretending. Sgt. Allen moved around behind him and pulled back the bolt carrier on his M-16 and let it slam forward with an alarming clash. The boy flinched and closed his eyes as if that would ward off the bullet he was sure was coming next. Sgt. Allen noticed my surprise.

"Just puttin' the fear of God in him. Ask him again," he said poking the muzzle of his rifle into the back of the boy's head. I did, but his denial was even more emphatic than before. Sgt. Allen picked up the round that had been ejected during his show of force and put it in his pocket.

"Probably more afraid of the VC than he is of us," he said. "Your call, El Tee."

"Keep 'em separate till I get back. I gotta check with higher." Sgt. Allen pushed the boy to the ground and then dropped his canteen into the boy's lap.

"Don't drink it all," he ordered, then looked at me. "Your mouth gets dry when you're lying' your ass off," he said. He sat down behind the prisoner and poked him in the back with the muzzle of his rifle just to let him know he was still there.

"Anything?" I said when I got to the tree line.

"No sir. Same same," Sgt. Little said and pointed his chin at the two mama sans returning to the village after visiting the ARVN camp. Their step was light as they scurried across the paddy dikes, their baskets swinging freely. “They didn’t stay long. What’s up back there?”

“One of ’em has a phony ID. The other’s just a kid.” Sgt. Little gave me a look that said I was still naïve. “He has a legit ID,” I said in my defense. “What do you think? I think we should ruin their day,” I said, looking toward the village.

“They’re gonna know we were here anyway,” Sgt. Little said. I held my hand out and Cisco gave me the handset.

“Somebody’s gonna get in trou-ble,” he sang. I pushed the transmit bar.

“X-ray Kilo, X-ray Kilo, this is X-ray One, over.” The reply was almost instantaneous.

“X-ray One, this is X-ray Kilo, go.” It was a voice I didn’t recognize.

“Is X-ray Actual there? Over.”

“Wait one.” A few seconds later Captain Messina came on.

“This is X-ray Actual, over.”

“This is X-ray One Actual. We’ve just taken two prisoners at our last location. One’s ID does not match. Lots of young men in the village. Requesting permission to check them out, over.”

“That’s not what you’re there for, over.” Cisco was giving me the ‘shame’ sign with his index fingers. I ignored him.

“We were spotted and had to take the two prisoner. They’re gonna know we were here sooner or later, over.” There was an uncomfortable silence while Captain Messina thought it over.

“X-ray One, X-ray Kilo. Roger, but step lightly. Technically that’s the ARVN’s A.O. Separate the good guys from the bad guys and I’ll check with higher, over.”

“X-ray One, out.”

We moved out from the tree line avoiding the dikes and slogging through the paddies. Within seconds everyone knew we were there. The children pointed at us and stared. Adults slapped their children’s hands and were conspicuous in their attempts to act like they didn’t see us. One of the men in a paddy near the river was drifting toward the tree line and I realized I’d made a mistake. I ordered Sgt. Burkholtz’s squad to double time over there and herd the people toward the village. The man near the river pretended not to see us, swinging his sickle in a wide arc and letting the stalks fall in the water as he worked his way toward the tree line.

Sgt. Burkholtz broke into a run, ordered him to stop. “Dung lai! Dung Lai!” The man dropped his sickle and broke for the trees. Murphy got off a short burst before the man disappeared into the jungle.

“No shooting! Hold your fire! Let him go!” I yelled. Sgt Burkholtz gave me a *what the fuck* look but quickly got his men under control, splashing through the paddies to cut off anyone else who might try to escape. The rest of the men spread out, yelling orders in English and crude Vietnamese as they shepherded the peasants toward the village. On the other side of the river, the ARVNs looked on from behind their barbed wire enclosure but made no move to leave their compound.

“Sgt. Little,” I yelled. “Set up a collection point in the village. Have the rest of your men pair up and clear the hootches. Everyone meet back at the collection point!” I had Sgt. Allen and PFCs Boyd and Murphy take their prisoners to Sgt. Little and wait for further instructions. I stood apart, watching the men doing their jobs, finally feeling that I was in control of things. I joined Sgt. Little by the village well where a contingent of villagers was already squatting on their haunches, waiting for what was to come next.

I tried to remember everything I’d learned about handling prisoners at OCS. The rest I made up as I went along. “Sgt. Little, I want the locals separated into two groups. Murphy. Take your buddy,” I said grabbing the younger of the prisoners we had captured earlier by his shirt and pulling him to his feet. “Take him over there and sit him down.” I turned to Sgt. Little. “Send the women and children and men with legitimate IDs to Murphy. Boyd!” I turned around and there he was, his blindfolded prisoner at his side. “You guard anyone who’s questionable over there,” I said pointing to a place on the other side of the well. “He doesn’t need this anymore,” I added, taking the sweat band from his prisoner’s eyes and giving it back to Boyd. “Keep ‘em quiet. Sgt. Allen, you help Sgt. Little separate the good guys from the bad.”

By then the rest of the stragglers had come in from the fields. I sent the Vietnamese to Sgt. Little and corralled the rest of my men not already searching the hootches. “The rest of you I want to cordon off the village,” I said. Someone muttered *a little late for that, isn’t it?* “Do it anyway,” I ordered. “No one out, no one in.”

I dropped my rucksack and headed to the west side of village.

Sgt. Little's squad had already cleared most of the hootches but I noticed Caulkins standing outside one hootch, his machinegun laying at his feet, an old mama san squatting in front of him. He saw me coming and quickly picked up his gun. He looked nervous. The old woman came to her feet and started jabbering at me. I held up my hand in an attempt to quiet her down.

"Sir," Specialist Caulkins said. His eyes fixed on me, went quickly to the ground and then back to me.

"Why isn't she at the collection point?"

"Still clearing the hootch, Sir," he said, his eyes darting to the hut that couldn't have contained more than two rooms. The woman was nonstop jabber, pointing to the hootch while drops of spittle spattered my fatigues. I put my finger to my lips and then pushed her to a squat.

"Who's in there?" I demanded. Caulkins swallowed. Hard.

"Nolan. Sir." I did not bother to ask how long he'd been inside. My anger was apparent.

"Take her to the collection point. Wait for me there." He pulled the woman to her feet but she resisted going, still trying to get through to me. "Di di," I said in a tone that was harsher than I intended. "Xin," I added in a gesture that I thought more polite.

The inside of the hootch was still cool from the night before and I stood just inside the doorway as my eyes adjusted to the gloom. Sleeping mats were still scattered along the walls and a rucksack leaned against a flimsy partition of bamboo that partially separated the main room from the back. I heard a voice speaking softly on the other side. There was no door, not even a curtain covering the opening between the two rooms.

At first all I could see was Nolan's broad back against the far wall, then became aware of the top of a girl's head just above his shoulder. In the corner, only a step away, leaned Nolan's rifle, his bush hat hanging from the muzzle as if it was a hat rack.

"What the hell are you doing?" The sound of my voice startled me almost as much as it did Nolan. I saw movement as his arms came down to his side and he turned toward me. I saw the girl's frightened face, not sure if this new intruder was a good thing, or if it was only going to make her horror worse. The top two buttons of her blouse were undone, not enough to show any of her still developing breasts.

"Checkin' for ID, Sir. Like you said." It was the first time he'd ever addressed me as *Sir* and I saw a flicker of fear in his eyes as he stared back.

"I said to clear the hootches. Checkin' IDs ain't your job." He said nothing. The girl tried to button up with shaking hands but made no move to get away, still uncertain of my intentions. She finally decided I was no threat, perhaps even a friend. She looked right at me, said something I didn't understand. "What do you think she's sayin', Nolan?"

"She's sayin' she ain't VC," he said.

"I ain't that new," I said. Again the stare but this time the fear had been replaced by hostility. "Get out. Wait for me outside." He turned to the corner and reached for his weapon. "Leave it." I said. He stopped, then continued reaching. I brought my rifle to a more ready position. "I said *leave it*!"

"Gettin' my hat," he said, taking it from the muzzle of his M-16. He took his time positioning it on his head. Everything he did or didn't do, everything he said or didn't say, was a challenge to my authority. He sauntered past me, barely missing my shoulder. It took every ounce of restraint I had to keep from butt stroking him in the side of the head. The girl just stood there. I took a step in her direction and her hands shot up to the top of her blouse. I stopped, held up my hand, said something softly, like I was talking to a cowering dog. I reached past her and retrieved Nolan's rifle. "Xin loi," I said and backed away, leaving her standing there.

Nolan was waiting outside, his rucksack on, looking defiant. "My rifle?" he said, holding his hand out. My mind was racing, trying to remember how you placed someone under arrest, how I would have to put a guard on him during our two day march back to Old Crow, what would I do if we were ambushed on the way back.

"You think I don't know what was going on in there?" I said.

"You didn't see nothin'," he said. "Wasn't nothing *to* see." He was right about the first part anyway, and before I could stop myself my eyes went briefly to the ground. I glared at him but he never blinked.

"Don't ever do anything like that again," I said and threw his rifle to him. He caught it without even breaking his stare. He held it a moment longer and, as he turned to go back to the collection point, I thought I caught a self-satisfied smirk on his fat lips.

Cisco came out to meet me. "There's a sergeant from the ARVN compound wants to talk to you," he said. "And Captain Messina called. Twice."

The men looked sloppy, hanging around the well, filling their canteens and bullshitting or lazily watching over their prisoners. I let it slide thinking, as they probably did, that no bad guys were going to be firing into a village filled with their own. The ARVN sergeant saw me coming and his face lit up like a Christmas tree.

"Ah, Trung-uy! Numba one," he said and I returned his salute quickly, scowling at his breach of security. "No VC," he said, sweeping his arm to take in the entire village. "No VC."

"Just a minute," I said. I walked over to the collection point where Murphy was holding the women and children, intent on letting the mother of the girl Nolan accosted go but I couldn't tell which one she was. It didn't matter. She jumped to her feet as soon as she saw me and was jabbering away even before I got to her. "Di di," I said, pointing in the direction of her hootch. She hurried off but did not shut up, assuring me of my number one status on her list of enemy invaders.

"No VC," the ARVN soldier said again as we walked back to the eight suspect prisoners. Until that moment I hadn't realized he had followed me. "Nooo VC."

"No, I'm sure you're right," I said sarcastically. "I'm sure you and your gung ho squad of airborne rangers have killed every VC for miles around. What about these guys?" I said when we reached the eight men being guarded by PFC Boyd. "This it?"

"Yes, Sir," Boyd said, handing me a collection of phony IDs.

"How 'bout these guys?" I said again, handing the ARVN sergeant the ID cards. "VC?" He barely looked at the IDs; didn't even give the prisoners a glance.

"No VC, No VC," he said, shaking his head emphatically.

"That's all he's been saying since he got here," Boyd said. "Even came to this group first, like he already knew what the groups were." I gave Boyd an appraising look. Perhaps there was more to him than I first thought. Cisco handed me the handset. "Captain Messina again, Sir" he said.

"No VC" the ARVN sergeant said again. He backed away, nodding his head and raising his hand in a gesture of good-bye. He had made his appearance and, his token obligation to the Viet Cong completed, he wanted no more to do with the situation.

"This is X-ray One Actual, over" I said into the handset.

"This is X-ray Actual. What's your current situation, over?"

"We have eight suspect Victor Charles in custody. Requesting either extraction or an interpreter on site for further interrogation, over."

"Negative. If they have an ID let them go, over." I thought for a moment I hadn't heard him right. Or maybe he hadn't heard me right.

"This is X-ray One Actual. The IDs don't match up at all, Sir. Request--"

"Let them go," Captain Messina said, overriding my transmission. I was stunned, lost my head. I'd never challenged Captain Messina's authority before but now…"

"Sir, could you check with higher because I'm quite sure--"

"This comes from higher. New S.O.P. We'll discuss it when you get back. Out." I handed Boyd the ID cards.

"Let 'em go," I said. Boyd looked mad but knew there was no point arguing.

"Di di mau," he said and threw the cards on the ground. Cisco was on them in a minute, gathering them up and putting them into a neat stack.

"You have to make sure everyone gets their correct ID back. Very important!" he said.

"Just give 'em back and let's get outta here," I said.

"Yes, sir," Cisco said and then, in a loud, clear voice he addressed the nervous group of prisoners. "When you hear your name, please step forward and get your ID card. Charles," he called, pretending to read from the top card. "Mr. Victor Charles!" A twittering of laughter from our platoon. Cisco looked up and scanned the prisoners but no one moved. "Oh, there you are, Vic. My God, your picture looks just like your father," he said, handing him the card. "When'd your teeth grow back. You look good, man." I was going to tell Cisco to knock it off but the men were laughing and I didn't want to spoil their fun.

"McDonald," Cisco called out. "McDonald? Is there an Old McDonald on this farm?" Again, no response except from his audience of entertainment-starved G.I.s "You know," Cisco said and started to sing. "With a trip wire here and a booby trap there--" and a few of the men joined in.

"Here a booby trap, there a booby trap, everywhere a booby trap." Cisco picked out a probable suspect and handed him the card. The man looked at it, confused, but held on to it.

"Minh? Mr. Ho Chi Minh?" Cisco called and a couple of the younger prisoners started to giggle, catching on. One of them pointed to a middle-aged man with a graying chin beard and pushed him forward. The man gave him a sharp look, but realizing any danger to them had passed, stepped forward and took the card. Cisco gave him a look of desperate shock. "Sir!" he said, turning to me. "We can't let this guy go. We can end this war today. We'll be fuckin' heroes, Sir. They might even make you a first lieutenant."

"Hurry it up, Cisco," I ordered. The rest of the villagers had gathered around, also giggling and enjoying the charade. I was getting nervous.

"Motherfucker," Cisco called. "Lie Ing Motherfucker. Is there a lying motherfucker here?"

"Enough!" I said. "Sgt. Little, form 'em up. Let's get outta here."

"Oh, hell," Cisco said, handing out the rest of the cards willy-nilly. "You're all a buncha lying motherfuckers. Here. Here. Here. Your mama san owes Sgt. ARVN Rock a blow job. All of you do. Ho, an honor to meet you," he said, shaking the older man's hand.

Sgt. Little set up the order of march and within a few minutes we had crossed the bridge over the Mu Dai, skirted the ARVN compound and disappeared into the jungle.

Chapter 22

"So what was all that with the mama san about?" Cisco said. We had put as much distance between us and Phu Gap as we could before stopping for lunch. I was eating cold beans and franks, heated only by the Tabasco sauce my mother had sent at my request. I didn't know what Cisco was spooning out of his can. Beef or pork slices by the looks of it.

"Whaddya mean?" I said even though I knew.

"The one you let go aheada the others."

"She reminded me of my mother," I said. Cisco looked up.

"Oh, yeah. I didn't notice the resemblance at first. Around the eyes." I put another spoonful of beans into my mouth and regretted the Tabasco sauce. Everyone else was enjoying the cool water from the village well but my mind had been so wrapped up with the Nolan thing I had forgotten to refill my canteens.

"Nolan didn't look very happy when he came back. You either," Cisco said. He didn't look up; acted like it wasn't a question.

"You know he's an R.A?" I said, meaning he enlisted.

"No shit? That what you were talking about all that time?" He was still fishing but I was not going to get into what had gone on in the hootch. Nolan was right. I hadn't *seen* anything. Nothing that would hold up in court anyway. I had seen his back and two unbuttoned buttons on the girl's blouse. That was it.

Nolan was a piece of shit and I disliked everything about him-- the way he looked at me; his fuck-you attitude; the way he thought every slight was because he was black; the way he posed for pictures holding the machine gun with belts of ammo crisscrossed across his chest like he was some kind of badass. The only time he'd carried the machinegun was after Stevens was wounded and he had to hump the broken one. He was not a good soldier and the way he was always talking that black power crap was having a detrimental effect on the platoon. Most of the other black guys bought into it and the white guys resented them for it. Not good for unit cohesion.

"No. I read it in his 201 file."

"Checkin' up on him, eh El Tee?"

"I read everybody's," I said. "He had two years of college and then enlisted. For the infantry! Now he's talking all that shit about fighting a white man's war against Asians." I was talking too much. Saying things I shouldn't say to an enlisted man. "Makes no sense," I said.

"Says he's gonna use all the things he learned in the army for the revolution," Cisco said.

"The revolution?"

"When the blacks take over the country," Cisco said and tossed his can aside. "It's all talk." I wanted to get away from the subject.

"Did you know Murphy and Boyd were drafted?"

"Uh huh," Cisco said and started digging around in his rucksack for something else to eat.

"I guess you never know," I said.

"Know what, Sir?"

"About people. Who will make a good soldier. Look at you," I said. Cisco had been drafted too and despite all his stupid shenanigans, he was a good RTO, a good soldier. He looked up, surprised at the first compliment I had ever given him.

"Thank you, Sir," he said, then, embarrassed, opened another pocket and started pulling more cans from his rucksack.

* * *

We put in five more miles before we set up an NDP for the night. This was all new country for us, even Sgt. Little. We crossed few trails and came upon only one village consisting of three or four hootches that wasn't even on the map. There were no rice paddies and only a few small gardens tended by women and old men. There weren't even any children to be seen. No one knew what to make of it. We watched it for half an hour and then skirted it in a wide arc. They looked harmless but we still didn't want to be seen.

There were no likely ambush sites around as dusk fell but there was a small knoll that provided at least the illusion of high ground so we set up there. We had to stretch our lines thin to cover it all but by setting up two man positions and a 50% watch it looked defensible. There was no C.P. Cisco and I took up a position on the perimeter.

I got little sleep. Nolan was on my mind, thinking about how I should have dealt with him; how I would deal with him when we got back. He had to be disciplined but as yet I hadn't caught him doing anything I could prove. I couldn't say for certain that he had fallen asleep on guard the night the two VC walked by his position any more than I could prove he was molesting that girl when I walked in on him. His insubordination was minor and ambiguous, the kind of thing an officer could either ignore or deal with in a way that didn't waste the time of the military justice system. I was mad at myself for my inability to deal with him and that made me even madder at Nolan, as if it was his fault I was an ineffective leader.

My thoughts turned to Audrey. Sometimes my mind drifted to Marlene, and Karen too, fanaticizing situations where I might find myself in a sexual relationship with them. My thoughts of Audrey were different. I found her attractive, but my feelings toward her were more complicated than that. I wanted her approval or--at the least--I didn't want her disapproval. I wanted her to like me, to think well of me, but whenever I was around her I seemed to accomplish exactly the opposite. At inappropriate times I found myself wondering who she was with, what she was doing, when my mind should have been on other things. It was a distraction I didn't need but was helpless to stop.

Time passed slowly. The moon had set about 11 o'clock and there was little light from the stars. It was as dark as a closet and there was little to orient myself except for Cisco's breathing and the hourly sit reps from the radio. I woke Cisco for his watches in the hope that I could get some sleep but if I did sleep, it was never for long. Shortly after four in the morning the sky to the east started to turn gray and the birds started their spring cacophony of sounds. When it was light enough to see I went to Sgt. Little's position.

"Let's get the men up. I want to be out of here in twenty minutes," I said. Sgt. Little went one way around the perimeter and I went the other. At the second position I found both men asleep. One was a white PFC, Voit, Hanson's replacement on his first mission. The other was Nolan. The PFC was curled up in his poncho liner, not even his head showing. Nolan was lying in the prone position, his head facing outward from the perimeter, his poncho liner underneath him, his back wet from the dew. I kicked the soles of Nolan's boots and nudged the poncho liner sheltering the new guy.

"Whose watch is it?" I demanded. I could see the fear on the new guy's face. He blinked twice, noticing the coming of dawn and his fear turned to terror. I glared at him even though I was fairly certain I knew what had happened. "When's the last watch you remember standing?"

"I…I had the second watch. I woke up Specialist Nolan and then…." That was the last thing he remembered. He looked at Nolan, hoping he'd take responsibility.

"It was my fault, Sir," Nolan said. It was the second time he'd called me *sir* me in as many days and I knew the next thing out of his mouth was going to be pure bullshit. "I woke him up for his watch. I axed was he awake and he grunted. I shoulda made sure he was fully alert before I went to sleep." Voit's mouth went dry.

"Sir, I never heard nothing'. I…He…" I gave Nolan a hard look but he said nothing, standing by his statement.

"Pack up. We're leaving in fifteen minutes. This isn't over," I said, making a promise I wasn't sure I could keep. *Fuckin' nigger* the voice in my head said as I walked away. I knew it was wrong as soon as the word popped into my head but I wasted no time dwelling on it. I wanted to be on the move as soon as possible.

PFC Voit hurried up to me as we were getting ready to move out. "Sir?" He was too new to call me El Tee and was smart enough to know it. "I stood my first watch, Sir. I swear to God, no one woke me up after that. I wouldn't do that, Sir," he said.

"Forget it. I'll take care of it," I said and looked at him just long enough to see he was totally bewildered by my response. "Fall in. Let's get outta here." Sgt. Little's squad had rear security and I saw Nolan grab Voit's sleeve and say something to him as he walked by. Voit jerked his arm free and stared him straight in the eye before taking his place in line, erasing any doubt I might have had that it was Nolan who had fallen asleep on his watch.

We stopped for breakfast around 7:30. There was a chill in the air and the men were still wet from the dew so I allowed them time for a hot breakfast. The glow of heat tabs dotted our line as men made coffee and warmed up their C-rats. Doc Ertel moved along the line, handing out malaria pills and asking after the men's well-being.

"You look like hell, Sir," he said, dropping the large, once-a-week pill into my hand. "You okay?"

"Monday already?" I said popping the pill into my mouth and washing it down. "Headache," I said. "Got anything for it?" Doc pulled a bottle of aspirin from his aid kit and gave me two.

"You taking your salt?"

"I was holding off a little. Forgot to refill my canteens at the village," I admitted.

"Shit, El Tee," he said and handed me two salt tablets. "You shoulda said something. Here. Lighten my load," he said, handing me his canteen. "I been peein' like a race horse since we left Phu Gap." I took him at his word and took a couple of long swallows. He pushed the canteen back to my mouth when I started to hand it back. "Tank up, Sir," he said. "We got a ways to go yet an' nobody wants to carry your ass." I drained what was left in his canteen and handed it back.

"We're gonna miss you, Doc," I said. His time was almost up and this was to be his last mission. "Any plans for when you get out?"

"I'm gettin' a SuperSport," he said. "Orderin' it through the PX before I leave. Figure I'll save a hundred fifty bucks just in taxes."

"I meant school or something? Got a job lined up?"

"Ain't thinking' that far ahead, Sir. Let me know if you need more water."

* * *

"The division is transitioning to pacification," Captain Messina said by way of explaining why we had been ordered to let the men with phony IDs go. "MAC-V thinks the days of major opposition in our A.O. are over and that we should me doing more hearts and minds stuff." I started to say something but he cut me off. "You don't have to *tell me*," he said. "The new S.O.P. was poorly written. Write up a report with your recommendations for changes to the policy pertaining to ID cards and I'll submit it to battalion." He was not in the mood to listen to me vent my anger. "Speaking of battalion, I got a reply about your suggestion concerning the corporal promotions."

"That was fast," I said.

"They can be very fast if they don't actually have to make a decision. They said all promotions will be considered on an individual basis."

"What does that mean?"

"It means put in your request regarding *each* person you want promoted to corporal and they will consider each one based on its own merits. That means you have to make your argument for each and every specialist you want to wear stripes."

"I made my justification in the original request," I said.

"Then do it again. This is the Army. By the way, I put Sgt. Little in for Staff Sergeant. I wanted to get that done before he leaves. I assume you're good with that."

"Yes, Sir." I said. "I wouldn't mind having him as my platoon sergeant. Permanently, I mean."

"Well, that's not going to happen," he said. He leaned back in his chair and stretched his arms behind his back. I could hear his tendons pop. "You know how many men you're losing in the next six weeks, beside Sgt. Little?"

"A lot," I said.

"Seven," he said and picked up a list he had made. "Ertel, Patterson, Rivera, Angus, Caulkins, Turner, and Burkholtz so you better come up with a recommendation for a new sergeant too."

"Any word on replacements?"

"We get 'em when we get 'em," Captain Messina said.

* * *

The platoon roster swam before my eyes. The headache I'd gotten on patrol hadn't gone away; it had gotten worse--a constant ache at the back of my skull that exploded into a piercing pain whenever I ventured into the sunlight. I was sure it had more to do with Nolan than my water consumption during our mission.

I had listed the men in descending order by squad based on rank and time in grade, crossing off everyone that was scheduled to DEROS within the next six weeks. From what was left I had to pick three specialist 4s to promote to corporal and two to sergeant to replace Burkholtz and Little.

I stared at the list but couldn't seem to see the big picture. Always my eyes came back to the name just below Sgt. Little's. I couldn't concentrate on the issue at hand with the Nolan problem hanging over my head. I did not have to promote the spec. 4 with the most time in grade. That was barely a consideration. The problem was that when Sgt. Little left, or if something should happen to him before the promotions came through, Nolan would automatically be in charge of the squad. I could not let that happen and I couldn't just move him to another squad. He had more time in grade as a Spec. 4 than anyone else in the platoon.

The ache at the back of my head started to throb and I closed my eyes, hoping it would go away on its own. I was already maxed out on aspirin. Doc said a small scratch and I'd bleed like a pig. I concentrated on taking deep breaths and relaxing my muscles. I didn't hear anyone come in.

"Lookin' stressed, El Tee." I opened my eyes and was surprised to see Stevens sitting across from me on Gary's bunk. I didn't recognize him right off. The scars on his face threw me at first but the empty eye socket gave him away. He smiled at my reaction.

"How ya doin'?" was all I could think of to say.

"Okay. For a dead man," he said. His smile revealed several chipped teeth where a fragment of the B-40 had torn through his mouth. "Hey, I'm new at this. You're gonna have to help me out," he said. I didn't know what to say. I had no idea why he was there either. We were not under fire and I had no orders to give or decisions to make that needed to be made in the next few seconds. I just sat there, staring at his disfigured face.

"Girl problems? Now tha's somethin' I know 'bout." I must have made a face because he said: "I'm jus' fuckin' with ya, El Tee. We don't get into that kind a shit. Got a guilt thing? 'Bout me getting killed an' all?" I thought about that before I answered.

"I don't think there's anything you can tell me that I haven't told myself a hundred times already. Unless you're here to forgive me or something like that."

"Naw. We don't do that, from what they tell me," he said. "But like I said…"

"Yeah. You're new at this." He rubbed his eye socket, then brushed away an imagined tear. "So how…why…"

"Jus' a option they give us. Hadn't finished my tour so I thought, *what the hell*. As to why I'm *here* here, you tell me. You ain't no fucking new guy no more. Unless it's a black thing. This about Sgt. Little?"

"No!"

"The brothers in general?" he guessed. I shook my head. "Nolan!?" His good eye went wide and he laughed when he realized he had it. "Shit, Sir. You ain't figured that out yet?" I wasn't sure what he was talking about. "You a good officer, sir," he said. "But in some ways you no different than Sgt. Nelson." He saw my reaction to this and cut me off before I could say anything. "'s true, Sir," he said. "Only difference, Sgt. Nelson *know he* prejudice."

"You don't know what you're talkin' about!" I said. "I go out of my way to treat everybody the same." Stevens laughed.

"You hear yourself, Sir? *You go outta your way*? You don't go outta your way to treat everybody equal, you jus' do. Nolan? He playin' you, man."

"He's not playin' me. He's playin' you guys. All that black power bullshit and that handshaking stuff."

"Black power bullshit? You think we need Nolan to tell us things fucked up? Sheeit. An' that handshaking got nothing' to do with black power. Tha's jus' brothers bein' brothers. You the problem, Sir, an' you can't put that on Sgt. Little."

"What the hell are you talkin' about?" I said. "I don't put anything on Sgt. Little that isn't his job."

"You really believe that, Sir? Ya know, until I got hit I bet you didn't say ten words to me the whole time I there. If it's third squad's turn for some shitty job, you tell Sgt. Little so he got to pick one of the brothers 'stead of you. You 'fraid it make you look prej'dice when in truth it only make you look chicken shit."

"I make all my assignments through the squad leaders," I said, almost certain that was true.

"Have it your way, Sir," he said. "But ain't nobody doesn't know Nolan ain't worth a shit in the fiel'. That's your problem an' you don't fix it ain't nobody gonna respec' you, black or white." Gary came in and flopped on his bunk, right where Stevens was sitting. I flinched.

"Startin' to rain," he said and, looking over, noticed the startled look on my face. "What?" he said.

It wasn't until I reached for my bottle of aspirin before I went to bed that I realized my headache was gone.

Chapter 23

I ducked into TOC and leaned my rifle against the wall.

"Hey, El Tee." It was Rivera, pulling his shift on radio watch. He spoke in a voice just short of a whisper so as not to wake Captain Messina, or Sgt. Little, napping on a cot at the back of the bunker.

"Hector," I said. "Anything going on?"

"Nada," he said. Sgt. Little sat up, embarrassed to be caught napping even though the Sergeant of the Guard was not expected to stay awake all night as long as he had left instructions with the radio watch to wake him for rounds and change of shifts.

"Hey, Lieutenant. Just catching a few Zs before--" I held up my hand to let him know I wasn't checking up on him.

"Can't sleep," I lied. "Everything quiet?"

"Yes, Sir."

"Why don't you take the rest of the night off. No sense both of us being up."

"Sure, Sir?" he said.

"Go," I said, as if it was something I did all the time.

"Thank you, Sir," he said and handed me the guard roster. "You know where everybody sleeps?" I assured him that I did. He looked at his watch. It was just after three. "I was going to do rounds on the next shift, but I can do them now, before I turn in."

"Forget it. I'll do them," I said. He gave me a curious look. Was this the first time I had done something considerate for him? For any of the men?

"Thanks," he said and left, taking his rifle and bandoleer.

"If you really want to feel useful…." Rivera said, giving a nod to the radios.

"Nice try," I said. I checked the guard roster again, disappointed to see that Sgt. Little had done rounds during Nolan's first shift, then thought it might be a good thing. He wouldn't be expecting another check during his next watch.

I waited a half hour, then told Specialist Rivera that I was going out to do rounds. "He had it scheduled for the next shift," he said.

"I know. Does he tell them when he'll be doing rounds?"

"No, Sir. Not even Sgt. Allen does that." Sgt. Allen was the easiest going of all the squad leaders.

"I'll be back," I said and ducked out the door.

From the roster I knew who was on watch but not which post they manned. It didn't matter. The wee hours of the morning were the hardest time for guards to stay awake, as was a half hour before change of shift when they had already been staring into the darkness for 90 minutes.

It was a clear night and I could see the silhouette of the guard's helmet just above the rim of his foxhole at post number one. I watched the back of his helmet for a full minute; never once did it turn, or even move for that matter. I moved toward him and only at the last instant did he jerk awake and turn so I could see his face.

"Oh, Sir. I--" he stammered.

"Shut up!" I hissed. *Shit.* Cisco, of all people.

"I--"

"Shut up, I said." He looked guilty as hell. "Everything quiet?" It took him a moment as he tried to figure out if I was giving him a break, or if I didn't know he'd fallen asleep in the first place.

"Yes, Sir," he said.

"Okay. Stay alert," I said and moved on to the next post.

Caulkins and Brokovitch were both awake at the next two posts. That left Nolan. I approached carefully and was rewarded by finding him asleep. I moved to the front of his position, noting that his rifle was leaning in the corner of his foxhole, the muzzle pointed toward me. I reached in, grabbed it by the barrel and started to lift it out when he awoke with a start. He lunged and I pushed him back pinning him to the back of his foxhole with my foot.

"Nolan!" He froze at the sound of his name and when he saw me it was down the wrong end of a rifle barrel. His eyes darted to the corner where he had leaned his rifle and when he realized it was *his* rifle pointing at his chest, he slumped back against the wall of his fighting position. "I coulda slit your fuckin' throat, you asshole," I hissed. He said nothing, just glared at me with those eyes of his. "You jeopardized the entire camp," I said, but he just glared back, said nothing. I don't know if he had guessed that I was gunning for him or not, but at that moment he knew it didn't matter. "Who's your relief?" I demanded.

"Voit," he said--the new guy he'd blamed when he fell asleep on watch on the way back from Phu Gap. It was all I could do to keep from smiling.

"Go get him," I said. "Tell him his watch starts early." He stood slowly and climbed from his hole. He held his hand out for his rifle. I removed the magazine, ejected the round in the chamber and threw it at his chest.

"You been out to get me since the day you got here," he said, not admitting anything. I noticed there was no 'Sir' this time.

"Now," I said.

When Voit got to the post it was clear Nolan hadn't admitted anything to him either. He was not going down without a fight.

"What's going on, Sir?" he asked, dropping into his hole.

"Wha'd Nolan tell you?"

"Nothin'. Said you had a case a the ass."

"Specialist Nolan was unable to fulfill his duties as guard. You're going to have to finish out the rest of the night. Can I count on you to do that for me, Private?" It took a moment for that to sink in. When it did a smile broke out across his face.

"Yes, Sir," he said. "You can rest easy on that, Lieutenant."

"I know I can," I said. I slapped him on the shoulder and went back to TOC. I stayed awake until after change of shift, then slept straight through until morning.

*   *   *

"El Tee. Hey." I rolled over, looked up into the gloom. It was Slick Slack, his hand on my shoulder, shaking me awake. "You wanted a wake up at 4:45?"

"Yeah, thanks," I said. I swung my feet over the side of the cot and rubbed my eyes. My excitement over last night had worn off and I started to wonder if I was doing the right thing. I leaned over, putting my head between my knees to ward off the beginning of another headache and then stood up. "I'm dismissing the guard," I said and then grabbed my rifle and left the bunker. The sun had not broken over the mountains but the birds were singing and day was upon us. PFC Voit waited for me to officially relieve him but the other guards saw me coming and waved me off as they left their holes and stumbled back to their bunkers to catch up on their sleep.

By the time I got back to my bunker I had decided that what I was doing was the right thing. Nolan was a bad soldier and a combat zone was no place to spend a lot of time trying to turn a bad soldier into a good one. Personal feelings had nothing to do with it. I pushed the incident with Cisco from my mind, a one- time thing.

Gary was still asleep when I got back so I got my shaving gear and took it outside. I poured half a canteen of water into my helmet, washed my face and shaved. I wanted to look presentable when I talked to Captain Messina.

"I'm awake," Gary said, when I went back inside. "How'd it go last night?"

"Caught him sleepin'," I said. He sat up immediately.

"No shit," he said. "What'd he say?"

"Nothin'," I said. "I was right in front of him and he never moved a muscle until I started to take his rifle."

"Jesus."

"No kiddin'," I said. "He lunged at me and I had to kick him back. Musta thought I was a gook. Wish I was. Save me a lotta trouble."

"Be a hard ass. Go for a court martial."

"Know how many men we'd have left if we court-martialed every soldier who dozed off on guard duty?" I did not mention Cisco.

"It's more than that. You said so yourself."

"Yeah, but last night is the only one I can make stick. I'm gonna ask Captain Messina for an Article 15."

"Whadaya hope to get?"

"Bust him. A Fine. I want to see what Captain Messina will go for, but I think he'll back me up on this."

"Don't go soft," Gary warned, knowing me. "This is long overdue."

* * *

The radio watch was gone when I got to TOC. Captain Messina was drinking a cup of coffee and Sgt. Little was sitting at the makeshift desk writing up the morning report. I thought of asking him to leave but it concerned a member of his squad and if he wanted to move up the food chain I wanted to see if he had the stomach for it.

"Got a minute, Sir?"

"Got more than that now that Sgt. Little is doing my dirty work for me. What do you need?"

"There was an incident with one of the guards last night," I said. "You might as well be in on this, Sgt. Little. It concerns one of your men." Sgt. Little looked alarmed so I got right to the point to relieve him of any fear that it had something to do with him. I turned to Captain Messina.

"I couldn't sleep last night so I relieved Sgt. Little as sergeant of the guard around, what? Three o'clock?" Sgt. Little nodded. "Anyway, I found Specialist Nolan asleep when I went on rounds. I even took his M-16 away before he woke up so there's no question he was asleep."

"What do you suggest we do?" Captain Messina said. Sleeping on guard was a serious offense, but given the demands of duty in a war zone, where sleep deprivation was the norm, it sometimes happened and was usually handled without a blemish on the man's permanent record.

"I think an Article 15 is appropriate." Neither Captain Messina nor Sgt. Little said anything. "I'm sure this isn't the first time this has happened," I continued. "There were at least two other times I thought he had fallen asleep. This is just the first time I can say it with complete certainty." I said nothing about the incident with the girl at Phu Gap. Captain Messina scratched the back of his neck.

"Sgt. Little?" he said. Sgt. Little thought it over before answering.

"Nolan's not a very good soldier," he said, hedging. "But if this is meant to make him a better soldier…I don't think any punishment will do that."

"I agree," Captain Messina said. "Of course that doesn't mean we can let this go unpunished." He took a breath and let it out slowly while he thought it over. "Okay," he finally said, looking at Sgt. Little. "Give us half an hour to get this thing typed up and then tell Nolan I want to see him. You can finish the morning report later. Why don't you grab some chow before then."

"We're putting a lot on him for an E-5," Captain Messina said after Sgt. Little left.

"I know," I said. "Any word on his promotion?"

"Not yet. I'll call battalion this afternoon and push them. There's no reason to turn it down. What are you thinking in the way of punishment?"

"Busted to PFC and a $50 fine for three months?"

"Okay. Type it up," he said, handing me an Article 15 form. "Do the specification but leave the charge blank. I'll call Lt. Avery and get the correct language for that." We went to work and were done by the time Nolan darkened the door.

"Sit down," Captain Messina ordered. Nolan sat in the chair by the radios. Captain Messina and I took chairs facing him only a few feet away. "I guess you already know what this is all about."

"No, Sir. Sgt. Little didn't say nothin'." He didn't even look at me. Like I wasn't there. *Let the games begin*, I thought.

"It's about you sleeping on guard last night," Captain Messina said. Nolan made a poor attempt at acting surprised, looked at me as if to say *what's he talking about?* "We're bringing Article 15 charges against you," Captain Messina continued. "Just to be clear, I'll read the charges for you--Charge one: Dereliction of duty. Specification one: That, on or about 30 May 1967 at about 0330, Specialist Four James D. Nolan, RA 11644995 did, while serving as an infantryman in C Company 2/605, 53rd I.D., fall asleep while on guard duty at post #4 at LZ Old Crow, Dinh Bihn Province, Republic of Vietnam, a hostile fire zone." He handed Nolan the form and waited while Nolan read it. "Lt. Sullivan's witness report is attached. You should read that too." Nolan read it through and handed it back.

"I ain't signin' that," he said.

"If you wish to dispute the charges you can do that at a court martial. Is that what you want?"

"Yeah. Tha's what I want," Nolan said. "Tha's my right."

"You know, of course, that a conviction at a court martial could land you in Long Binh Jail for a long time?"

"An' when I get out, I'm outta this motherfuckin' place. Outta this motherfuckin' army." I wanted to slap the grin off his face but Captain Messina never missed a beat.

"That's not how it works," he said. "Jail time is bad time. It won't count toward your tour *or* your time in the service. It all has to be made up, unless they want to give you a dishonorable discharge, but that's up to the judge."

"I get a jury a my peers, right? Enlisted men."

"All senior NCOs," Captain Messina said, and now his tone turned nasty. "Sergeants who have spent a lifetime putting up with third-rate soldiers, and when they pass judgment it won't be just on sleeping while on guard duty. It will be on wasting their time when they could be doing something important." Nolan pursed his lips, pushed his tongue through and wet them. "And who are you gonna call to refute Lt. Sullivan's testimony? To testify on your behalf?"

"Sgt. Little. He know me."

"You mean Sgt. Tom? Isn't that what you call him behind his back?" I don't know who was more surprised, Nolan or me. How did Captain Messina know that? I didn't know that.

"I want to consult a lawyer," Nolan said.

"And you can. You can have one all to yourself if you choose not to sign the Article 15." Nolan's eyes went dark.

"What's the punishment?" he said.

I could see that Captain Messina was getting weary with his nonsense. "You know that's not how it works. I saw your record."

"I was two hours late coming back from a three day pass," Nolan said. "That was over a year ago."

"You were AWOL," Captain Messina said.

"Not everything in there is acrate," Nolan said, referring, I supposed, to my witness statement.

"You can debate the facts at your court-martial if that's what you want," I said. He gave me the Nolan stare and when I didn't blink he snatched the Article 15 from Captain Messina's hand, laid it across his knee and scribbled something that didn't even look like a signature. He handed it back and without waiting to be dismissed stood up and headed for the door.

"Oh, Nolan," I said, and when he turned I tossed him the magazine I had taken from his weapon the night before. "I believe this is yours." He fumbled it, had to bend down to pick it up. When he was gone, Captain Messina witnessed Nolan's signature and handed me the form so that I could type in the punishment.

"For a moment there I almost wished he'd take the court-martial," he said.

"Me too," I said as he disappeared behind the curtain that separated his sleeping quarters from the rest of TOC.

Chapter 24

The next day a helicopter arrived with the battalion XO on board. As part of my training, Captain Messina had appointed me pay officer for the month and I signed for the money, took the pouch, and ran clear as the chopper took off for Wild Turkey.

A line formed outside TOC while I set up a desk inside. The men were eager for their pay, even though they had nowhere to spend it. One by one they reported to me; they signed their voucher and I gave them their money. Several men had questions or complaints about their pay but I had no answers for them. "Take it up with finance," was my standard response.

"Let me go back to Hardscrabble and I will," was their standard response.

An hour later the chopper was back and I hopped on for the ride back to Hardscrabble to turn in the vouchers and any money that had not been paid.

The finance office was closed by the time we got to Hardscrabble so I reported in at the company orderly room, taking a moment to admire the new company logo and motto hanging above the door. PFC Fisher had created a three foot high, two and a half foot wide replica of his entry out of cut plywood, this time painted with striking colors instead of the pencil and ink sketch he had submitted for the contest. Lt. Avery signed for the pouch and locked it in the company safe.

I vowed I wasn't going to go out of my way to run into Audrey but realized I was lying to myself when I lingered at the mess hall until it closed without seeing her. Disgusted with my lack of resolve, I grabbed a shower and crashed in the transient tent.

It was almost nine o'clock when the pay officer from A Company stumbled into the tent and woke me up. "Fuckin' thing!" he mumbled, fumbling with the light bulb that hung from the ridge pole.

"Chain's broken," I said. "You have to screw it in." I watched as he turned the bulb the wrong way.

"Shit," he said when it came off. "Easy, easy," he mumbled trying to replace the bulb in the socket without electrocuting himself. "Now turn, turn. Righty tighty." he giggled, then started singing. "There is a season, turn, turn…I don't remember the rest." The light flickered on. "You know how hard it is to find this place in the dark? When you're shit-faced?"

"I'm guessing….hard?" He laughed and dropped unto his cot.

"You like girls?" he asked. I didn't like the sound of that.

"Very much," I said.

"Then you should go to the O-Club. Big party. Place is crawlin' with nurses. Makes me want to shoot myself in the foot."

"Then what are you doing here?"

"Even more crawlin' with ossifers. The man kind. There's even a fucking Lt. Colonel sniffin' around. He suggested it was time for me to leave. Who you think stands a better chance, a tight ass lieutenant or a fat ass colonel?" He was having trouble getting his boots off.

"Try untying them," I said.

* * *

"Hey, you came!" Audrey said. She must have seen me as soon as I opened the door to the O Club and ran over to greet me. She threw her arms around me and gave me a short, but enthusiastic hug. "Come on. You know everyone," she said. She ushered me to a group of tables pushed together in the middle of the room and started introducing me as one of our gallant men-in-arms. She was clearly drunk. I shook hands with a young captain Audrey introduced as Doctor Ben Casey *because he was both a doctor, and a Ben.* She slapped me on the chest in appreciation of her humor.

"I hope you're not one of those gung ho assholes who keeps filling up my operating room," Dr. Ben said.

"Now, now," Audrey scolded, directing her comment at Dr. Ben. "Sorry," she said, turning to me. "Ben's a mean drunk. Like you!" she remembered happily. "No mean drunks on my birthday," she ordered, this to both of us. Dr. Ben wandered off toward the bar.

"Is that what all the celebrating is about?" I asked.

"That, and today I am officially short. One more month to go. Ironic, huh?" She had a beautiful smile that made her eyes sparkle. Alcohol agreed with her.

"Ironic?" I said.

"Not the short part. I meant me being born on Memorial Day." I didn't get it. "Being born on Memorial Day, and then being a nurse?

Here? Trying to keep people from being honored on Memorial Day?"

"You're leaving in a month?" I must have looked disappointed.

"Aw, you're gonna miss me," she said. "Buy the birthday girl a drink?"

"What are you drinking?"

"Whatever nice people bring me. And people have been very nice to me tonight. But nothing for you," she warned, wagging her finger at me. "No mean drunks, remember?"

I brought our drinks and gave one to her. "Sean, you remember Karen and Bill," she said.

"Only Karen," I said and shook the Engineering Captain's hand. "Sean Sullivan." Bill just grinned, the only person at the celebration who appeared to be as drunk as Audrey.

"Bill, you tell him," Audrey said. "An Army nurse being born on Memorial Day--that's ironic, right?"

"I wasn't an English major but I think the word you're looking for is *onomatopoeia*." That made Audrey laugh and that made her bend over and cross her legs.

"That reminds me. I gotta pee," she said, slapping Bill's arm.

"Want me to show you where the piss tube is?" I said.

"I can find it," she said, not getting the joke. When she did she laughed and slapped me.

"Piss! Now that's an onomatopoeia!" Bill exclaimed. Audrey laughed and squeezed her thighs together as she shuffled to the ladies room, taking her drink with her.

"Who designed those things anyway?" I asked, meaning the piss tubes. "I can't hit them sober."

"Not me," Bill said. "I suggested we use a twelve inch pipe, but they wouldn't listen."

"Good idea," I said.

"Thanks. Actually I got the idea from the motor pool guys. They put big funnels in their piss tubes. Very efficient."

"What are we talking about?" Audrey said when she got back. I noticed her drink was half gone.

"Urine," Karen said, clearly bored. "Feel like I'm back at work. How was your output?"

"Good," Audrey said, taking another sip. "This is good. What is it?"

"Bourbon and coke," I said. "The official drink of Second Battalion."

"Is that what you're drinking?"

"Just coke," I said. "With some bourbon mixed in." Another laugh and slap for me.

"Well, if you turn nasty I'm going to have to ask you to leave," she said seriously.

"Speaking of which," Karen said. "I've got first shift tomorrow, and so do you." She drained the rest of her cup and set in on the table.

"I'll be along as soon as I finish this," Audrey said and I felt my heart drop. Bill chugged the last of his drink and then kissed Audrey on the cheek."

"Happy birthday, Aud," he said and followed Karen to the door, clearly a couple.

"Karen, Karen, Karen," Audrey said. "The happiest girl in Vietnam." And tonight Bill's the happiest guy I thought. The ice in Audrey's glass had melted to fragile slivers and her drink had gone pale.

"Ready for another?" I asked, trying not to sound as desperate as I felt.

"Maybe one more," Audrey said and drained her glass.

* * *

I awoke suddenly, a feeling of dread washing through me. I reached for my rifle, trying to remember where I was. I was not used to alarms.

"Ohhh, God," Audrey moaned. She reached over me, feeling her nightstand until she found the clock and shut off the alarm. "Oh, God," she moaned again, suddenly aware of my presence.

"Good morning," I said, turning so I could see her face. She looked like hell, in a pretty sort of way. She pulled the sheet over her head and held it down. Tight.

"Oh, God. Get up," she said. "I've got to be at work in 45 minutes." I pulled the sheet from her face.

"You've got plenty of time," I teased. I put my arm around her, bent over to kiss her neck.

"I'm serious," she said, pulling away. She sat up, wrapping the sheet around her just above her breasts. I could see the pain in her bloodshot eyes. "Oh, God." I swung my legs over the side of the bed and sat up. It was a small, cubicle of a room with no window and the bare minimum of furniture, but it seemed like heaven to me. The walls and floor were made of wood instead of dirt. I put on my pants and then sat in the folding chair by her nightstand.

"Could you hand me my bathrobe? Please." I picked her fatigue shirt from the heap on the floor and touched the embroidered lieutenant's bar on the shoulder.

"Gold or silver?"

"Silver," she said. "Now get me my bathrobe." She was not in a playful mood.

"Yes, ma'am," I said and tossed her the robe from her wall locker. I caught a glimpse of a breast as she let go of the sheet and caught the robe which she managed to put on without further exposing herself. I was hoping she'd broach the subject of last night but she avoided it like the plague. She opened a small refrigerator, took out a coke, then shook two aspirins from a plastic container into her hand. Then one more. Then, carefully, one more. She popped them into her mouth, then opened the can and washed them down. "I'm being a bad host," she mumbled. "Help yourself." My head wasn't even fuzzy, nothing a shower and breakfast wouldn't cure. I took two aspirin anyway, an attempt to absolve myself in her eyes of any blame she might want to put on me for last night.

"Needs bourbon," I said, after several swallows.

"Not funny," she said. I sat down in the chair. "Really, you've got to go. *I've* got to go." She reached into her locker for her shower bag. I looked at the swell her buttocks made in the robe as she pulled the bag from the top shelf.

"Afraid your mother will catch us," I teased, trying to cover my arousal.

"Worse," she said. "Marlene."

"So what's up with her anyway?" I said, hoping to keep the conversation going.

"She's my best friend. And she's very protective of me." She slipped into her clogs, grabbed a towel, and headed for the door. "Really. Don't be here when I get back."

When she got back, I was still there. She just rolled her eyes and pushed past me. I couldn't seem to please her no matter what I did. I held up my hand in apology.

"I'm leaving," I said. "I just need to know…" and then I paused, pretending to be concerned even though I assumed a nurse would have taken the proper precautions. “Did you do anything? About birth control, I mean.”

“I’m not Karen,” she said, whatever that meant.

“And I’m not…” I was thinking about the guy Marlene mentioned--the other asshole in her life--but I didn’t know his name and decided this was not the time to bring him up.

“Don’t worry about it,” she said, just a hint of compassion in her voice. “My period’s due tomorrow. Now, really, I’ve got to get dressed.” I took one of her hands in mine. She startled but didn’t pull away.

“Okay,” I said. “Well…” Thank you did not seem the appropriate thing to say. “I hope I see you again before you DEROS.”

“Me too,” she said, then rose up on her toes and kissed me on the cheek.

* * *

A resupply chopper was leaving for Old Crow at eleven o’clock so I had breakfast, turned in the company’s pay vouchers and undistributed money to Finance, then found myself wandering over to the hospital. I knew trying to see Audrey again was a bad idea but I went anyway. I looked into Dr. Fletcher’s office as I walked by and as I did he looked up. I stopped, took a step back.

“Sean!” he said. “Come in. I was just thinking about you.” I went in and he motioned to the chair in front of his desk. As I sat he started toward the door.

“That’s, okay. I can’t stay,” I said. “Gotta catch a chopper back to Old Crow soon.” He closed it anyway, took his seat again and leaned back in his chair.

“So what brings you here today?” he said.

“Returning pay vouchers.” I smiled to show him I was fine.

“No. I meant here here,” he said. I thought quickly. Why had I looked into his office as I passed, stopped when he looked up?

“Well, I never thanked you for our talk last time I was here so…thanks. It was very reassuring. Knowing I’m not crazy.” He nodded his head. The old waiting game. “You said you were just thinking about me?” I finally said.

“I’m working on a paper about the various ways people cope with the stresses of combat. Yours is somewhat unique. Have you had any more…what shall we call them?" When I couldn't think of an answer he made suggestions. "How do you think of them? As spirits? Apparitions? People?"

"Visitors."

"Good enough," he said. "And have you had any more…visits since we last spoke?" I told him about Stevens and was comfortable enough with him now to tell him about my father's visit too. I didn't tell him I had withheld that part the last time I was there. I was starting to trust him and wanted him to trust me.

"And you took their advice?" I told him I had. "And it worked out well?" I told him it did. He nodded his head. "Do you mind if I jot down a few notes?"

"No, go right ahead," I said. He picked up a pen and pulled a pad in front of him. "You said you were writing a paper? You won't be using my real name, will you?"

"You'll be Lt. Leary for the purpose of the paper."

"Lt. Leary?"

"A mnemonic device to help me remember who my subjects are. Like Timothy Leary--the doctor who advocates the use of hallucinogenic drugs to enhance self-awareness?" He looked up to see if I was offended by the comparison. I wasn't.

"So you think my *visitors* were hallucinations?"

"Technically, any sensory impression that's not real is a hallucination. Do you think the people you saw, heard, were real?"

"No," I said assuming that was the right answer.

"You can tell me what you really think."

"No. I don't think they were real," I said. I don't know if he believed me but he didn't question my answer further.

"I'd like to get some background information on you if you don't mind."

"Actually, I better get going if I'm going to catch my ride," I lied, but for some reason I did not want to leave yet. I liked talking to him. "Is this for another doctorate or something?"

"Just want to make some kind of contribution to the science. Feed my ego," he said.

"So what did you do your doctoral thesis on?"

"I worked on it during my first tour. My research project was designed to find the optimal lighting conditions for maximum office efficiency. I compared light levels at three different finance offices and compared them to the number of mistakes reported on the vouchers--typos, computation errors, things like that."

"Sounds boring," I said.

"It was."

"And what did you find?"

"I concluded that skills requiring manual dexterity and eye-hand coordination are best performed when the subjects can see what they're doing."

"That must have been hard to defend," I said facetiously.

"I didn't even submit it," he said. "It was poorly thought out and implemented from the start. But I came across something even more interesting during my research. Turns out that the unit with the fewest pay complaints also had the worst working conditions of the sample group. Crummy office, outdated typewriters, a mishmash of various adding machines, you name it. So I did a new thesis on that: *Influences of efficiency: a study of morale and unit cohesion within the military*."

"And what did you find?"

"Nothing new--that morale starts from the top. It was the specifics that made it interesting. The Finance officer called everyone with the rank of Sergeant or above by their rank and last name. Everyone else he referred to by their first name. He was a stickler for a clean barracks and clean fatigues around the compound, but let the men wear T-shirts and even shorts at the office so they'd be comfortable. He kept the door to his office open so the men could see that he was working as hard as they were. He was quick to correct poor performance, but even quicker to give praise when it was warranted.

"But the most important thing he did was to require his record clerks to take turns going to the forward bases and outposts to take pay complaints and answer questions the men had about their pay. They took their weapons because they were often required to stand guard if they were stranded overnight at a firebase. They ate what the grunts ate, slept in their bunkers, and pulled guard duty just like everyone else.

"The men in the field became actual people to the clerks, not just names on a voucher. And the grunts treated them like royalty. They'd never had a REMF come to them before, asking what *they* could do for *them*. A mutual respect grew between them. The clerks felt more a part of the unit. They saw how important their job was to the men on the lines and took pride in doing it right. Going to the field took time away from the rest of their work but there was never a shortage of volunteers to hitch hike around on helicopters to see the men. What's the old adage? Morale is to all other factors as ten is to one?"

* * *

When I checked in at Aviation I was told that the resupply chopper was grounded for repairs and that it would be at least another hour before it could fly. As I left I was stopped by a PFC just outside the door. He must have been there when I went in but a PFC in new jungle fatigues at Hardscrabble barely registered on my radar. "Excuse me, Sir, but I couldn't help but overhearing," he said. It was clear he was new to Vietnam but he showed none of the signs of a FNG, saluting or standing at attention. "You Lieutenant Sullivan? Lieutenant Avery said I might run into you here. I'm PFC Cook. I'm your new Medic." Doc's replacement. I shook his hand.

"Welcome to the platoon," I said. His handshake was neither firm nor weak and he showed no sign of gratitude for my friendliness. In fact, he said nothing. "So Lt. Avery got you all squared away at Company? Got all your gear?" I said.

"Yessir," he said. He had been issued a new rucksack--now bulging with equipment and leaning against the wall of the aviation shack--and Doc Ertel's old aid kit which he had placed beside the rucksack. I looked around for the rest.

"Where's your rifle?"

"I'm a medic," the PFC said, as if that explained it. It would have in World War II, but not here.

"You qualified? On the range, right?" I said. "Until someone needs your attention you're just another grunt. Go see Staff Sergeant Dozier and draw a weapon. You've got time."

"I'm a conscientious objector, Sir" he said. I was momentarily stunned, didn't know what to say.

"You a Quaker?" I asked. "Or a Mennonite?" I had seen Mennonites riding in their horse-drawn buggies in southern New York. I'd even seen one once in traffic right in Hornell, pissing off all the people trying to get to work in cars and I'd heard that they too were exempt from military serviced based on their religious beliefs.

"No sir. Just a personal decision on my part."

"Did you apply for a deferment as a conscientious objector?"

"They turned me down," he said, a simple statement of fact.

"So why–" He had clearly been asked this question a hundred times before.

"I was about to get drafted so I enlisted instead. As a medic. I figured I could do that." It was then I noticed that he was a little older than the usual draftee. And smarter. He'd probably put a lot of thought into his decision.

"What was your major? In college?" I asked.

"Liberal arts."

"Good choice," I said.

* * *

I left Private Cook at the aviation shack and went to the division finance office thinking how fucked-up the platoon was getting. "I'm here to see Specialist DeFrance. He's expecting me," I lied. The specialist took in my lieutenants' bars and unlocked the gate in the counter to let me in. Spec. 5 DeFrance was busy posting the May pay vouchers into each man's finance record when I stopped in front of his desk. He looked up, surprised to see me again so soon.

"Got a minute?" I said. He motioned me to the same chair I sat in earlier that morning when I turned in the company pay vouchers.

"What's up?" he said.

Chapter 25

Something was different when I got back to Old Crow, something I couldn't put my finger on. The usual contingent of grunts was on hand to help unload our supplies, but something was missing. The mail bag, the boxes of C-rations, the jerricans, the box of sundries from the Red Cross, were all ignored after they were unloaded and the chopper left. Cook, of course, didn't notice. It was his first time out.

"Leave your shit here," I said. "Cisco–"

"Shooting contest," Cisco explained. "Sgt. Henry challenged Boyd." Boyd had been getting a lot of ribbing about his M-14, none more cutting than from Sgt. Henry, a squad leader from Gary's platoon. Apparently it had come to a head while I was gone. "They each get fifteen seconds to get as many shots in the target as they can," Cisco continued as we joined the mob headed toward the other end of the compound. "Sgt. Henry has to use his M-16 and keep it on automatic. Everyone's betting, if you want to get in on it."

"Who are you betting on?" I asked. "By the way, this is Doc Cook. He's our new medic." Cisco nodded to Doc, but just barely.

"Boyd," he said, giving me a strange look.

"Who do you think is gonna win?" He shrugged. Platoon loyalty. Like everyone else he was starved for entertainment, had just been paid, and had nothing else to spend his money on.

"Hey, you're just in time," Boyd said, coming over. "Easy money if you bet on me."

"You really think you can beat him with that?" I said, nodding to his M-14. He noticed the new guy, then walked me a few yards from the crowd.

"I suckered him into thinking he challenged me, but I laid down all the rules. Fifteen seconds at a hundred yards. Look at the target," he said and laughed at the 8½ by 11 inch piece of paper tacked to a piece of plywood. "I've killed elk at twice that range. One shot."

"That's a lot smaller than an elk," I said.

"Not the vital area. Look, I know these guys. He's going to put as many rounds down range as he can in fifteen seconds and think the law of averages will work in his favor. Plus he'll have to waste three seconds, minimum, changing magazines while I put one round in the target every one and a half seconds. I'll put 11 rounds in the paper. At a hundred yards he'll be lucky to get five. After his second round he'll be off the paper until he puts in a new magazine and aims again."

"He'll get off fifty rounds to your eleven," I said.

"And most of them won't hit anything but air. That's why I picked a piece of paper as the target instead of a silhouette." He seemed disappointed in my lack of confidence in him. "Tell you what," he said. "I'll make a bet. I win, you recommend me for sniper school. He wins, I stop pestering you about it. What do you say?"

"That doesn't mean you'll get accepted," I warned him. He stuck out his hand.

"I'll get accepted," he said, and we shook on it. His confidence was infectious and before the first shot was fired I made a ten dollar bet with Gary.

"You getting in on this?" I asked Captain Messina.

"I've got five bucks on your boy," he said. The betting was clearly along platoon lines and I thought he would have stayed neutral. He saw the look of surprise on my face. "Hate to see marksmanship get beat by firepower," he said. "If he's as good as he says he is, he just might do it."

Sgt. Henry shot first and before his first magazine was empty I could see the look of concern on Boyd's face. Sgt. Henry was not following Boyd's plan. He was firing in short, three to four round bursts, correcting his aim after each burst. The barrel of his rifle nestled in a groove he had pounded into a sandbag and I could see little movement in the muzzle as he fired. He changed magazines quickly and got off a final, five round burst before Captain Messina counted down to zero. He cleared his rifle and the mob charged down range to count the hits. Two rounds barely broke the edge of the paper but he scored ten hits.

Boyd's poker face couldn't hide the hard swallow he took when the number of hits was announced. Gary's platoon was pounding Sgt. Henry on the back as we walked back to the firing line. My platoon had been shaken by Sgt. Henry's score, but Boyd had promised them he would could get off eleven round in fifteen seconds, all of them on the paper. One miss would mean a tie. Two misses and he would lose.

Boyd used the same standing position Sgt. Henry had but with a different sandbag, grooved to his liking. He had his rear sight up, the crossbar set at one hundred yards. The clock started at his first shot. I watched the muzzle and the kick was twice what Sgt. Henry had to cope with. But Boyd settled the rifle quickly and kept squeezing off rounds. He was nervous, shooting faster than he had intended and after eleven rounds he still had three seconds left and used them to get off three quick shots.

"How many rounds did I get off?" he asked as the rest of the men charged down range.

"Fourteen," I said. "Were you trying to shoot faster?"

"Not really," he said. "But that's good. I think I missed twice. At least," he said. "I wish I could do it all over again." A cheer went up from the target and it took a long moment before either of us realized it was our platoon that was cheering.

Boyd had missed twice, but that was all. One round just barely cut the edge of the paper and was disputed by Gary's platoon but it didn't matter. Even Sgt. Henry called it a hit and Boyd won 12-10. "Nice shooting," Sgt. Henry said, shaking Boyd's hand.

"You too," Boyd said.

"Very nice," Captain Messina said. "Both of you."

* * *

"I forgot to tell you. Remember that friend of mine? The one who wanted to know if he should get married to stay out of the draft?" Gary had rolled up his poncho liner and was stuffing it into his rucksack. Second Platoon was due back at Wild Turkey later that day and his platoon would be going out first thing in the morning.

"Uh huh," he said. I could tell the pre-mission jitters were setting in and thought he might need a little distraction. Finally he looked up, my question finally registering. "Yeah. So'd he get married or what?"

"Oh, he got married. A week after he got his notice to report for his draft physical. Took a copy of his marriage certificate to the draft board the day after the ceremony and asks for a deferment." I heard a chopper come in and then take off with barely enough time to set down. Someone coming in or going out, I thought without much interest.

"His bride must have loved that," Gary said. "Marrying her just to stay out of the Army, I mean."

"I doubt he told her that. Doesn't matter. He gets drafted anyway and I get a letter from him from Fort Dix. You know how basic is--drill sergeants yellin' about how you're gonna die in Vietnam because you can't remember to button all your buttons? What are you looking for?" I said. He was turning around in circles, picking up articles of clothes and tossing them aside.

"My poncho liner. Where'd I put it?"

"You already packed it," I said. "Jesus, relax. What's wrong with you anyway?"

"I don't know," he said, sitting on his bunk. "I've been getting spooky lately. Does it show? I still got three months to go. Too early for that shit."

"Just noticed it. How long has it been going on?"

"Not long. It's nothing. I'm fine once we get outside the wire. It's weird. It's like I'd rather be out there looking forward to getting back than being back and dreading going out again. You ever feel like that?"

"All the time," I lied. I thought about suggesting he talk to Dr. Fletcher next time he was back at Hardscrabble, but let it go for now. The last thing he needed to think about now was the possibility that he was losing it.

"So, anyway…" he said.

"So anyway, he's scared he's going to Vietnam as a ground pounder if he doesn't do something, so guess what he does?" Gary saw the smile on my face.

"He reenlists so he can go to OCS."

"Four more years," I said. "They told him with his education, for sure they'd put him in administration. He'd probably never even leave the states."

"What a moron."

"Yeah, not like us," I said. "He'll probably be my replacement." The doorway went dark and someone stuck his head in.

"Lieutenant Sullivan?" he said, his eyes adjusting to the gloom. I didn't recognize him at first and when I did I was too shocked to speak."

"What…" I finally said. He ducked his head and took a step inside.

"I talked to Major Tibbits and he said it was okay. Me coming out and all. It's okay, right?" he said, noticing my surprise. He had an M-16 in one hand, a satchel slung over his other shoulder, resting against his hip. A bandolier of ammo crossed his chest.

"I don't believe we've met," Gary said, extending his hand. The man looked at him for only a moment.

"Lt. Holder," he said. "Yeah we have. Specialist DeFrance. I'm your finance clerk. Wow! You guys really are out in the boonies."

*　　*　　*

Specialist DeFrance was all I'd hoped for and more. He gave a half hour talk on how the finance office worked, how to read their pay vouchers, and the importance of keeping Military Script out of the hands of the Vietnamese. He then spent the rest of his time resolving pay complaints, filling out allotment forms, and explaining anything the men didn't understand on a one to one basis.

He brought money for partial payments but he needn't have bothered. The men had more money than they could spend. Instead they gave him *their* money to send to their wives or parents for safe keeping. He advised them to allocate a certain amount of their pay to go to a soldier's savings account where it would accrue 10% interest. He also encouraged them to draw only the money they would need, the rest to be carried forward and paid to them when they needed it. He also converted military script into piasters for those who wanted Vietnamese currency.

As Dr. Fletcher said, the men treated DeFrance like royalty. They shared their C-rations, kidded him about being a REMF--Rear Echelon Motherfucker--and took pictures of him with his camera standing by the wire with his M-16 in hand for the people back home. When the chopper took him to Wild Turkey (where he would spend the night on guard duty) he left with the promise that he would try to get back every other month or so.

*　　*　　*

June was a month of change. Not only had the weather gone from a constant wet to a throat-parching dry, our platoon went through changes as well. Doc Ertel's departure was followed by Specialists Rivera, Angus, and Turner. Patterson also left and Slick Slack refused to walk second to anyone else so new point and slack men had to be trained. Romansky took Rivera's place as first gunner and started breaking in a new replacement as his assistant.

Spec. 4 Simpson took over as acting sergeant for second squad when Sgt. Burkholtz left but the biggest holes came from third squad. Caulkins left leaving no experienced machine gunners and when Turner left, Brokovitch had little to choose from for his new slack man. Even as a PFC, Nolan was the next most senior man in the squad and he didn't want the job any more than Brokovitch wanted him for it. The biggest loss, though, came when Sgt. Little left.

His promotion to staff sergeant came a week before his DEROS. I was in TOC when Captain Messina gave him his exit interview. Captain Messina congratulated him on his promotion and asked him his plans for the future. Sgt. Little wasn't sure. Captain Messina told him that when his time was up a reenlistment officer would try to talk him into another hitch; he encouraged him to consider it. Senior NCOs were the backbone of the army and Captain Messina and I both told him he was a good leader and would be missed. I never felt those words were more true than the day the resupply chopper took away my acting platoon sergeant.

After Sgt. Little left Captain Messina sent in more requests for promotions. All PFCs with a good record and more than three months in country were recommended for promotions to specialist 4 except PFC Boyd. Even though Murphy had more time in grade as a PFC, Sgt. Burkholtz had by-passed both him and Spec. 4 Merrit to recommend Boyd for the rank of corporal. Boyd was still relatively inexperienced but he had earned everyone's respect as a level-headed soldier who quickly mastered the skills he would need as an NCO. His initiative in capturing the two Vietnamese who had spotted our platoon outside Phu Gap was considered by Captain Messina as reason enough to promote him above his peers. Corbert and Romansky were also put in for corporal slots, and acting sergeants Simpson and Brokovitch were to have their acting sergeant positions made permanent.

Chapter 26

I turned at the sharp slap of flesh against flesh. Nolan looked at the bloody remains of the mosquito on his arm, showed no regret. Noise discipline had deteriorated after an old woodcutter saw us as we moved through the jungle just east of Gia Hoi.

Still mad about the loss of Stevens, Captain Messina wanted us to patrol in the area of Phu Nu but I had talked him out of it. With acting sergeants taking the places of Sergeants Little and Burkholtz, and six new guys filling the ranks of other veterans who had left, I wanted something a little less dangerous. A sort of shakedown cruise, I told him, and if he didn't approve of the analogy he accepted the logic.

"I thought the mosquitoes disappeared after the rains," I said, studying the village from the tree line.

"No, Sir," Cisco said. The rice paddies had all but dried up but the mama sans were still threshing and winnowing the grain while the men bagged the finished product for storage or market. Or the VC. A young boy stood at the edge of the village, staring right at us until his mother grabbed his arm and yanked him away.

"Get Allen, Simpson, and Brokovitch up here," I said. Cisco slipped his rucksack off and disappeared into the foliage, returning a minute later with the squad leaders.

"We're going to search the village," I said. "They already know we're here so there'll be no surprises. They've had plenty of time to hide anything they don't want us to find but this is a good opportunity to break in the new guys. Everything by the book."

"Even the hearts and minds crap?" Brokovitch said. Allen and Simpson laughed."That goes double for the hearts and minds crap," I said. "In case you haven't noticed, we've got enough enemies around here. Let's not do the VC's job for them. Brokovitch, your squad will set up the cordon. Everyone else will search the hootches. Have your new guys paired up with a veteran. Except for Nolan," I said looking at Brokovitch. Nolan was the reason I wanted third squad to cordon off the village. I didn't want him out of my sight. More than that, I wanted Nolan to know I was watching him. Brokovitch nodded that he understood.

We moved out across the paddies. The sun was blistering and the muck sucked at our boots as soon as they broke through the thin layer of dried earth. One of the new guys tried to escape the mud by walking on a dike and Acting Sergeant Simpson jumped in his shit, grabbing his sleeve and yanking him back into the paddy. "You new guys listen up," he yelled. "If you were a gook, where would you set up your booby traps? On the dikes," he said. "To get some lazy ass American who doesn't want to get his boots dirty." He slapped the new guy gently on the back of his head. I couldn't help but smile. Simpson was going to make a good sergeant.

The village gave up nothing but an ancient shotgun and a dozen shells, the cardboard casings mushy from the damp. Boyd had found the gun leaning against the wall of a hootch in plain sight. An old papa san sat on the dirt floor and watched as Boyd broke open the gun and tried to extract the shell that had rusted itself into the chamber. The papa san grinned and mimed shooting a bird. "Good luck," Boyd said and put the gun back where he found it.

We broke for lunch just east of a trail that followed the Mu Dai River. Normally we might have followed the trail, the point man moving slowly to find any booby traps, but I wanted to make the point to the FNGs that trails were to jungles what dikes were to rice paddies--booby-trap alleys.

The plan was to ambush a footbridge to a large island in the river about three miles upstream from Gia Hoi. I had never been there but it was on the map and a couple of the older guys had crossed it early in their tours when they were mapping out a ground route to Wild Turkey.

My plan was to cross the bridges and familiarize myself with the terrain on the other side of the river, but the bridge to the island had been washed away by the monsoons and had not yet been repaired. Old timbers and newly cut logs lay like pick-up-sticks on the bank; otherwise there was little sign that repairs had begun.

"Who's responsible for fixing the bridge?" one of the new guys asked.

"The Gia Hoi Highway Department," Cisco said. I gave him a look that said I was not in the mood for his humor. "I saw their truck about a mile back," he said. I looked at my watch. It was too soon to set up an ambush so I decided to push upriver a ways, then return and ambush the trail at the bridge after dusk.

The vegetation was thicker upriver from the island where the Mu Dai backed up onto a large floodplain during the monsoons. Corbet had to drop his rucksack several times to hack his way through the vines and creepers with a machete. Twice he relinquished the blade to his slack man to give his arm a break. Half an hour in and I gave second squad the point. Boyd was their new point man with Murphy walking slack. Right from the start Boyd paced himself, handing off the machete as soon as his arm started to ache; Murphy did the same, the rest of the platoon sitting down until enough of a path was cleared to make getting up worth-while.

Even sitting was enervating in the June heat and Doc Cook was constantly moving up and down the line making sure everyone was taking their salt and getting enough water. I called a halt just before four thirty and gave the men twenty minutes for supper before heading back. I ate my supper on the fly, chewing date nut bread as I met with each squad to tell them the plan.

"Keep the noise down," I said, coming up to Simpson's squad. "The trail is just over there," I said, pointing toward the river. The old guys had pointed out the steep slope of Mount Everest on the other side of the river and were razzing Dell and Newell, telling them they would remain FNGs until they climbed it. Despite my assertion that I made my decisions without regard to race, I had put Dell in Simpson's squad to avoid another black clique from forming after Stevens and Sgt. Little left. Nolan, I thought, would be an even worse influence on him after he'd been busted.

"We're going back by way of the trail," I said, directing my remarks to Dell and Newell. "We try to keep off trails for the same reason we keep off dikes. The other place they're likely to booby-trap or ambush is the way we came. That's why we're using the trail on the way back. Got it?" I said.

"Yessir," Newell said. Dell just nodded, his eyes dull, like there was little there. I couldn't tell if he was tired or hostile, like I had insulted him by telling him something he had already had hammered into him in AIT.

We made good time back to the bridge, arriving while there was still enough light for setting up an ambush. Too much light some would argue, but I wanted the new guys to set up the claymores under the supervision of the veterans and for that we needed descent visibility. I didn't want half the platoon blown away by a misplaced claymore. Darkness fell quickly and the moon did not come out until just before midnight, long after the mosquitoes.

* * *

"El Tee." It was the hand shaking my shoulder, not the voice that woke me up. Cisco gave me the handset. "Old Crow's getting hit. Mortars." I listened; the radio had gone silent but I could hear the explosions off in the distance. I tried to tune them out and listened for the sound of a mortar round leaving the tube. Nothing. I counted four more explosions before they stopped, then listened to the radio long enough to wonder if TOC had taken a direct hit. I was just about to call them when the radio came to life. Captain Messina was requesting an urgent dust off for a WIA. Choppers did not fly at night unless it was serious so I knew the situation was life-threatening.

Within five minutes the dustoff pilot came on the net saying he was on the way, ETA twelve minutes. It was still Cisco's watch but I couldn't sleep, waiting for word of the extraction when another voice--not Captain Messina's--canceled the dust-off. The WIA was now a KIA. They could pick him up in the morning.

Losing someone from your own company hurt whether you knew him or not. You had seen him around, would recognize his face, maybe even have exchanged a few words in passing. He was a brother, if not a friend. It might even be Gary.

Cisco nudged me with the handset. "Captain Messina," he said. It had been fifteen minutes since the dustoff was canceled. I pressed the transmit bar. "X-ray One Actual, over" I said.

"This is X-ray Actual. How soon can you get to Gia Hoi? Over." I had no answer, wasn't even sure what he was asking. Did he mean how long it would take us to get there if we left now--at night--or in the morning? I was about to ask him for clarification but he came back to me first. "I know your objections but I want you to get to Gia Hoi ASAP and set up an ambush on the east side, preferably on a trail where you can still see any activity from the village. I'm hoping to get that mortar squad returning to their village; if they're from Gia Hoi you're in a good position to do that. Over."

Gia Hoi was two klicks away; it was night with just a sliver of a moon and the only way to get there was by bushwhacking or taking a trail. And I had a platoon full of FNGs and acting sergeants with little experience as NCOs. I squeezed the transmit bar.

"This is X-ray One. At least two hours, over."

"Then get a move on and keep me informed. X-ray Actual, out." I took that to mean I had just been given an order without the option for discussion.

"You're shitting me," Cisco said.

"Start packing," I said and went to notify the rest of the platoon.

"Any word on who got wounded?" Simpson asked after I gathered the squad leaders.

"He died before the chopper got there," I said. "I don't know who it was."

"Bastards," someone said

"Captain Messina thinks they might have come from Gia Hoi. He wants us to get over there ASAP and maybe catch them on the way back." I was waiting for their resistance. Instead I saw heads nodding in the moonlight. A flash of a smile.

"Payback is a motherfucker, eh El Tee?" Brokovitch said.

"Oh yeah!" Simpson said. Only Sgt. Allen said nothing. If he had an objection, he didn't voice it. I decided not to let the moment pass.

"The only question is how to get there." This I threw out for discussion. Everyone looked to Brokovitch.

"No way can we bushwhack through this shit at night. Gotta be the trail," he said.

"I hate to ask this…" I said. Brokovitch must have known what was coming.

"I know. Back on point," he said. He probably thought he'd left that job behind when he accepted the acting sergeant position.

"You don't have to do it if you don't want to."

"Shit," he said. "Still need a couple more grenade pins for that necklace."

"Okay. We leave in five. Get those claymores in. No new guys. Brokovitch, it ain't a race. No more KIAs tonight."

* * *

Brokovitch's blood was up and he moved at a pace I thought too fast for the meager light of the moon and his flashlight. Still, we made it to Gia Hoi without incident until the village curs announced to all that all was not as it should be.

"Good job," I said. Brokovitch had insisted that no one walk slack, reasoning that he would not be able to see an ambush ahead anyway and there was no sense putting another man at risk should he trip a booby-trap. "How many trails coming in from that side?" I asked, pointing to the east side of the village.

"Two, three," he said.

"I want to set up a backward L-shape ambush, the long side paralleling one of the trails, the short side facing the village," I explained. The two sides would then be covering differing fields of fire so there would be no friendly fire incidents should we catch anyone out after curfew.

He moved out, staying in the moon shadow of the tree line looking for a break in the jungle once he was opposite the village. After a few minutes he stopped and waved me forward.

"Wait here. I'll check it out." He disappeared into the dark of the jungle and was back in less than a minute. "Trail takes a sharp turn twenty yards in," he said and without further discussion he moved on. We went through the same routine at the next trail only this time it took several minutes before he returned. "This looks good," he said.

The dogs started up again as we set up the ambush--the sergeants setting up machine gun positions at both ends of the ambush. I ordered a 50% watch. Sergeants Brokovitch and Simpson positioned their men along the trail while I settled in with Sgt. Allen's squad in the tree line facing the village. We were spread thin so I had Cisco leave the radio with me while he joined Simpson's squad. The village stood out in dark silhouette against the paddies and, as the moon continued its rise, I heard a small ruckus behind me. I turned to Sergeant Allen.

"Tell those guys to keep the fuckin' noise down," I hissed. He turned to move away just as Sgt. Simpson reached our position.

"Anybody seen Murphy?" he said, excited.

"Shit," I mumbled under my breath. "Where is he?" A stupid question, directed at Simpson. "Anybody seen Murphy?" I said, this time to the rest of Sgt. Allen's squad. No one had seen him since we broke the last ambush site. "Did anybody wake him at the bridge?" This to Acting Sergeant Simpson. Simpson seemed flustered.

"Last I saw him was just before we left. I had him on rear security."

"Well, who was next in line?"

"Newell, Sir. He didn't know. He was just followin' the guy in front of him." Newell was a new guy and no one had told him that he was responsible for the man walking rear security.

"Shit," I said.

"We goin' back for him?" Simpson asked. He felt responsible, and he was. I didn't spend much time thinking about it. The platoon was already jittery enough, moving around at night. I remembered a story I had heard in basic training about how the VC would sneak up on a unit, slit the throat of the last man in line, then ambush the platoon when they came back looking for him. I'd always regarded the story as drill sergeant bullshit. Now I wasn't so sure.

"No," I said. "Check again. Make sure he's not here and then report back. And make sure everyone else is here," I added as an afterthought. "Sgt. Allen?"

"We're all here," he said.

"Well, thank God for that." I'd already called in the new ambush site and spent the next few minutes figuring out how to cover my ass on this one. It didn't take long to realize I couldn't.

"No Murphy. Everyone else is here," Simpson said when he got back.

"Okay. Nothing we can do until morning. Just let everyone know we got a man out. No shooting at a single man unless they're sure it's not Murphy." Simpson left and I picked up the handset.

"You want to make the call?" I said to Sgt. Allen.

"Way above *my* pay grade," he said. I pressed the transmit bar.

"X-ray Kilo, X-ray Kilo, this is X-ray One, over."

"X-ray one, this is X-ray Kilo, over."

"X-ray Kilo, X-ray One. Be advised we have one MIA, over." There was a long pause.

"Say again, over."

"Be advised, we have one Mike India Alpha, over."

"Stand by, X-ray One…." The next voice I heard was Captain Messina's.

"X-ray One, this is X-ray Actual. Understand you have one MIA, over."

"Affirmative, X-ray. Over."

"Please report last known position of MIA, over."

"Last seen in transit from our last position, over." There was another pause while Captain Messina considered the situation.

"X-ray One, please give phonetic initials of MIA, over." Every one called Murphy *Audi*. I didn't remember his real first name.

"Anybody know Murphy's real first name," I whispered to anyone who could hear.

"Audie," PFC Williams answered eagerly. Williams was the black replacement I had assigned to Sgt. Allen's squad. I could hear the rest of the squad laughing quietly, calling Williams a dip shit for not knowing who Audie Murphy was.

"Knock it off," I said and pressed the transmit bar. "X-ray Kilo, X-ray One, regarding initials of MIA – nickname *Alpha*, last name *Mike*, over."

"Roger, X-ray One. Stay put for tonight. Keep me informed, over."

"Roger. X-ray One, out." To my surprise, Captain Messina sounded more down than mad. I guessed he felt some responsibility for the situation he had put us in too. In this case, at least, there was plenty of blame to go around. Only time would tell if some of that blame could be shared by PFC Murphy as well.

Chapter 27

"Murphy?" Silence. "Murphy, that you?" No answer. I sat up, trying to locate the voice. The calm was shattered by machinegun fire. I buried my face in the dirt. Several M-16s joined the racket. The rest of Sgt. Allen's squad was also making love to mother earth, unable to join the fray behind them and trying to become as small a target as possible. Someone blew their claymore. Then another. The machinegun fired another long burst, then a series of short bursts. I heard no rounds passing overhead, felt no vegetation fluttering down around me.

"Stay down," I said. I worked my way behind Simpson's and Brokovitch's squads and dropped down next to Caulkins. Caulkins had taken over as gunner when Stevens was killed and Voit was now his assistant. I let the shooting continue until I was sure there was no return fire before calling a halt.

"What's going on?" I said in hushed tones. Caulkins jumped up from behind his gun.

"Stupid motherfucker!" he screamed. He grabbed Voit by his shirt, lifted him almost to his feet and threw him sprawling on his back. Voit was bigger than Caulkins but the enraged black man must have seemed like a giant as he loomed over him. "You almos' got me kilt, motherfucker! Stupid cherry motherfuckers gonna get us all kilt!" Voit was scurrying backwards like a crab, afraid Caulkins would follow up on his assault.

"Knock it off," I said but it was like Caulkins didn't even know I was there.

"You think Murphy's gonna be coming down *that* trail?!" he demanded, spittle flying from his mouth. "You see someone coming down that trail at night you waste him! Callin' out like that! What the fuck you thinking' man?!"

"Knock it off," I said. "What happened? Voit, you first."

"I saw someone coming down the trail," he sputtered, arranging himself into a less ridiculous posture. "I thought it might be Murphy. I didn't want to shoot Murphy."

"Twice he calls out!" Caulkins said. "Twice! Wakes me up. I knock him out of the way and open up on the motherfucker."

"Just one?"

"Didn't catch but a glimpse of him. He was jumpin' off the trail jus' as I opened up on him," Caulkins said. His voice was becoming more modulated as the fear and adrenalin started to subside.

"Think you got him?"

"Hell, I don't know. I shoulda shot *him*!" he said, looking at Voit.

"Don't kill him. Train him," I said. I looked at my watch: 4:38. "Okay, 100% watch for the rest of the night," I ordered and returned to my position.

"What the fuck was that all about?" Sgt. Allen said, talking quietly but not whispering. It was no secret where we were now.

"Gook on the trail. Everyone on watch til morning."

"They get 'im?" Romansky asked.

"Hope so," I said. "Only thing that will save this from being the most fucked up mission ever."

"Proud to serve under you, Sir." I recognized the voice. Slick Slack.

"Thought I was going to get a break from Cisco's bullshit," I said. "One fuckin' night. Just one fuckin' night is all I ask."

"Not a chance, El Tee. Not a chance." Muffled laughter all around.

* * *

The sun wasn't yet over the mountain but it was already light. I kept the ambush intact a while longer, hoping the mortar squad that attacked Old Crow had waited until morning to return to their base, but there was little hope of that now. The best I could hope for was that the gook last night was part of that crew and that we would at least get a blood trail, if not a body, out of it. I also wanted to give Murphy a chance to show up on his own before going back to look for him, but I was getting itchy. Sitting around with a man missing did not sit well with me. Others felt the same. Cisco came through the brush.

"Caulkins wants to check out the trail. See if he got that gook," he said. I was getting anxious too.

"Not alone. Have him take Brokovitch. And Boyd."

"Boyd?" Boyd was not in Brokovitch's squad but I thought his supposed tracking skills might be helpful.

"Yes. Boyd," I said. "Tell everybody to pack up. We're leaving in ten minutes."

The villagers were getting anxious too. The breakfast fires were burning and several women were already threshing rice. The dogs, already used to us, were sniffing around the cooking fires while children wandered to the outskirts of the village, staring in our direction. An old man was walking across the paddies to the south. He stopped where I thought there was another trail into the jungle and started hoeing the dried earth. He faced the trail and appeared to be going through the motions rather than doing any real work. We'd been there too long. Cisco nudged me in the side.

"Your lucky day, Sir," he said, pointing toward the river upstream of the village. Murphy was standing at the trail head, his hand shielding his eyes from the sun as he scanned the tree line looking for us. I stood up and, stepping into the open, waved. He was a quarter mile away but I could still see his smile when he waved back and started walking across the paddies toward us.

PFC Voit came up, took a moment to watch Murphy before he spoke. "They found a blood trail, Sir. They're following it now."

"Well tell them to hurry up," I said. My irritation was quickly replaced by the hope that they'd recover a body. An enemy kill would help mitigate all the other things that had gone wrong.

"Miss me?" Murphy grinned, still ten yards away. Word had spread quickly and the ambush disintegrated into a clusterfuck of happy soldiers, none happier than me. Cisco had already notified Captain Messina that our MIA had returned.

"Where were you?!" I said. "We were freakin' out."

"*You* were freakin'?" he said.

"What the fuck happened?"

"I thought I heard something behind us so I stepped off the trail and waited until I was sure no one was following us," he said. "I hurried to catch up but I couldn't find you. Finally realized I must of gotten lost on some side trail so I figured I better stay put til morning. Soon as I could see I made my way back to the river trail and just followed it. I knew you'd be here somewhere so…I heard shooting last night. That you guys?"

Brokovitch was coming down the trail carrying Boyd's rifle. I went to meet him; he answered my question before it was asked.

"They're right behind me," he said. "It was just a deer."

"A deer?!" I said. "What took you so–"

"Boyd wanted to gut it out." At that moment Boyd and Caulkins came out of the jungle dragging a small deer by its front legs."

"What the hell do you think we're going to do with that!?" I demanded. I could see that it had been hit once in the hip and at least twice in the gut.

"Give it to the village," Boyd said.

"You gutted a deer so you could give it to the gooks!?"

"Indigenous personnel," Boyd, corrected me.

"He fuckin' crazy, El Tee," Caulkins said. "Mother fucker slits 'im open an' pulls out all his shitty guts an' then…an' then," he went on, as if he wouldn't have believed it if he hadn't seen it with his own eyes, "an' then he saves some a it. Look at this shit," he said opening up the abdominal cavity with the toe of his boot so that I could see inside.

"Hearts and minds. Isn't that what you said, Sir?" Boyd said.

"Yeah, hearts an' *minds*," Caulkins said. "Not hearts an'… what you say that other thing is?"

"Liver."

"I just wanted to get out of there," Caulkins said.

"Sergeant Allen."

"Yes, Sir."

"Take your squad and bring that papa san back here. The one pretending he's gardening. The rest of you, saddle up. We're leaving as soon as they get back."

The old man did not come willingly; Romansky and Slick Slack each had an arm, propelling him along as fast as his old legs would carry him. He picked me out as the leader and started jabbering, begging, I assumed, for his life. All I could make out was *no VC*.

"No crocodile. No crocodile," I said to calm him, but the man kept blabbering.

"Already told him, El Tee," Sgt. Allen said. Boyd took the man's hand and pulled him over to the dead deer.

"Take. Take," he said, pointing to the animal. "For you and mama san. Baby sans." The man gradually quieted down--no longer in fear for his life, but not sure what was wanted of him. Boyd lifted the deer's leg and placed the man's hand around it. "Take. Di di," he said, shooing him toward the village with his hand. The man pointed to himself, then the deer, and then the village.

"cho toi?"

"Yeah, yeah, for you," Boyd said. The man broke into a toothless grin.

"Cam on Ong. Cam on. Cam on," he repeated, bobbing his head and smiling.

"See, Sir. He's happy," Boyd said.

"Happy it ain't his grandson we killed," Caulkins said.

* * *

Captain Messina was still pissed off. He canceled our mission, ordering instead that we patrol Mortar Mountain until we found the enemy mortar or we ran out of time, whichever came first. I told Boyd to stay off trails, trying to make up for all the rules we'd broken the day before. I could only imagine what the new replacements thought of us. Boyd followed the contour of the hill for almost an hour and my right hip had taken on an ache that wouldn't quit. I stopped to give my muscles a break and waited for Cisco to catch up.

"You find out who the KIA was last night?" I asked.

"Heard some chatter, but I can't figure it out," he said. "Echo Five Hotel?" I immediately thought 'Holder,' but Gary's first initial would have been sent as *golf*, not *echo*. And why did they use *five* instead of *foxtrot*?

"You sure you got it right?"

"Pretty sure," Cisco said. "Maybe one of the new guys. Whaddya think, Sir? Time for a break?" I was just thinking the same thing when Doc Cook hurried forward.

"What is it?" I said.

"Williams is lookin' pretty whipped," he said. "Some of us aren't up to this yet."

"Tell Boyd to take a ten minute break," I said. "Actually, just tell him to take a break. He's been pushing us pretty hard. Breakfast if anyone wants it." I sent the signal back and sat down, my feet pointing downhill. "Dijya notice he never calls me *Sir*?" I asked.

"Who?" Cisco asked.

"Doc," I said. "Nolan too."

"Not really. Why? You getting a thing about that? Sir."

"Just an observation," I said. I took a drink of water.

"Sergeant Henry!" Cisco said suddenly.

"What?"

"Sergeant Henry. Echo Five Hotel. Echo Five isn't his initials, it's his rank. E-5 Henry." There was a moment of silence while that sunk in.

"Shit," I finally said. Sgt. Henry was well thought of not only as a good soldier, but also as a good guy.

"So that's why Captain Messina's got such a case a the ass."

It took a while for Doc Cook to work his way back to us as he was handing out salt tablets on the way. "By the way," I said after I took mine. "When you stop a column, do it from the front, back. Not from the back, forward." He gave me a look that said *what difference does it make?* "Did you notice how spread out the men were on your way back?"

"Not really." he said. Again no *Sir.*

"Well, notice how much closer together they are from here back," I said to make my point. He just looked at me. "And get that thing off your dog tag chain," I said, indicating the peace sign he had around his neck.

"Other guys are—"

"Not with their dog tags. If you have to wear it, put it on a separate rope."

"That'll teach 'im. *Sir,*" Cisco said after Doc moved off.

We spent the next four days patrolling the side of the mountain but found nothing that looked as if it had been used as a mortar site. The new men performed as well as could be expected. Even Doc Cook, whose politics and mother hen manner of looking after the men had earned him the distinction of being the first medic in the history of the U.S. Army to be nicknamed something other than *Doc*. The men called him *Hippie*.

Chapter 28

"Hey." I dropped my ruck just inside the entrance of the bunker.

"Hey," Gary said. He was laying on his bunk but I could barely see him. He had stuffed his poncho into our one small window cutting off both light and air.

"Sorry about Sergeant Henry," I said.

"Thanks." He hooked up the Christmas tree lights to the battery pack and lay back down. The lights cast soft shadows across floor.

"What happened?"

"He was checking the guards. First round hit about twenty yards from him. One piece of shrapnel. That was it. Took a piece out of his throat about the size of a quarter." There was nothing for me to say. "You should have seen his eyes. Doc was tryin' to blow air into his lungs but Henry kept spittin' up blood. Drowned was what Doc said. Not a good way to go." A long time passed.

I took off my boots and peeled my socks from my feet. "God I stink." I took my towel from around my shoulders and rubbed the dead skin off as best I could. "Boyd didn't take it well," I said.

"Um," Gary grunted.

"At first I thought it was you," I said. "Echo Five Hotel was all we heard. Hotel? Holder?" Gary said nothing. "You okay?"

"Just peachy," he said. He forced his shoulders back, stretching, then relaxed. "He was going to get married when he got home. Go to college. You know that?"

"No," I said. The lights went out; Gary fiddled with the wire. I pulled the poncho from the window. "Get some air in here." Gary squinted against the harsh light, then tossed the wires aside and accepted his fate. "My imagination or is the mortar pit smaller?"

"Not your imagination," he said. "The second round landed right in the pit. No one was in it yet but it fucked up the mortar. Nothin' left but the baseplate. Twisted the tripod all to hell, holes in the tube. Spooked the mortar guys so they made the pit smaller. How'd you make out? Who was it, the MIA? New Guy?"

"Murphy. He was walking rear security. Thought he heard something so he hung back to check it out, then couldn't find us. Bad part is, I had this idea of breakin' the new guys in right. Do everything the way we're supposed to, ya know. Then we do everything we told 'em *not* to do. We tell 'em never move after dark, then we move after dark. We tell 'em stay off the trails an' we walk the trails. We tell 'em not to set up a pattern, then spend five days searchin' the mountain in a pattern." Gary laughed.

"Don't forget Viet Bambi," he said. "That's what my guys are calling it."

"Oh God," I said. I noticed the mail on my bunk.

"Nothing from her," Gary said.

"Who?" I said, even though I knew who he meant.

"Abby?"

"Audrey," I said. "It wasn't like that. We didn't exchange addresses or anything."

"I think she knows where you live."

"You know what I mean," I said. The truth was I *was* hoping to hear from her. I wanted to see her before she went home but didn't want her to think I wanted anything more than what we already had. I told myself our last time together was just two people in need of human contact, and it was. We didn't really know each other, the time we'd spent together measured in hours rather than days. But there was something about her I couldn't put my finger on. She was pretty enough, but it was more than that. There was a sadness about her that brought out something in me. Gary read my mind.

"Don't get hung up over here," he said. "You're too vulnerable. You know Merry had a whore in town? Wanted to marry her?"

"You're shittin' me. Merry?" I said. "What happened?"

"She married some black guy instead. First ticket out."

"Not the same thing," I said. "But I know what you're saying."

"I'm wise beyond my years," Gary said. There were two letters from my mother and one from my uncle. I rarely heard from my old friends. They were too busy moving on with their lives. I tossed the letters aside, saving them for later.

"I guess I better get my debriefing out of the way," I said, looking around for my sandals. I couldn't bring myself to put my boots back on. "Captain pissed?"

"Not at you," he said.

"He's not mad that I just led the most fucked up patrol ever?" Gary turned on his side, propped his head on his hand like we were at a sleepover.

“Connors--he was on radio watch--said the captain didn’t get any sleep that night. Kept wakin’ up an’ asking if the MIA was back yet. Guess he felt responsible, makin’ you move your ambush in the middle of the night like that.”

“He was,” I said. Gary gave me a look that said I wasn’t being fair, but he wasn’t the one that had to put his entire platoon at risk. To be honest, I wanted to get the VC mortar crew as much as anyone. The question was, what price would we have to pay to get them, and who would pay it?

* * *

We could see the Chinook lifting off from Wild Turkey, its two top rotors lifting the behemoth off the helipad before turning in our direction. When it landed the back ramp came down like the front of a landing craft. We waited for the men from Second platoon to disgorge and then ran up the ramp, taking their places on the webbed seats lining the sides of the chopper.

Lt. Petros’s platoon had been scheduled to patrol on their side of the Mu Dai but Captain Messina was serious about finding that VC mortar site and changed the assignment. Sgt. LoPresti was convinced the mortar rounds came from Mortar Mountain despite the fact that we had been aggressively patrolling the area for as long as I’d been there.

The plan had been for second platoon to hump it from Wild Turkey to Mortar Mountain, but upon learning that the bridge over the Mu Dai was out and the river would not be fordable for another month, Captain Messina decided to chopper them to Old Crow and start the patrol from there while I took part of my platoon to cover Wild Turkey.

Life was good at Wild Turkey. Even though I saw things in the defenses that I would have done differently, it was Lt. Petros’s base and I was in no position to change things. I set up the night LPs and tended to the duty roster but otherwise spent my time reading, catching up on my letter writing, listening to the chatter on the radio, and following second platoon’s progress on the map.

On my second day there I got a call from Captain Messina. He wanted me to go to Hardscrabble to supervise quartermaster inventory while Lt. Avery was at Vung Tau on an in-country R&R.

It would be my last chance to see Audrey before she DEROSed but I fought the urge to see her one last time. I told myself not seeing her was the best thing for her but the truth was I was taking the coward's way out. I wanted to avoid the inevitable talk of the future. Gary was right.

I spent all day on the inventory--eating C-rations in the orderly room rather than risk running into Audrey at the mess hall--and caught a chopper back to Wild Turkey in the morning.

I was surprised to find that I liked being in charge at Wild Turkey and even more surprised at my feelings when Captain Messina called to tell me my new platoon sergeant had arrived. Sgt. Nelson had left a sour taste in my mouth and, having gained both experience and confidence in the five months I'd had the platoon I did not like the idea of having to share my authority. Ever so gradually, it had become *my* platoon. I'd earned the respect of the old guys, and the new guys looked on me as an old salt. I did not want things to change.

As it turned out, Sergeant First Class Poole was not at all what I expected.

Chapter 29

Lt. Petros had no better luck finding the mortar site than Gary or I had. Their mission had accomplished little other than to familiarize second platoon with new territory and to add more doubt in Captain Messina's mind that we were looking in the right place.

SFC Poole was at the helipad when we returned to Old Crow. At first sight I thought he was a new replacement. I had expected someone older, or at least older looking. I assumed an E-7 would have been in the Army at least a dozen years but the man who introduced himself to me appeared to be no more than twenty-five years old. We shook hands and I asked him to meet me in my bunker in an hour.

Sgt. Poole was black, his fatigues new guy green, and he put me off right from the start. "So what's the platoon like?" he asked, as if he was conducting the interview.

"It's a good platoon," I said. "Lots of new guys, so we've got some work to do."

"That can be a good thing," he said, as if I didn't know the advantages of getting replacements that hadn't had time to get into bad habits. I had just decided to take control of the conversation when he startled me with his next comment. "I'm sort of a new guy myself, so I look forward to learning from your experience."

Normally, senior NCOs give young officers the benefit of *their* experience. Sgt. Nelson delighted in *not* giving me the benefit of what he knew. Now Sgt. Poole was suggesting that I had more to offer him than he had to offer me. I took in his fatigue shirt at a glance. He had the 53rd Division patch sewn onto his left sleeve, but the right sleeve was bare and there was no CIB.

"How long have you been in the Army?"

"Almost 16 years, Sir." He saw my confusion. "I got drafted right after the Korean War started but I ended up on occupation duty in Germany. I re-upped to be a drill sergeant. Liked it. Seemed to have a talent for it. Spent the next thirteen years stateside, training troops or getting trained myself, and here I am." I didn't know what to say.

"Married?"

"Three kids," he said. He did not pull out pictures.

"What other training did you have?"

"Six months at Fort Sill, artillery forward observer school. Jump school, pathfinders, five weeks of ranger school, til I broke a leg. Platoon Sgt. with the 82nd Airborne until I got sent here." Aside from a lack of combat experience it was an impressive resumé.

"You aren't wearing your jump wings," I observed. He shrugged as if it wasn't a big deal.

"You didn't want an airborne unit?"

"I go where they send me," he said. I didn't know if that was a sign of acquiescence, or laziness. I would find out soon enough.

* * *

Three days later the promotion orders for those we recommended for the ranks of specialist 4, corporal, and buck sergeant came through. Everyone we recommended got their promotion, even PFC Boyd, who got a corporal spot ahead of more experienced spec. 4s. The army is not a union shop.

Captain Messina had bought both cloth and medal insignias of rank which he handed out at an informal ceremony with the entire platoon assembled. When he was done he announced that there was one more promotion and called me forward and presented me with a small blue box with the silver bars of a first lieutenant inside.

"Congratulations, Lt. Sullivan. Well deserved." He shook my hand and the platoon joined in with a chorus of cheers and well intentioned--I hoped--jabs. Promotions to first lieutenant are often routine after paying your dues as a second lieutenant so I was more pleased with Captain Messina's *well deserved* comment than with the promotion itself. And one other thought popped into my head that both surprised and startled me--the idea that the one thing missing to make the moment perfect would be if Audrey had been there to share it with me.

* * *

Sgt. Poole pointed to a spot on the map, touched it with the tip of his finger. "You're sure?" I said.

"Sure," he said.

"What difference does it make?" Slick Slack said and he was right. I was stalling.

"You saw the guns?"

"They were wrapped up in something," Slick Slack insisted.

"Coulda been guns. What else could it be? Look at him!" He was frustrated with my lack of decisiveness but I didn't want to make a mistake and shoot an innocent civilian. From our cover in the tree line I looked at the man/boy--he was too far away to tell which--but he was certainly acting suspiciously. He was behind a paddy dike, pawing away at the dirt and looking around like a kid raiding the cookie jar.

"What do you think?" This addressed to Sgt. Poole.

"You saw as much as I did, Sir," was all he said. I felt my anger flare until I recognized that he didn't want to be responsible for a wrongful death any more than I did. And when it came right down to it, it was my responsibility no matter what he thought.

Gary's mission had yielded nothing regarding the VC Mortar site. Captain Messina had them check out every place we might have missed on previous patrols--low marshy spots, areas of thick vegetation we might have skirted because the going was too tough and the terrain deemed it an unlikely place for even the gooks to go. He even had them walk the ridge line along the top of Mortar Mountain where the treeless, rocky slope made it an unlikely place to set up a mortar pit as it was too visible.

Captain Messina decided he couldn't justify spending any more time looking for ghosts and sent us back to the bridge site to see if it had been repaired and to look for likely fording places on the way. We found one place we thought was fordable but the water proved too deep and too fast and our scout had to turn back before getting halfway across. Nothing had been done to the bridge since the last time we were there. I decided to ambush Gia Hoi that night but while bushwhacking our way to the back side of the village we came upon an extensive paddy network that didn't show on the map.

Slick Slack was walking point and he called us forward when he saw someone walking across a dike carrying a bundle about the size of a bunch of rifles.

"He's going to get away," Slick Slack said, impatient. I considered trying to take him prisoner but he was a long way off and if we were where Sgt. Poole said we were, Gia Hoi was less than a half mile away. I didn't want to get surprised by any of his buddies who might be providing cover.

"Get Boyd up here. Leave the radio," I said. Cisco hurried off. I looked at the map again. The paddies were dry now and we were a good ways from the river. "Where does the water come from? For the paddies?" I thought aloud.

"Who gives a shit?" Slick Slack muttered. He saw an easy kill and his blood was up. Sgt. Poole ran his finger over a broken blue line where an intermittent stream ran off the back side of Mortar Mountain. During the monsoon the place would be flooded.

"Hey," Boyd said, dropping down next to me. His request for sniper school had been turned down and he still carried his M-14.

"Can you hit him from here?" I asked.

"Yessir," he said. He asked no questions. Instead he started clearing away any vegetation in his way and took up the prone position.

"Why don't we just blast him with everything we got?" Slick Slack said. "The guy's 500 yards away."

"Because he's 500 yards away," I said. "First round passes over his head an' he'd be behind the dike, low crawlin' it to the trees." The man in the paddy stood up, wiped his forehead with the bottom of his black pajama top.

"You better be right about those guns," I said to Slick Slack. He hesitated.

"I didn't say I actually saw—"

"Anytime," Boyd said.

"Whenever you're ready," I said before I could change my mind. Boyd held his breath and steadied himself just as the man bent over to work on the dike.

"Shit," Boyd muttered. It was then the thought occurred to me that the bundle the man was carrying might be tools and that he was there to fix a break in the dike. The man stood up again. I was about to say something when a shot made me jump.

"You're low. You hit the dike about six inches from the top." It was Sgt. Poole, spotting with his binoculars. I felt a wave of relief wash over me.

"Huh? Shit!" Boyd muttered. "Forgot to adjust the fuckin'—" I looked to see what Sgt. Poole was seeing. "What's he doin?" Boyd demanded as he fiddled with his rifle.

"Just lookin' around. He don't know what's going on." Boyd flipped up the rear sights, fumbling the ladder up almost to its maximum range.

"Waitin' to die of old age." Slick slack, sarcastic.

My mouth was open, nothing coming out. Boyd tightening down the sight screws. Sgt. Poole saying something. I leaned toward Boyd as he took another breath, let half of it out. I put my hand on his shoulder, said *wait* but heard nothing but another shot exploding in my ear. I looked toward the paddy. For a full second I thought Boyd had missed again. Then the man's torso snapped back, a pink mist blossoming from his chest. He staggered--fell from sight.

"Nice shot," Sgt. Poole said. Something uncertain about his voice. The man in the paddies rose to his knees, only his head and shoulders visible above the dike.

"Again! Again!" This time Slick Slack. I looked again but there was nothing there but paddies and sky.

"He's done," Boyd said. My heart was pounding, my breath coming in short, shallow pants.

"Let's get him." Slick Slack was on his feet.

"Wait!" I said. Should we just leave him? Make up some reason why we didn't check for weapons? How would I explain that? Besides, I had to know. "Wait here. Cover us. Boyd," I said.

Boyd and I ran across the paddies, over one dike after another. I lost track of which dike the man was behind but Boyd didn't. He slowed to a walk once we were in the paddy before the dike. He stopped. I stopped. I kept looking at him as if he was in charge. He pointed to the spot on the dike where the man had fallen and made a wide circle to the left, his gun at the ready. I circled to the right, flipped the selector switch on my M-16 to full automatic, remembered to make sure Boyd wasn't in my line of fire if the man was still a threat, if he ever was. We mounted the dike and I knew immediately. The man was dead. Boyd covered me from the top of the dike while I dropped into the other paddy.

I could see a break in the side of the dike, the fresh dirt that had spilled around the burlap bundle. I laid my rifle next to the bundle and pulled the loose edge of the burlap. Three guns tumbled out into the dirt. I had never felt more relieved in my life. Not even when my girlfriend in college finally got her period.

Boyd came down off the dike and I joined him at the body. The boy--and that's what he was, sixteen or seventeen at most--was laying on his side, one arm pinned at an awkward angle beneath his body, his head facing the dike, as if he were trying to reach it before he died. A pool of blood had accumulated under his armpit. Boyd was standing above him, staring at what he'd done. If there was an expression on his face, I couldn't read it.

"Not like shooting an elk, is it?" I said. Boyd put the toe of his boot under the boy's arm and gave it a flick so that the body flipped over onto its back. Pink bubbles gurgled from the hole in his chest forming a frothy dome above the entrance wound.

"Actually, sir, it's almost exactly like killing an elk," he said.

* * *

The hole in the dike was large enough to hold a small man, or a stash of weapons. We pulled out a plastic bag containing over a hundred rounds of ammo, an unexploded 105 millimeter artillery round, a tangle of wires, and a U.S. issue battery pack for a PRC 25 radio. We took the guns and blew the rest in place after Boyd dragged the boy's body far enough away that the gooks could see his handiwork.

We tossed Gia Hoi too, and this time Corporal Corbet confiscated the old papa san's ancient shotgun that Boyd had let pass the last time we were through. We spent the next two days getting to Phu Nu. On a hunch, we made our approach from the back side of Mortar Mountain, not dropping down to the village until just before dark. We set up an ambush on a trail far enough away from the ville that the dogs didn't make so much as a whimper, but the night passed with nothing but negative sit reps.

At first light we went into the village and rousted the inhabitants, gathered them at a collection point and, while one squad checked IDs, the rest of the platoon searched the hootches. I searched the same hootch as the last time I was there. The old woman was no longer in the back room. Only her smell remained. Two young men we hadn't seen before had suspicious IDs, but again we were denied permission to send them back for interrogation. Even the new guys were pissed.

We refilled our canteens at the village well and headed back but before we had gone very far Captain Messina ordered us to check out the low ground between Mortar Mountain and the Crow's Nest--the name the men had given the mountain Old Crow was on.

Even well into the dry season the ground there was damp. The mosquitoes were vicious and so was the vegetation. We moved in two columns to cover more ground and we were making so much noise hacking our way through the prickers and wait-a-minute vines that I didn't even try to stem the stream of curses from the men as they struggled forward. Eventually I declared nature the winner and went to a single column, rotating the point every ten minutes while the rest of the platoon rested. Our mission deteriorated from finding the VC mortar site to just getting the hell out of there. Even Sgt. Poole said we were wasting our time, that the floor of the narrow valley was the last place he'd pick if he wanted to mortar Old Crow. The angle was just too steep.

By the time we got back the men were thoroughly drained--frustrated by our failures, but also pleased to be bringing home some booty--two captured M-16s, a Chinese SKS, a breach-loaded, shotgun with a shell rusted into the barrel, and one enemy KIA to credit to our company's account.

Only two shots had been fired but that was enough. SFC Arthur Poole had finally earned his Combat Infantryman's Badge along with six new replacements, none of whom hadn't been in the army a full year.

Chapter 30

Sgt. Poole quietly took over such jobs as sergeant of the guard, setting up duty rosters, inspecting weapons, and making sure everyone was properly equipped before going out on ambushes or LPs. He took it upon himself to make sure the men maintained a proper interval on patrol and enforced noise and light discipline at all times. In other words, he did his job, but for some reason it felt like he was intruding on my territory. Although he had no more combat experience than I had when I arrived, the men accepted his authority without question, recognized him as a leader without him having to earn it the way I did.

I resented the effortless way in which he earned the men's respect. He was the kind of platoon sergeant I had wanted Sergeant Nelson to be. But I had grown accustomed to being the sole man in charge. Sgt. Little had been more like a trusted assistant. Sgt. Poole had become, in the eyes of the men, my equal and I didn't like it.

On top of that, Cisco was mad at me. This was nothing new and whatever real or imagined slight I gave him, he usually got over it quickly. Not this time. At first I paid it little mind, but when his mood didn't improve after a week or so, I confronted him on it.

We were working Mortar Mountain again, ambushing trails two klicks east of Phu Nu. In Captain Messina's mind it was the pinkest of the hamlets in our AO and he suspected it was the hub of the mischief we had been getting from the VC mortar crew. We had taken a break after fighting through some particularly tough terrain and his sullen mood was getting on my nerves.

"So what's buggin' you?" I finally said, screwing the cap back onto my canteen.

"Nothin'," he said. Not *what do you mean?* or *about what?*, just *nothin'* so I knew he knew what I was talking about.

"Where's the old wiseass the platoon's grown to know and love?" I said. He said nothing for a long moment.

"Why didn't you put me in for sergeant?" he finally said. I was taken aback. Putting Cisco in for a promotion to sergeant had never occurred to me. Despite his sarcasm and lack of respect for radio protocol, I felt he was the best field RTO in the company. He was cool under fire and knew every frequency and call sign in the battalion by heart. But a squad leader? I couldn't see it.

"I didn't think you'd be interested in being a squad leader," I lied.

"Why didn't you ask?" I did not want to answer that.

"Are you? Interested?"

"Not really," he admitted. "But not all sergeants are squad leaders. Sgt. Nelson's in supply." He saw I had no answer for that. "Forget it," he said, but I wanted to make things right. Or at least not get blamed for my insensitivity.

"He's a senior NCO," I said. "It's different for buck sergeants."

"Whatever you say," he said. I was suddenly mad at him, wanted to tell him to grow up and get over himself, but didn't want to make things worse.

"Look, I'm sorry," I said. "And you're right. You deserve a promotion. I'll put you in for spec. 5 when we get back."

"Can't be a spec. 5 with an infantry MOS. I checked with Merry." He was right. The RTO at Wild Turkey who never left the firebase was a specialist 5--the same pay grade as a sergeant--but his MOS was that of a Radio/Telephone Operator. The RTOs humping the boonies were just infantrymen lugging around an extra 26 pounds of radio equipment. Not fair, but fair wasn't a big priority in Vietnam. "Forget it, Sir," he said. "Don't mean nothin'. I'm outta here in 31 days no matter what."

"I thought you were going to extend. Get an early out from the army."

"Fuck it," he said. "What's six months back in the world compared to another 23 days in this shithole?"

*   *   *

We worked the side of the mountain for two more days. It was the farthest away from Old Crow we had ever been the day before returning home and the men were grumbling. It had been almost a given that the last night in the field would be spent within a few hours of base camp so that our six day outing would actually be five days and a wake up. I heard someone mumble *who's he tryin' to impress?* The answer was, of course, Sgt. Poole. Once again I had put my own petty needs ahead of the men, but I didn't feel guilty. I told myself it was all about the mission.

For his part, Sgt. Poole considered it a soldier's right to

complain, but the one time I heard criticism directed at me within his hearing he told the man to knock it off. He always took the high road.

The morning of our last day we were still eight hours away from Old Crow. We broke ambush just after dawn and I allowed the men a half hour for breakfast after pushing them for more than an hour in the rising heat of the day. The temperature was in the nineties by eleven o'clock and the humidity was stifling. The sun broke through the jungle canopy only in scattered flashes but any relief the shade provided was negated by the foliage's ability to keep the heat from rising above our heads. The sweat clung to our skin and our skin stuck to our clothes.

Sgt. Poole worked his way forward from the back of the line. "Rough country," he said, falling in beside me. "Guess I'm not used to it yet." He didn't look any more tired than anyone else but I got his meaning.

"Me either," I said, feeling magnanimous. He was ten years my senior and I had no doubt he could walk me into the ground any time he wanted. "Cisco," I called ahead. Cisco turned. "Half hour for lunch as soon as he finds a good spot." I had no idea who was walking point. Sgt. Poole had taken over those duties as well. Cisco passed the word forward and two minutes later the line stopped. Apparently, this was as good a place as any. Sgt. Poole and I sat down and started pawing through our rucks. Cisco found someone else to eat with.

"You've done a good job with them," Sgt. Poole said. He sounded sincere and I believed him because I wanted to.

"Appreciate that, Sergeant," I said. I opened a can of pork slices and started cutting them into eatable pieces with my plastic spoon. "Ever wonder why anyone bothered to invent the fork when the spoon is all you need?"

"You been in the army too long," Sgt. Poole said.

"What about you? Sixteen years?" He shrugged.

"Different here," he said. "Everything here seems so…"

"Real," I said when he couldn't find the right word.

"Yeah," he said. "Good in a way, though. Like all that training wasn't for nothin'." In the line behind us Romansky laughed.

"Keep it down," Sgt. Poole said, just loud enough for the words to carry.

"Cisco's got a case of the ass," I said.

"I noticed. What's his problem?"

"Ever feel like you were dealing with a bunch of kindergarteners?"

"Most of 'em ain't that far from that," he said.

"Yeah, well. He's pissed I didn't put him in for sergeant. I asked him. He doesn't want to be a squad leader anyway," I said, not mentioning the fact that I didn't asked until after the promotion list came out.

"Not everyone's cut out for telling other people what to do," Sgt. Poole said, leaning against his rucksack. "That don't mean they ain't worth more than they gettin'." I felt a sudden flash of anger.

"You agree with him?"

"Jus' sayin', they's other ways a showin' 'preciation. Try slipin' another promotion to corporal past battalion. Put him in for a Commendation Medal. He a ditty-bopper, but he's a good RTO. And he's good for morale. Every unit needs a jerk-off to take the tension off every now and then, ya know?"

I was amazed at how quickly he had gotten the pulse of the platoon. I took another slug of canteen water and screwed the cap back on.

"Go ahead an' crap out if you want," I said. "I'll wake ya when it's time."

* * *

Fifty minutes after our lunch break Sgt. Brokovitch stopped the platoon, signaling it was time to switch point men. He was walking slack, breaking in PFC Colon on point--a gung ho type with less than a month in country. I took a seat on a downed tree and checked my water. Doc Hippie was working his way down the line, handing out malaria pills.

"How do the men look?" I asked, holding my hand out.

"Like they been carrying a bag of cement on their backs for five hours in ninety degree heat. Other than that, good." He said it as a statement of fact rather than as an accusation. He put a pill in my hand. The big yellow one.

"Monday already?"

"Time flies when you're havin' fun," he said. I popped the pill in my mouth and unscrewed the cap on my canteen.

"I expected better than that from you," I said and washed the pill down.

"Mind's a little fried," he said and started to move on.

"Sit down," I said. "You've got time." He looked reluctant, but sat anyway. "Ever wish you were just a grunt 'stead a running around lookin' after everyone else while they get to crap out?"

"No." he said, then smiled. "How 'bout you?"

"Every day," I said. He laughed. "You said you had a degree in liberal arts? From where?"

"Actually, I didn't finish. And liberal arts is just what I told the college. I was really majoring in girls, grass, and civil disobedience. What about you?"

"Just girls and beer. I couldn't handle three majors."

"Me either," he said. "That's how I lost my deferment." Sgt. Poole was coming our way, walking faster than usual.

"Sir, you're gonna want to see this," he said. There was a tinge of excitement in his voice. Not much, but the first time I'd ever heard it.

"Go ahead and finish your rounds," I said to Doc and then followed Sgt. Poole. "What's up?" I said.

"You're not gonna believe this, but I think we just found the mortar site."

"What! Who…?"

"Nolan was just going off to take a crap," he said. "It's a miracle he even saw it. It's nothing'. You'll see." We walked quickly, past several men, each wanting to know what was going on.

"Just stay alert and keep the noise down," Sgt. Poole would say.

We angled uphill from the line and I was surprised when I saw Nolan. I expected to see him standing smugly in a clearing amid the stumps of several downed trees, maybe in a shallow pit, maybe surrounded by a low wall of sandbags. Instead, there was nothing to distinguish the spot but a ragged oval of light on the jungle floor about seven yards long and four yards wide. He looked at me, the trace of that tell-tale smirk I hated so much. *Anybody but Nolan*, I thought.

"This is it?" was all I could think of to say. Sgt. Poole showed me where Nolan had brushed away a bunch of leaves and dead branches revealing a rectangle of flat concrete.

"Check it out sir," he said. He knelt down and pointed out a two foot wide depression about an inch deep in the concrete slab. "They put the baseplate in and then removed it before the cement dried so they could set it up in the exact the same spot every time. Even the bipod," he said, pointing to two small divots near the front corners of the rectangle. "And look at this." He got up and walked forward about a dozen yards. "Aiming stake. That's how Nolan spotted it."

"Reminded me of the aimin' stake Sgt. LoPresti showed us that time," Nolan said.

"I bet if you drew a line from the center of the baseplate to this stake it would point directly to Old Crow," Sgt Poole said.

"Noticed somepin' else," Nolan said, making sure he got full credit. He pointed up into a tree where a small platform had been erected where a man could look out across the valley to Old Crow and call down corrections to the mortar team. I looked at the site again. Only a single tree had been cut down plus a few branches from surrounding trees. Just enough to allow a mortar round to be fired through the canopy at a high angle.

With the sun directly over head the ground below was conspicuously brighter, but within an hour the sunlight would be diffused through the trees so that the site would be undetectable to someone more than a few yards away. We'd probably walked within a few yards of it several times without suspecting a thing. Even from a chopper, it was unlikely anyone would notice anything out of the ordinary.

"Good job, Nolan," I said. He replied with nothing but his smirk. "Okay, let's get a man up there and get a back azimuth from Old Crow. Sgt. Poole, I want every bit of litter from our guys picked up. No cans, no spoons, not so much as a cigarette butt. Tell the sergeants it's their ass if one of their men leaves so much as a trace that we were here. Nolan, you go with him. Tell Cisco to get up here. Everybody walks lightly from now on."

I called Old Crow to tell Captain Messina the good news and asked him to have Sgt. LoPresti and his crew standing by in the mortar pit. When the rest of the platoon arrived Sgt. Poole organized a search of the area for any sign of trails leading to the site, weapons caches, or anything else that might prove useful. They were instructed to be thorough, but to create as little disturbance to the area as possible. Murphy volunteered to climb up to the platform.

"Here, take these," Sgt. Poole said, giving Murphy his compass and a metal hand mirror.

There were no notches cut into the tree; no steps nailed to the trunk so we boosted Murphy as high as we could and from there he had to shinny up another twenty feet before reaching branches strong enough to hold his weight.

"Holy shit! You wouldn't believe the view from up here," he called down once he reached the platform.

"Never mind the view. Get a reading," Sgt. Poole said. Murphy pulled out the compass and sat with his legs dangling over the edge of the platform.

"Where? I can see the whole fucking camp."

"The mortar pit. Dead center." Murphy pulled his elbows into his sides to steady the compass.

"Just like shooting a rifle. Hold your breath," I called up. "We can't be even half a degree off."

"One…ninety……two. One ninety-two," he called down.

"Are you sure?" He went through the whole procedure again while Sgt. Poole figured the back azimuth.

"One ninety-two, Sir." Murphy yelled. "You should see--"

"Never mind that," I yelled. "Flash the mirror at them." I raised Captain Messina again and waited while the mortar crew got a fix on us.

"Zero one two," Sgt. Poole told me.

"They're all waving' at me!" Murphy yelled.

"Jesus Christ," Sgt. Poole grumbled. "Why don't we just carve *Kilroy was here* on the trunk of the tree." On the radio I could hear Captain Messina yelling for the men at Old Crow to knock it off.

"Oh, now they stopped," Murphy said, disappointed.

"Zero one two," Captain Messina said.

"Hear that?" I said. Sgt. Poole smiled.

"Good job," Sgt. Poole called up.

"Keep flashing," I yelled to Murphy when he started to put the mirror away. "They need to get a second reading so they can triangulate for distance."

When Murphy returned to earth his forearms were abraded and bleeding from sliding the last fifteen feet down the tree when his arms gave out. They looked worse than they had my first week at Old Crow when he got tangled up in the barbed wire.

"Jesus, Murphy," I said as Doc Hippie cleaned and dressed his wounds. "You've lost more blood since you got here than most people with a purple heart."

"More than yours, El Tee. That's for sure." Sgt. Poole looked at me.

"I'll tell you later," I said.

I decided to leave a squad of men behind to ambush the mortar site for two days in hopes that the VC would be back. It was a long shot, but not so long that just about everyone wanted in on it. Even Sgt. Poole. Especially Sgt. Poole. But I pulled rank. I wanted this for myself.

"I thought you were leaving for R & R in four days," he said.

"I've got time," I said. I wasn't sure if the disappointment on his face was because he couldn't get in on an easy kill, or if it was because he thought I lacked confidence in him. Either way, I told myself it would give him a chance to lead the rest of the platoon on his own. I picked the men to stay behind with me. I took Boyd because my confidence in him was growing every day; Calkins and Voit for the firepower, and Cisco. And Nolan, only because he said I owed him this and I had no argument for that. It was a small but deadly group and everyone was high on the possibilities.

The rest of the platoon gave us all the food they had and as much water as they could spare before leaving. We then picked our ambush site and settle in for the long wait.

Chapter 31

Picking an ambush site proved harder than I expected as we had no idea which direction the mortar crew might come from. We decided on a position forty yards away behind a downed tree. We kept two people on watch at all times, one keeping an eye out behind us so we didn't get ambushed ourselves. It was a waste of time.

After two days we were out of water and had to abandon the mission. We left the site as clean as possible and made it back to Old Crow, taking only one break along the way.

Captain Messina was happy though. Our mortar crew had zeroed our mortar on the coordinates they had worked out and had fused twenty rounds for the correct distance. Already they had rehearsed their response five times. They would drop the first five rounds exactly where they determined the mortar to be and then use the traverse and elevation knobs to cover a 75 yard square around ground zero.

Sergeant Poole had pre-registered a two hundred yard square around the site with a 175mm artillery battery ten miles away that could blanket the area within two minutes of his call. Given its distance from any villages or friendly positions, he had gotten permission to fire for effect without the usual precaution of firing a smoke round first. Captain Messina gave orders that no patrols were to go within a mile of the mortar site after dark. We were probably the only Americans in Vietnam looking forward to being hit by enemy mortars.

I caught a chopper to Hardscrabble the next morning to pick up my R & R orders and catch a ride to Cam Rahn Bay. Spec. 5 Merry was gone, his duties temporarily taken over by Master Sergeant Fowler who was not happy with his new job. I introduced myself, turned in my .45 and M-16, showered, changed into a clean set of fatigues, and checked in at Aviation. I was told my best bet was to catch a ride to Phu Cat and catch a flight out from there. I checked the time to see if I had time to get breakfast before the mess hall closed.

The cooks had already shut down the line when I got there but they gave me the last three shriveled sausages on the griddle and a piece of French toast. Two majors were enjoying their last cup of coffee in the officers' section. The only other person there was Karen, happily putting down her paperback and waving me over. I was surprised at how glad I was to see her. I guess I needed that R & R more than I thought.

"Hi," I said, putting my tray down opposite her. She shoved her hand in my face and wiggled her fingers. I had to lean back to see the tiny engagement ring on her finger.

"Oh," I said. "Congratulations. Who…"

"Bill, silly," she said. "I thought he was never going to ask me."

"When–"

"Yesterday," she said.

"No, I meant when are you getting married?"

"After we get home. Bill's a lifer so I don't know what I'm going to do. Probably get out, maybe work at a base hospital as a civilian until I have kids; then stay home and do the mom thing. Marlene's agreed to be my maid of honor. She DEROSed last week so I haven't asked her yet but I'm sure she will. I would have asked Audrey but she won't be there. And we'll have to find a place once Bill gets his orders. There's so much to work out and I haven't even told my mother–"

"Have you heard from her recently?" I said, finally getting a word in.

"My mother?"

"No. Audrey,"

"Have I heard from her?"

"Yeah. Has she written you or–"

"Didn't she tell you?"

"Tell me what?"

"She extended. Took a thirty day special leave to go home. She got back, what? Two weeks ago. I thought she told you."

"No." I was stunned. "Why didn't she say something?"

"It was kinda a last minute thing," Karen said. "Ask her yourself," she said, leaning over the table to punch me in the arm. "She's probably on the surgery ward." I had no choice but to see her, now that I'd talked to Karen; I wasn't sure I wanted one.

* * *

"Is Audrey around? I was told she might be here." At first the nurse didn't know who I was talking about but she was new, one I hadn't seen before.

"Oh, you mean…yeah. She's in her office." She pointed to a door at the end of the ward.

"Thanks," I said. The plaque on the door said *Capt. Audrey Kostanciak.* I knocked. The door was open but I stayed outside. Audrey looked up from her paperwork. At first she showed no reaction, then a slight smile creased her face.

"Congratulations," I said, commenting on her promotion.

"Come in," she said. She started around her desk like she was going to hug me, then changed her mind. An awkward moment passed before she motioned me to a chair.

"Have a seat," she said. "Got a minute?"

"Just," I said. "I'm leaving on R & R. I just ran into Karen and she told me you were still here. Why didn't you tell me?" She had cut her hair into a pixie with bangs halfway down her forehead, her ears showing. It made her hair look fuller, thicker, and it was all I could do to keep from reaching out and touching it.

"I didn't decide until the last minute," she said. "Major O'Shaughnessy had been after me to extend. Then, when he offered me a promotion and the head nurse's position…." She shrugged.

"Captain Kostanciak. Sounds like a super hero," I said. "How do you like it?"

"It's okay. Different. I don't do much in the way of patient care anymore and I miss that, but I still assist on surgeries so…. How about you? Where are you going?"

"Sydney. I hear it's nice." Actually, the guys who went there didn't say much about the country. What they said was the girls were *friendly*.

"It is," Audrey said. "Don't miss the zoo." Yeah, that's what I'm looking forward to, I thought. The zoo.

"That's where you went?"

"Uh huh," she said and smiled. "If you can tear yourself away from the Texas Tavern." Apparently that was *the* place to get drunk and meet girls. I started to say something when the ward nurse stuck her head in, apologizing for the interruption.

"That's okay. What is it?" Audrey said.

"Casualties coming in, ma'am," she said excitedly.

"How many?" Audrey. Calm.

"Three."

"I'll be right there," Audrey said. "Get Karen and Linda back here too." She came around the desk, came right up to me. "Sorry. Gotta go. Have fun in Australia. You deserve it," she said and rose up on her toes to kiss me on the cheek. I turned as she did, her lips brushing my cheek and coming to rest on the corner of my mouth. She held it there for only a second. More than a peck, but only a little more. *Shit*, was the word that popped into my mind as she hurried out the door.

* * *

The gate MP checked my orders, then ignored me as I asked drivers leaving the compound where they were headed. The fifth vehicle was a jeep with a PFC at the wheel, the passenger seat empty; the rear seats were filled with several unmarked crates.

"Where ya goin'," I asked as the MP checked his authorization to leave the base.

"Phu Cat," he said. "Want a lift?" I told him I did. The MP gave the boxes in back a cursory inspection and gave him back his papers.

"You know how to use this?" The PFC asked, indicating the M-16 on the passenger seat. I assured him I did. "Then climb in," he said.

Chapter 32

"Hey! Lieutenant Sullivan. Come on in!" Dr. Fletcher came around his desk, slapped me on the shoulder and waved me to my seat. "You look happy for a change." I was taken aback. I had always considered myself a happy person and the idea that he thought me being happy was not the norm surprised me.

"Just got back from R & R," I said.

"Ah! So how was it? Where'd you go?"

"Australia. Great. Hard to come back. Have you been?"

"I went to Hawaii."

"Oh, you're married," I said. Married men got to go to Hawaii on R & R so they could meet up with their wives.

"Very. I'm glad you stopped by."

"I stopped by earlier but your door was closed so…."

"I was talking to someone else." I noticed he didn't say he was seeing another patient. Very diplomatic. I had stopped to see Audrey first but she was in surgery and I was just passing time. He had stopped talking. Apparently it was my turn.

"Actually, I wanted to thank you for all your help and apologize for not getting that bio to you. I'm afraid I'm going to wreck that paper of yours. At least my part of it."

"Oh."

"Yeah. I'm fine. I mean, I haven't had any of those little visits since the last time I saw you so I figured… you know. I'm fine." He looked at me for a long moment, waiting for me to say something more.

"Why do you think that is? That you no longer have any more… visitors?" I had no answer so I made a joke of it.

"'Cause you cured me, Doc. No more Looney Tunes. Thea, thea, thea, that's all folks!" He smiled.

"Funny, I don't recall doing that. Curing you," he said.

"Well, it's not like you did anything, no offense. But you listened to my nonsense. That's what you guys do, isn't it? Listen? While we talk about our feelings and shit?" He just looked at me. "I mean, I know it's more than that, but you know what I mean." Was I babbling? I decided to shut up.

"I do," he said. "In fact, I've been working on a talk I'd like to give at jungle school to incoming troops. You know, tell them what they might expect in the way of mental stress; that it's normal; that it's good to talk about it; that I'm available if they don't feel comfortable talking to anyone else about it." He stopped, perhaps waiting for me to comment. "I'd like to do the same for troops going back home too," he said when I didn't say anything. "The transition back to civilian life can be even more traumatic than the stress of combat." He didn't know what the hell he was talking about but I didn't say that. "I even thought about giving classes to medics in training. Once I DEROS. What to look for in combat stress. How to talk to men with problems. How to listen." He looked at his watch. "Just a minute," he said and went to the door; I could hear him mumbling to someone outside.

"Sorry," he said, coming back. "I have someone waiting but I want to continue this conversation, hear your thoughts. And I still want that bio. I can still use what I learned from you."

"You want to learn something about life in the field?" I said. I could see the suspicion in his face. "Come out to Old Crow. You can give my guys your talk, maybe stay the night. Pull guard duty. Maybe even tag along on an LP." He looked as if I had just challenged his manhood. Maybe I had.

"Set it up," he finally said, probably thinking he was calling my bluff. But I wasn't bluffing.

"Nothing to set up," I said. "Just hitch a ride out whenever you want. If I'm in the bush, third platoon will be there. You can work your magic on them." I wasn't being snotty, but I could see how he might take it like that. He smiled and walked me to the door. I left it open when I left. Whoever had been waiting outside was gone.

* * *

I felt her lips against the back of my neck. "Gotta get up," she whispered in my ear. I rolled onto my back and she kissed me again. On the lips this time. She pulled away, a rare smile on her face. She was beautiful when she smiled and it made me feel good that I was the one who put it there. "Gotta go to work. And you, Sir--are a tiny bit AWOL? Come on. Move," she teased, nudging me to the edge of the bed with her knee. I sat up while she pulled the sheet around herself and climbed over me.

"Why do women always do that?" I said as she went to her wall locker.

"What?" She opened the locker, dropped the sheet and put on her robe before turning around.

"Cover themselves up like that. We just spent the night naked together. What do you think I'm going to see I haven't already seen? Nice ass, by the way."

"Is that what the Australian girls do? Cover up after sex?" She turned on the light next to the bed and I pulled her to me and kissed her long and slow on the lips. She let me enjoy the moment; then pulled away, combing her hair with her fingers. The short cut fell quickly into place.

"I like it like that, your hair," I said. I couldn't get enough of looking at her. I wanted to pull her back into bed and spend the rest of my life there.

"So you said last night. Many times. So?"

"So, what?"

"Do the Australian girls cover up too?" she said, fishing.

"Actually, I met a nice girl on my second night there, but we never got that far." She stopped gathering her shower supplies and turned, giving me a disappointed look.

"Why do men always do that after sex?" she said.

"What?"

"Lie," she said.

"Actually," I said, trying to make light of the subject, "we're more likely to lie *before* sex." She was not amused. "I'm not lying," I said truthfully. I saw no need to tell her that the fact that I didn't have sex was through no fault of my own. I certainly tried hard enough. She smirked. I could tell she wanted to believe me. "I'm not," I said. "It's the truth."

"Yeah. You were pining away for me the whole time," she said, probing. I got up but suddenly felt very exposed myself. I slipped my hands inside her robe and pulled her to me, our bare skin pressing warm against each other.

"I thought of you often. I can't tell you how many times I wished you were there with me," I said.

"Especially when you weren't getting any from Sheila," she said.

"I am kind of a guy," I admitted. She pulled away, kissed me quickly on the lips and told me not to be there when she got back from the shower.

"With rank comes responsibility," she said. "And use your best grunt skills to sneak out. I'm supposed to set an example around here." With that she put on her flip flops and slipped out the door. I was still there when she got back.

"I mean it, Sean," she said. "I don't want anyone to see you here. And I've got twenty minutes to get to there."

"It's a short commute," I said.

"Turn around," she said. She dropped her robe and started putting on her undergarments. I had spent my alone time poking around and now held up a framed picture she kept on a shelf.

"Who's this?" I asked.

She turned, no longer self-conscious now that her bra and panties were on. "Me," she said.

"No, really?" I said. The picture was of a chubby girl with long, dark hair, standing in front of the hospital entrance. It looked nothing like the pretty girl buttoning up her fatigue shirt in front of me. She stopped buttoning and turned serious.

"Really," she said, looking me in the eye. "That's what I looked like when I got here, and that's what I'll look like six months after I get back home." She held my gaze like a challenge. I didn't know what to say.

"It doesn't have to be," was all I could think of. I could see her eyes go all puffy. "I'm sorry. I didn't mean–"

"Jesus, Sean," she said, trying not to cry. "Sometimes…."

"I know. I'm an asshole. I'm sorry. I just meant–"

"I know what you meant. But that's the real me," she said, meaning the girl in the picture. "I've always been the fat girl–"

"You're not–"

"–and I always will be. I didn't try to lose weight here, it's just with all the stress and work… Diets never worked for me and when this is all over…" She turned around and her hands went to her face.

"I don't care–" I started to say, then stopped before I found myself in a lie.

"Look," Audrey said and wiped again at the corner of one eye. "I don't want to fight. This is… whatever it is. Let's not pretend it's something it's not. Let's just get through this Goddamn mess and–"

At that moment I loved her more than anyone I had ever loved in my life but didn't want to say anything I might later regret.

Instead, I took her in my arms and pulled her close while she cried into my chest. I didn't say a word, just let her cry for as long as she wanted until she pulled away and left for work.

* * *

Captain Messina welcomed me back, but not with the enthusiasm I expected. Apparently I was not greatly missed. I shouldn't have been surprised. My platoon hadn't come up for a mission during my absence and Sgt. Poole was capable of handling the day to day routine of life inside the wire. More than capable as it turned out.

Without consulting me he had run two training seminars on land navigation while I was gone. All infantrymen are trained in the use of map and compass but it is little more than an introductory course. Sgt. Poole's idea was to give all the sergeants and corporals in the platoon a class designed to teach them skills specific to their jobs as team leaders in Vietnam. When Captain Messina heard about the class he had him give it to, not just my platoon, but to every NCO in the company.

"He did a good job," Captain Messina said. "We should have done it long ago." I took that as a rebuke although it probably wasn't meant that way. Sgt. Poole was just carrying on the training programs I had initiated months ago. The only difference was that he didn't get someone else to give the class. He taught it himself.

"Yes, Sir," I said.

"It wasn't a criticism," Captain Messina said. "You've done a good job on the training program. I just wanted to let you know it rubbed off. How are you two getting along? You and Sgt. Poole."

"Good," I said.

"Good?" He must have picked up something from my tone. "I would have thought that after Sgt. Nelson you'd be thrilled with Sgt. Poole."

"No, I am. Really. He's good. Knows his job. It's just that…I guess I'd gotten used to running things by myself. I'm adjusting."

"You *are* running things," Captain Messina reminded me. "If you aren't you need to let Sgt. Poole know who does. Is there a problem there I should know about?"

"No. Nothing like that. He's a team player. The men like him. Respect him." A smile passed his lips.

"Sit down, Lieutenant. Let me tell you a story." I took a seat.

"Right out of college I took a job at a financial firm--reading company prospectuses and analyzing their financials to make recommendations our salesmen could pitch to their clients. My boss was a couple of years older than me and we hit it off, hung out after work; shit like that.

"I was there less than a year and the firm was having problems. They were consolidating to save money and had to let some of the supervisors go, but not Sam. I asked him how he managed to keep his job when so many men senior to him were being fired. He said you have to make yourself indispensable. Other managers delegated most of their work to subordinates who eventually learned to do the job as well as their supervisors. These managers took long vacations and when they did their sections moved along efficiently without them.

"Sam didn't do that. He kept his people in the dark about much of the things he did so that when he took time off his people were constantly calling him for instructions. When it came time to make cuts, management realized they couldn't let him go. He was too valuable. Without him certain work wouldn't get done or would be done poorly. Other supervisors were let go, but Sam kept his job."

I didn't get his point and my face showed it. "Sam was not a good manager," Captain Messina said. "He didn't train his people to work independently without him to guide them. That served Sam well, but not the company and upper management wasn't smart enough to see that. Our company is the United States Army and we do not have the luxury of protecting our own positions to the detriment of the unit. If you were to get killed in action, there's no time to train someone else to take your place. If you haven't trained your people to carry on when you're gone, you haven't done your job. And people might die because of it. I judge you not only by how well you do, but by how well your platoon does. Whether you're there or not."

Chapter 33

"Sir?" It was PFC Johnson. "Foxtrot Two. They want to know how far away we are." I started to take the handset, then changed my mind.

"Half a klick," I said. "Maybe twenty minutes. You tell 'em." I saw the panic on Johnson's face. Johnson was a serious black kid just out of AIT who had the bad luck of being the latest FNG when Cisco was getting short. Not only was he on the small side to be humping the radio, he was also a quart low on confidence.

"Foxtrot Two, this is X-ray One," Cisco coached. "Then just tell them we'll be in position in two zero." Johnson swallowed hard, licked his lips and squeezed the transmit bar.

"Foxtrot…"

"Two."

"Two. This is X-ray One. We'll be in position in two zero…."

"Over," Cisco said, shaking his head.

"Over," Johnson said and looked to Cisco for approval. Cisco told him to drop back into line.

"You sure you don't want me to do this?" he said.

"You gonna extend?"

"Nope," he said. I didn't know if that was because he was still mad at me about the promotion thing or if he was just getting spooky with only a few weeks left on his tour.

"Then get him up to speed before you leave," I said.

"That's not going to happen," he said.

"He'll catch on," I said. "You probably weren't any better when you first started."

"I doubt that," he mumbled, dropping back to shadow Johnson.

We were on our second day out, 12 klicks from Old Crow and our first time out of our AO. B Company had taken three casualties around the village of Lang Tai in the past month without anything to show for it and wanted us to provide a blocking force to the south while they came in from the north to search the village. Because our platoons would be facing each other from opposite sides of the village there was to be no shooting unless it was absolutely necessary. B Company was already in position and they were getting antsy that they would be discovered before we had time to set up. I moved up to consult with Sgt. Poole.

"B Company's nervous. How much farther, you think?"

"Not long. We're close." He was telling me not to rush things. Better to have B Company stew than to be discovered ourselves.

"Who's on point?"

"Boyd."

"Okay," I said and dropped back to the middle of the platoon. Fifteen minutes later word came back to halt and I went forward with Johnson and Cisco. Lang Tai was like an island in a sea of dried up rice paddies. The village was bigger than Gia Hoi and Phu Nu combined and there was a hundred and fifty yards of open space between us and the nearest hootches. There was little movement in the village and the paddies were deserted. Even the dogs were lying in whatever shade they could find to escape the afternoon heat.

"Whaddya think?" Sgt. Poole asked even though the situation couldn't have been any more straightforward.

"Spread 'em out so we cover the length of the village. Just make sure everyone knows the situation. No shooting unless they see a gun and then only if they have to. A prisoner is as good as a kill. We don't want to hit anybody in B Company. Stress that."

"I'll put the fear of God in 'em," Sgt. Poole said. I turned to Johnson. "Tell Foxtrot Two we're on the south side of Lima Tango--Lang Tai," I said when he looked confused. "And tell them to stay put until we give the word that we're in position."

* * *

You could see the change in the villagers. A stiffening in their posture, a turn of the head, the pretense of normality. An old cur barked twice, struggled to its feet and slunk off to the far side of the village. Only then did I notice the flashes of olive drab on the far side of Lang Tai. An old mama san tried to look casual as she put out her cooking fire. Kids stopped playing, moved to their mothers' side. Three papa sans pulled thatch from the side of a hootch, then pretended to repair the damage. Anything to look busy. I scanned the space between the village and the tree line where we lay hidden but no one was trying to escape.

The first of the B Company soldiers entered the village. Orders were yelled; rifles were pointed, villagers were herded toward the center of the town. No one hurried. No one screamed except the soldiers. It seemed like a well-rehearsed play until I noticed a disturbance at the base of one of the hootches on our side of the village. A boy poked his head through the thatch, then forced the rest of his body through. My heart was pounding. The boy was up and running in an instant, right toward our line. I saw movement in our line but nobody fired.

A soldier from B Company fired a burst from the village that went high off to my right. I heard swearing from our line and then another burst that sent the boy sprawling just as he crested another dike. He fell on our side, out of sight from the shooter, but not us.

A woman screamed. The shooter stayed put, waiting for another soldier to join him before he advanced. They spread out and moved forward, joined by a third soldier with an M-79. *This is not going to end well*, I thought, then saw Doc Hippie running into the field, his arms up.

"It's okay!" he yelled. The assassination squad stopped, stunned by the sight of an unarmed G.I. running toward the injured man. "He doesn't have a gun. I got this." He ran with his medical kit in front of himself, the black cross facing forward.

I found myself running as well, yelling for Doc to stop but he either didn't hear me or ignored me. He got there first, just before the three soldiers from B Company. By the time I got there Doc had pulled the boy's pant leg above the knee and was assessing the gunshot wound to his calf.

"Doc! Check him for weapons first!" I said. For the first time Doc seemed to realize the foolishness of his actions. When he started to pat him down the boy reached into his shirt pocket. Guns came up all around and if Doc hadn't been in the way the boy would have been wasted. Instead he pulled his hand free and, jabbering away, held out his I.D. card. One of the B Company men took it saying it was probably a fake before he even looked at it.

"Give me that," I said; he reluctantly handed it over. Doc had his medical bag open and was swabbing the wound while I examined the I.D. "Hein," I said. The boy looked up at the sound of his name. "He look about fourteen to you, Doc?" Doc ran his fingers along the ridge of his shin bone, feeling for breaks.

"Somewhere around there," he said. From the village I heard three shots, followed by the yelp of a dog. Assholes! A woman came running up, hands to her mouth, tears staining her cheeks when she saw her son on the ground. She knelt at the boy's head, brushed his hair with her hand. I was suddenly aware that the B Company platoon leader was standing next to me, a deer-in-the-headlights butterbar with no idea what to do.

"I thought there was to be no shooting!" I lit into him. "You're lucky one of my men wasn't killed!"

"He was running away," the shooter said. I lunged at him, grabbed his shoulder straps, tried to throw him to the ground. Hands grabbing at me, pulling me off; the other Lieutenant yelling; Doc pushing at my legs, trying to do his work; Romansky's voice, yelling, prying hands off me. I shook myself free.

"You better get your men under control, Lieutenant," I snapped, ignoring my own loss of restraint. He turned, thinking I meant the men in the village. Men were running toward him, eager to see what was going on.

"Get back there and finish your search!" he ordered and then noticed that the hootch the boy had snuck out of was starting to burn, several mama sans beating at the flames with their brooms. "And put that fire out, Goddamn it! I mean it! Now!" He yelled. "Jesus Christ, as if it ain't fucked up enough."

Doc had cleaned the wound and was applying a battle dressing. "You're fuckin' up, Hippie," Romansky said.

"My first real gunshot wound," Doc said, not even looking up. "You rather I practice on him, or one of our guys?"

"How bad is it?" I said.

"Not bad," Doc said. "Through and through. No bone, no major vessels involved. Gonna need surgery though." I turned around to wave Johnson up but he was already there.

"Cisco said–"

"Yeah, good. You know how to call in a dustoff?"

"I think so. Yes," he said, fumbling in his pocket for the notebook that held the battalion frequencies and call signs.

"Tell them we have one civilian WIA," I said. The shooter glared at me.

"VC suspect," he snarled. I glared back.

"Possible VC," I said to Johnson. "Got it?" I looked to the tree line and waved Cisco forward. "Stay with Romansky and Doc," I said when he got there. "Have Johnson direct the dust off." I went back to the tree line. "Jesus, what a fuckin' mess," I said. I opened my canteen and took a drink.

"Coulda been worse," Sgt. Poole said. I looked at the village. Half of an entire side of the hootch was a smoldering, black mess, the villagers throwing buckets of water around the edges to keep it from reigniting. The men of B Company did nothing to help.

"A lot worse," I agreed.

* * *

Johnson was in trouble. We had spent the last two days since leaving Lang Tai patrolling the back side of Mortar Mountain with nothing to show for it but sore muscles and abraded skin from the frequent slides along the steep slope. But the worst was the heat. We took frequent breaks; Doc Hippie passing out salt tablets and making sure we drank enough water while the rest of us rested.

The temperature was over 110 degrees and there was little shade on the rocky back slope of the mountain. Everyone suffered, but no one more than Johnson. There was a stiffness to his legs, a widening of his gait as the mission progressed but he refused to admit anything was wrong. The pain on his face every time he took a step told me otherwise.

"Doc, take a look at Johnson, will ya?" I said at one of our breaks.

"I'm fine," Johnson insisted. "Really."

"I think he's got crotch rot," I said. Johnson protested but Doc prevailed.

"That's your problem, man," Doc said when Johnson dropped his pants. "Didn't anyone tell you not to wear underwear and pants at the same time? Freaking sauna in there." He pulled out his bandage scissors, cut off Johnson's underwear and threw it aside. He had Johnson lay face down on his poncho liner and spread his legs. "Jesus," he muttered. "Sir?" I went over and looked. His inner thighs and scrotum were raw and swollen, oozing blood and clear liquid. Doc spread the cheeks of Johnson's buttocks; it was even worse there. "He can't walk. He needs to go to a hospital."

"I can walk," Johnson insisted. "A little ways anyway." He was embarrassed and further humiliated that he was lying face down while another man probed his private area.

Doc's response to the situation helped. He cleaned the area and applied ointment, treating the problem with no more hesitation than if it was a shrapnel wound to the leg. The rest of the platoon was surprisingly sympathetic. Men who normally jumped at the opportunity to razz another soldier, turned their heads, said nothing. The jokes and verbal abuse would come later, but for now everyone acted as if nothing unusual was going on.

"You good, Johnson? You make it til we find an LZ?" Doc said when he was done.

"Yeah, no problem," he said.

"It is a problem," Doc said, not unkindly. "Next time say somethin'. Coulda fixed this two days ago with scissors and talcum powder. One more thing," he said as Johnson pulled his pants up. Doc took his scissors and cut away the inside of both pant legs and the lower buttocks to reduce chaffing and increase air circulation. "I'll have Lt. Sullivan post a rear guard on ya til you're safely aboard the dustoff," he said. "Some of these guys are pretty horny and I ran out of salt peter three days ago."

And so the jokes began.

Chapter 34

"Sullivan! You know a Major Fletcher?" Captain Messina never called me *Sullivan*. It was always Lt. Sullivan or, rarely, *Sean*, so I knew he was mad. Plus, he was standing in the doorway of my bunker. Before, if he wanted to see me, he sent for me.

"I've met him. A couple of times," I admitted, my mind racing.

"Well who the hell is he and why's he coming here?" I knew who, but not why.

"He's the division psychologist," I said and tried to think of a good reason, other than the truth, as to how I knew him.

"Well he's coming out on today's re-supply. Something about a request from you?" Now I remembered.

"Oh, yes Sir. Sorry. I didn't think he'd do it, just like that. I approached him a few weeks ago about giving a talk to our guys about the stresses of combat, things like that. You know, their feelings like…as a part of our training thing." Not exactly the truth, but close enough.

"Their feelings?" he said. "I'm just spit-balling here, but I'm guessing some of them might be scared shitless."

"Yes, Sir. And feeling ashamed because of it. He deals with this kind of thing all the time and thought it might be helpful if they could talk about it. Or he talk to them. Let them know it's normal an' all that." Captain Messina gave that some thought.

"Well, Lieutenant, next time you invite a field grade officer to my firebase I'd appreciate a heads up."

"Yes, Sir."

"Well, too late now. Get your men moving. I want this place policed and looking good before he gets here. The men too. Everyone clean shaven and clean fatigues. No T-shirts. And helmets. Everybody wears a helmet."

* * *

"Tough audience," I said after Dr. Fletcher's talk. "They're usually more animated at these things."

"It's no more than I expected," Dr. Fletcher said. "I didn't expect them to open up in front of everybody. Just wanted them to know they're not alone. That their buddies are probably feeling the same things they are. I'd also like a moment with your medics if I may. Tell them what to look for in combat fatigue. Let them know they should send them back to see me, just like any injured soldier."

"Well, thank you for coming," Captain Messina said, extending his hand. "A good talk. I'm sure you gave the men a lot to think about. Lt. Sullivan, if you'll take Major Fletcher to see Doc Cook, I'll see about getting him a chopper back to the base."

"That won't be necessary," Dr. Fletcher said. "Lt. Sullivan suggested I might stay the night. Get a taste of what it's like out here in the boonies."

"Ummm," he said, and gave me a sideways glance. "If that's what you want. Just let me know if there's anything I can do to make your stay easier," he said. Then, without another word to me he turned and walked back to the commo bunker.

"Jesus, Sir," I said, when he was gone.

"What? Something wrong?"

"The overnight thing. I think Captain Messina…never mind," I said, still upset that he brought it up like that. "You really want to get a feeling for what it's like out here?"

"I think it would help me understand what the men are going through," he said.

"You want to spend the night outside the wire?"

"Well, I didn't say that," he said.

* * *

It was dusk when we left--Cisco and Romansky, Boyd and Murphy, and me and Dr. Fletcher. Cisco and Romansky were to set up their LP along the main trail to the base. Boyd and Murphy had the west side of Old Crow and Major Fletcher and I took the east. We had reverted to our bush hats once we realized Major Fletcher was no threat to what we called *jungle rules*, which differed greatly from Division S.O.P. Only Major Fletcher wore his helmet, not having brought a bush hat with him. "Keep that strapped on," I whispered. "It falls off, you know what it sounds like?"

"Like a steel helmet falling off someone's head?"

"You catch on fast," I said. We hadn't made enemy contact anywhere near our base camp since my arrival but I didn't tell Major Fletcher that. I wanted him to feel the same stress the rest of us felt when facing the unknown. Dr. Fletcher had his .45 and Captain Messina had loaned him an M-16 in the unlikely event we came under attack. I had a round chambered but I hadn't yet told Dr. Fletcher to chamber his. Captain Messina didn't like the idea of a REMF major manning an LP and the last thing I wanted was to have him shooting up the jungle at the first sound.

We alerted the perimeter guards there were friendlies outside the wire and set off. I led Major Fletcher along the apron wire to the east side of the camp, gave a wave to the guard and started down the slope. When we reached the edge of the jungle I leaned close to Major Fletcher and whispered.

"Were going to drop down into the jungle til we're far enough over the lip that we can shoot in any direction, and the perimeter guards can shoot toward us and their rounds will go over our heads." He nodded that he understood. I led him down the slope until we were out of Old Crow's line of fire and then looked for a place that afforded some protection from an enemy attack. We settled in and I took the radio frame from my back and pressed the transmit bar. "X-ray Kilo, this is X-ray One, we are in position, over." It was a second or two before I heard Johnson's voice.

"X-ray One, this is X-ray Kilo. Roger that, over." Johnson's chatter was still tentative but I put him on radio watch every chance I got and I could see improvement every day. I signed out and reiterated what I had already told Major Fletcher before we left. "We're not here to shoot anybody. You hear something, you wake me up. Got it?"

"You do this every night?" I could hear the tension in his voice.

"Not every night," I said, not mentioning that, aside from platoon missions, I hadn't spent a night outside the wire since my first month in-country. "Look, every noise is gonna sound like a gook at first but most of the time it's nothing. Just wake me up if you're unsure of anything. I'll stay awake til you get through your first sit-rep."

* * *

In my dream Audrey had just turned around. She was wearing a black nighty showing just a hint of breast at the top and lots of thigh at the bottom so when the first mortar round hit I was as confused and disoriented as Major Fletcher. It was close and bits of dirt and debris drizzled down through the leaves. Major Fletcher was bug-eyed; I could only hope I did not look as terrified as he did. He grabbed up the handset.

"Should I call and tell them?" he gasped. I put my hand on his helmet and pushed him down.

"I think they know," I said.

"Of course," he said. Another round hit, farther away this time. We could hear shrapnel and litter falling to the ground but none of it reached us. My heart slowed. They wanted Old Crow and the closer the rounds got to the compound, the farther away they were from us. It was then I remembered. This was what we were waiting for. "Come on, come on," I said to myself, waiting for the answering thud of our own mortars. "Jesus Christ, what are you waiting for?"

Finally, the first whump of a friendly mortar round leaving the tube. Then another and another. It was all I could do to keep from jumping up and yelling at the top of my lungs. An enemy round hit Old Crow. I could see the blast from the explosion, then the sound of our own rounds finding their marks on Mortar Mountain. My mind was racing. I grabbed Major Fletcher's M-16 and chambered a round. "Be ready. They sometimes coordinate a ground attack with mortars." I'm sure that was all he needed to hear. More explosions coming from both Old Crow and Mortar Mountain. Were we missing?

Another round fell on Old Crow, then stopped. Our mortar continued to fire, less frequently now that they were traversing the slope, changing elevation and traversing again. I started to explain what was happening but was interrupted by an explosion that reverberated through my body. Unlike our mortar rounds, I could see and feel the explosions as our 175s pounded the VC mortar site. Our mortar crew stopped firing and I heard the cheers from Old Crow as our artillery chewed up a small patch of Mortar Mountain. Two minutes later and it was all over but the shouting. The radio buzzed to life. Johnson.

"X-ray One, X-ray One, this is X-ray Kilo. If you have a negative sit-rep, break squelch twice, over." Major Fletcher looked at me.

"Nothin' they don't know about," I said. Major Fletcher squeezed the transmit bar twice, then listened as Johnson called the other LPs.

"X-ray One Two, X-ray One Two, this is X-ray Kilo. If you have a negative sit-rep, break squelch, over." It was a long moment before I heard Cisco's voice.

"Oh, yeah, X-ray Kilo. Sorry, I must have dozed off there. Yeah, no, nothing here. Everything's quiet, over." There was a moment while Johnson tried to figure out how to respond to that, not fully aware of the extent of Cisco's humor. I kept listening to see if a dustoff would be called but there was nothing. It was almost three o'clock but I was too keyed up to sleep. I told Major Fletcher to get some sleep but I don't think he did either.

* * *

We were back at first light, Captain Messina and Sgt. Poole at the gate to meet me. "Get something to eat and be ready to head out in two zero," Captain Messina said. "I want you to take a squad and check out that mortar site. See if we got anything. Major Fletcher, I've got a chopper coming out in about an hour to pick you up. I trust you got what you needed last night?" Captain Messina was smiling. No one had been injured and he had high hopes of having wiped out the mortar crew that had killed Sgt. Henry and the medic from Gary's platoon.

"More than enough," Dr. Fletcher said. "I'll tell Major Dempsey what great hosts you were."

"Please don't," Captain Messina said. They both laughed and shook hands.

"Thank you too, Lieutenant," Dr. Fletcher said, shaking my hand. He shook hands with Sgt. Poole, told him to stop by his office if there was anything he could do for him, and left.

"Want me to take the squad?" Sgt. Poole offered. "You've been up all night."

"No. I got this," I said. "Put together a squad for me while I get ready. Six men. Boyd, Johnson. Four others. Better take Cisco too." I was too taken up with my own wants to notice how Sgt. Poole took my brushoff. As it turned out, leaving him behind was the right move, but not for the right reason.

* * *

Traveling light and fast, we reached the mortar site in two hours. Everyone was psyched. Even Boyd lost his usual cool and set an unusually fast pace. At first I thought we had missed it. I expected to find several acres of mass destruction--trees down, huge craters from the 175s, smoldering embers from dying fires--but there was none of that. I was about to call for our mortar crew to drop a smoke round on the site when Boyd spotted a few flashes of white where broken limbs disrupted the green canopy just ahead of us.

There were no dead bodies on the ground and no twisted remains of a mortar tube. At first I thought our mortar and artillery rounds had missed their mark, but they hadn't. Pieces of the observation platform littered the ground and the aiming stake was nowhere to be seen. The cement slab that had been set to level the mortar baseplate was chipped and cracked where shrapnel had rained down upon it.

"What the fuck!" Cisco said.

"Air bursts," I said when it finally dawned on me. Sgt. Poole had ordered airbursts for the artillery shells so the shrapnel would explode outward in an ever widening cone to cover a larger area. Everywhere the ground had been chewed up, the tree trunks bristling with jagged chunks of metal. There was not a square yard in the kill zone that had not been hit and yet--

"Where are they?" Johnson asked.

"Look around. Maybe the gooks dragged them off already. Look for blood. Cisco, Call TOC. Tell them we found the site. We're looking for blood trails now." I'd forgotten Cisco was no longer carrying the radio. Johnson was studying an artillery fragment sticking a full six inches from the trunk of a banyan tree.

"Rash!" Cisco yelled. Johnson had been nicknamed *diaper rash* after getting medevaced for crotch rot and the name was quickly shortened to just *Rash*. Cisco relayed my instructions and Rash made the call.

"They said to never mind," Rash said. "They want us to go back." I held out my hand and he handed me the handset.

"X-ray Kilo, this is X-ray One Actual. We have no bodies at this time but I--"

"Five minutes," Captain Messina interrupted. "Then get out of there. I'll explain when you get back. Be alert to ambushes. They probably expected a recon after that pounding."

* * *

Captain Messina escorted me to the helipad as soon as we got back. "They weren't there. I didn't get it either," he said when he saw the look on my face. "It was Sgt. LoPresti. See the toilet paper on the bushes out there?" he said, pointing. "That's where the first two rounds fell. The third round landed where that stake is, just outside the wire. Remember how the last few times we were hit not a single round landed outside the wire? Not this time. After you left, LoPresti took his crew out and marked every place a round hit, then connected the dots." I looked, but couldn't see any pattern. "See that one, the farthest down the slope and off to the left? That's where the first round hit. Forget that one, and the next one too," he said pointing to another piece of toilet paper closer to the perimeter. "They were just adjusting for range and line of fire. That's why there was more time between the first few rounds and the rest. Come here," he said and led me to a small crater near the middle of the compound. "Sgt. LoPresti figures this is where the fifth round landed. See that other crater directly in line between this one and the stake where the third round hit just outside the wire? Those are the only three hits that form a straight line. After that the rounds fell all over, but always inside the wire. LoPresti figured that line is an azimuth to their new mortar site."

"Want me to take a look?"

"Sgt. Poole already did. With LoPresti and a few others. They were dead on, about a third of the way up that mountain over there," he said, pointing to a mountain somewhat smaller than Mortar Mountain off to the east. "Cement slab for the baseplate, aiming stake, observation platform. Same as before. Gotta be the same crew. Musta known we found the other site."

"I hope they didn't leave any sign that they were there," I said, meaning the squad Sgt. Poole took out.

"I don't think you need to worry about your platoon sergeant," he said. "Sgt. Allen said he lead them right to the site."

"They're back?!"

"About a half hour before you. They moved fast. Whenever they had to change course because of some obstacle, Sgt. Poole just noted a landmark on the other side of the obstacle, went around it and picked up the azimuth from there. Walked right to it."

"So we're back to square one," I said.

"Back to square one. Send out a couple guys to take down that toilet paper. We'll get 'em next time," he said. "I just hope I'm still here to see it."

Chapter 35

Instead of the usual disoriented look, the replacement that jumped off the chopper appeared confident, happy even. He saw me waiting at the edge of the helipad, slung his rucksack over his shoulder and made his way over, back hunched like a veteran.

"Hey, Lieutenant," he said like he was glad to see me. "What the hell's going on? I haven't used one of these since AIT," he said, holding up his grenade launcher. It was then that I recognized him.

"Nellis?" I said.

"They didn't tell you I was comin'?" I was surprised I even remembered his name and that was because he was the first man wounded under my command, shot in the ankle on my first mission.

"I knew I was getting a new guy but…we thought you'd gone home?"

"That was my plan, but I decided to come back."

"*You* decided?" The chopper was unloaded and we turned our heads as a wave of dirt and debris blew past us during the takeoff. Nellis waited for the noise to subside so he wouldn't have to yell.

"I spent the last six months in rehab at Cam Rahn Bay. After that they said I could get reassigned back to the states if I wanted, but if I did I wouldn't get credit for a full tour and they could send me back for another year."

"And now?"

"All the time I spent in rehab is good time and I DEROS on my original date. Two months and I'm outta here."

"Well, good to have you back," I said. "Check in with Sgt. Poole–"

"I was hopin' I could go back to Sgt. Burkholtz's squad."

"Burkholtz is gone. Sgt. Poole's the new platoon sergeant. Simpson's got your old squad."

"No shit?"

"Lots of changes."

"So I see," he said, noticing the unfamiliar faces hauling the supplies off the helipad. "Angus, still here? Merrit? Murphy?"

"Angus DEROSed. Merrit and Murphy are still here."

"Cisco?"

"Cisco left last week. You'll get caught up," I said, not wanting to go through the whole roster. "That's Sgt. Poole over there. The black E-7. He'll get you squared away. New SOP for M-79s."

"Yeah, about that--"

"You'll get the hang of it. Sgt. Poole thought each squad should have one. I don't have time to discuss it now. We're moving out as soon as third platoon gets back and that should be in about an hour."

"Me too?" he asked, hoping for some time to settle in before going on a mission.

"You too," I said.

* * *

"Sir, it's higher. There's a chopper down at Phu Gap. They want us to go there to assist," Rash said, handing me the handset.

"Phu Gap?! Dell, tell them to hold up," I told the PFC in front of me. I pressed the transmit bar. "This is X-ray One Actual. I understand you want us to go to Phu Gap to assist in a rescue, over."

"Affirmative, X-ray One. How soon can you get there?" I recognized Major Dempsey's voice. My mind was racing. We'd only been to Phu Gap once, only to be ordered to release the men we'd found with questionable IDs. I had no idea how far away we were. We were two miles north of Gia Hoi, not even on the same map as Phu Gap.

"Uh, that's more than ten klicks from us. It would take five hours at least. Please advise, over."

"Never mind that. We're inserting a ranger unit for the rescue but we have no idea what this might turn into. Just get there ASAP."

"Uh, Roger that, Sir. Uh, has the ARVN unit there been notified, over?"

"Just get moving, Lieutenant. We'll keep you advised. Two Bravo Actual, out." I filled in Sgt. Poole and he took it in with his usual stoic resolve. I would run out of map before we got five miles. Fortunately all we had to do was follow the Mu Dai downstream so it would not be hard to find. We turned around headed back the way we had come.

The bridge above Gia Hoi was still not finished but it was near the end of the dry season and we were able to ford the river without getting our rucksacks wet. I did not like staying on the trail after being seen by the gooks working on the bridge but there was nothing I could do about it. Higher was constantly asking about our progress and never happy with my answer. I told Boyd to pick up the pace, a decision I was soon to regret.

The explosion came from the front of the line. People were yelling for a medic but Doc Hippie was already running past me before I knew what had happened. I followed, Rash right behind me, asking if he should call for a dustoff. There was no shooting, only the screams of the wounded and unwounded alike. Sgt. Poole was already setting up security on the trail ahead. I could see one man down, Doc opening his aid kit. Boyd was in a daze--stumbling around as if in a trance--mumbling over and over that he never saw it. I was peripherally aware that Sgt. Poole was setting up a security team behind us in case trouble came from that direction.

It was Nellis, his legs a bloody mess. His glasses were clouded with sweat and dirt so I couldn't see his eyes but I knew he was in a lot of pain. "The same fucking foot!" he kept saying. "The same fucking foot!" He knew this was not going to be a case of a few months rehab. His right foot was completely gone.

"Call dustoff," I said to Rash and pulled out my map. "Here," I said tapping the point on the Mu Dai where I guessed we were. Sgt. Poole came up beside me.

"There's a place 200 yards up the trail I think we can get a chopper in. Just two palm trees in the way. Should be able to cut them down." I looked down the trail to where the river took a slight turn. I couldn't see the spot, but I could hear the sound of an axe doing its work. Boyd was still in shock, apologizing to Nellis while Murphy tried to pull him away.

"It wasn't a trip wire," Murphy was saying. "It was pressure. Nobody coulda seen it."

"Boyd!" I yelled but he appeared not to hear me. "Corporal Boyd!" He turned, seemed to be looking somewhere beyond me. "You know your way around an axe?"

"Huh?"

"Are you any good with an axe? You know how to cut down a tree?" Again, a moment for him to process what I was saying.

"Yes, sir," he finally said.

"Then get forward and help with the LZ. Make sure those trees fall where you want them. I want them down in twenty minutes."

"Dustoff's on the way," Rash said. I looked at Nellis.

"How ya doin'?" I said. He seemed calmer now that the initial shock and confusion was past.

"Okay, I guess. You can't get a chopper in here."

"We're clearing an LZ up ahead. How soon can we move him, Doc?" Doc had finished with the leg and was checking for other major bleeders.

"Anytime," Doc said.

"What about my foot?" Nellis said. Murphy picked up what was left of his boot and held it up for him to see. Nellis held out his hand and Murphy gave him the shredded mass of rubber, canvas, bone, and flesh.

"Maybe they can sew it back on," Nellis said.

By the time we got Nellis to the LZ one of the trees had already been felled and Boyd and Newell were working on the one bordering the river, Boyd notching the soft palm on the river side with a machete, Newell cutting into the back side with the axe.

"Sir, the ranger unit has already extracted the chopper crew," Rash said. "Dustoff's five minutes out." I didn't even acknowledge that I'd heard him. My mind was on other things. The "LZ" was barely thirty yards long--a washed out depression where the Mu Dai overflowed its banks during the wet season and held enough water to prevent most large trees from taking root.

"Boyd, Newell! Take a break. Dustoff will be here in five minutes." They handed their tools to Murphy and Dell and dropped to the ground, exhausted. "You sure this is big enough?" I asked Sgt. Poole.

"It's tighter than I first thought. Worst case, we can get a basket in here," he said, looking at the oval of sky overhead. I heard the drone of the chopper off to the south. Sgt. Poole yelled to one of the men up the trail to pop smoke. I told Rash to tell the dustoff to look for our smoke.

I had started toward the palm tree when I heard a sharp crack. Murphy dropped his machete and jumped back. The tree started to lean toward the river, then stopped. Dell started pushing on the back side of the tree, joined quickly by Murphy, Boyd, and Newell. If they were on the other side of the tree it would have looked like the flag raising at Imo Jima. They pushed and relaxed in unison, rocking the tree three times before there was a long, sustained cracking noise. They jumped back as the tree splashed into the river. The men cheered and two seconds later the Huey roared overhead. It came back and circled, surveying the tight spot we had put them in. I had a sinking feeling as Rash hurried over, handset in his hand.

"He wants everyone to move back fifty yards and take cover behind trees in case something goes wrong." In my mind I pictured the blades of the chopper hitting the trees, the fuselage spitting out crewmen and wreckage. I heard Nellis groan as he was wrenched from the ground, saw Doc preparing a syringe. The chopper came in through the notch in the trail, his rotors just above the tops of the trees. He dropped down once he was clear and settled into the middle of the clearing. The crew chief held up his hand, keeping us away while the pilot lifted up a few inches off the ground and crabbed sideways until he was as close to the edge of the landing zone as he could get. He made it look easy but I knew the hardest part would be getting out.

The crew chief waved us forward, the door gunners alert to any danger. Nellis gritted his teeth as his bearers ran forward and slid him onto the deck before running off to take cover.

The chopper lifted up, then slid backward until the tail was half way over the river. He came forward and stopped again, almost at the same spot where he had landed in the first place. He backed up again, this time angling his tail up river and as close to the far bank as he dared. The engine whined; the rotors accelerated. He came forward again, faster this time, gaining altitude and banking to the left until he made a complete circle around the clearing, gaining speed and lift as he did. He made another circle, accelerating quickly on the last leg before pulling back on the stick and shooting over the trees on the far bank of the river. Even though none of us knew anything about flying a helicopter, we all sensed that we had just witnesses a great exhibition of flying. Everyone was whooping and cheering.

"Nice job, Sergeant," I said. Sgt. Poole looked even more relieved than me.

"We better get going," he said. "If the gooks didn't know where we were before, they do now." The only question in my mind was, which way? I turned to Rash as the men started filtering back onto the trail.

"You said the rangers got the chopper crew out?"

"Yes, Sir. The pilot was killed in the crash. The co-pilot had been shot a short distance away. They want us to continue to Phu

Gap as fast as possible. They're sending in an ARVN company."

"What for!?" I could think of no reason to send a company of South Vietnamese Soldiers and a platoon of Americans to an action that was already over.

"They didn't say, Sir" Rash said.

* * *

It took us another three hours to get to Phu Gap. Boyd was in no condition to walk point so Corbet took over. When we got there the air was faint with the smell of C4 and aviation fuel, the rangers having blown up the two man observation helicopter before leaving. We deployed along the tree line, being careful not to be seen even though the village seemed to be abandoned.

"Fast response by the ARVN," Sgt. Poole said sarcastically.

"Are you sure they haven't come and gone already?" Rash shook his head.

"Ain't sure a nothing', Sir," he said. "Las' I heard they was on the way."

"Well, call higher. Tell them we're in position."

"Already did, Sir." Good man, I thought. A woman came out of her hootch, trying to look natural as she looked around. On the other side of the river several ARVN soldiers were sitting atop their bunker, watching. No one, it seemed, thought this was over.

Two Chinooks appeared like giant wasps on the horizon, their double rotors slapping the air with their staccato beat. I hurried along the line, reminding everyone to sit tight, that we were not to get involved unless we were needed. The Chinooks made their approach over the ARVN outpost and set down on our side of the river. The rear ramps were lowered and the troops, one platoon in each chopper, ran out and assembled in a ragged gaggle. Through my field glasses I could see their captain, a short, bird-like man looking around, wondering, I guess, where everyone was. Us, the villagers, anyone.

Rash was on the radio, telling their interpreter we were to their right front, in the treeline. The officer looked our way and, still not seeing us, waved.

"Jesus," Sgt. Poole said. The Captain formed his men into two columns and they double-timed toward the village, their gear banging and rattling as they went.

"Sounds like a Goddamn tinker's parade," Sgt. Poole said.

"What's a tinker's parade?" Rash said.

One column cordoned off the village while the other herded the inhabitants to the outskirts, pushing and shoving anyone they thought was lollygagging. They separated the women and children from the men; then the ID checks started. A soldier pulled one man from the group and dragged him to the ARVN captain. The soldier handed the captain the man's ID. The Captain looked at it, stuck it in his pocket, then calmly drew his pistol and shot the man in the head. The man dropped like a sack of rice.

Women screamed. Children clung to their mother's sides. One woman dropped to her knees, covered her face with her hands and wept but no one came forward to claim the body.

The Captain started yelling orders; the soldiers spread out, setting fire to hootches and shooting the village dogs. A water buffalo lowed and started pacing in his pen. A sergeant emptied an entire magazine into its side. Several soldiers started chasing chickens which, once caught, had their necks wrung before disappearing into an ARVN rucksack. It was total mayhem. I thought about stepping in but an image flash through my mind--my men in a Mexican standoff with the ARVNs. This was their country, their show, and I was not in a position to get into a fight with a South Vietnamese captain. I had my orders.

Every structure was now in flames, the heat shimmering everything around it. I flinched at the sounds like gunshots coming from the village.

"Bamboo," Sgt. Poole said. I looked at him. "It's the air pockets in the bamboo exploding," he said. I wondered how he knew that.

Within twenty minutes there was nothing left of the village but the burning skeletons of bamboo frames, the smoke and soot marking where the hootches once stood. The Chinooks came back, the ARVNs disappeared into their gapping maws and then they were gone. All was quiet except for the crying of women and the occasional popping of bamboo.

"Let's get the hell out of here," I said.

"You want me to tell higher we're leaving?" Rash asked.

"No," I said, as if that would erase any evidence that we were even there in the first place.

Chapter 36

"You're quiet tonight," Audrey said. I was surprised that such a simple statement of fact could leave me so speechless.

"Yeah?" I said. "Sorry." I moved closer, kissed her cheek.

"You don't have to apologize. Everyone's entitled," she said laying her head into the curve of my shoulder. "Sometimes it's just nice to talk though." I could feel her lips moving against my skin, wanted to stay this way forever.

"About what?"

"Anything. It doesn't matter." I pulled away so I could see her better and ran my fingers through her hair.

"Your hair's growing back," I said. She laughed.

"*That's* what you want to talk about? My hair!" She threw her leg over my hip and sat up, straddling me. She leaned forward so that her face was inches from mine, her breasts swaying just above my chest. "Well since you brought it up, you could use a haircut, Lieutenant," she teased.

"Tomorrow," I promised. She leaned closer so that her bangs brushed my forehead.

"So you never said if you liked my hair short."

"I do. A little short at first, but I like the way the ends frizz up, like now," I said, brushing my fingertips along the edges of her ears. She gave me a big kiss, the kind that smacked when she pulled her lips away from mine.

"That's not what a girl likes to hear. About her frizzy hair. Anyway, it's the humidity." She went back to her former position beside me. "You can hardly see it, you know. Your scar," she said, kissing the place on my bicep she had stitched up so long ago.

"Did you ever wear it short for the other asshole?" I asked, trying to keep the conversation away from my day job.

She lifted her head. "What are you talking about?" she said.

"Nothing. Just something Marlene said. Right after we met."

"Marlene!?"

"She told me you didn't need another asshole in your life. I was just wondering who the other asshole was." She pulled away, propped her head on her hand so we were looking right at each other. "If you don't want to talk–"

"Derek," she said and waited for the surprise to leave my face. "How perfect is that. Sounds like the name of a doctor on *General Hospital*?"

"He was a doctor?"

"I was talking about the soap opera. He was a helicopter pilot. Gunships. Cobras."

"You're making this up," I said. As stories go, this one was such a cliché.

"No! What? You don't think I could attract the dashing type?"

"I always thought I was the dashing type," I said, trying to weasel out of my mistake.

"Well, you're not." She sounded like that was the end of the story but I wasn't about to let it go at that.

"So what happened?" At first she seemed reluctant to go on.

"First of all, I should have seen it coming. Marlene warned me he was a hound dog. I think he put the moves on her before I got there. He never even noticed me until…well, you saw the way I was before."

"You met him at the officer's club?"

"Uh huh. He had me pegged right away. Told me he had just gotten a Dear John letter from his fiancé and how that made him a better pilot because he didn't give a shit anymore. God, it sounds so stupid, saying it out loud. Makes *me* sound stupid."

"No it doesn't," I lied, trying to remember if I had ever used a similar pick up line. Certainly not one that blatant, I told myself.

"Anyway, we became an item, like we had some kind of future together. It's a long story but basically, just before he DEROSed he tells me his fiancé wrote that she had made a horrible mistake and wanted him back and all that crap."

"And you believed him?"

"I'm not *that* stupid. I didn't need Marlene to tell me *I told you so*."

"So wha'd you say. To him. Derek."

"Nothing," she said, regretting it. "He thanked me for giving him a reason for living when he didn't have one and I wished him the best because he deserved it. I should have told him what I really thought but I was so…stunned."

"He was an asshole. You didn't deserve that," I said, and I

meant it.

"But I'm not that girl anymore so you better not pull any of that crap with me, Mister," she said, trying to sound playful. She looked as if she was about to cry and she did. I rolled her onto her back and, without bothering to wipe the tears from her eyes, kissed her softly on the lips.

"I love you, Audrey," I said, and for next several minutes forgot all about what it was that had been bothering me for the last couple of days.

*   *   *

Major Fletcher ran his hand over the top of his bristly head, waiting me out. "Why do I get the feeling that's not really why you're here?" he finally said.

"No, really," I said. I had just told him I hadn't had one of my visitations in a long time and I had no need to see him anymore.

"Because that's what you told me last time you were here," he said.

"I don't remember," I said. "Lots of things on my mind, I guess." I didn't elaborate.

"Well, I'm glad you stopped by anyway," he said. "I was going over my notes for my paper and I noticed something I hadn't thought of before. It seems, and I could be wrong, that you stopped having those events about the time Sgt. Poole got here. I'm not exact on the timeline but....what do you think?"

"Maybe. Around that time I guess. Why?"

"Well, I was trying to pin down the cause of your *visitations*, as you call them, and I remembered you saying how when you first got here that your platoon sergeant wasn't any help at all running the platoon. That must have put a lot of stress on you."

"Yeah?" I said.

"Well, you seem to hit it off with Sgt. Poole. It must have taken a lot of weight off your shoulders, having someone you could count on to share in the responsibility." I just nodded, not seeing what difference it made now. He read my mind.

"Well, that probably doesn't matter to you at this stage, but I found it interesting. Not that one case proves anything, but together with others....You know. A pattern. A cause and effect sort of thing. For my paper."

"How's it coming?" I said.

"Good. Good," he said without much conviction. "Mostly antidotal at this stage, but interesting. From a psychological perspective. Good." I didn't want to go on but didn't want to leave either.

"So, it's going good?"

"Yeah. As good as can be expected," he said.

"So is that what you see most? From the people who come to see you? Problems with stress?" He was watching me closely so I tried to make my face as unreadable as I could.

"Yeah, stress. Mostly. The root problems vary but stress is the number one cause of most problems I see. And the way it manifest itself. Like with you." He leaned back in his chair, his way of telling me it was my turn.

"What else? Besides stress, I mean?" He leaned forward like he was making some breakthrough.

"Guilt is big too. Lots of guilt." He waited but I wasn't ready to commit just yet. "The survival instinct is the strongest instinct we have. Sometimes it makes us do things we would not normally do. Or fail to do." He studied me carefully.

"And how does that usually manifest itself?" I asked

"Depression, usually. At first. Ultimately….Well, I've been reading a lot of reports about the suicide rates of veterans--from Vietnam." I had to laugh.

"Why would anyone kill themselves over here? Just wait and someone will do it for you."

"They usually don't do it over here," he said. "It's usually after they get back home." That took the smile off my face. I had a hard time imaging someone fighting just to stay alive over here, then going home and putting a gun to their head.

"Why?" was all I could say.

"We don't know," he said. "We just know that the suicide rate among veterans is much higher than among other men in their same age group." He watched me while I tried to process that.

"What?" I finally said, having heard him say something that didn't register.

"I asked if you ever felt depressed."

"Do you?" I said.

"Fair enough," he said and looked at his watch. "Look. Sean. I've got another appointment, but I'd like to continue this conversation. Could you come back in an hour?"

"Can't. Gotta get back," I said, grateful for an excuse to escape. I started for the door without my usual thank you and handshake. I sensed him following me.

"I'm serious," he said as I opened the door. "Will you stop by again? Next time you can?" I turned and saw the concern in his eyes. I forced a smile.

"Sure," I said. A Spec. 4 was waiting outside, staring at his feet to avoid eye contact.

"Next," I said and started down the corridor toward the exit.

* * *

"I am such an asshole," I said, tossing my hat on my mattress.

"I know," Gary said. "Any particular reason this time?" A look of disappointment suddenly appeared on his face. "You didn't ask her to marry you, did you?"

"I'm not that stupid," I said.

"But you told her you loved her?" I shrugged, a tacit admission. He smirked but said nothing.

"What? No lectures on the dangers of getting involved over here?" He grinned sheepishly.

"I asked Beth to marry me when I got back," he said. I was stunned. "I know, I know," he said.

"What….When?"

"I mailed the letter last week. I was in a bad place, I don't know…I think I really want this. I'm not saying *you* should do it. You shouldn't. Not now. This is different. It's just that…."

"What?"

"She sounds like a nice girl, Audrey. Don't fuck it up."

Chapter 37

August turned into September and September melded into October. Gary DEROSed, and so did Captain Messina and PFC Nolan. Lt. Avery became acting CO and Lt. Petros became acting XO but everybody stayed where they were. Lt. Petros was still platoon leader of second platoon and Lt. Avery decided he could command the company better from the same cushy office he occupied at Hardscrabble as XO than he could at Old Crow.

Gary's replacement was Lt. Franklin Taggert, a hard-charging 2nd Lieutenant who had been cadet captain of his ROTC unit. Gary's former platoon sergeant was also gone, replaced by an SFC from West Virginia itching for his third rocker. Already their platoon had racked up six kills in two actions around Phu Nu but had taken five casualties themselves, two of them KIAs. At a platoon leaders' meeting, Lt. Avery wondered aloud why a green 2nd lieutenant was getting more kills than Lt. Petros's and my platoons combined. Lt. Petros noted that Lt. Taggert's platoon was also taking more casualties. Lt. Avery scowled. He too was itching for a promotion.

I did not like Frank, Gary's replacement, and the feeling was mutual. Although I outranked him, he made it clear he did not take orders from me when he was in the field and Lt. Avery backed him up on that. As the highest ranking man at Old Crow, though, I moved out of the bunker I shared with Frank and took over Captain Messina's quarters at TOC.

By the second week in October the monsoons were upon us again. The gooks took advantage of the weather to ramp up their activities. D Company was reporting lots of movement in the A Nang Valley and on our last mission we discovered a large cache of peanuts and rice hidden along the trail between Gia Hoi and Phu Nu. No one knew what that meant but it seemed an odd place to store food. We ambushed the site for three days with nothing to show for it but mosquito bites and boredom; then we doused it with used motor oil choppered in from Hardscrabble and set it on fire.

The VC seemed to know our every move. We hadn't been mortared since the night of Dr. Fletcher's visit and the general feeling was that the VC had been scared off after seeing what our artillery did to their former mortar site. Sgt. LoPresti, though, was confident that the next attack would come from the same place as the last one and that we were just one mortar round away from blowing them off the face of the earth.

That round landed in the middle of our helipad on a moonlit night during a break in the weather. Another round landed; then a break while they adjusted their aim. "Raise artillery," I ordered as I pulled on my pants. Sgt. Poole burst inside.

"I got it, Sir," he said, brushing the radio watch aside.

The third round landed just outside the mortar pit. I could see sandbags rupturing; the silhouette of a man running toward the pit tumble to the ground. He tried to get up, then dropped like a rag doll. I was halfway to the pit when our first round left the tube.

Another enemy round landed on the other side of our pit. A crewmen was blown sideways, toppling our mortar as he fell. Other men pulled him off; struggled to set the tube right again. Another silhouette clambered into the pit just as our first round landed on the distant hillside. I scrambled to a trench outside a bunker and watched. It seemed to take forever but eventually the rhythmic whump-whump of our return fire soothed my fears. There was no more return fire from the VC. Third platoon's medic was already working on the wounded soldier outside the pit. Doc Hippie was tending to a dazed trooper inside.

Everything seemed to be taking place in another world. The first artillery round landed on the far hillside, the shock waves wrenching my guts. I ran to our pit, yelling for our mortar crew to cease fire but they ignored me. Or maybe they just couldn't hear for the ringing in their ears. I grabbed the shoulder of the loader, yelling and drawing my finger across my throat. Behind me men were cheering as the artillery barrage lit up the mountainside. I grabbed one of the mortarmen and told him to have TOC get a dustoff in the air and stand by. Sgt. Poole was standing beside me, watching as our artillery turned a city block-sized patch of jungle into hell on earth.

"That should do it, Sergeant," I said. I could barely hear myself for all the noise. Two minutes and fifteen rounds later it was over. Sgt. LoPresti lay dead outside the pit, his carotid artery having been sliced open by a piece of shrapnel that barely slowed down as it ripped open the side of his neck. Doc Hippie reported that Specialist Kimmel most likely had a ruptured ear drum and a mild concussion.

He would monitor him throughout the night but could wait til morning for the dustoff. I told Frank to do a sit-rep on our LPs and give me a status report on the rest of his men; he disappeared without comment. I had Sgt. Poole do the same for our platoon and the mortar crew.

* * *

"Just LoPresti and Kimmel," Sgt. Poole said and dropped into one of the lawn chairs. I had sent Frank on a bullshit assignment as soon as he had given his report and put Rash on radio watch for the rest of the night. He was no Cisco. He had been up to snuff until Battalion changed everyone's frequencies; now he was playing catch-up again.

"Cancel the dustoff until morning, Sir?" he said.

"Yes. Thank you," I said, that detail having slipped my mind.

"Think we got 'em?" Sgt. Poole said. His boots were unlaced, the tops flopping over like dog's ears.

"I don't know. I think so. I don't think they got off any more rounds after our first one hit. Either it hit them, or convinced them to get outta Dodge. They knew what was comin'. You get anything outta our mortar crew?"

"They're pretty messed up just now," he said. "Lt. Taggert wants to take a squad to recon the site tomorrow."

"Fuck him! He ain't claimin' nothing on this, the bastard," I said. "You hear that Rash?"

"No Sir."

"You want it?" I asked Sgt. Poole, knowing he did.

"Yes Sir,"

"Take someone from the mortar crew--someone who can still see and think straight--and whoever else you need from our platoon."

"They did pretty good tonight, huh?" he said, meaning the mortar crew. Doc Hippie stuck his head in the door.

"VanDorn caught a sliver of shrapnel in his back," he said. "No biggie. I pulled it out but he should go back tomorrow too."

"Okay, thanks. Good job tonight," I said.

"Too bad about Sgt. LoPresti," he said. "Nothin' we could do."

"I know. Let me know if Kimmel or VanDorn turn bad. Have third platoon's medic spell you. Don't try to stay awake all night by yourself."

"No Sir."

*   *   *

Sgt. Poole left at first light. They traveled fast, not wanting any VC to beat them to the mortar site. As he later described it, the site must have looked just like their previous site after our artillery pulverized it, the only difference being four enemy bodies, all quite dead. One of the dead was directly under the tree where the observation platform, now just litter on the jungle floor, used to be. Another lay next to the jumble of steel that used to be a mortar, probably a victim of the first round out of our tube. The other two were found a short distance away, heads facing away from the mortar site, which was probably as far as they were able to crawl before our mortar crew righted our tube and finished them off. They were probably dead before our artillery chewed their remains into ever smaller pieces.

Sgt. Poole dropped a handful of blood-soaked papers on my desk. "Don't know if they're worth anything," he said. I pawed through them, pausing only once at a picture of a pretty young woman dressed in a cream colored ao dai.

"I'll send them on to higher," I said, putting them aside. "What did you do with the baseplate?" He had brought back the bent and broken tube and bipod from the enemy mortar as a trophy for our mortar crew, but not the baseplate.

"We dumped it in the marsh on the way back. Too heavy." They had also brought back one AK-47, two SKSs and a pistol no one could identify. The unused mortar rounds they blew in place.

"It was a good job," I said. "Thanks."

"Too bad Sgt. LoPresti wasn't here to see it," he said.

"Yeah. Captain Messina too."

I spent the rest of the day writing the after action report and a recommendation for a bronze star for Sgt. LoPresti, and army commendation medals for both him and Sgt. Poole.

I could not bring myself to enjoy our success. It had cost too much. The best I could do was take satisfaction in the small part I played in helping to even the score, if even just a little bit.

Lt. Avery was thrilled.

Chapter 38

A new Spec. 5 was sitting at Specialist Merry's desk. He looked up from his typing, searching for a sign of rank but I wasn't wearing any. "Yeah?" he said.

"Lt. Sullivan," I said. "Lt. Avery wanted to see me."

"Oh, yessir," he said, getting up. "He's in his office. You can go right in." He unlatched the gate in the counter and opened it. I knocked on Lt. Avery's half open door and stepped inside.

"You wanted to see me, Sir?" We were now the same rank but he was acting CO and made that clear every chance he got.

"Shut the door," he said and motioned me to a chair. "There's been a complaint filed by one of the elders of Phu Gap," he said, forgoing any pleasantries. "You're familiar with the village?" I felt my blood run cold.

"Yes, Sir," I said.

"The alleged incident took place on or about the afternoon of 28 August, 1967. I believe you were there with your platoon?" The legal jargon and his formal approach put me on my guard. I had been trying to forget that day for the past two months and felt a knot growing in my stomach. I thought carefully about my answer.

"Yes, Sir. We were ordered by Major Dempsey--"

"Just answer the question that was asked," he said.

"Should I have a lawyer with me?" I asked. I could see me being used as a scapegoat for something I had nothing to do with.

"It's alleged--and we have no reason to believe any of this is true--but it's alleged that after an American helicopter crashed in the vicinity of Phu Gap, a unit of South Vietnamese soldiers descended on the village and in the course of searching it they executed one of the villagers and burned the village to the ground." He said nothing about a lawyer. I sat silent. "The elder claims that before the ARVN arrived, a group of Americans came and took the bodies of the helicopter crew and blew up the helicopter. They made no mention of any other Americans. To the best of your knowledge, were you at any time observed by the villagers?"

"No. We left the--"

"And was the ARVN unit aware of your presence?"

"They knew we were there but we didn't make contact. Except for once on the radio to confirm our position."

"Good," he said. I noticed he wasn't taking notes.

"Should I--"

"So far, from what I've been told, this is purely a Vietnamese matter and that we should keep out of it. If that changes, you'll be notified. Until then, this is a very sensitive matter. Don't speak of it to anyone. Your people either. But that's not the only reason--"

"This was two months ago. Why did it take them so long--" He stopped me with a withering glare.

"On to other matters: I've made some observations and in the interests of our mission I'm instituting some changes in company SOP." He handed me a sheet of paper outlining his decree. I took it, noticing for the first time a new, cloth, Combat Infantryman's Badge sewn onto his faded fatigue shirt. "Actually, only a couple are changes. Most are already division SOP that previously," he said, meaning under Captain Messina's command, "were largely ignored. Helmets, for example--steel pots are to be worn at all times when out of doors. That means on patrol *and* in the fire base."

"Sir--" I protested.

"If these rules were followed in the first place," he said, cutting me off. "Sgt. LoPresti would still be alive today!"

"Sgt. LoPresti was hit in the neck," I said, angry that he didn't even know the details of one of his men's death.

"I'm not here to argue. If you have issues, submit them in writing. Number two: everyone is to shave *every* day. Of course, I realize that isn't practical when you're on patrol," he said in a lame attempt to appear reasonable, "But as soon as they return to base camp. Number three: night ambushes and LPs are no longer an either or situation when in the firebase. I want one ambush and two LPs out every night."

"Not possible," I said. He started to speak but I cut him off. "I have 31 men in my platoon. If third platoon is in the field and I have an ambush and two LP s out, that leaves me what? Nineteen men in camp? Two on radio watch leaves seventeen men for guard duty. No one will ever get a full night's sleep." He paused only briefly.

"Of course," he conceded, "That only applies when you have the manpower. But I know there are times when you have the men to do it and in those situations I expect it to be done. Number four…Well, you can read them yourself," he said, glancing at his watch. "I have a meeting. I just need you to sign that copy for my records. Here are copies for Lieutenants Petros and Taggert. Have them sign and return their copies in the next mail pouch." *So my ass is covered* I thought, finishing his sentence. I signed my copy and headed for the door.

On the way out I ran into Master Sergeant Fowler, our new company sergeant. "Sergeant Fowler, I need a word. Got a minute?"

"Eaten yet? I'm on my way to the mess hall." I fell in beside him.

"I see you got a new company clerk?" I said, starting off with small talk.

"Thank God," he said. "And not some infantry short-timer either. Types and everything. How's everything with you Lieutenant? How's Sgt. Poole working out?"

"You know Sergeant Poole?"

"We go way back," he said. "Old Army."

"Good," I said. "Very good. We work well together."

"That's what he says. He says you got no ego. That's a compliment, in case you didn't know." I nodded that I recognized a compliment from an enlisted man when I heard one. "He's way overdue for his third rocker, by the way."

"A CIB should take care of that," I said. I noticed that Sergeant Fowler wore a combat infantryman's badge, with a star to boot. "I notice Lt. Avery has one now?" Sgt. Fowler laughed.

"Is that a question?" he said but didn't wait for my answer. "From what I hear he put in for one twice when Captain Messina was here, both times for mortar attacks on Hardscrabble. Messina turned him down. Told him if he wanted a CIB he'd be glad to give him an infantry platoon, but apparently Wild Bill wasn't wild about that idea. So after Messina leaves, he clears it with division to take a recon patrol outside the wire. He puts together a platoon of unassigned FNGs and out-processing veterans, all eleven Bs. Hard to say who's more spooky, the new guys or the old guys. Anyway, the buck sergeant on point is jumpy as hell. See, he thinks he's home free and now this green lieutenant--first time outside the wire--is in charge of this menagerie of grunts thrown together at the last minute for what he probably thinks is a real mission for a real reason.

"So he sees this spot up ahead that looks like a great place for an ambush and he wants no part of it. He calls up Avery and of course Avery agrees. Avery brings the entire unit on line and orders a recon by fire. They go through enough brass to recast the liberty bell and then return to base without even checking for enemy KIAs because he knows there aren't any. He writes it up as a firefight and puts himself in for a CIB. Of course, by the time it reaches battalion all the witnesses have either gone home or scattered to forward units. Probably wasn't even a record of who all was there in the first place. Bingo. He gets his ticket punched." He opened the door to the mess hall and held it for me. "You look like a slob, Lieutenant, so feel free to join me on the enlisted man's side."

We went through the line and to an out of the way table. "So what's on your mind, Sir? I know it's not the state of Lt. Avery's career."

"He called me in for a talk today," I said. "You know anything about an incident at Phu Gap a couple of months ago?"

"It ain't no secret, but I thought nobody was making a big deal about it. Art said it was the ARVNs." Sgt. Poole's first name was Arthur.

"It was. But we were there. But I guess you already know that. Anyway, Avery's all hush hush about everything and made it clear he did not want to know the details. Told me not to discuss it with anyone. You got any experience with this sort of thing?"

"Not personally. But I got lots of experience with Lt. Avery. His kind, anyway. Get a lawyer, Sir." I felt my heart skip a beat.

"He said I didn't need one."

"All the more reason to get one. My guess, someone's making a fuss and I can guarantee you one thing--Lt. Dickhead's number one priority is to make sure none of the shit that's sure to hit the fan lands on him."

"But we didn't do anything. We were--" he held up his hand.

"I knew this guy, an advisor to the ARVN back in '64. An E-7. They were supposed to cordon and search this village. They had taken some casualties earlier in the day from booby traps so when they found a stash of hand grenades and twine and shit the ARVNs went berserk. Worse than what you saw. Anyway, when word got out they threatened to court-martial him for war crimes. He protested; said it was all the ARVNs an' that he tried to stop it. Even had a couple of ARVNs willing to back him up but it didn't matter.

They said it was a crime and he didn't report it."

"So what happened?"

"Nothin'. I don't know the details, but the army didn't want the publicity so they kept everything quiet. Point is, that was then and this is now. Talk to a lawyer, Sir."

*   *   *

The JAG office was closed for lunch so against my better judgment I went to see Audrey. I thought it best--for both of us--to let things cool down a bit. But people from the hospital had seen me at the mess hall and if word got back to her…Well, I didn't want to hurt her either. Luckily, she was in surgery at the time so I left a note on her desk saying I was sorry I missed her, signing it *S*.

A staff sergeant was sitting at a desk by the door when I went back to the JAG office. "Help you?" he said, another reminder that I was not wearing my lieutenant's bars.

"I'd like to speak to a--" What? JAG officer? Lawyer? "Lawyer," I said.

"Nobody in right--" I heard the door open behind me. "Oh, Sir, this man would like to speak with you." He was a young second lieutenant, probably a reserve officer fresh out of law school. He looked at his watch, then around the office as if there might be someone else who could handle it. There wasn't.

"Follow me," he said and led me to his cubicle. "Lieutenant DeVoist," he said, extending his hand.

"Sean Sullivan," I said. No rank.

"Have a seat," he said taking his chair behind the desk. "So what brings you to JAG today….Sean?"

"I was advised that I should talk to a lawyer."

"By?"

"My company sergeant."

"Have you talked to your company commander?"

"He advised me not to talk to a lawyer. Or anyone else?" This piqued his interest. He looked at me for a moment, then pulled a yellow legal pad in front of him. "Mind if I take notes?" I nodded my consent. "Sean Sullivan, you said?"

"Yes," I said, looking at the pad. "That's S-E-A-N. Everybody gets that wrong." He crossed out the *Shawn* and wrote the correction above it.

"Rank?"

"Lieutenant." He looked up. "First." I knew what was coming next so I didn't wait for him to ask and gave him my serial number.

"Unit?"

"C, second of the 605th." He wrote it all down, then laid his pen on the pad and leaned back in his chair.

"And why does your company sergeant think you should talk with a lawyer?" I filled him in on the circumstances surrounding the events at Phu Gap. He jotted a few things down but mostly listened, betraying no judgment regarding my actions, or lack of action.

"Did you report the actions of the South Vietnamese?" I thought over my answer.

"My after action report stated that in the course of the search of the village by the ARVN, a villager was killed and the village caught fire." He did not ask why my report was so vague or misleading.

"There's a lot to digest here, Sean. And I have a brief to write by three o'clock. I want to be honest. If you were completely honest with me, should you be brought up on charges, I think we can mount a credible defense." That unnerved me. I had been hoping he would tell me I was only following orders and that I had done nothing illegal; had nothing to worry about. "One thing you should know. I spent four years in law school, but have had only an eight week training course on the Uniform Code of Military Justice. I've never tried a case. As of now, I'm your lawyer and everything you've told me is privileged. If you want another lawyer instead of me, that privilege remains in effect. Do you want a different lawyer?"

"No," I said.

"Good," he said and handed me his card. "Just sit tight for now and let me look into things. In the meantime, don't worry about this. That's *my* job. I'm sure you've got other things to worry about." Not very reassuring.

"What do you think will happen?"

"Nothing," he said. "There's been talk about the Phu Gap thing, but nothing official here at JAG. If anyone was contemplating charges against an American, I think I would have heard something. If fact, this is the first I heard that an American unit, other than the rangers, was involved. My best guess… It's not in the Army's best interested to investigate this. As far as I know the Vietnamese are handling the complaint and my guess is that's as far as it will go. I'll keep you up to date on any developments. Until then, don't make any statements to anyone without me present, okay?"

Not until I got to the door was I aware of the dull roar that filled the office--rain pounding on the roof so loud that it could have been gravel. I was completely soaked before I got to the aviation office. I did not go back to the hospital.

Chapter 39

It was like looking at the world from behind a waterfall. Water streamed off my helmet, onto my shoulders and down my back. Everything was wet. Our packs and clothes took on extra pounds; our feet squished in our boots when we walked and the mosquitoes were everywhere again. So were the snakes. A water snake rippled by me on his way downstream. When it drew next to the man ahead of me he dipped the barrel of his rifle under the reptile and flicked it onto the bank.

"I hate those fuckin' things," he said. I couldn't remember his name. There were just too many new guys taking the places of the old guys. All the old sergeants were gone. Corporals Boyd and Corbet were now sergeants. Corporal Colon was our best point man but hadn't lived up to my expectations as a leader. Sgt. Poole had suggested Spec. 4 Murphy take over third squad.

I couldn't shake the image I had of an overeager Murphy tangled up in the barbed wire while trying to repair the perimeter during my first month at Old Crow but Sgt. Poole insisted he had matured since then. He never ragged on the new guys; instead he took them under his wing. Like Sgt. Poole, Murphy was a natural teacher and he proved his worth as a sergeant right from the start. He rarely yelled and when he told someone what to do he explained not only how, but why. Already his squad was performing better than the other two despite having more new guys in the ranks.

Everyone in the platoon looked up to Sergeant Boyd but Sergeant Poole made me see that he was still a bit of a loner and that Murphy was the better leader. Sgt. Poole had a knack for getting a quick fix on every new man in the platoon but that didn't keep him from changing his mind as things changed.

The training classes we had started so long ago were now in their second run. Doc Hippie was now giving the medical sessions and Rash was doing communications. Rash was a better RTO than teacher--his shyness holding him back--but Sgt. Poole kept things moving by asking the right questions to clarify points Rash missed or did not explain clearly. My men thought they had the best platoon in the company and so did I.

We were moving downstream in a shallow creek bed. Dry except during the monsoons, the water ran wide and slow, the rocky bottom often exposed above the waterline. The line slowed, the men bunching up as they came to a stop. *El Tee to the front* passed back in hushed voices. I hurried forward, the splashing of my feet drowned out by the rain. Sgt. Poole was kneeling in the creek, crouched against the low bank. He signaled me to stay low and ushered me in front of him so I could talk to Colon.

"Sentry. See him," Colon said, pointing to where the creek started a lazy turn to the right thirty yards ahead. With the rain I could see nothing but the dark trunks of trees tiger-striping the gloom. "On the far bank. Keep watching," he said.

It happened so fast I wasn't even sure I saw it—a sudden movement followed by the sound of a hand slapping flesh. "God help us if they ever get ahold of our DEET," Colon said. He was grinning like an idiot, proud of himself.

"Anybody else?"

"Not that I seen, but he ain't guardin' himself." I scanned the area, my mind racing to come up with a plan of attack. If we were to attack. How many are there? How long can we count on the rain to cover our movements? What kind of–

There was more movement. A shadow coming out of the gloom toward the sentry, his shoulders hunched against the rain, his rifle hanging limp from one hand. He said something as he drew close; the other man answered, leaning over to retrieve his rifle leaning against a large tree. A few more words and the first man started to leave, two targets about to become one. I could feel my gut tighten. The first man stopped, then froze. He seemed to be looking right at me, his mouth opening.

My rifle came instinctively to my shoulder and I emptied an entire magazine at them. One man dropped, the other stumbled. Colon and Sgt. Poole were firing in short, measured bursts.

There was a muzzle flash from the bank farther downstream, then another and another. Sgt. Poole was waving the men forward, bringing them on line. I grabbed a gun team and showed them where I guessed the encampment was; soon they were laying down a withering fire. The muzzle flashes from downstream stopped and I saw another figure running through the trees away from us. I raised my rifle and fired but by then he was gone.

"Move up, move up! Stay on line!" I yelled and we started moving forward, across the stream. Colon fired a long burst into the brush where he had first seen the VC to make sure they were dead before scaling the bank. The platoon moved quickly, shooting at anything that moved until I called a cease fire.

A low fire burned in a pit underneath a small lean-to. The place smelled of sardines and nouc-maum sauce. Cooking gear, tarps, and pieces of canvas littered the ground.

"Got a blood trail!" someone yelled. I looked in the direction of the voice. Others were running to get in on the kill.

"Leave it!" I yelled. "Sgt. Murphy, set up a perimeter."

"The blood trail's gonna wash away if--"

"Leave it!" I yelled even louder. Lt. Avery wanted every blood trail followed until we found a body or lost the trail but I saw that as a losing proposition. If the man died we had done our job. If he was still alive I didn't want one of my men walking toward a trapped animal lying in wait.

Colon and two new guys were searching the dead for documents. Everyone else was searching the campsite for souvenirs and contraband. Musty web gear, nylon backpacks, clothes, tire tread sandals, were thrown into the fire. It smoldered and smoked and stunk. Tin plates, porcelain cups, spoons, an aluminum tea pot, were all smashed and thrown into the jungle. A cache of 17 mortar rounds and eight B-40 rockets was found and blown in place along with several boxes of ammo, some of it the size used by Russian heavy machineguns. In addition to the two SKSs found with the sentries were an AK-47 and several old Bangalore-type torpedoes that Sgt. Poole recognized as the type used to blow gaps in barbed wire in World War II and Korea. They too were blown in place.

"What do you think?" I asked Sgt. Poole.

"Fits with everything else we been hearing," he said. The marines had been reporting a lot of movement in the DMZ not to mention the ongoing siege at Khe Sanh. Recon units had been seeing so much traffic along the Ho Chi Minh Trail that they were bombing with B-52s. Closer to home, D Company had gotten into a fire fight with what they were certain was a battalion of North Vietnamese Army regulars even though the numerically superior NVA pulled back before their suspicions were confirmed.

Judging by the campsite, we guessed there were between 10 and

15 men involved--not enough to justify the kind of ordinance they were carrying. "Something's brewing," I agreed. "Let's get the hell out of here." The light was fading fast and I wanted to put as much distance between the campsite and us as we could before dark.

* * *

The rain had stopped and I could hear the murmur of a sit-rep being called in. One o'clock. There was no moon and no stars. Everything was black. Someone snorted as he was nudged awake for his watch. I hadn't yet fallen asleep--lying awake and second guessing myself for initiating contact earlier that day. Had we really been spotted, or was I getting spooky? I had 40 days left in country and my nerves were shot. I was jumpy. At Old Crow I kept looking at the calendar and mission rotation schedule, figuring out how many missions I had left before I rotated to the rear. One, I figured. Two at the most.

I finally started to drift; I hoped Sgt. Poole would take part of my shift as he sometimes did. I felt his hand on my shoulder.

"Your watch, Sir," he said. I sat up, trying to orientate myself in the dark. I waited for the rush of blood in my ears to stop, listening for the rustle of water around rocks to regain my sense of direction.

"Got it," I said. The temperature had dropped into the 60s and I felt a shiver run through me. I wrapped my poncho liner tighter around my neck and pulled my arms in close to my side.

"Think I fucked up today?" I whispered. Sgt. Poole said nothing for a moment.

"I don't know. You see something I didn't?" That wasn't the answer I was hoping for.

"I thought one of them saw us. I just reacted." Another silence. Did he believe me? I wasn't sure I believed myself.

"I saw him turn," he said. "Colon said something about it. Things get confused. Happen so fast. I guess ya just gotta go with yer gut," he said, letting me off the hook. "We got two enemy KIAs and a WIA an' nobody hurt on our side. Tha's a good day in my book," he said and lay down with his head on his helmet. Something occurred to him and he raised his head again.

"Merry Christmas, Sir," he said.

"Merry Christmas, Sergeant," I said.

Chapter 40

Dear Shawn,

Sorry I missed you too. I was in surgery XXX most of the day but I guess Jill told you that. Jill is the new nurse you talked to. We've been very busy lately because we lost a nurse who found out she was pregnant before she even got here and had to go home. Plus we've been very busy and when we aren't all I do is try to sleep. We had a 13% increase in XXXXXX wounded just this month.XXX XXXXXXXXXXXXXXXXXXXXXXXXXXXXXXXX. But Enough of that.

I wish I had been here when you stopped in to see me but I was in surgery XXXXXXXXXXXXXXXXX when you stopped by. XXXX My DEROS is January 29. I hope you can find some business to bring you back to Hardscrabble before I go because I would like to XXXXX say good-bye and thank you for being my friend but if not I understand.

When we're busy it's usually because you're busy too and I will always remember the last time XXXX I saw you XXXXXX. Anyway, I know you are getting short too and I hope XXXXXXX everything goes well. Be careful and don't do anything stupid.

Love,
Audrey

P.S. Sorry this letter is such a mess.
P.PS I drink to much.

The letter was on my bunk when I got back from the mission along with several others.

Lt. Avery believed that the more miles we covered, the more likely we were to make contact with the enemy and the more kills we would get that he could take credit for. That was why we had been in the creek bed when Colon spotted that sentry--it was faster to walk in the water than through the brush, although I caught hell from Doc Hippie as it was wreaking havoc on the men's feet.

Still, the extra miles were not enough for Lt. Avery and he kept us out another day. We were patrolling a small valley south of where the VC had set up their last mortar site. The area was new to us because the valley floor was so narrow and the surrounding hills so steep that it was not suitable for agriculture and therefore no villages showed on the map. Lt. Avery concluded it would be a good place for the VC to hide and it turned out he was right for a change.

We found only two Vietnamese living there--an elderly couple whose hootch perched above the high water mark on a low hill. There was only one barely visible trail leading to the place. They had a small garden and a few chickens, but how they survived there was a mystery to us. They probably just wanted a quiet place to live out their remaining years away from the war. Now, even that was taken from them.

We couldn't get re-supplied, but the old couple showed us a spring where we could refill our canteens and we were able to pool together enough C-rations to repay their kindness. The VC probably did no less when they passed through.

When we got back Lt. Taggert met me at the TOC doorway. "Sean, come on in," he said as if it was his place, and apparently it was. Lt. Petros had DEROSed three days earlier and, in anticipation of that, Lt. Avery had pushed through an early promotion for Taggert to 1st Lieutenant and appointed him acting XO. "Sorry about that," Frank said, apparently not sorry enough to let me stay in the TOC bunker. "I put your mail on your old bunk."

I read Audrey's letter again, trying not to read too much into what little was there. At every cross-out I held the letter to the light to see what was underneath but she had been so diligent in her attempt to hide what she had written that her pen had almost worn through the paper. I read the letter again and again, feeling a warm rush in my chest each time her sadness seeped through. Still, as much as I wanted to see her I knew that it was for the best that she would soon be going home. For her, and probably for me too.

Gary had been right the first time. Wartime romances had little chance of surviving the long term. How well did we really know each other anyway? She had said nothing when I told her I loved her the last time we were together. Did she think it was just bedtime talk? Did she even hear the fervent whisper I murmured into her hair? What did the *love* in the closing of her letter mean? Was that her usual closing, or was that special for me? How well could she know me, anyway? We'd never even been on a real date, never seen each other under what most people our age would consider normal circumstances. Hell, she didn't even know how I spelled my name.

*   *   *

D company had been seeing a lot of action in the A Nang Valley and Lt. Avery wanted in on it so he sent second platoon out with orders to repeat our feat of climbing Mount Everest for the purpose of watching for enemy troop movements on the other side of the mountain. I told Lt. Avery that the mountain was so steep and the soil so unstable that it was too dangerous to attempt during the monsoons. Of course, he didn't listen and probably gloated when Lt. Churchill, the green 2nd Lieutenant who took over for Lt. Petros, reached the top. It took them two days though, and they spent only one night on lookout before having to return. They reported seeing the headlights of what appeared to be a small convoy heading east which turned out to be six deuce-and-a-halfs full of soldiers from South Korea's Tiger Division sent to reinforce our badly depleted D Company.

During their descent from Mount Everest, a dustoff had to be called to evacuate a trooper with part of his femur protruding from his thigh after he broke it sliding down the slope. They had to use a jungle penetrator to get him out.

*   *   *

I was typing up my monthly report for December when I heard Rash roger a transmission on the radio. I had moved back into TOC while Lt. Taggert was on patrol so I would be closer to the radio while I was in charge of Old Crow. At least that's what I told myself. A bigger reason was that I felt increasingly isolated in my old bunker and found that the company of the radio watch helped, even though we rarely spoke.

"Lt. Taggert's about an hour out," Rash said.

"Okay," I said and kept typing. I wanted to finish the report before he got back and reclaimed his bunker. I'd had ten days to finish the report but I kept finding reasons to put it off. Procrastinating was nothing new to me but as my tour came to an end I found it harder and harder to perform the more tedious duties of a platoon leader. Or any other duties for that matter. Sgt. Poole noticed and he asked if I wanted him to delay his R&R until after I left. I did, but I couldn't ask that of him. He hadn't seen his wife in six months.

"Where are they now?" I asked, meaning third platoon.

"Just past Gia Hoi," Rash said. I went to the map. I had to hand it to Frank, he could hump the boonies. Lt. Avery had told him to search Gia Hoi and then patrol the front side of Mortar Mountain on the way to Phu Nu where he spent two days setting up ambushes in hopes of catching some VC on the move. From there he was supposed to return the same way he had come but Lt. Avery had a bug up his ass and ordered him to return by way of the back side of the mountain--a more rugged, steep-sloped route that taxed their endurance.

On the way they encountered a young man in civilian clothes who immediately raised his hands and started chatting amiably to the uncomprehending Americans. He had no ID and Lt. Avery sent a chopper to pick the man up for interrogation.

They later found a series of new foot paths in the scrubby wilderness. They followed one of the trails which led to a deserted campsite. Returning to their patrol on a different trail the point man stepped on a land mine and lost both legs. The slack man was killed instantly and another man received minor shrapnel wounds. The point man died before the dustoff got there. Frank had more men killed on that one mission than I had lost in my entire tour but Lt. Avery didn't seem to notice. He liked aggressive patrolling. Frank was still the golden boy.

"Long hike," I said.

"Too long," Rash said.

It took second platoon almost two hours to get back after passing Gia Hoi. My platoon was out in the yard when they dragged themselves through the gate looking tired and defeated. There was little for my platoon to say. That would come later. For now it was a knowing nod for what they had been through; a reassuring pat on the back instead of a hearty slap.

"Frank," I said. He looked past me, like he couldn't focus. He looked exhausted. More than that. Drained. *Older* was the word I was looking for. I followed him into TOC. He leaned his rifle against the wall and I helped him off with his rucksack.

"Shouldn't of gone on the trail," he said. "But the men were tired. I know better," he said.

"You were being pushed too fast. That's what happens," I said.

"Yeah," he said. It was the first time I heard him say anything against Lt. Avery. He sat in one of the lawn chairs and dropped his helmet to the floor. He didn't seem to want to talk anymore. I went to a shelf, pulled down two bottles of Old Crow and handed them to him.

"From Major Dempsey. Two bottles for each platoon. The brand depending on your fire base. A belated Christmas present. Or New Year's. Whatever." He looked at the label, then forced a smile.

"First time I wished I was at Wild Turkey," he said.

"It gets the job done," I said, meaning the Old Crow. "Enough for a couple shots per man. Enough for a good night's sleep." He gazed at the cool brown liquid. "I left my monthly report on your desk," I said and started for the door.

"Hey, Sean," he said. I stopped and turned. He raised a bottle in a toast-like gesture. "Thanks," he said.

"You're supposed to share that with the rest of your platoon," I said.

"That's not what I meant," he said.

Chapter 41

It was just like before except the creek was higher this time. The water was almost to the top of our boots but I kept to the creek bed anyway. Not to appease Lt. Avery's belief that more miles yielded more contact with the enemy, but because it was unlikely the gooks would booby trap the water. This was to be my last mission and I wasn't taking any chances. Miraculously, Stevens was the only man to die under my command and I wanted it to stay that way. Besides, Lt. Avery wasn't in command anymore.

A new captain had finally arrived. Captain Ford was on his second tour, his first served as a platoon leader in 1965 when the 1st Air Cavalry was deployed as the first fully operational army division in Vietnam. His first official act was to send Lt. Avery, now XO again, to Old Crow to take over the day to day operations. Frank Taggert and I were again bunking together.

The line stopped and word came back for me to come forward. "This it?" I asked. For the last mile, every time the creek took a turn to the right, it looked like *it* to me.

"Yeah," Colon said. "I remember that tree." The tree had a distinctive, gnarly shape but I had no memory of it. S-2 wanted the camp site we had stumbled upon on our last patrol checked out and the area patrolled for signs of new activity.

"Get Boyd up here," I said. "Tell him to bring his RTO and one other man. Sgt. Poole too." Cpl. Colon returned a few moments later with the men, the RTO's whip antenna flopping a foot above his head. "Tuck that fuckin' thing in in," I said.

"That's the old camp site. Check it out," I said. "Watch out for booby traps." Boyd deployed his men on a wide front and crossed the creek. After checking out the other side he waved us forward.

The camp site was as we left it, minus the two bodies that had been dragged off by the VC. Charred web gear and melted plastic formed a blackened mound where the fire pit used to be. The old poles and thatch of the lean-to lay as broken and scattered as we had left them. It was just what intelligence thought--a temporary camp for resting and having a hot meal before moving on.

We spent the next two days searching the area in no particular pattern other than to avoid the vicinity where the old couple lived. We had no doubt they would be as cooperative with the VC as they had been with us. We found nothing that looked like new trails but a company of NVA could have cut their way through that jungle after we left it three weeks ago without us seeing it. The jungle grew fast during the rainy season.

"Looks like you just might get out of here alive," Frank said when we got back.

"Looks like it," I said and for the first time I started to believe it myself. I had been lucky. By Nam standards I had not seen a lot of action, but it was more than enough for me. And I took comfort in the fact that, by Nam standards, my platoon hadn't taken a lot of casualties. Each one was a tragedy, but getting everyone through without a scratch was not realistic. No platoon leader got through a tour without blood on his hands.

* * *

Three days later Sgt. Poole left for Hawaii. Good soldier that he was, he had arranged it so he would be back before our platoon was scheduled to go on our next mission. I said my good-byes in case I was gone before he got back. My DEROS was in ten days and I hoped to rotate back to the rear for a leisurely out-processing well before that. Captain Messina let DEROSing soldiers rotate to the rear several days early so they had time to decompress and soak up some sun before catching a plane back to the world. It was a common practice and I was all but certain Captain Ford would let me go early.

* * *

"Have a seat," Lt. Avery said. I assumed he had called me in to finish up some last minute business before I left; maybe even complement me on the job I had done; tell me he had put me in for a commendation medal or a bronze star. I put my helmet on the floor, noticing there was nobody on radio watch, never a good sign.

"I hope you're not going to tell me I'm not outta here today, 'cause I'm already packed," I said. I was smiling; he was not.

"I'm sorry," he said as if he really meant it. "I spoke up for you, I really did. But Captain Ford said no rotations to the rear more than three days from DEROS. I'm sorry," He saw my protest coming and cut me off before I could open my mouth. "It's only four more days. That's the bad news. The good news is the chopper that was going to take you back will be bringing your replacement--a Lieutenant Hoffman. Three weeks out of OCS. You can turn the platoon over to him as soon as he gets here. The only duties you'll have is to bring him up to speed as best you can in what little time you have left. You won't even have to unpack." I said nothing, started to get up.

"It's not an arbitrary thing," he said in Captain Ford's defense. "Intelligence believes all this activity is a build-up for some big offensive to coincide with the Tet holidays."

"That's bullshit and you know it," I snapped. "Jesus Christ! They say that every time the gooks have a holiday, or *we* have a holiday, or Ho Chi Minh has a birthday--or even a good crap for that matter, and it never amounts to shit." I started for the door, expecting him to try to calm me down, but he wouldn't give me the satisfaction.

* * *

The chopper came in low, under the clouds, the windshield wipers going even though the rain had stopped. My guys were there, eager to unload the Huey and see what goodies it might contain to brighten their miserable lives. Today it was mail and four green thermite containers of hot food, hopefully not one of the same entrees offered by the folks who brought you C-rations.

Lt. Hoffman hopped off first, carrying his rifle and dragging his rucksack behind him like a reluctant puppy, my men sizing him up while they unloaded the chopper.

"Lt. Hoffman?" I said.

"Yuh," he said, glancing around at his new surroundings.

"Sean Sullivan," I said, extending my hand. "You'll be taking over my platoon." He dropped his rucksack and shook my hand.

"Jesus, so this is it," he said, a sad statement of fact. It had been my life for so long I couldn't imagine what he'd been expecting.

They finished unloading and the chopper lifted off, scurrying across the Mu Dai Valley toward Wild Turkey. "That's Wild Turkey over there," I said, pointing toward the gray and brown scar on top of the smaller mountain two miles away. "That's where the rest of our company camps out." He looked at it as if appraising which firebase might be the better deal.

"They name everything after birds?" he asked.

"Bourbon," I said. He nodded. Apparently he knew his drinks. He was shorter than me and had the round, soft face of a man who once weighed more than he did now.

"Hey, El Tee. Macaroni and cheese!" Murphy yelled from the helipad.

"And green beans," another man yelled, opening a second container.

"What color were they supposed to be?" someone yelled back.

"Everyone's a comedian," I said. "Come on. Let's get you squared away and get some chow. You never know when you'll get another hot meal delivered." He picked up his rucksack and I led him toward the bunkers. "You'll be bunking with Sgt. Poole till I leave. He's your platoon sergeant. Then you move in with Frank Taggert. He's got Third Platoon. You're first."

"So what's it like around here?" he asked.

"Days and days of boredom, interrupted by brief moments of absolute terror," I said. The look on his face made me want to say something reassuring like *it's not so bad*, but I couldn't bring myself to do it.

*   *   *

"Any news?" I asked. Sgt. Poole was due back yesterday but so far we hadn't heard a thing from him. Lt. Avery looked up from his morning reports.

"He's hung up at Tan Son Nhut."

"Tan Son Nhut!? What's he–"

"The airfield at Cam Rahn was under a mortar attack so they diverted his flight. Captain Ford said he'll be back tomorrow." Tomorrow! Frank's platoon was one mile out and First Platoon was supposed to go out as soon as they got back.

"Can you wait till Sgt. Poole gets back to send my platoon out?" I said. I had spent the last two days briefing Lt. Hoffman on the men in his platoon and the tactics the VC were using in the area but it was clear from his questions that he was not yet up to taking over. He lacked confidence and the men would pick up on that in a minute. Bad as Sgt. Nelson was as a platoon sergeant, he was better than nothing when I first took over the platoon almost a year ago. Murphy and Boyd were both good sergeants, but neither one could take the place of Sgt. Poole. Or Sergeant Little for that matter.

"Negative. Captain Ford…Division, wants maximum G.I.s in the field until this Tet thing is over. Seems like half the ARVN army is on leave for the holiday, so that leaves us." I wasn't above kissing a little ass when it came to the safety of my men.

"Sir, Lt. Hoffman--"

"Lt. Hoffman is an infantry lieutenant in the United States Army. This is what he was trained to do. If he wasn't ready, he wouldn't have gotten his commission," he said and then softened. "Look, I sympathize. It isn't an ideal situation. But nothing is. I'm sorry. There's nothing I can do." Nothing short of going out yourself, I thought. I started to voice my objections again but he cut me off.

"If you feel so strongly about it you can take them out yourself. Your ride gets here at 1500. Be on it or not. It's up to you," he said.

"This is fucked up, ya know that?" I said and stormed out. I went to my bunker, threw myself on my air mattress, stared at the ceiling and looked at my watch.

"FUCK THIS SHIT," I yelled at the top of my lungs. Sgt. Murphy stuck his head in.

"You okay, El Tee?" he said. I was embarrassed by my outburst.

"Yeah, Murphy," I said. "I'm fine."

"Didn't sound like it, Sir. Don't be goin' ape shit now. You gonna come out and say good-bye? I'm sure the guys--"

"Yeah," I said. "Just give me a minute. Don't leave until I get there. You good with Lt. Hoffman?"

"We'll be fine," he said, and smiled. "Me an' Boyd, we know every safe place to hide in the entire AO. We could take him to Vung Tau for an in-country and he wouldn't know no different."

"Seems like you have it all figured out. Ten minutes," I said. I thought that would give me enough time to think things through and make the right decision.

I couldn't have been more wrong.

Chapter 42

I heard thunder in the distance but it was the hand on my shoulder that woke me up. I opened my eyes, wondering why I was being woken up. I had made it clear that I was only along as an advisor, that Lt. Hoffman was in charge. Not that that helped. No sooner were we outside the wire than I gave the order to stay off the trail while we came off the mountain. I wanted Lt. Hoffman to learn how to do things the right way and, to be honest, I felt I was pushing my luck by going out on one more mission. I wasn't taking any chances.

"Is that ours?" Lt. Hoffman whispered. I looked up and saw stars. It wasn't thunder after all. Artillery. I looked beyond the ripening rice paddies, beyond the dark silhouettes of Gia Hoi, beyond the even darker mass of Mount Everest to the flickering sky above the A Nang Valley.

"Gotta be. They don't have anything that big," I said, but wondered. With all the activity in the area, who knew?

"Any chatter on the radio?"

"Nothing," Lt. Hoffman said. "Just sit reps."

"Tune that thing to D Company," I said. Rash bent over the radio, adjusting dials. "We're supposed to keep at least one radio on the company frequency at all times," I explain to Lt. Hoffman. "But this will be for just a minute." Already teaching him bad habits, I thought. It was more than a minute because I couldn't break away from what I was hearing. Rash turned the volume up a notch and held the handset so we could all hear. Jim Beam was under attack. Mortars, rockets, small arms fire. Something big was happening. Big enough that they were calling in artillery around their own base camp, blindly searching for the bad guys. Dustoffs were in the air. One had been shot down trying to get in, the other limping back to Hardscrabble with a damaged tail rotor, their door gunner wounded.

"Get back on our push," I told Rash. Are they going to send in choppers to pick us up and go to their assistance? Is that even feasible? There was no traffic on our frequency. I heard voices along the line of our ambush. "Go tell them to keep it down!" I said and Rash scurried off into the darkness. It took him some time to get back, probably having told everyone what he knew.

"Wake me if anything happens," I said and went back to sleep, or what substituted for sleep in situations like this.

First light came with the sound of fighters screaming overhead. There were four of them, flying in pairs. They swooped above the mountains to the west, banking and dropping out of sight again and again looking for targets. I had originally planned on searching Gia Hoi in the morning as a training exercise for Lt. Hoffman but I had a sense of dread about me. I was spooky and more than anything in the world, I wanted out of there. We pulled back deeper into the jungle and then turned north. Captain Ford wanted us to check out Lang Tai and since he didn't share Lt. Avery's philosophy of *more miles equals more contact* we were free to pick our own route. I put Newell on point, saving Colon in case things got dicey. Slowly, my sense of dread lessened. For once I felt like the jungle was my friend, wrapping me in its protective cover. After an hour we heard more explosions off to the west. More fighters screamed overhead. The bombing continued for almost fifteen minutes but we could see little through the jungle canopy. We broke for breakfast, hoping to get a hot meal before it rained.

"Go see if any of the RTOs were listening in on D Company last night," I told Rash. "Tell them they aren't in trouble. I just want to talk to them. I'll keep an eye on your food," I said. There were Ants everywhere. I explained to Lt. Hoffman that we usually kept only one radio on at all times. "If we kept all the radios on we'd be carrying an extra 30 pounds in batteries," I said. The delinquent Rash brought back was PFC Cruz.

"First of all, don't do that again," I said while Rash flicked ants off his chopped ham and eggs. "So, Wha'd you hear?"

"Sounded like, from what I could make out, Jim Beam got its ass kicked. B-40s, mortars. They found dead gooks in the wire this morning. They had four KIAs an' nine wounded bad enough to evacuate. Got off easy, you ask me, from the sounds of it. They got the ROKs sweepin' the area now but I don't know what they find. I turned my radio off after that."

We continued north, moving slowly. At around nine o'clock we got a call. "Captain Ford," Rash said, handing me the handset. I envisioned us being choppered into the fight and my blood ran cold.

"Tell them to hold up," I told Lt. Hoffman as if he was just another enlisted man. I listened as Captain Ford explained what he wanted. I had no questions. I knew exactly what he wanted. The men were all sitting down, grabbing a smoke or a drink, bullshitting. When Lt. Hoffman got back I sent him on another errand--"Get all the sergeants. And Colon too. Change of mission."

*   *   *

I had the map out for Lt. Hoffman's benefit. Everyone else was familiar with our destination and how to get there. "The ARVN compound at Phu Gap hasn't been answering their sit-reps since early this morning. They had a chopper do a fly over and they reported five bodies inside the compound, presumably dead. They want us to check it out. That means, if we want to get there before dark, we're going to have to use the trail. Colon?"

"Fuck," he said, but I sensed in his tone the same relief I felt that we were not being inserted into the blood bath going on just over the mountain.

"Is that bridge above Gia Hoi still there?" he asked.

"I guess we'll find out," I said.

"What about the one at Phu Gap?" Boyd said. "If we cross now, we gotta cross back once we get there."

"I don't know," I admitted. "That one's higher. And pretty sturdy. I don't think the river's high enough to take it out. Any other questions?" Murphy raised his hand as if he was in school . "Yes. Sgt. Murphy."

"At what point, Sir, did you realize how big a fuckin' moron you were to go on this mission instead of going home?" It occurred to me that Murphy was the only man in the platoon who had been here longer than me. He would be home himself by now if he hadn't extended his tour by twenty-six days so he could get an early discharge from the army when he returned home.

"Probably the same time you did, Murphy," I said. Even Lt. Hoffman was laughing.

*   *   *

The bridge above Gia Hoi was still standing, but just barely. The water was splashing against the center of the span where the bridge sagged the most. The bridge on the other side of the island was better, but not by much and I felt we had dodged a major bullet when everyone made it across. We crossed one at a time but the extra caution had been worth it. Only our feet got wet. Still, time was short.

Colon kept up a good pace and we didn't stop to rest until we reached the clearing we had made to medevac Nellis months earlier. The river was almost over its banks, the tree we felled already washed away. Only the stumps remained to bear witness to the events that happened there. The old guys told the new guys the story. The moral: if you have the chance to get out with all your limbs attached, get out while the getting's good.

All morning we had been hearing artillery in the distance and seeing the contrails from fighter-bombers going to or coming from missions, but our radio was silent as to what was going on. All we knew was that it was something big. Intelligence had been right on this one.

One of our RTOs was monitoring the battalion net but all he got from it was that B Company was in contact above Lang Tai and A Company was choppering in a platoon of grunts to run a sweep out of Jim Beam in support of the Korean troops.

By then it was almost two o'clock, three hours until sunset. We were making good time but within half an hour Colon found a booby trap. Ten Yards further on he stepped on a trip wire but the pin on the grenade did not come out all the way. Colon was badly shaken, not to mention the slack man. The message was clear. Whoever was up ahead knew we were coming. We left the trail. Colon insisted he was okay and we continued toward Phu Gap at a much reduced speed. A half hour later we saw light filtering through the trees ahead. Phu Gap.

It had been five months since I'd last seen Phu Gap, although it had never been far from my mind. I'd stopped in to the JAG office to see Lt. DeVoist the last time I was in Hardscrabble and he had nothing new to report. It was, he said, almost like it had never happened; looking at the village now it was easy to make believe nothing had.

There was no evidence of the charred remains that once marked the site of the village. Instead a new village--indistinguishable from the old one--had sprung up in its place. New thatch replaced the old as seamlessly as the lush green of the rice paddies had replaced the sunburned earth of the dry season.

The inhabitants appeared to be going about their business in the village, but the paddies, except those closest to the village, were vacant. They knew something was coming; they just didn't know it was us. The bridge to the other side of the river was intact, the water still a foot below the lowest beam. I could make out little of the ARVN compound--a few puzzle pieces of wire and bunker seen through the trees that lined the riverbank; not enough to suggest what the picture as a whole looked like.

The Vietnamese tensed when we came into the open, then started drifting back into the village. A couple of older men stayed put, watching with a combination of fear and curiosity as we angled away from them toward the bridge.

Colon crossed first. I went next, as soon as he was across. The tree line along the river was too narrow to hide an ambush and the abandoned paddies stretched so far upstream and down that I feared little in the way of surprise from that quarter. Beyond the fallow paddies and the old millet field however, lay the edge of the jungle where the original village of Phu Gap was located before the soil played out and forced them to move. If we were to be hit, I thought, it would be from there.

I stayed at the bridge as the rest of the platoon crossed, spreading them out so as not to present an inviting a target to anyone lying in wait. We moved through the paddies, muddy from the rains, and stopped after reaching the old millet field. From the top of the last dike I had seen the dead ARVN soldiers the chopper had reported inside the compound. Other than the bodies, though, I saw no sign that anything resembling a battle had taken place. They were all in the open. Not a single body was near anything that could be considered a fighting position. It was like whoever had killed them had simply walked up to the wire and gunned them down before they realized they were in danger. Maybe, I thought sardonically, they should have put their unwritten agreement with the VC in writing.

"Colon," I yelled. "You and Dell, check it out. Watch out for booby traps. AND DON'T GO IN THE BUNKERS!" I knew I was overusing Colon but it seemed every situation was critical enough to require the best man for the job.

Colon took his time clearing the entrance to the compound before he waved Dell in. "Don't touch the bodies!" I yelled as they worked their way toward the bunkers. Colon didn't even acknowledge that he heard me, as if to say *I'm not that stupid.*

Taking a grenade from his belt, he pressed his back against the wall outside his bunker's entrance. He looked to see if Dell was in position, then yelled as the Spec. 4 took a step inside his bunker.

The explosion threw Dell back several feel and an instant later the jungle, only a hundred yards away, erupted. Colon tossed his grenade into his bunker, then ran to help Dell. Bullets riddled the field across our front. I saw one of my men fall, then another; a mass scramble back to the paddy, men toppling over crumbling dikes, seeking cover; One man still down in the millet field, another lying prone, firing into the tree line; Lt. Hoffman just standing there, paralyzed with fear.

"Get back! Get back!" I screamed, surprised to find that I was already behind the dike myself. Bullets were cracking over my head, hitting the ground around Lt. Hoffman; more men returning fire, entire magazines being emptied in a single burst; the sound of our machinegun chattering off to the right; Lt. Hoffman falling over the low wall of the dike, one man still on the field--motionless, another behind the dike, holding his arm and screaming for a medic; Doc Hippie nowhere to be seen. Lt. Hoffman was right next to me gulping air, his eyes wide, his skin pale.

"We need artillery!" he yelled. "Call in an air strike!" I looked for Sgt. Poole, but that was the reason why I was there in the first place. I felt alone, but of course I wasn't. I looked to the ARVN compound. Colon was pinned down behind the bunker, sitting with his back against the sandbag wall. Doc Hippie was next to him, leaning over Dell. His hand came up, full of bloody bandages, throwing them to the ground, his shoulders slumped.

A rocket skipped off the millet field and exploded on the dike. Romansky ducked, pulling his machine gun off the embankment. He pulled the bipod from the barrel, stole a peek at the tree line.

The man still in the field--I couldn't tell who it was--turned his head, looking for help. He didn't call out, raised his hand a few inches. *I'm still alive,* he seemed to be saying. Someone yelled for him to lie still. Doc Hippie saw him, was throwing his supplies back into his aid kit, slinging it over his shoulder. I yelled for him not to go out there but he showed no sign that he heard me.

Lt. Hoffman had crawled over to Rash, was grabbing at his shoulder, yelling at him to call in artillery. Rash shaking him off, returning fire to the tree line. Doc Hippie was out of the compound;

making ready for his run to the wounded man in the field. I yelled for cover fire and our line erupted. Doc ran. He pulled the man's arms from his rucksack, grabbed his shirt collar and started dragging him toward the dike, his legs pumping. The VC zeroed in. Spatters of mud danced around him. Doc fell to the ground, taking cover behind the wounded man, Sousa I now saw. Sousa's body jerked with every hit. His helmet came off with a loud smack, a red flow spreading down his cheek in a dark sheet. Doc Hippie running, diving over the dike, swearing, crying.

A moment of relative quiet as men changed magazines, gathered their wits. The enemy fire dropped off but never stopped completely. Lt. Hoffman was crawling toward me--Rash just ahead of him, as if being chased.

"You call it in?" I said.

"Yes, Sir." Rash's radio voice. Calm, deliberate.

"Okay," I said. "Let's see where we are." I looked at our line, the position of our guns--studied the ARVN compound twenty yards to our front. There was no sign of Colon. I noticed a window the size of a shoebox in the side of the bunker closest to me; assumed there was another one facing the tree line. I hoped Colon was inside, manning the gun port.

Lt. Hoffman crawled over on all fours. I pushed his head down when it bobbed above the dike. Every glimpse of us drew fire. He shoved his map under my face. "We need artillery! I can't figure out where we are!" He kept turning the map, trying to orient it. I took the map, oriented it to the river and pointed.

"Here," I said. "The map's outdated. This village?" I said, pointing to a cluster of black squares on the map just to the east of our position. "It's now over there." I pointed to Phu Gap across the river. He looked at the lay of the land, then the map.

"So they're here?" he said, his finger drawing the enemy's position on the map. I had to give him something to do.

"I'll take care of that," I said, taking his map. A rocket sizzled over the dike near one of our gun positions, exploding harmlessly behind them. "See where our guns are? I want them on our flanks. If the gooks--" He nodded that he understood. "And tell the other RTOs to turn their radios on," I yelled after him as he crawled off. I watched as he reached the first cross dike, paused, then rolled over it into the next paddy.

We were pinned down with no way out. I looked at the sun, low in the sky behind dark clouds. We had about an hour before sunset and I did not want to be caught out in the open after dark. Lt. Hoffman was right--we needed artillery. Sgt. Poole was the expert on that but the bridge gave me an exact fix on the enemy position. I was confident those we didn't kill would be driven off with a few well-placed rounds on the tree line

Our radio crackled. "Cruz is on," Rash said.

"Ask him if he can get to us?" Rash relayed the message.

"On his way," Rash said. I watched as Cruz toppled over one cross dike after another, low crawling the intervals between. Farther down the line I could see Lt. Hoffman on his way back, and Romansky and Williams settling in one of our machineguns at the end of the line. "Want me to raise artillery?" Rash asked. His rucksack was off, lying flat on the ground so the radio's antennae wasn't exposed above the dike.

"Not yet," I said. Doc Hippie had just finished bandaging the man who had been hit in the arm. "Who got hit?" I said when Cruz reached us.

"Warner," he said. "Bleedin' like a motherfucker, but no bones broken. Doc stopped it for now."

"We need your radio. You stay on the company net." I turned to Rash. "Let's get some firepower." I was grinning like a maniac. Rash changed frequencies and made the call.

"Bravo Zulu," he said, handing me the handset.

"Bravo Zulu, Bravo Zulu, this is X-ray One, over."

"Bravo Zulu. Go ahead X-ray one." I could hear his battery firing outside his bunker.

"This is X-ray One. Fire mission, over."

"Go ahead, X-ray One."

"Requesting H.E. Troops in a tree line. Grid coordinates 8312 4763, over." There was a moment while he found the coordinates on his map.

"X-ray One, say again grid coordinates, over." I read the grid coordinates again. "X-ray One, I have a village at those coordinates. Please confirm, over."

"Negative, Bravo Zulu. That village is no longer there. The village is now about a klick to the west of those coordinates, over." It wasn't that far, but close enough.

"Negative on the fire mission, X-ray One. I can't fire within 200 meters of a village, over." I was barely able to control myself.

"I say again," I said, ignoring the call signs. "The *village* has been *abandoned*. It is no longer occupied. No longer *there*!" I said. Lt. Hoffman had joined us from the right side of our line but I waved him on--*tell the rest of the platoon*. He indicated that he'd wait, he wanted to talk. Jesus! Couldn't he see that we were bunched up!? Two officers and two radios in one spot!

"I'll need confirmation on that, X-ray One," the battery commander said. "From an O-4 or higher, over." His voice was flat, dispassionate. One of our men down the line popped up and emptied half a magazine toward the tree line. I tapped Rash on the shoulder and made a shooting gesture with my left hand. Rash looked quizzical, then got it. He stuck his rifle over the dike and squeezed off several short bursts while I talked. Background noise for the battery commander's benefit.

"Bravo Zulu, this is X-ray One Actual." I yelled above the sound of Rash's firing. "We are pinned down by a large enemy force. I already have two KIAs and a WIA in need of evacuation. Need you to expedite fire mission, over." Rash stopped shooting so I could hear his response. The artillery commander repeated what he said before, word for word. "Stupid motherfucker," I spat. "If it was his ass out here we'd be seeing all hell breaking loose out there. Even if there was a village. Cruz--get Captain Ford. Tell him our situation, see what he can do. WHAT!?" I said, seeing Lt. Hoffman was still there.

"O'Brien's radio is finished. Bullet hole right through the middle of it."

"Shit! He okay?"

"Loosened a coupla teeth when he got knocked on his face is all." I took my helmet off and wiped my eyes.

"Okay. Finish up with the rest of the line then stay there with the RTO," I said. "Get air," I said and Rash changed frequencies again. Shit.

There was another machine gun, this one in the middle of the enemy line. Had it always been there, or were the VC getting reinforced? I heard the whump of an M-79 and looked down our line. Corporal Semmler was crouched behind the dike, the butt of his grenade launcher planted on the ground, using it like a mortar. I stuck my head up in time to see the grenade land behind and to the left of the machine gun.

"Is third squad on the air?" I said to Cruz. He nodded and handed me the handset.

"Captain Ford ain't in the orderly room," he said. "Hardscrabble's being probed an' him and Sgt. Fowler are on the green line." Shit. I pressed the transmit button and raised third squad's RTO. "Tell Semmler his last shot was thirty yards behind the machine gun and twenty yards to the left," I said. "Tell him no more grenades unless he has a spotter. That goes for everyone with a launcher." I took another look; all I saw was muzzle flashes. The VC were just inside the vegetation, either dug in or behind cover. From the sound of things, we hadn't diminished their fire power in the least.

"Thomas is trying to get Major Dempsey," Cruz said, finishing what he was trying to tell me before. Spec. 4 Thomas was the new company clerk at Hardscrabble, but Cruz's words barely registered with me. I was having trouble concentrating.

"Anything on air support?" I said to Rash. He was listening to the handset and held his hand up, signaling me to shut up.

"Keep trying," he said. "Let me know as soon as you got something'. We getting' our asses kicked out here bro. X-ray One, out." He put the handset down. "Nothin', Sir. Sound like the whole fuckin' country wants air support." I looked at the sun, resting on the tops of the trees lining the river.

We started taking small arms fire from the tree line off to our right but they were 300 yards away and not dug in. A few bursts from Romansky's gun drove them off but not before an AK round kicked up dirt at Cruz's feet.

"Fuck this shit!" He said, changing frequency on his radio. "Bravo Zulu, Bravo Zulu, this is Two Bravo, over." I wanted to laugh but did nothing to stop him. Two Bravo was Major Dempsey's call sign. Just maybe he would give the chicken shit artillery commander what he needed to cover his ass.

"This is Bravo Zulu, go ahead Two Bravo." Cruz smiled.

"This is Two Bravo *Actual*, confirming X-ray One's transmission. There is *no* village at the grid coordinates requested for the fire mission. I say again, NO village at said coordinates. You are clear to commence fire mission, over." Cruz put his hand over the mouthpiece and told Rash to get back on the company net.

"Roger, Two Bravo," the artillery commander said. "Please provide password to confirm identity, over." Cruz looked to me but all I could do was shrug my shoulders. "Two Bravo, I say again, please confirm password, over." Again, I shrugged my shoulders. I didn't even know Major Dempsey had a password. Cruz panicked.

"The password is *fuck you, you chicken shit motherfucker. I'm gonna be dead in ten minutes an' my blood will be on your hands. PFC Raymond fuckin' Cruz, you rear echelon motherfuckin' hijo de un puta.*" He threw the handset to the ground and slumped against the paddy dike. There was no reply from Bravo Zulu and no artillery barrage.

"I take it that wasn't the password," I said.

"It was a long shot," he said. "Sorry, El Tee."

The sun was dropping quickly. I looked down our line; saw a trooper laying on his back, his feet toward the dike, his helmet three feet behind him. Another trooper was crouched against the dike next to him. He made no effort to attend to the other man and had not called for Doc.

Some of the men were returning fire, getting their licks in while it was still light. Others were conserving ammo. Romansky and Williams were using an entrenching tool to carve a battlement out of the dike so they could have some protection while they fired their machine gun.

No one knew what the VC were going to do after dark. One thing was sure, they weren't going to pull back. Only Boyd wasn't shooting. The two to three second window he had after sticking his head up was not enough to locate a target--let alone take aim and shoot--before getting his head blown off.

"Get Boyd over here," I yelled. The word was passed down and within two minutes Boyd was by my side.

"Those guns are killing us," I said, meaning the VC's machine guns. "The sun should be in their eyes. You think you can make it to one of those bunkers?" He looked at the ARVN compound and smiled.

"Yes, Sir," he said, reading my mind. I told him anyway.

"There should be a gun port in front. That should give you enough cover that you can see movement long enough to get a shot off. What do you think?"

"I think the gooks are in a world of shit," he said.

"Don't be too cocky," I warned. "Once they figure out what's going on they're going to be putting everything they got at you. Don't take any chances," I said after I'd ordered him to do just that. "Wait till we put down some cover fire before you make your run."

Boyd worked his way along the paddy dike until he was directly across from the ARVN compound. He waved when he was ready and I gave the word to open fire. Our line erupted. Grenade launchers thumped, machine guns chattered, M-16s crackled, and Sergeant Boyd ran. He made it to the gate and barely slowed as he ran the zigzag path through the barbed wire.

Boyd was not the only one running. Sgt. Murphy also ran forward. At first I thought he was trying to retrieve Sousa's body, still lying in the millet field; instead he grabbed the belt of machine gun ammo around his neck, his men cheering as he tumbled back over the dike to safety.

I called a cease fire, hoping the VC hadn't seen Boyd. Again, I wondered about Colon. I didn't even know if he was still alive inside one of the bunkers. There was so much shooting I couldn't tell if any of it was coming from him.

The back and forth continued--the crack of the AKs, the chatter of machine guns, the short bursts of the M-16, the whump/boom of the M-79s, and now the occasional bang of a single M-14. Another B-40 sizzled our way. It skipped off the millet field to the right of Romansky's machine gun and exploded on top of the dike, spraying Specialist William with shrapnel. Romansky screamed for a medic, pulled his gun from the notch he had carved in the dike, and started tending to him.

Rash's ear was plastered to his handset. He shook his head. Nothing. An explosion to my left. A plume of smoke and sand rose up from the front wall of Boyd's bunker. Several sand bags slumped and fell from the top row but the wall held. The fire from the tree line increased, much of it directed at the ARVN compound. If nothing else, Boyd was taking some pressure off the rest of the platoon. I caught a glimpse of movement--a flash of black pajamas headed for the VC machine gun on the right, the bark of an M-14, another B-40 headed Boyd's way along with a burst of enemy machine gun fire, an explosion and a collapse of the bunker's roof line. An agonizing minute, then Boyd coming out of his bunker and disappearing into the other. Another rocket, this one sailing over our heads and landing near the bridge--getting their range in case we tried to retreat across it, reading my mind.

The sky was clearing and a three-quarter moon was rising in the east as the sun fell in the west. The river was too high to ford and a bottleneck at the bridge would allow the VC to pick us off if we tried to cross. With the wounded we'd have to carry, we'd be lucky if half of us made it. I was out of ideas, pinned down, dead and wounded on my hands, and no help in sight. And that's what I needed—help.

The VC opened up with another fusillade of gunfire. Bullets cracked overhead and launched sprays of dirt from the top of the dikes. I saw a rocket hit the dike in front of the machine gun on our left flank, heard another explosion to the front. I stuck my head up in time to see part of the wall on the second bunker crumble. I never saw the rocket that hit the dike right in front of me.

Shrapnel rattling off my helmet; my head spinning; the yelling of a thousand men. I opened my eyes, saw the tread of a hundred ragged shoes hurrying past, legs trousered in gray and butternut marching in quickstep. The line stretched a thousand yards to either side of me, men in rout step, thirty to forty deep. I had never seen so many men on the move--so fast, so urgent, their muskets tipped with the hot steel of their bayonets. Another cannonball hit near-by. Three men went down, another half dozen faltered. An officer's horse panicked, charging to the rear, blood streaming down its flank, its rider dead on the field. I looked in the direction of the fire, across the dirt road, beyond a rail fence, up the slope behind a low stone wall where the Union line waited, the Confederates not yet in musket range. Higher up, just below the crest of Cemetery Ridge, the federal batteries worked to a frantic rhythm. Off to the left, the spires of Gettysburg watched in silent witness.

I got to my feet, fell in beside a pimply-faced private. A cartridge pouch bounced against one hip while his canteen, slung by a piece of twine, banged against the other. His slouch hat was torn and greasy, his face a portrait of fear. Sweat ran down his sunburned face, his eyes fixed on the Union infantry behind the stone wall.

"Where are they now?!" he yelled to the heavens. "Now's when we need them!" I stumbled on the uneven ground, looked behind me to see the last of the confederate artillery disappearing into the trees.

This was insane.

"Who?" I screamed. "What are you trying to tell me?!" I knew how this ended. What could I possibly learn from this? The federals fired, the blue line disappearing into a cloud of smoke. The rebel line staggered, its ranks decimated. The shock wave from the union muskets hit me like a sledgehammer. The rebels still standing picked up the pace, trying to close the gap while the Union line was blinded by its own gun smoke.

Tears were running down the teenager's face, the salt stinging his parched lips. I wondered how many times he'd relived this moment in the hundred years since it had taken place, how many others he'd recreated it for, how many times he'd died for…what? What was he trying to tell me? What to do? What not to do?

An officer yelled *Charge* and the rebels answered with a blood-curdling yell. They charged, muskets at the level, and I ran to keep up, waiting for an answer. I grabbed the boy by the shoulders and turned him to me. "Who!? Who do you need?" I demanded.

"Our artillery! They should have saved enough ammunition for our advance! Now it's too late!" he yelled, shaking himself free from my grip. He turned, his eyes wide. The smoke was clearing as the last of the federal troops withdrew their ramrods from their muskets. We were now close enough to see the bayonets spiking the ends of the federal barrels, to see the determination in their eyes as they leveled their guns for another blast, hoping there would be little need for their bayonets once their mini-balls ripped through what was left of the gray line. They fired. The confederate line faltered and fell, their yells turning to groans as they were knocked off their feet. I was down too, uninjured but down on my hands and knees. The boy was among the few left standing, the few left charging forward, the few left to meet the enemy's steel.

"Sir! Sir! I've got someone." My head was reeling. I looked past the black face, our entire line down, firing only sporadically. Bullets hitting all around, Doc tending to Williams, Warner feeding a belt of ammo with his good arm while Romansky sprayed the enemy line from the cover of his battlement. "Sir, I've got someone! They want to talk to you," Rash said.

"What?"

"A cobra! I got a cobra. They want to talk to you." A handset in front of my face. I reached out slowly, not sure….

"Who?"

"Hellfire Two One."

"Hellfire?" Everything was coming back now.

"Yes, Sir. Two One." I tried to swallow, clear my throat.

"Hellfire Two One, this is X-ray One Actual, over." It came out like a croak and I tried to work up some saliva in my mouth.

"Good evening X-ray One Actual. I understand you're in need of a little help. A little is all I can give you. I'm down to two rockets and one or two hundred rounds in my mini-guns. You want it?"

"Uh, affirmative, Hellfire. How soon can you get here?"

"I'm on my way back to Hardscrabble. I'll be there in zero five. Have smoke ready to mark your position, over." A flashback to the Union line, blinded by their own gunsmoke.

"You can count on that. Stand by," I said. I looked down our line and what I saw was a group of exhausted men, near the end of their ropes, desperate enough to try anything. "FIX BAYONETS!" I yelled and then yelled it again when everyone looked my way, not reacting. Most of them didn't even have bayonets. Those that did started pulling them from their scabbards or ripping into their rucksacks to find them, trying to remember how to fix them to the ends of their rifles. I was down to twenty four effectives. Minus the men I would have to leave behind--Rash, Doc Hippie, Colon and Boyd, if they were even alive--I would have only twenty men to make the assault.

I moved down the line explaining what was expected of everyone. No one was happy, but to a man they were willing. Anything was better than the status quo. By the time I got back to the radio I could see the gunship in the distance, approaching from the southeast.

"Hellfire Two One, I have you in sight. We are about four klicks to the northwest of your position. Hold off your advance, over." I saw the gunship turn to the west, gain altitude and circle while I explained our position and what I wanted, that timing was critical and that I wanted him to use all the ordnance he had in one pass. Under no circumstances was he to make a second pass; that by then I hoped to be inside the enemy position.

"Roger, X-ray One. Am proceeding to my point of attack, over." By this time the VC had spotted the cobra and a few desperate tracers arced up in a vain attempt to stop what was coming. The helicopter dropped to treetop level, staying far enough away that he was out of their line of sight.

"Pop smoke!" I yelled and two dozen smoke grenades were hurled toward the enemy line. They landed in a ragged line, sparked, and started to ooze smoke.

"Looks like you got a whole rainbow out there, X-ray One," The cobra pilot said.

"Give it another minute," I said. The smoke billowed, Blue and green and yellow and red. For once luck was with us and a gentle breeze out of the north filled the gaps. I could feel the nervous energy from the enemy line. Off to the right I saw a flash as a rocket exploded just inside the smoke screen. Bullets cracked high overhead or hit the ground in front of the dike. The gooks were getting nervous. I nodded to Rash.

"Hellfire Two One, this is X-ray One. Execute. I say again, execute." I rose to a crouch, my eyes on the cobra as it accelerated, gaining altitude as it advanced.

"Get ready!" I yelled as the cobra lowered its nose and started its run. "Charge!" I screamed, scrambling over the top and pumping my legs as fast as they would move. The cobra's first rocket exploded before I was lost in the fog of our smoke screen. I was through it in a second, in time to see hellfire's second rocket explode just inside the tree line, heard the electric hum of its miniguns. He was past the target in a matter of seconds, faster than I'd expected. Those VC still left after the first run recovered quickly. The machine gun in the middle of their line spewed a continuous stream of lead. I thought I was the first one through the smoke but already I could see people ahead of me. One went down, then another. The men were returning fire as they ran. The cobra was a quarter mile off, its tail swinging up into a half cartwheel, then roaring back for another pass. *No* I screamed, aloud or in my head, I didn't know.

There was nothing I could do to stop him. Murphy was almost to the tree line, his mouth a dark hole as he screamed. The cobra screamed forward, the VC taking cover. Several broke and ran, then more and more. The cobra flashed past without firing a shot, having blown his wad on the first pass. M-79s boomed as they blew holes through the vegetation with the 00 buckshot in their canister rounds. I crashed into the tree line, turning left and right but the only VC I saw were already dead, the cobra's mini-guns having done their worst in my section of the line. Off to the left there was intense shooting, all of it M-16s.

Hellfire Two One circled, assessing the situation from a distance. Doc Hippie was in the millet field, tending to one of the wounded. Rash was running across the field, headset to his ear, talking to….someone. He stopped, checked on one of our men lying in the field and then moved on. Hellfire flew over our position, did a helicopter version of wagging its wings, then turned to the south and disappeared into the darkening gloom.

The shooting was dying off, a few shots here and there, the men making sure the dead were really dead. The wounded too, probably. I didn't care. Lt. Hoffman was calling men back from blood trails, trying to set up some semblance of security. I walked toward the end of the enemy line. It was clear where the mini guns chewed up their line. The dead having at least three holes in each body. The bodies thinned out suddenly, dramatically. Many had escaped, enough to have handled us easily had they not been scared off by the unarmed cobra's second run. The only other concentration of dead lay at the end of the line where five bodies lay in a machine gun pit.

"That one's still alive," the PFC standing over the pit said. He was a new guy, his first mission. Three of the bodies had large caliber bullet holes in their heads, a fourth a fatal chest wound. The fifth was still very much alive. His head was bent at an unnatural angle. A small amount of blood oozed from the back of his neck. "I don't think he can move," the boy said, shaken by the sight.

The man was neither young nor old. He was wearing the typical black pajamas and Ho Chi Minh sandals of the Viet Cong. His eyes followed me everywhere.

"Trung-uy?" he said. He ran his tongue over his lips.

"Yeah, I don't know what the fuck that means," I said.

"I think he wants water," the PFC said. I stepped into the pit.

"You VC?" I said. I thought I saw a twinkle in his eye.

"No VC," he said, and smiled.

"Well at least you still got a sense of humor," I said. "How 'bout my boy, Boyd? Pretty good shot, huh?" I said, taunting him. The man said nothing. I turned to the PFC. "Gather up any weapons and documents they might have and take them to Lt. Hoffman."

"What do you want me to do with him?" I considered the wounded man for a moment, the PFC I was entrusting him to.

"Nothing," I said. "He's not going anywhere." I turned and walked away. After a few steps I turned back, wanting to say something more. The PFC was kneeling by the wounded man, unscrewing the cover on his canteen. I remembered myself, the person I used to be a lifetime ago, and then walked away. I met Rash in the millet field.

"Who's that?" I said, pointing my chin at the man he had stopped to check on.

"Semmler," he said. "He's dead, Sir. Sorry." I let that sink in. Semmler. A good kid. Quiet. Always under the radar, but a good soldier.

"Anybody else?" He shook his head.

"Not that I know of. Doc's working on Nixon and Cruz. A couple others got minor wounds. I got two dustoffs on the way."

"Good job," I said. "I ever tell you that before?"

"No sir."

"Stay with me," I said. Aside from the usual scavenging for souvenirs, everyone was doing his job. I put Lt. Hoffman in charge of gathering up all documents and any weapons that hadn't been claimed as souvenirs, then checked on the wounded. Nixon had a nasty abdominal wound and Cruz caught one in the thigh that had nicked an artery. Newell had a fragment to the shin that he removed himself and Romansky had a deep laceration to his scalp that Doc said looked a lot worse than it was. Romansky pulled his battle dressing from the top of his head when I came to see how he was. Blood and dirt were encrusted in a gash that went from his forehead to the middle of his scalp. At first there was no more bleeding, then the blood welled up and started flowing down his forehead. I took the hand that was holding his battle dressing and put it back on top of the wound.

"It's bad, huh El Tee?" he said hopefully.

"Doc says no," I said.

"I'm gettin' medevaced though, right, Sir?"

"No promises. Those birds are gonna be crowded," I said and turned to walk away.

"An' a headache too, Sir," he called after me. "Bad. Like splittin'. Like what they call a migrant."

"Migraine," I said and kept walking. Murphy and Colon carried Dell out of the ARVN compound, then went back for Boyd. I could tell by the way they were carrying him that he was dead. They laid him next to Dell. Murphy dropped to his knees next to Boyd, his head in both hands.

Boyd had a single gunshot wound just above his right eye. The blood had already been wiped away.

"Murphy," I said. He looked up, his face smeared with mud, his eyes puffy. He looked right past me. Rash turned away, talking on the radio. "Sgt. Murphy, I need you to set up an LZ. Dustoffs will be here any time now." He just stared, trying to process what I had said.

"We made a deal," he said. "If either of us got killed, the other would be his body escort." I could have given the job to anyone but I wanted to get Murphy's mind on something else.

"That comes later," I said. "Right now I need--" Colon put his hand on my shoulder.

"I got it, Sir," he said and hurried off.

"Five minutes," Rash said.

The only light came from the moon and with a heavy cloud cover moving in it wouldn't last long. Lt. Hoffman was still at the tree line next to a growing pile of pith helmets, canteens, machine guns, rockets, loose ammo, food, and cooking gear.

"How 'bout it, El Tee? I going out?" It was Romansky, his machine gun hanging from one hand, less than ten rounds on the belt dangling from the feed tray.

"Sorry, Romansky. Can't afford to lose you tonight," I said, hoping to soften his disappointment with flattery.

"You're shittin' me, Sir. I got shot in the head, man."

"You should have had your helmet on."

"I did!"

"Then what caused that wound?"

"How the hell should I know!? Maybe it fell off. I wasn't keeping' a fuckin' diary!"

"Tell you what. You stay tonight, we'll call it a gunshot wound. You'll get a purple heart and I'll try to get you out on a chopper in the morning."

"That's fucked up, Sir, an' you know it!" he said and stormed off toward the perimeter. "Tha's a gunshot wound," he said, pointing to the battle dressing tied to his head like a bonnet. "Tha's a fuckin' purple heart."

Lights appeared in the south. Security was in place and Colon fired a parachute flare to guide the chopper. Sgt. Corbet stayed with the pile of enemy equipment, setting charges of C-4 for demolition.

"El Tee, what about the ARVNs?" It was Doc Hippie.

"No room this trip," I said. "We'll see what higher wants to do with them tomorrow." The flare drifted away as the choppers came in low over the river, their landing lights casting Corporal Colon as a Christ-like figure, hands raised to the heavens in the middle of the millet field.

The wounded were loaded on one chopper and as it took off the dead and whatever equipment they had that we hadn't taken for ourselves was loaded onto the other. Corporal Romansky trotted away from one of the choppers, two belts of machine gun ammo draped over his shoulders, a donation from a sympathetic door gunner. The chopper lifted off the ground, spun on its own axis, and raced across the clearing, gaining altitude as it cleared the trees along the river before turning for Hardscrabble. Its departure left us in a weirdly dark and quiet place.

"Sgt. Corbet's ready anytime you are," Lt. Hoffman said.

"Where is he?"

"In one of the machine gun pits," he said. While we were getting everyone else behind the paddy dike Rash came up to me. He did not look happy.

"Lt. Avery called. He wants you to ambush the VC dead tonight and follow any blood trails first thing in the morning."

"Where's Captain Ford?"

"Don't know, Sir. Want me to try to raise him?"

"No, never mind."

"You want to talk to Lt. Avery?" Again, hoping for a change of orders.

"No. Time to seek shelter." I yelled across the millet field for Sgt. Corbet to do his thing.

"Fire in the hole!" he yelled. The explosion was so bright you could see the VC's equipment spinning into the sky. Cheers erupted from our raggedy line behind the dike and when everything but the dust had settle Sgt. Corbet ran back, giggling like a school girl.

"Jesus! Did you see that? It was like a whole NVA supply truck was raining down on me. Lucky I wasn't killed," he laughed. *Like a bunch of fuckin' kids,* I thought.

We took a head count and when the numbers were right I gave my orders. We were going to cross the bridge and get into the jungle bordering Phu Gap's rice paddies where it would be almost impossible for the gooks to find us.

I had planned on going at least a hundred yards into the brush but it was so dark in the jungle I called a halt twenty yards in. With the nineteen men we had left we set up a cramped NDP with a thirty percent watch. I gave Lt. Hoffman the first watch and before I fell asleep he got a call on the radio.

"Artillery, Sir," he said, handing me the handset. "He says you're cleared for your fire mission." I should have taken the handset--told him he was too late, that I had five KIAs. That Dell and Sousa were on me, but Fine, Semmler, and Boyd were all on him. I should have called him a chicken shit officer who cared more about his own career than he did about the lives of the men who were real soldiers; that every one of my men were worth a dozen of him and that he should pray to God none of my men find out who he is. But I didn't. I was exhausted, whipped. I just wanted to close my eyes and have everything go away.

I was sick of it. All of it. I was sick of living like an animal. I was sick of eating cold spaghetti out of a can and drinking warm water out of a canteen. I was sick of wearing the same clothes for a week without once taking them off. I was sick of squatting when I took a crap and keeping my rifle cleaner than myself. I was sick of taking orders from people who knew less than me and giving them to people who knew more than me. I wanted to be lying face down in a clean pool, eating hot dogs at a Pirate's game, drinking cold beer on a hot day, lying next to Audrey on clean sheets in an air conditioned hotel room. I wanted to know that the elements held little sway over me, that I could come in out of the sun or the rain as my heart desired. I wanted to take a walk in the woods without worrying what was behind every tree or bush. I wanted to be anywhere but where I was, doing anything but what I was doing. I wanted to live like a human being. I wanted to go home.

"Tell him it's too late," I said. I laid my head on my helmet and pulled my poncho liner over my head in a vain attempt to keep out the mosquitoes. The last thing I remember before I woke up the next morning was the feel of a cold rain drumming against the outline of my head, its rhythm oddly reassuring as it lulled me to sleep.

Chapter 43

I woke up on my own. The jungle was so shrouded in fog I could barely see the men on the other side of our tiny NDP. One thing was clear though--I was the only one awake. A few men changed position in their sleep but there wasn't an eye open, a head held up by its own power. I checked the time. Almost six o'clock. A murmur came from the radio. I reached out from under my poncho liner and grabbed the handset.

"This is X-ray One, over." My mouth was dry, my words thick. Rash sat up, a look of horror on his face.

"X-ray One, this is X-ray. You've missed the last five sit-reps. Report your situation, over." Lt. Avery's voice.

"Sorry, X-ray. Forgot to change our battery last night, over." Rash was signaling frantically, something he had to tell me.

"X-ray One, cancel all previous orders. Return to Oscar Charlie ASAP."

"Stand by, X-ray," I said. People were starting to stir around me. Rash signaling he needed to talk to me. "What?"

"Wild Turkey got hit bad last night. Captain Ford was supposed to chopper out there this morning with a relief force. That's all I know. I fell asleep. Sorry." I needed more, but I would ask later.

"X-ray, this is X-ray One. I'm down to 19 effectives, all of them exhausted. Low on ammo. Requesting extraction, over."

"Negative X-ray One," Lt. Avery said. "No birds available. You're going to have to hump it. How long do you think it will take? Over." It had rained most of the night; I doubted the bridge above Gia Hoi had survived which meant we would have to cross here and make our way through the jungle.

"All day, at least," I said, not wanting to make promises I couldn't keep.

"Before nightfall, X-ray One. No Later! Keep me posted."

The men were rousing from their sleep and a small knot had gathered around our CP. Lt. Hoffman sat up, wondering what was going on, why he had only pulled one watch.

"So what happened last night?" I asked Rash.

"Just before ten Wild Turkey reported they were under attack.

Rockets, RPGs, small arms. I could hear it all on the radio. Anyway it was real big. They called in artillery. They couldn't hit the front slope so our guys at Old Crow hit that side with mortars. They must have been all around. Anyway, it sounded pretty fucked up. Last thing I heard was there was gooks in the wire and then nothing' till I heard Captain Ford come on saying to hang on, he'd be out with a relief force at first light. That's probably why Avery wants us back before dark. He's afraid Old Crow will be next."

"Jesus," someone moaned.

"Okay, pack it up, let's get out of here before the fog lifts," I said. I thought there might still be a chance we could take the trail back, but the Mu Dai was already slapping the support beams at the Phu Gap bridge. No way was the bridge above Gia Hoi still intact.

The fog was particularly thick on the river so we closed our interval as we crossed the bridge. No one made a sound. We had no idea what had happened to the VC after they had time to lick their wounds and recoup. One thing was sure--they still had more men than we did and in this fog our aircraft would be grounded. We headed upstream staying close to the river, every head turning as we crept past the fog-shrouded ARVN compound.

Three hundred yards further on the old rice paddies ended and we disappeared into the jungle, angling away from the river on a direct azimuth to Old Crow. Within an hour we found a small knoll that provided relief from the slop of the jungle floor were we could have a hot breakfast. We hadn't eaten in more than twenty hours and the warm food and hot coffee restored a small part of our energy.

We reached the back side of the Crow's Nest an hour before sunset. Lt. Avery wanted us to split up and circle the mountain just below the firebase, making sure there were no enemy in the area. If they *were* there that would be a good reason *not* to split up, but we were tired and wanted to get inside the wire as soon as possible.

I sent Lt. Hoffman around the left side with half the platoon while I took the other half around to the right. It had rained on and off throughout the day and the back slope had given way again. Deep gullies furrowed the loose soil and the perimeter wire sagged down the incline like a swollen udder. I looked to Sgt. Murphy.

"I believe you have some experience with this sort of thing," I said, recalling the first time I saw him.

"Yes, Sir," he said.

"You don't have to do any work yourself. Just something to last the night. Get a squad from third platoon."

"Looks like Avery didn't want to send out his own patrol," Rash said. It did not escape me that the men referred to Lt. Avery as simply *Avery*.

Lt. Avery tried not to show the relief he felt at our return, and probably not for our sake. He showed little interest in my report on the battle of Phu Gap, instead stressing the perilous situation Old Crow was in with a play by play of what happened at Wild Turkey the night before.

Wild turkey had been alerted that something was up by their LPs who started breaking squelch frantically a half hour before the scheduled sit-rep giving the men inside the wire time to get to their fighting positions before the attack started. Still, they were outnumbered and out gunned. A sapper got through the wire and destroy TOC with a satchel charge before he was gunned down. Six VC were killed in the wire and another 28 died in the jungle or in the open ground between the jungle and the compound from claymores, small arms fire, and artillery and mortar rounds. Still, second platoon had eight men killed and thirteen wounded including Lt. Churchill who was blown up in TOC while trying to adjust artillery fire. Only one man from the three LPs out that night made it back alive, himself badly wounded from our own artillery fire.

Captain Ford did not make it to Wild Turkey at first light, all air crews being grounded until the fog lifted. When he finally arrived he informed Major Dempsey that he could still hold the base despite the fact that he had only been able to get five replacements to accompany him on the rescue mission. Lt. Avery, I later found out, had earlier requested that Wild Turkey be abandoned, the survivors choppered to Old Crow to reinforce our defenses there which he expected to be attacked any minute.

"So you can see our situation," he explained. "That's why I needed you back here. I'm putting out three LPs tonight. Everyone else will be sleeping in their fighting positions–"

"Is that really necessary, with three LPs out? Isn't that why they're there, to give us advanced–" He sighed, fed up with my insubordination.

"You and Sgt. Poole apparently–"

"He's back?"

"He came in on yesterday's resupply chopper and apparently thinks he knows--"

"He probably does--"

"Enough!" he snapped. "Those not actually on watch will sleep in their fighting positions. That includes you, Lieutenant." If I wasn't so tired I would have laughed.

"Not me," I said. "I've got to pack. I'm outta here on the first bird that flys anywhere near this place. Need I remind--"

"You don't need to remind me of anything. Apparently I need to remind you that you owe me." Now I did laugh.

"*I* owe *You?*" I said. He asked Lt. Hoffman and the radio watch for a few minutes alone.

"I covered for you!" he said. I didn't know what the hell he was talking about so he spelled it out. "Phu Gap? Have you forgotten about that?" It took me a minute to realize he meant the time the ARVN captain shot an unarmed villager in the head.

"You weren't covering for anybody but yourself," I said.

"Me!? I didn't witness any crime. It was you who failed to report it."

"You knew--"

"I knew no such thing. Your report said nothing about it and when I questioned you, you--"

"You wouldn't let me say anything because you didn't *want* to know. You told me to keep my mouth shut and let the South Vietnamese handle it." He was about to say something but I'd heard enough. "I'm going to pack. If you have any questions, contact my lawyer."

"Your--"

"Lt. DeVoist. He works out of the JAG office. He knows everything. Including our 'talk' about the Phu Gap thing," I said and left.

"I think he's done with us for tonight," I said, steering Lt. Hoffman away from TOC. "I can't remember. Have you met Sgt. Poole yet?"

Chapter 44

Lt. Hoffman shook me awake. "Resupply chopper will be here in fifteen minutes. You can catch a ride back on that." He looked ten years older than when I met him a few days ago. His face was unshaven and still caked with mud from the day before. His eyes were sunken beneath heavy lids and I felt guilty that I'd dodged guard duty the night before.

"Shit," I said. I emptied my rucksack and started repacking the things I needed to take with me. There wasn't much. With few exceptions, everything I had was owned by the army. I threw in the items I'd signed for--minus my air mattress and a few things others could use--and cinched my pack tight.

"Is it always like that?" Lt. Hoffman asked. "The other day, I mean."

"The worst day of my tour. My life," I said. "Before that I'd only lost one man, KIA." That seemed to ease his mind only a little.

"I couldn't do what you did," he said. I sat on my bunk.

"Neither could I my first time out. You did fine. Really," I said.

"I panicked," he said.

"Not like the movies, is it?" I said and now he smiled; not much--more like a grimace--but a little. "That's what it's like for everybody their first time. If you're up against a squad, it feels like a platoon. A platoon feels like a company."

"Felt like the whole NVA army out there." I said nothing for a long time, trying to figure out the best way to say it.

"You're not expected to do it alone. Sgt. Poole is the best NCO I ever met. He's made our platoon what it is today. Don't be afraid to ask his advice." There was more, but I couldn't find the words. I remembered Gary's medic, dead before I got there. I remembered Smitty on my first mission, my father in New Guinea. I remembered Stevens, the major in Korea, the sergeant at Bull Run, the Confederate private at Gettysburg.

"There are others too, ready to help," I said. "You just need to be open to it." He nodded that he understood, even though he had no idea. How could he? I didn't understand it myself. He cocked his ear toward the door.

"Your ride," he said. I heard the familiar whump whump whump of the Huey making its approach. I grabbed my rifle and rucksack and ducked through the door.

"I got that, El Tee," Sgt. Murphy said, relieving me of my rucksack. I let him take it. Voit was there too, and Colon. Sgt. Corbet and Rash. Doc Hippie and the rest of the platoon minus the few who had crashed too hard after being on watch all-night. "I almost forgot. I promised you a ride, didn't I?" I said. Romansky touched the clean bandage on his head. "Guess we didn't need you after all."

"Good to have me along anyway though, huh El Tee?" he grinned. He took his place on the helipad, a small bag of personal items he would need during his hospital stay in his hand. O'Brien was there too, one tooth missing in front, the other moving in and out as he worried it with his tongue. A trooper from third platoon was standing on the helipad, yellow smoke drifting away from him as he guided the chopper in.

Others ran forward, pulling supplies from the chopper. A new guy in unfaded fatigues climbed down from the deck. Dragging his rucksack behind him, he looked around as if he had just been dropped on an alien planet. Business as usual.

I took a nostalgic look around Old Crow one last time--the pools of water where mortar rounds had landed, now breeding grounds for mosquitoes; the bunkers, their roofs sagging from the ravages of time and the weight of waterlogged sandbags; the men, weather-beaten and aged beyond their years. I looked across the valley to Wild Turkey, battered but not broken--like the undermanned platoon that defended her until more replacements arrived--and thought how glad I was to be getting out of there alive. Sgt. Poole saw my expression, extended his hand. "Go home, Lt. Sullivan," he said, misreading my thoughts. "We got this."

"Come on! Come on!" the crew chief yelled, waving me onboard. I took Sgt. Poole's hand and shook it.

"I know you do," I said, then turned and ran to the chopper, leaving Sgt. Poole with a mistaken belief in my nobility.

Chapter 45

I dropped my rucksack on the orderly room floor loud enough to be heard. "Oh, Lt. Sullivan," Specialist Thomas said, coming out of Sergeant Fowler's office. "Heard you were coming. Jesus. Sorry about….you know."

"Where is everybody? I stopped at supply to turn in my equipment but there was no one there."

"Captain Ford took everybody to Wild Turkey with him-- Jimmy, Sgt. Fowler, Sgt. Manson, some new guy. Said he needed every man he could get. Everybody but me," he added sheepishly. I knew how he felt. "You can leave your equipment with me. Sgt. Mason said not to worry if you were missing anything. He'd write it off as a combat loss. Except your rifle of course. You're gonna want to keep that until you actually leave. Kinda hairy around here the last coupla days. Nothin' like you seen, of course. Jesus. They brought in a couple of tanks yesterday. You see 'em?"

"I saw 'em." I pulled a clean set of fatigues and my toilet kit from my rucksack and went to the shower room, looking at all the logos that appeared above orderly room doors since the contest I started to appease Captain Messina so many months ago: *Night Stalkers; Semper Vigilantes; Grimm's Reapers*, after Colonel Grimm, our regimental commander.

I showered, shaved, brushed my teeth, put on clean clothes and, feeling somewhat human again, went to the hospital to check on the wounded. Audrey and I hadn't seen each other or been in touch for over a month, both of us thinking, perhaps, that that was the best way to end it. Her DEROS date was about the same as mine and I half-hoped she was already gone, then felt an emptiness in my chest when she was.

It took twenty-six stitches to close the laceration in Romansky's scalp. The doctors gave him a break, admitting him on paper even though no beds were available in the overwhelmed hospital; telling him to stay in the transient tent and check in every day to have his head looked at.

The doctors stitched O'Brien's lower lip, packed his mouth with gauze, and put him on the first flight to Phu Cat air base where they had a dentist. Nellis had been evaced to Cam Rahn Bay but the rest of my guys were still at Hardscrabble, the medical facilities at Cam Rahn having since been stretched beyond their limits.

Nixon was asleep in the recovery ward, tubes going in, tubes going out. I didn't wake him. Warner and Cruz were there too—Warner on a cot in the center aisle, Cruz two patients ahead of him on a floor mattress. Williams had multiple fragment wounds from head to toe but they weren't serious enough to rate a space in the ward. I found him on a cot in the corridor near Dr. Fletcher's office. Dr. Fletcher was making the rounds among the wounded and he approached me after I was done talking to Williams.

"Sean, you're alive! Got a minute?" He put his hand on my back and ushered me into his office. "Sit, Sit," He said shutting the door and taking his seat behind the desk.

"I see you've been demoted to nurse?" I said.

"It's been crazy," he said. "Rumors are flying. I checked with Graves this morning and they said it wasn't you." I didn't know what he was talking about. "Everybody's talking about C Company, second of the 605. A bayonet charge? Was that you?" The very thought of it embarrassed me.

"It's not like it sounds. There was no hand to hand or anything like that. It was more of a way of getting the men psyched up. The spirit of the bayonet and all that shit."

"Still," he said. "I'm sorry about your losses. I know how you must feel." He couldn't, but I let it go. "We heard that the platoon leader was killed," he said by way of explaining his greeting.

"That was Lt. Churchill. Defending Wild Turkey," I said.

"It's bad all over. They took over our embassy in Saigon for Christ's sake. Sounded like the gunfight at the O.K. Corral before we took it back."

"Sounds like we're getting our asses kicked," I said.

"Not to hear the staff officers tell it. I sat with a bunch of them at breakfast. We've taken a lot of casualties, but nothing like the NVA and VC. They make it sound like this is the best thing that could have happened, having them all concentrated in large units for a change where our artillery and air power can chew them up. They say the war will be over in a year. Two tops." I let that sink in. At least something good would come out of all our sacrifices. "But a bayonet charge?" he continued. "Your idea or…."

"Gettysburg. Pickett's charge."

"They got slaughtered," he reminded me.

"I think it was more like a cautionary tale. What they did wrong."

"I guess that shoots down my theory about why you stopped having those visions after Sgt. Poole arrived."

"He wasn't there. R and R."

"Oh," he said. I couldn't tell whether that pleased him or not. "Anyway, I was hoping you'd stop by before you left. I've been looking over that bio you worked up for me and I noticed that you majored in history. In college."

"Uh huh."

"Well, I've been going over my notes and it struck me that those episodes you experienced didn't just materialize out of thin air."

"I thought that's exactly what you thought," I said. "Don't tell me you think they were real."

"No, that's not what I meant. I mean that you seemed to have known what kind of help you needed before you actually experienced your…whatever you want to call them. I haven't decided on the right word myself yet." I didn't get what he was talking about and told him so. "Your first episode, for example. Consider this–it was your first time under fire. You were understandably…unsteady."

"I panicked," I said.

"Yes," he said, glad to see he didn't have to mince words. "You once said you were a Civil War buff. That you studied many of the battles, visited several battlefield." I didn't remember telling him that, but it was true. "So when you needed help your first time under fire, you already knew where to look. In your mind. You didn't pick just any battle, you picked the battle that was the testing ground for both sides–First Bull Run. Nobody told you what battle it was. How did you know?" I'd never thought about that.

"I don't know. I just did. I saw Bull Run Creek, church steeples off in the distance."

"But how did you know it was Bull Run? Manassas Junction? Because that's where your mind needed to go to get the answers you needed," he said, answering his own question. "Does that make sense to you?"

"As much sense as anything else, I guess. Is that what you think? That it wasn't just happening in my mind? That I made it happen?"

"Not consciously, of course. Anyway, it's just a theory. Something to think about. The advice you got wasn't anything new in the annals of military science. You already had all the information you needed to come up with a rational response to whatever position you were in. You just needed some way to remind you where that information was stored and your brain presented that information in a way that was relevant to your situation."

"So how long have you been nursing this theory?"

"It's been an ongoing thing. At first there weren't enough incidents to draw any conclusion."

"So for some time then." He made a *more or less* gesture with his hands. "And you decided to wait until now to let me in on it?"

"First of all, it's just a theory. The mind is very complex and I'm not arrogant enough to think I have all the answers. At best, it's a place to start; at worst, I'm totally off base."

"And second of all?"

"Second of all, we were dealing with a coping mechanism that was working pretty well for you. Why would I risk taking that away from you by making you over-think it?" I had to give him that one.

"Anyway," I said, standing up. "I've got a lot of shit to do. I just wanted to stop by--"

"I won't keep you," he said, pushing his chair back and opening his top drawer. "Audrey asked me to give this to you if I saw you," he said, handing me a piece of paper, folded in two. I felt a warm flush at the sound of her name.

"You know?…I mean, how did--"

"It's a small camp," he said. I unfolded the paper. There was no note, just her name, phone number and her address in Bradford, just a couple of hours south of where I lived. I sat down.

"What did she say?" I asked.

"Just to give it to you." He let me think about that for a while. "Do you remember when I told you about all the problems--adjustment problems--veterans were having when they returned to the States? Your problems don't magically disappear the minute you get out of here," he said. "You had someone to talk to over here; maybe it would help if you had someone to talk to when you get home."

"So, what?!" I said, the anger rising in my chest. "So you thought you'd enlist her to…What did you tell her about me anyway!?"

"You know me better than that. Everything you said in here is confidential."

"Then how…." Then it dawned on me. "Was she seeing you too?"

"What you saw in the field? What you saw in a month out there, she saw every day. *Every day.* Because that's what she did. Is it different from what you did? Absolutely! But make no mistake about it--the doctors? The nurses? They feel every bit as responsible for the men that end up on their table as you did for the men in your platoon. And sometimes…sometimes things don't go well and when that happens they question themselves. What did they do wrong? What could they have done differently? Should they feel responsible for losing a patient when they did everything they could? Of course not. No more than you should. But trust me, the emotions you've been suppressing all this time? It's going to surface at some point in your life unless you deal with it now. The people back home? You're not going to feel comfortable around them at first because they haven't been through what you've been through, what Audrey's been through. Talking's the best medicine. And your old friends? You won't want to talk to them about it because they weren't here. They won't get it. Can't get it."

"So that's what this is all about?" I said, holding up the piece of piece of paper. "She wants to *help* me!? Like I'm some kind of project for her?"

"Did you not hear what I just said?" he said, angry for the first time since I'd met him. "We don't have time for me to let you figure this out for yourself so I'm going to break one of my rules and lay it out for you. I don't know the extent of your relationship with Audrey. What that's for," he said, pointing to the paper in my hand, "I don't know. What I do know is that Audrey's a wonderful person and she cares about you, but whatever. She's not looking for a project. She's hurting too and if you think helping *you* is what this is all about….Well, that helping thing is a two way street."

Something Audrey said when she came back from her leave--after Karen and Marlene had gone--popped into my mind. She'd said she no longer had anyone to talk to, just one friend. I had no idea at the time that she was talking about Dr. Fletcher. Now she didn't even have him. I felt like shit.

"You both have your own lives to live," he said, reading my face. "It's not an obligation. It's just an option," he said, referring to the note. "I think that's all she was trying to say."

* * *

I wanted to get away as fast as I could but there were no flights out until the next day. I went back to our orderly room and spent the rest of the afternoon writing up recommendations for medals. I thought back on what we did in the millet field and I could not escape the fact that everyone had gone above and beyond what was expected of them. I recommended Boyd and Doc Hippie for silver stars. Everyone else I put in for bronze stars with a "V" for valor. I also put Rash in for an Army Commendation Medal for his work on the radio. Romansky would get his purple heart as would the other twelve who had been killed or wounded.

I also wrote a letter to the commander of the aviation battalion recommending that the pilot and co-pilot of the cobra that provided us with air support be awarded the Distinguished Flying Cross for their skill and heroism. I would not find out until the next day that the day after they made an unarmed "strafing" run on the tree line bordering the millet field, Hellfire Two One was shot down while supporting D Company in the A Nang Valley. The pilot and Co-pilot were officially listed as missing-in-action.

The next day I boarded a Chinook to Phu Cat Air Base and from there caught a ride on a C-130 to Cam Rahn Bay. Two days later, Three days after my original DEROS date, I walked up the steps of a Continental Airlines 727 and took a window seat just forward of the wing. No one sat next to me. Apparently more men were coming over than were going back.

* * *

Wooden barracks, trucks, warehouses, water towers flashed by my window; then--as the wheels left the ground--mortar pits, sandbag bunkers, rows of barbed wire. The plane banked, the starboard wing dipping toward the South China Sea. Golden beaches and concrete piers; cranes lifting cargo from heavy freighters; tiny sampans, navy lighters shuttling men and supplies from ships to shore, from shore to ship. We gained altitude quickly, the sea changing from gloomy green to dark blue. In less than a minute we were in the clouds. Wispy tendrils streaked by my window, engulfing us in an ever changing sea of gray and white until the sky turned blue again. It was like being transported to a new world. The clouds dropped farther and farther away. At 30,000 feet we leveled off and a minute after that the pilot announced that we had just left Vietnam air space. Some men cheered, others just stared at the seatback in front of them.

I unbuttoned the pocket of my fatigue shirt and pulled out the piece of paper I'd put there three days ago. I unfolded it and stared at the small, cramped handwriting.

"Can I get you something?" The cart was full of cans and bottles, plastic cups and a bucket of ice, swizzle sticks and a stack of white napkins. The stewardess had a smile that you could tell came naturally and often. She was short and cute, her hair cut in a bob with bangs that stopped just above eyes that shined in a way I hadn't seen in a long time. There was something familiar about her. Familiar, and yet different at the same time. A hint of the way things could be. Should be.

"You have Old Crow?"

"We have bourbon," she said.

"That will be fine," I said. "Just ice." I lowered my tray and she handed me the cup and a napkin. A napkin! I put it on my tray, then looked at Audrey's name and address one last time before folding it up and putting it in my wallet where I wouldn't lose it.

50890797R00202

Made in the USA
San Bernardino, CA
08 July 2017